To
Brother Ron
Best Wishes
Brian

CW00405276

FROM UNCLE RON

0474 3510-27.

or 0474 371 594.

THE KILLING

Also by Brian Todd:
One Step At A Time

THE KILLING

Brian Todd

The Book Guild Ltd.
Sussex, England

The Book Guild Limited
Temple House
25 High Street
Lewes, Sussex

First published 1993
© Brian Todd 1993

Set in Baskerville

Typesetting by Dataset
St Leonards-on-Sea, Sussex

Printed in Great Britain by
Antony Rowe Ltd
Chippenham, Wiltshire

A catalogue record for this book is
available from the British Library

ISBN 0 86332 807 5

1

The old cliché about London having streets paved with gold has for centuries been responsible for drawing people from all over the globe. Many come on holiday to satisfy their curiosity and enjoy the sights, the pageantry and the history, while thousands more arrive each year hoping to find fame on stage or screen. A few, however, come to make fast fortunes from crime.

London has its share of home-grown criminals, ranging from gem and bullion thieves to big-time shady arms dealers, and from organized super-frauds to cold, calculating contract killers and drug barons.

In years gone by it was considered absolutely taboo to kill a policeman; it was not uncommon for members of the underworld to seek out anyone so doing and hand him over to the law, or even to exact an appropriate punishment themselves. Today, of course, things have greatly changed. As the quality of life has improved, the level of respect for the law has dwindled with the meting out of more lenient sentences.

Today there are no crime overlords to maintain a limited control over the city's villains. Such gangs as there are do not choose to police themselves so as to maintain an acceptable amount of order, and thus keep the long arm of the law at bay for the general good of the community. Now it is every man for himself; small territorial gangs are forever looking to extend their boundaries and muggers will use lethal weapons rather than risk failure or apprehension.

One such man was Ferdinand Rodriguez, who had been born and bred in London's East End and, like his

5

hardworking parents, came from good Catholic stock. There the comparisons ended, for Ferdinand, who had suffered the modern stigma of racism, learned at an early age that a show of strength, power, wealth and brute force could overcome almost any obstacle or enemy. Tall, dark and very handsome, he had found that young female hopefuls fell easily for his charms – only to be manoeuvred into becoming hostesses in his nightclub. From there they moved automatically into the world of prostitution, working from flats, massage parlours and sex shops.

Rodriguez' main business competitor was Max Stoddart, a much older man, well-established in the same business, with narcotics as the mainstay. As always, this kind of wealth brought with it envy, treachery and mistrust, invariably the forerunners of murder.

On the surface it was business as usual. Soho was its normal, colourful self, with crowds flocking to enjoy the gaudy night life of theatres, clubs, pubs, bars and restaurants. Under the bright neon signs promising a multitude of thrills and exotic delights, a gleaming golden Corvette pulled in at the kerbside opposite the Pearly Queen nightclub, which belonged to Max Stoddart. In the rear seat sat Rodriguez, looking through the tinted glass windows. His adrenalin was rising in anticipation of a great coup which would either put Stoddart in jail for a long time or force him into exile in Spain, with whom the British had no extradition treaty. His gaze flicked to the man in the front passenger seat, an actor named Wise who had never achieved any great success in his profession. With a little aid from make-up he was now about to pass himself off as Max Stoddart.

'Time to go,' encouraged Rodriguez, 'and remember: don't get involved in any long-winded discussions with anyone. Call anyone you don't really know bonny lass or bonny lad. Everything has been set up, so there's nothing for you to worry about. If the unthinkable should occur, stay schtum until I can spring you.'

'You will spring me?' asked Wise anxiously.

'Mister, this operation is costing me an arm and a leg. If you get caught and found not to be Stoddart, it'll blow the

6

lid off my plans to get rid of him and take over his operation in the city. Just get moving and do exactly as we planned and you'll be on the plane to New York with the rest of your money before you know it.'

With a deep sigh, Wise swung out of his seat to stand on the pavement, butterflies fluttering in his stomach. As he slammed the door, determined to give his best performance, someone spoke to him from across the Corvette's bonnet. A police patrol car had stopped alongside and for a moment Wise froze. His heart skipped a beat then started to pound like a big bass drum. In a split second he went from icy coldness to a burning heat which brought more colour to his already ruddy complexion. This, he guessed, was the unthinkable that no one had expected to happen, and he knew that if he failed in his performance and was searched, the half kilo of poor-grade cocaine that he was carrying would condemn him just as easily as it would the real Max Stoddart.

'Come on, move yourself, bonny lad!' he yelled at his chauffeur in a faded Yorkshire accent, and continued with a smile: 'Sorry officer, it wasn't our intention to cause an obstruction.'

With a look of disgust, the officer wound up his window and the patrol car eased back into the traffic. Moments later the Corvette followed, leaving Wise standing alone in the throng of pedestrians, his legs turned to jelly. Gazing at the large neon sign while gathering his wits, he searched his pockets irritably for his cigarettes and in the process touched the two packets of cocaine and the wrapped bulk of the Beretta automatic pistol which had once belonged to Stoddart. He drew deep on the cigarette, sucking the smoke down hard before expelling the blue-grey plume into the night air through tightly-puckered lips.

'Christ,' he muttered, 'I feel like a jelly going back to the kitchen and I haven't even started yet. Lord knows what it's going to be like when the curtain goes up.'

Turning to cross the street he became acutely aware of an itch on his stomach which he couldn't scratch because of the flak jacket he wore beneath his shirt to give him the bulkiness of the real Stoddart. All he could do was rub the thick padding hard against himself, only to feel another

7

itch, this time beneath the false receding hairline covering his own scalp.

In profound irritation, he crossed between the two lines of waiting traffic at the lights, resisting the temptation to scratch for fear of disturbing his disguise. He was not surprised to feel the urge to pass water, brought on, he knew, by the anticipation of the performance to come. Gritting his teeth, he forced himself to think of the large fee he would soon collect and the new life awaiting him across the ocean.

'Good evening, Sir,' smiled the uniformed commissionaire, doffing his cap. 'Packed house tonight.'

'Nice to hear, bonny lad.' Fooling the commissionaire boosted his confidence enough to press his luck a little further so that the man should remember him later. 'How long have you been with us now?' he asked as the commissionaire opened the door for him.

'Six months next week,' replied the man in surprise.

'Come and see me in the morning – I'm sure we can find you something a little more rewarding than this.'

'Yes, Sir,' beamed the commissionaire, hardly daring to believe that he had even been noticed.

Wise found the foyer to be exactly like the replica set up by Rodriguez in an old dockland warehouse where he had rehearsed the part. As a result, he began to feel more comfortable. He proceeded to the door leading to the club proper and the manager, who had been most instructive during the rehearsals, swung into step alongside.

'Nice to see you, Max,' he beamed. 'I wasn't expecting you to pay us a visit tonight.'

'First nights have never been my thing, bonny lad, but tonight is special, so I guess I'll have to suffer in silence. How's the cabaret going?'

'The first show finished about five minutes ago and the punters loved it. Give it a couple of days and word will get round – we'll be packed to the doors every night, I should think. Those girls certainly know how to flaunt their charms. Wouldn't mind some of that to pass the time of day with myself.'

'Bad for business,' Wise reproached him. 'Play with one and the others will think you're giving special favours.

8

Remember, they're here to get the punters spending at the bar and gaming tables.'

They passed the cloakroom where Wise gave the scantily-clad check girl a lecherous smile which she forced herself to return. Inside, the bar spanned the whole length of the room to the left. Both men and women sat on tall, swivel, armchair-style barstools and were served by handsome Latin barmen and barmaids in revealing dresses. At one side of the room were gaming tables where the crowds were far too engrossed in increasing their fortunes to pay any mind to anyone else. The remaining space was filled with tables and chairs for those who came to drink amid the reasonable privacy offered by cascades of exotic artificial flowers and vines.

Moving to a reserved table close to the bar as planned, the manager beckoned a young waitress who smiled a silent hello and immediately headed for the bar.

'It's all set and I can see no reason for anything to go wrong. Just await your cue, as we rehearsed, and it will be just fine,' the manager assured him quietly. 'So far as I can see, six of the serious crime squad are here – and they're armed, so be careful.'

'You should tell me that,' commented Wise, swallowing hard. 'Which ones are they?'

'There's a couple by the door where we came in whose job will be to see that you don't escape through it. Pay them no attention. At the far end of the bar there are two more waiting to block any attempt by you to reach the stage exit. The two to worry about are sitting at the bar – the woman in the red dress and her boyfriend. He'll come in first to make the arrest while she stands back to cover him. Don't try any heroics because she won't hesitate to shoot.'

'Thanks a bundle,' said Wise, looking up at the hanging vines as the voluptuous young waitress leaned over provocatively with his drink.

'Can I get you anything else?' she smiled, and the manager gave Wise a knowing look of encouragement.

'There is,' said Wise, reaching under the hem of her black satin mini-dress to feel the soft, pear-shaped buttocks, 'but if my wife were to find out, she'd skin me alive.'

The girl laughed happily and obviously enjoyed the attention, knowing that she was safe from any lecherous designs he might have on her as long as his wife was around.

'And you, Sir?' she asked the manager.

'Not for me,' he replied. 'I've got things to do.'

Sipping his whisky and ginger on ice, Wise toasted a silent toast and then, under cover of taking a packet of cigarettes from his pocket, he unwrapped Stoddart's Beretta. Placing the cigarette between his lips, he flicked his lighter but as the flame flickered into life another intruded to light the tip.

'Thanks,' he said, recognizing the buyer for the cocaine.

'You're welcome. The name is Dainty, Tom Dainty. Mind if I join you?'

'Be my guest. I hate drinking alone.'

'I'm told that you have something for me?'

'And you,' Wise responded quietly.

'Half a million in counterfeit twenties as arranged,' Dainty assured him in a hushed voice. 'I dropped it off at the hat-check and your manager is checking it out – he should be here with confirmation in a minute or so. I'd like the opportunity to check the merchandise before I leave.'

When Wise offered the use of his office, Dainty looked at him carefully as though trying to fathom whether he was being led like a lamb to the slaughter now that he had completed his part of the delivery.

'No thanks,' he decided. 'Just pass it under the table. My tastebuds are good and I can tell rubbish at once.'

With a shrug, Wise reached into his coat pocket to retrieve the first packet and passed it as discreetly as possible to Dainty who, thinking himself safe from treachery, bowed his head and furtively opened it. He dipped the very tip of his finger in and as he raised it to touch it on his tongue the detective took his cue and sprang forward to stand crouched behind Wise. One hand gripped Wise's left shoulder, while the other, holding a gun, threatened the back of Wise's head and Dainty's face.

'Hold it right there,' he warned. 'Police.'

10

As his lady colleague made her presence known by crouching at the bar and bringing her weapon to full cock in the hushed, astonished silence, both men froze. At once the plain clothes men by the stage and the main exit moved to cover the crowd, calling: 'Freeze, this is the police!' as they, too, crouched with their weapons pointing.

Stunned, the crowd watched as the culprits were ordered to stand with their hands held high. The first detective, covered by his lady companion, frisked Wise and when the incriminating evidence from his pockets lay on the table for all to see, the two switched roles. As the woman moved forward to search Dainty, a stun grenade exploded on the stage and the lights went out, plunging the club into chaotic darkness. Panic broke out and Wise grasped one of the heavy vines hanging down from the high ceiling and, exactly as rehearsed, was quickly and silently whisked up through a trap-door into a large closet above.

'Hurry,' urged the manager in a hoarse whisper as the lights came back on. On the verge of panic, Wise shed his disguise and put on a neatly-pressed dark suit and tie, while the manager hid those he had just discarded.

'How do I look?' he asked.

'Nothing like Stoddart,' replied the manager. 'Follow me.' And making a quick exit they crossed the hall to the office – only to be caught in the act of leaving as the two detectives pounded to the head of the stairs.

'What the hell's going on?' shouted Wise. 'Get the hell out of here, this is private accommodation!'

'Police!' yelled one of the detectives, brandishing a weapon. 'Where's Stoddart?' and he barged his way into the office.

'He was downstairs having a drink the last time I saw him,' explained the manager.

'Well, he isn't there now,' panted the second detective. 'And he hasn't left because we have all the exits covered inside and out. He just disappeared when the ruckus started. He's got to be here somewhere and we'll find him if it means taking the place apart, one brick at a time.'

'What's he done?' asked Wise innocently.

'Trading cocaine for counterfeit £20 notes,' said the detective shortly.

'Not much future in that,' the manager retorted sarcastically. 'What was that explosion?'

'Don't act so dumb,' said the detective coldly, 'you know the score. Where have you got him hidden?' But before the manager could respond, his colleague returned from a fruitless search.

'Nothing,' he declared, 'absolutely nothing. We'll block every entrance and check everyone out in single file, then we'll call the rummage crew to take this place apart at our leisure.'

'I'll hold you responsible for any damage,' retorted the manager.

'Mister,' growled the first detective, who seemed to be in charge, 'we have enough evidence to warrant the demolition of this whole building if we have to – and make no mistake, we would do just that. If you want to protect your job, you tell me where Stoddart is.'

'If I knew, I'd tell you,' the manager promised. 'As for my job – well, there's little chance of my having one, after this. The club's gaming and liquor licences are due for renewal next week and I can't see them being granted, can you?'

'That's just breaking my heart,' scowled the detective. He'd been eyeing Wise with obvious interest, and said: 'Your face seems to ring a bell. What's your name and what is your business here?'

'I work for the BBC,' Wise told him confidently. 'We were discussing the possibility of doing a live show here – which would appear to be most unlikely under these present circumstances, wouldn't you say?'

'At a guess, I'd say that you have more chance of getting bitten by a daffodil in mid-July,' he scoffed. 'Now, get yourselves downstairs. You can go home after your statements have been taken. Is there anyone else here?'

'No,' the manager assured him, 'and I'd like to collect some things before I leave.'

'Later. After you've given your statement, come and see me and I'll arrange an escort. It wouldn't do to have you wandering around on your own, would it? Now, move

12

your butt downstairs before I decide that you're in need of a strip search.'

On the lower floor they found utter chaos. The floor where Wise had last stood had been ripped up and a gaping hole now gave access to the cellar. The stage was a wreck – scenery and drapes hung in tatters and several customers in deep shock were lying on tables being comforted while waiting for ambulances. At every exit was a table, where detectives patiently took statements from disgruntled patrons before allowing them to leave.

Four nerve-racking hours of listening to the same questions and answers, the same speculations and the same complaints, passed before the manager stood before the table.

'Name?' groaned the weary detective.

'Travis.'

At the curt response, the detective looked up and scowled. 'Don't try my patience,' he warned, 'or would you like to find yourself still here come lunchtime?'

'Michael John Travis,' sighed the manager.

'Occupation?'

'I'm the manager of this place.'

With an expression saying all too clearly, 'So what?' the detective let his eyes wander once more over the scene of destruction, before returning to his paperwork. 'And where, pray, were you when this crap hit the fan?' he asked, with pen hovering.

'In my office upstairs.'

'How very convenient. Witness?'

'Mr Ernest Wise – he's standing next in line.'

'That's nice,' the detective groaned. 'Did you see Stoddart?'

'Yes, I met him in the foyer when he arrived – around 8.30. I accompanied him into the club and saw him to his table over by the bar where Yvonne – that's the waitress – served him with a drink. Mr Wise came in then, so I left Mr Stoddart and took him into my office to discuss a business matter.'

'Did you see Stoddart after leaving him at the table – like after the lights went out, for instance?'

'No.'

'And you didn't know about any deals concerning counterfeit £20 notes, or cocaine?'

'Certainly not,' replied Travis haughtily.

'Thought as much,' came the sarcastic reply. 'Sign at the bottom. Full name and address and telephone number at the top. Block letters, if you please, and don't leave town without letting us know. I would just hate myself if I was the one chosen to come and find you, you know what I mean? Leaving all this paperwork would just about crack me up,' he concluded hopefully. 'Next!'

But instead of leaving, Travis said: 'I was told that someone would accompany me to my office so that I could pick up some things.'

The detective repeated his earlier performance of fleetingly meeting Travis's gaze before glancing around the room and then back to him. 'Mister,' he said tiredly, 'can't you see that we're all up to our necks in it? Come back in the morning, there's a good chappy. Next!'

With a brief smile and a knowing wink, Travis made for the exit. Outside he faced a battery of newspaper and television reporters and scowled. 'No comment,' he snapped and shouldered his way through to an alley which gave access to the parking area at the rear of the club.

Aware that he had now served his purpose and, as far as Rodriguez was concerned, could be a dangerous witness, he checked his car thoroughly for bombs before getting in. Then, after taking the time to light a cigarette, he called Stoddart's second-in-command on the car telephone.

'Can I speak to Hank?' he asked when the familiar voice of Hank's wife answered. 'It's Travis.'

'Hello,' said Hank, moments later. 'What's the problem?'

'There's been trouble at the Pearly Queen and the law have shut us down. They caught Stoddart dead to rights trading in cocaine and £20 counterfeit notes.'

'Are you drunk, or out of your mind?' Hank shot back. 'I spoke to him less than half an hour ago. He was at a hotel in Southend, so there's no way he could have been at the club – even without the traffic it would take longer than that to get here from there.'

14

'I'm telling you he was there,' insisted Travis. 'I met him in the foyer at half-past eight. The law closed in while he was doing a deal with Dainty a few minutes later. Christ, there must have been two hundred witnesses.'

'Okay, okay,' stormed Hank. 'So where is he now?'

'I don't know. I was in my office at the time. Someone let go with a stun grenade and hit the lights just as the Old Bill pounced. When they came back on, Max was gone. He seems to have just disappeared into thin air. The club's full of coppers and they're threatening to take it apart to find him.'

'Something smells fishy. Where are you now?'

'In the club car park.'

'Go home and stay there until I get back to you,' said Hank. As soon as the line was clear he dialled the number Stoddart had given him earlier and waited with bated breath until the night porter answered.

'Put me through to Mr Peter Cumming's room, please – number 257.'

'Hello?' replied Stoddart's familiar voice.

'It's Hank.'

'I've been trying to ring you,' ranted Stoddart. 'Have you seen the news? What the hell's going on?'

'I was hoping you might be able to tell me. Travis was just on the phone.'

'The hell with Travis! Some bastard has set me up.'

'Haven't they, though! What are you going to do?'

Since seeing the newsflash, little else had been on Stoddart's mind. If he produced witnesses to prove that he'd been fifty miles away at the time he was supposed to be at the club, the truth of his infidelity would come out – and his wife would carry out her longstanding threat to inform the police of his many misdeeds. The information she could give would ensure that he remained faithful for many years to come; yet facing trial for something he hadn't done would be equally as bad.

'I'm going to make a run for my villa in Spain, where the law can't touch me,' he confessed hopefully. 'Call me there in a couple of days. Better get Lily to fly out too. In the meantime, try to find out what's going on and see if you can arrange a quiet passage back for me when things cool down. If anyone asks about my movements today, you know absolutely nothing, my bonny lad.'

2

Once Stoddart reached the sanctuary of Spain, safe from extradition, he shed his veil of secrecy in the hope that this would satisfy the law that he was not hiding out in one of his own establishments, and thus relieve the pressure on his organization. Rodriguez, who had been busy in Stoddart's absence, anticipated this and began putting the next part of his planned takeover into action.

At four o'clock in the morning the Soho streets were reasonably quiet after the previous night's revelry. As the early summer dawn began to break there was a smattering of early shift bus and train crews. Postmen, milkmen and night market traders going home after the auctions closed. At 4.15 a fleet of minibuses conveying the cleaning crews which serviced clubs, restaurants, cinemas, theatres and office blocks began to cruise quietly through the maze of streets to drop off personnel and equipment.

Rodriguez, in the front passenger seat of a Transit minibus, ordered his driver to pull into the kerbside at the corner of Oxford Street and Charing Cross Road. There the first of his crew disembarked, carrying what looked like a small lunch-box. Disguised as a plumber he was to enter the Hawaiian Isle restaurant and hide the pre-timed bomb. This would emit such a foul smell that not only would it empty the restaurant at once, it would remain that way for at least a week. A second small device would release a thousand cockroaches into the kitchen area, timed to occur when the health officials would be there investigating the cause of the foul odour.

Moving off, the driver continued along Charing Cross Road into Shaftesbury Avenue and stopped at the corner of Walda Street, centre of an area where Stoddart had a concentration of several video shops. Six men disembarked here, one of them an expert locksmith who would open up the shops for his colleagues to enter and plant hardcore pornographic video tapes among those intended for viewing by young children. As the morning wore on, several young mothers would hire these films and then, pretending to be horrorstruck, would call the police and have the premises closed down, their stocks discarded.

As this group dispersed, two more men alighted. Their task was simply to wait for the early morning deliveries of newspapers and magazines to two newsagents and tobacconists belonging to Stoddart. When the delivery men had dumped them outside the shop and departed, Rodriguez' men would insert several tiny folds of paper containing cocaine between the pages, making it look as though the shops were being used as distribution centres for addicts.

Anxious to know the results of his handiwork, Rodriguez found an early morning cafe and ate a hearty breakfast to pass the time. At seven o'clock he called the police to inform them of the narcotics racket at the newsagents, and within thirty minutes the suspect premises had been raided, trade suspended and the staff taken in for questioning. At ten, the police sirens wailed again through the streets of Soho as the law took its toll on the video hire shops, and three hours later there was pandemonium at the Hawaiian Isle restaurant as patrons flooded out on to the crowded street, complaining about the stench that had forced them to abandon their half-eaten lunches.

Wondering what to expect next and loathing the sound of the ringing telephone, Hank picked up the instrument and called Stoddart in Spain.

'What can I do for you, bonny lad?' asked Stoddart amiably.

'Probably nothing,' replied Hank in despair, 'but the way things are going somebody had better do something or by the end of the week there'll be nothing left of the organization worth a damn. My day began with two telephone calls, one from Winthrop, the other from

18

Crosby. Both were enjoying the company of the serious crime squad, who raided their shops early this morning after an anonymous tip-off about their being involved in drug-pushing. Needless to say, they found packets of cocaine inserted between the pages of some of the magazines and newspapers. Both premises have been shut down while a thorough search is carried out, and Warburton has been down to see both managers to arrange bail. Crosby and Winthrop and their staff claim to know nothing about it.'

'Sounds like a plant job to close the shops down,' observed Stoddart mildly. 'Any idea who might be behind it?'

'That's only the thin end of the wedge,' Hank continued, ignoring the question. 'By mid-morning, all of our video shops were shut down and the stocks confiscated. On the face of it some idiot mistakenly put hardcore pornographic films in with those meant for children. They even had titles like Superman and Yogi Bear. An isolated incident in one shop I could believe, but not all five.'

'It's got to be . . .' began Stoddart, but Hank cut him off in mid-sentence.

'There's more,' he blurted out. 'The Hawaiian Isle had to close down because of a mysterious smell so foul that it emptied the place. The local council got to hear about it and called in the health department. God only knows what they're going to find, but I can tell you this: there's no way anyone is going to go in there until it is found. From what I can make of it, it smells like someone let a whole cartload of skunks loose in there.'

'Is there anything else?'

'No – but don't hold your breath waiting.'

'I need time to think,' said Stoddart. 'Stand by the telephone and I'll call you back within the hour. One thing is certain: the incident at the Pearly Queen was a set-up to get rid of me. Well, whoever is behind this is in for a shock because I'm coming back to sort out this little bag of tricks.'

'Are you mad? Haven't you seen any news bulletins at all since you arrived?'

'No,' admitted Stoddart, 'but I have a distinct feeling it's all bad news. Go on, bonny lad, enlighten me.'

'One of these left-wing factions has threatened a bombing campaign against all cross-Channel ferries and aircraft, so everyone and everything is being searched – and apart from that, the serious crime squad are on the alert for an expected billion pound narcotics haul. You'd be lucky to make it back undetected, even if you swam across. Every coastguard and radar station is on full alert.'

'I'll put a question to you and you tell me if I sound paranoid,' said Stoddart. 'I'm convinced that the man behind our troubles is Rodriguez. Do you think he could have instigated this trouble at the Channel ports to keep me out of his way while he takes over my territory?'

'You do sound paranoid,' agreed Hank, 'but you could be right.'

'In that case, give me an hour and I'll call you back.'

Replacing the telephone, Stoddart poured himself a large, cool drink and, too worried to sit, went and stood in front of the open patio doors of his luxury beach villa. Outside, the sun shone and not a single cloud sailed the clear blue skies. Not twenty feet away, his beautiful wife lazed on a sunbed close to the swimming pool. She believed the things said about him and cared nothing for his reasons for being in Spain.

From behind mirrored sunglasses he gazed at her, the sun's bright reflection from them touching on her long, shapely legs before travelling along her thighs to the flat of her stomach, the trim waist and the proud swell of her voluptuous breasts. As she raised her head to stare back at him her stomach muscles tightened and her nipples stood proud as the sun glinted on her long, champagne-coloured hair.

'You want I should take my bottoms off too?' she teased huskily.

'Sure,' he replied, clinking the ice against the side of his glass.

Unabashed, she stood up and tweaked at the bows securing the bikini bottom which fell to the ground, leaving him wondering why he ever strayed to what he always hoped were greener pastures. She was everything a

20

man could want in a woman both in body – and the promise it held – and in mind.

Smiling at the thought of what he was thinking, she walked slowly towards him with her long, well-manicured fingertips tracing a line from her pubic hair to her proud breasts.

'Are you hungry?' she breathed.

'No,' he replied in all honesty. 'I don't need your body for sex. I want you to hold. I want to feel like I belong somewhere and to someone.'

'What you need is seducing,' she smiled, pressing her body close to his. 'You've been like a cat on a hot tin roof since we arrived. Relax – let Hank take care of things in the big city. He can handle it.'

He folded his arms round her until the cold glass touched her warm skin and she flinched, moulding her body even closer. 'Don't do that,' she purred. 'You know it does things to me.'

As her long fingers began to slide beneath the elasticated waistband of his shorts, he felt a growing need to make love to her right there on the carpet. But just as his muscles tensed prior to making his move, a great shadow sailed silently into view and splashed into the swimming pool.

'What in hell's name?' he exclaimed.

She turned, fearing the worst, then sagged back into his arms. 'It's only someone with one of those hang-gliders,' she sighed. 'I'll be waiting for you in the bedroom when you've got rid of them.'

'I'll be right there,' he promised, thinking that the uninvited guest might hold the key to his problem. Hurrying to the poolside, he reached for the soggy, light-blue sail and was pulling it out as its young pilot spluttered to the surface.

'I'm sorry to intrude,' he apologized. 'I intended landing on the beach, but the currents suddenly dropped and dumped me here in your pool.'

'That's okay,' smiled Stoddart, offering the youngster a hand. 'I guess flying those things is not as easy as it looks.'

'It takes a lot of practice. The best way to start is by being towed over the sea by powerboat – that way you don't get hurt if you make a boob on landing. People can usually cope with landing on the beach first time so long as they're not still hooked up to a towline from the boat. Running free, as I was, takes a little more practice.'

'How far can you glide with that thing?' asked Stoddart.

'With a towline, as long as you like,' came the friendly reply. 'Without it depends on how high you can get and on the wind.'

'Supposing you wanted to land on a particular spot twenty miles away – could you do it?'

'Oh, sure. The wind would have to be in the right direction, of course.'

'You're not hurt, are you?' asked Stoddart thoughtfully.

'No, the water cushioned the impact. If you want to travel this way without worrying about winds and currents, the next best thing is a microlight – that's a hang-glider with an engine – although you need a licence for it.'

'I guess a man of means could keep himself amused all through the summer season out here,' mused Stoddart, and added: 'From your accent you're obviously a Londoner – on holiday, I suppose?'

'Sort of. I own a watersports business back in Woolwich but with our inclement weather not being very encouraging, I thought to myself: why the hell should I stay there to do my thing, when the taxes out here are much more acceptable?'

'My name's Max,' Stoddart smiled, offering his hand. 'Can I offer you a drink?'

'James Scott,' the young man told him, 'but mostly I get called Randy, as in Randolph, because I'm crazy about country and western music.'

'I have a friend called Tony Snow. Everyone calls him Hank for the same reason. Come to think of it, your face rings a bell. Have I met you before?'

'I doubt it,' said Scott. 'You've probably seen me on television. I race 1000cc Japanese ski-bikes on the Thames.'

'Now I recall, bonny lad,' beamed Stoddart. 'Look, I've just remembered a call I should make. Maybe we can get together later for a chat. You're not leaving for home just yet, I hope?'

'No, I've got two more days.'

Feeling as though a great weight had been lifted from his shoulders, Stoddart went inside and as he reached for the telephone he ogled the naked beauty of his wife who stood framed in the bedroom doorway.

'Dinner is getting cold,' she cooed seductively.

'Keep it warm for a few minutes, bonny lass; the circus has just come to town and the old lion is on the prowl.'

'Hurry then, because the monkey is due for a nosebleed and there'll be no show tonight,' she grinned. Unaware though she was of his earlier conversation with Scott and the anxiety it had caused, she sensed an upsurge in his mood and remained to listen.

'Hello, Hank,' he began chirpily. 'Any more developments?'

'Sadly, yes, and it's becoming obvious that Rodriguez is behind our troubles. Some of his boys have been offering protection to our girls and our sex aids shop in St Martins Road has been told to cough up five hundred a week or be put out of business. Have you any ideas about how to tackle him without starting a gang war?'

'Right now that's just what I have in mind, bonny lad – although whether or not I cool down by the time I get home is another matter. But never mind that for now. A young chap literally dropped in a few minutes ago, and I hope he may be the one to solve my travel problem. He goes by the name of James Scott and owns a watersports business of some sort in Woolwich. I want you to research him with a view to putting him out of business – I want him so broke that he'll lick my boots clean for a pound.'

'That sounds a bit vicious,' commented Snow. 'What's he done to deserve that and how will it help us with our present problem?'

'He races one of those motorbike things that go on water,' explained Stoddart. 'If we can reduce him to a state where he'll be glad to accept any kind of deal just to get himself back on his feet, he could get me across the Channel. One of those machines would hardly be visible on radar, and even if it was picked up it would probably be dismissed as a freak thing. As far as I recall they can do sixty miles an hour so I'll be across before anyone can react.'

'It still seems a bit dramatic,' persisted Snow. 'Why not make him an offer for his services?'

'Because I don't intend taking the chance of a refusal, bonny lad. You strip him clean, and then make him an offer he can't refuse.'

'Have you got a figure in mind?'

A refusal could be devastating, thought Stoddart. On the other hand if he chose to pick up a consignment of narcotics on his way, the trip, no matter how costly, could more than pay for itself. 'Be generous,' he said at last, warming to the idea. 'Offer him ten thousand up front.'

'Jesus wept! Are you serious?'

'Never more so,' Stoddart assured him. 'In fact, the more I think about this young man the more I wonder about his usefulness.'

'You're the boss,' said Snow. 'For what it's worth, what does he look like?'

'He's about twenty-five years old, six feet tall, weighs in at a good two hundred pounds, got a body like a Greek god – I'd say he does a lot of swimming and is probably good at it – blue eyes and looks intelligent. No facial hair, no rings, no scars or tattoos. On the face of it he looks like a clean-living lad. Better go easy on your approach, though.'

'When's he due home?'

'He leaves in two days.'

They rang off and, cradling the telephone between his chin and shoulder, Snow began tapping out the digits of another number. With his free hand he pulled open the top drawer of his desk and fumbled for a sweet-like tablet which he placed on his tongue in the hope of quelling the acid that rose from his stomach to burn the back of his throat.

'Wicks,' he said, manoeuvring the tablet to the side of his mouth, 'it's Snow. I've got a job for you.'

'Sounds like you want a dentist,' Wicks replied.

'Sorry,' Snow apologized. 'I've got a mouthful of Rennies. The worry of this damn business is giving me ulcers.'

'That's the name of the game, unfortunately,' sighed

Wicks. 'When I was your age I always told myself that I was going to make the mythical killing and get out of crime for ever. Even dreamed of making it real big and spending my days on a yacht out on the Mediterranean somewhere – and look at me: a middle-aged has-been who never was, whose capabilities don't go beyond lock-picking, petty theft and doing general jobs for you. Take some good, well-meant advice that's based on thirty-five years of kidding myself,' he said. 'Get out with whatever you can lay your hands on while the getting's good – and the way things are looking, that isn't going to last long. No matter which way you read the signs, the gang war is almost due and it's going to leave a lot of dead in its wake.'

'That's for sure,' Snow agreed. 'But unfortunately, it's a question of alternatives. Anyway, let's get on with the business in hand, shall we? I want you to go down to Woolwich and locate a watersports business owned by a young chap by the name of Scott, James Scott. He races those waterborne motorcycle things and also sells them. Max wants him put out of business; every stick and stone he possesses has to go. If he doesn't live on the premises, try to locate his home through the telephone directory and strip that too. You shouldn't have any trouble because Scott's in Spain and won't be back for a couple of days. You'd better take Walker and Golder along to give you a hand.'

'Is there anything in particular that you want done with the things?' asked Wicks.

'Let's put it this way,' said Snow. 'If they can't be found, they can't be traced back to you.'

'Suits me fine,' agreed Wicks. 'What's Max's beef with Scott?'

'Who knows,' lied Snow. 'The job is worth three thousand to you and two thousand apiece to Walker and Golder. I'll stand by on the telephone. Keep me informed and call if there's a problem.'

Replacing the receiver, Wicks thought about the fee and mentally added it to his meagre savings and the five thousand he'd already been paid for aiding Rodriguez in his bid to take over Stoddart's organization.

'That sounded like Snow,' observed Rico Fernandez,

25

Rodriguez' hatchet man.

Wicks' arm remained resting on the arm of his chair. Still holding the telephone, he turned to face Fernandez, a small, slight, wiry man with dark, close-set eyes who made Wicks' skin crawl.

'Stoddart wants someone by the name of Scott put out of business. He operates from Woolwich. Snow says he doesn't know why.'

'Do you know him?' asked Fernandez.

'Name doesn't mean a thing to me.'

'Is your business with him going to interfere with our business?'

'Depends on how long it takes,' replied Wicks. 'But one thing's for sure, I can't give your job precedence over Snow's. I've always worked exclusively for him and if I start making excuses for not doing jobs he's going to start wondering why.'

'In that case you'd better get on with it,' advised Fernandez. 'Call me if you think this Scott business might be of any interest to us. Failing that, I'll see you for the pay-off in two days' time.'

'Yes, but do us both a favour by not coming here again. Snow's no fool. I wouldn't put it past him to have some of us watched to find out who's collaborating with Rodriguez. It must be painfully obvious by now that someone is.'

Swallowing the last of his beer, Fernandez eased himself out of the comfortable armchair. 'Sure,' he agreed. 'I'll let myself out.'

3

When he returned home to England, Scott was devastated to find that his dream had become a nightmare. Every stick and stone had gone, simply disappeared from the face of the earth. The chance he had taken with his meagre fortune and the hard work building up his business had been for nothing. All that remained was an ageing series D Citroen and a few months' lease on his business premises – now housing no more than the advertising literature of his departed wares.

For two days he scoured the city in the hope of finding some of his stock on sale but without success. None of his many friends and contacts were able to help and, blurry-eyed from too much drink the night before, he rang the police to see if they'd had more luck then himself only to be told, cordially, that a large plastic bag, believed to contain some of his belongings, had been retrieved from the River Thames.

At their request he presented himself in hopeful mood at the police station for the purpose of identification. For several minutes he waited alone in a spartan interview room on a hard, wooden seat, and then Chief Superintendent Haynes entered, carrying the suspect bag.

He was a tall, good-looking man with dark hair and friendly eyes which seemed to smile and accuse at the same time, almost making Scott feel guilty of a crime he had not committed.

'So, you're Scott,' said Haynes, emptying the contents of the shiny black bag on the table before him. 'Do you recognize any of these?'

There were some items of clothing which had been

daubed with paint during the renovation of the houseboat he had been preparing for his own use before embarking on the venture into Spain. Curious how the police had connected them with himself, Scott began to inspect them more closely.

'Well,' urged Haynes impatiently, 'are they yours?'

'Sure,' said Scott. 'I was just wondering how come you managed to make the connection. There's nothing there to identify them as mine.'

The hint of a cold smile touched Haynes' face as he produced several colour photographs from his breast pocket and handed them to Scott. 'You have some interesting friends,' he said accusingly. 'Richard Montgomery, professional gambler; Spiro Deiger, international arms dealer; Cameron, racehorse breeder.'

Looking at the pictures, Scott saw himself with the people mentioned. Each one taken at the end of a race he had won on his much-prized powerful ski-cycle.

'They sponsored me in the early days,' he said, 'when I first started in the business. Naturally they won large amounts of money whenever I won. So what?'

'And when you lost?' queried Haynes suspiciously.

'I never did,' declared Scott proudly.

'So, tell me about your trip to Spain,' said Haynes, changing the subject.

'I already have – several times, in fact. It's all in my statement,' replied Scott, somewhat impatiently.

'So tell me again,' Haynes invited stonily.

'I went to Spain for a holiday and to research the prospect of moving my business out there,' Scott said curtly. 'If you want any more detail than that, read my statement.'

'Why should you want to move a highly successful business to Spain? I understand that you owed virtually nothing and paid promptly for all your stock.'

'They call it saturation,' he replied shortly. 'In my view I had gone as far as I could, considering the circumstances.'

'Tell me about them.'

'First, the weather in this country is so unpredictable for the watersport enthusiast. When someone spends several thousand pounds on a ski-cycle, for instance, he likes to know that he's going to get the fullest possible enjoyment out of it. The average punter is a working man or woman so they're limited to holidays and weekends – how many weekends of fine weather can you recall in the last year? Then, of course, there is the aspect of expansion itself. Another centre in London would simply mean competing with myself. If I opened up in any of the coastal towns or resorts I'd have to commute to and fro to supervise my stocks and managers – which would mean employing two managers in order to open up one more centre. That is always supposing that I could find two that I could trust, let alone who knew the business. Customers like to have test runs, just as they do when buying a car, so the insurance for that aspect alone would treble straight away.'

'Okay, okay!' said Haynes, holding up his hands in mock surrender. 'So what does Spain have to offer that we don't? Apart from the weather, that is.'

'Have you ever been to Spain?'

'No.'

'Well, over here I feel like a mouse living in a cage and running on one of those treadmills,' he began to explain. 'The faster you run, the faster the wheel turns but you never seem to get anywhere. Out in Spain the lifestyle is different. There isn't any rat race, there's no hustle and bustle. You don't feel the need to accumulate vast fortunes that you won't ever live to spend. There's enough scope for someone like me to make a good living and still have time to enjoy life.'

'You seemed to get a little uptight when you mentioned insurance,' commented Haynes. 'You were well covered for your losses, I take it?'

'Sure,' said Scott, 'although my policies were taken along with everything else. However, once I've sorted every-thing out I should get around fifty thousand for the loss of my stock, and the same again for any personal effects and the houseboat that I'd just finished renovating.'

'That was very convenient,' observed Haynes sarcastic-ally. 'Saved you the trouble of selling your stock at cut prices to get rid of it, or paying to have it transported to Spain.'

'Are you accusing me of organizing this caper so that I could claim against the insurance company?' Scott challenged hotly.

'No, but you must admit it doesn't look good.'

'Looks can be deceptive!'

'Sure they can, but supposing they found all your things at the bottom of the river; how would that affect your claim? Taking into consideration your planned move to Spain, of course.'

'It could result in a long drawn-out battle with the insurance company and, to be honest, I don't have the funds to fight them if they choose to take the view that I've tried to swindle them in any way.'

'I was involved in a case recently where a man like yourself sold all his stock and then claimed it had been stolen,' Haynes reflected innocently. 'He never got away with it, of course; a nasty business.'

Scott leaned on the table with arms straight and fists clenched, his tanned face sallow, the hard stoniness of his voice well-matched by the ice-diamond glint in his eyes. 'If you would care to step outside,' he warned, 'if you have the guts, that is, I'll make you eat those innuendoes and take great pleasure in doing so!'

The same irksome smile leered back from Haynes and seemed to be deliberately provoking him. 'I have a point, though, you must admit.'

'I don't give a damn about points!' Scott shot back angrily. 'I've been robbed of everything I own. As far as I'm concerned it's your job to find the culprit, not make wild accusations against me.'

'Now that's an interesting point. Maybe you can help me and, in so doing, even up an old score for both of us as well as clearing up this mess. Why not sit down and we'll get down to cases? Smoke?' he added, offering a packet and taking one for himself. Reaching across to light Scott's, he studied him. Anger still showed in his eyes, but not the kind that flared up quickly and ran out of control. Despite the way the interview had gone, Haynes found himself liking the man. 'Don't you remember me?' he asked after a short pause.

'Generally speaking, remembering faces isn't my thing,'

confessed Scott.

'I used to be with the river police,' said Haynes.

In an instant, bad memories came flooding back into Scott's mind. It was six years ago and he had been a guest on a tugboat captained by his father, with his eldest brother as first mate. It was midnight and warm, and the sky was crystal-clear with a full moon, the heavens twinkling with a myriad stars. Just a few miles upstream the bright lights of the city glowed like a great dome above the hustle and bustle of the streets below. His father gave the order to go slow astern and the tugboat's massive rope fender began to draw close to the bow of a giant, ocean-going container carrier, which they were gently manoeuvring into its berth.

As it towered high above, a crew member signalled to a powerboat lying several hundred yards away and, as many over-curious onlookers sometimes do, the powerboat came in close to the line astern. A warning voice called out from above as it inched in to collect a consignment of illegal drugs from the courier stationed at a porthole on the lower deck. Then a searchlight from a police river patrol boat zeroed in from a distance and a second police boat, which had been hiding behind the ship anchored in mid-stream, came into view with a powerful beam probing and loud-hailers ordering the powerboat to heave to.

It answered by coming to instant full power and in the excitement the crewmen on the liner released the giant anchor – though whether by a deliberate act or by accident had never been established. Scott's brother had been crushed to a pulp under its massive tonnage and the impact sent the tugboat to the bottom in seconds. Scott, who had always been a powerful swimmer, was the only survivor despite the police abandoning their quarry to assist.

'I remember you now,' Scott reflected. 'It's been a long time. Did you ever catch the smugglers?'

'Oh we know who they are, but if you can't prove anything, arresting them is a waste of time. As I recall, it was you who said you would recognize one of the culprits anywhere; yet you couldn't describe him or pick him out of our mugshots – and, believe me, he was among them.'

31

'Maybe. Anyway, what's this skill that you hinted at earlier? And what's more, how does it help me?'

Haynes groped in his breast pocket for yet another photograph, which to Scott's surprise had been taken at Stoddart's villa in Spain, with himself as the subject.

'What is your connection with this man in the background?' asked Haynes, side-stepping Scott's question.

'There isn't any connection to speak of,' he said. 'I got caught in a sudden gust of wind when I was hang-gliding and ended up in his swimming pool. Apart from that, we only met once when he invited me to a party the following evening. His friends were a bit highbrow for me so after a couple of hours I made my excuses and left.'

'Did Stoddart talk about himself?'

'No, he just seemed to be interested in my business. I'd already mentioned that I planned to move out there to start afresh and he gave me the impression that he wanted to help – provided he got the lion's share of the profits. Mind you, to be fair, he was probably thinking in much grander terms of business than I am.'

'Oh he is,' Haynes assured him. 'What's more, he didn't really have your interests at heart. You see, we have a couple of men out there watching him and they have his villa bugged. What else do you know about him?'

'He claimed that he had business interests both here in London and on the continent. However, he didn't elaborate on what or where. Apart from that, I don't know a thing about him.'

'Well for what it's worth, he's one of two gangland bosses in London. You name it, he's got a finger in the pie. Now,' Haynes went on more seriously, 'if you repeat the information I'm about to disclose to you, or try to act on your own in any way, I shall personally crucify you. Is that understood?'

'I understand that,' said Scott, adding after a moment's thought: 'What I don't understand is why you're trying to involve me in something which doesn't appear to be any of my business.'

'Patience,' advised Haynes quietly. 'Give me your word that you won't do anything on your own and I'll fill you in on how it concerns you.'

'Okay, you have my word.'

'Good,' Haynes sighed. 'As I said, there are two main gangs operating in the city and at the moment one is trying to take over the other. Its boss, whose name I won't divulge for the time being, is the one responsible for the death of your father and brother and I am quite sure you will meet him eventually. Anyway, he set Stoddart up so that he would get arrested, leaving the way clear to take over his business interests. Unfortunately, Stoddart managed to flee to Spain – where you dropped in on him like a saviour from heaven.

'He may well be interested in your business, but not for the reasons you think,' Haynes continued. 'I have tape recordings of telephone conversations to substantiate almost everything I am about to tell you – and please don't go flying off the handle because we didn't do anything to save you. We were after much bigger fish as you will soon hear. I hope you'll appreciate our reasoning. Stoddart must have realized very soon that you held the key to his getting back into the country at will, and out again, without being discovered. He would have reasoned that if he had propositioned you, you might well have refused since you were doing all right anyway. The obvious solution was to first bring you to your knees and then get one of his colleagues to proposition you.'

'Hold on,' said Scott, bewildered. 'What exactly do you mean by "propositioning" me, and to do what? You're on about me bringing him secretly into the country and, to be honest, I don't have a clue what you're talking about.'

'You race waterborne ski-cycles,' explained Haynes, 'which are so fast and so small that you could make a return trip across the Channel in an hour without being detected. That is the extent of your usefulness to him and for that, through his colleague, he will make you an offer of ten thousand pounds.'

'Christ! He must want to get back here pretty badly to pay that kind of money.'

'Oh, he'll make it pay. I happen to know that he intends bringing in two kilos of cocaine to make it worthwhile.'

'Just what are you getting me into?' asked Scott, ragged by the thought of Haynes' knowledge of his being robbed, even before the robbery had taken place. Haynes, in turn, realized that here was the one man who could help him if he handled himself properly.

'Ten thousand pounds would just be the tip of the iceberg,' he said. 'The big fish we're after runs an international drugs ring. With your help, through Stoddart, we can break up the biggest ring operating in Europe. You, a little nobody from nowhere, are going to be my key man. Your life will be at risk, I'll make no bones about it, but at the same time I can promise you that all the cash you make will be yours and, due to the nature of your earning, it will not be subject to taxes. Eventually, of course, you will also meet the man responsible for your grief in the past.'

With a great effort Scott kept his feelings under tight control while he tried to understand Haynes' actions and his expectations. How can I help this man, he wondered? He has obviously stood by and watched while parties known to him have taken everything I own. If the truth be known he could probably reach out and touch everything that was mine if he chose. He has acted like a god over me and now he expects me to be a puppet on a string. Jesus Christ! Some people have got some gall.

'Have you ever seen what heroin and cocaine can do to people?' asked Haynes, guessing that Scott was weighing up the odds. 'Can you even begin to guess what some addicts will do in order to maintain the habit? Whole families just fall apart; some go crazy; some kill their parents when they get found out; some just kill for the price of a single fix.'

While Haynes' voice droned on, Scott's mind moved to the sanatorium where his mother now lived in tormented grief over the loss of her husband and son. A beautiful young woman emerged from the shadows of his mind. A blonde whose blue eyes were vacant, she slouched rather than walked, her arms hanging loosely at her sides and her shoulders slumped without pride or purpose where narcotics had drained her young life away.

'I know,' he said at last. 'As I see it you want something from me in return for the name of the man who was responsible for the deaths of my father and brother.'

34

'Now hold on, I didn't say that.'

'No,' Scott agreed, 'but I'm saying it and I want to know where my things are and who stole them. I want those people so badly I can taste it.'

'If you're not going on my terms in my way,' Haynes said meaningfully, 'the only thing you're likely to taste is a large portion of my boot as an hors d'oeuvre and a whole mountain of lumpy prison porridge for a main course.' Haynes' tone suggested that he was playing a game where he knew all the angles and made up the rules as he went along. Scott thought about what that meant for a moment and decided that he too could play the game.

'I suppose that means that I get arrested for an insurance fraud,' he retorted angrily.

'You'd better believe it! So, what's it going to be?'

'Your way, I guess. So what do I do now?'

'If my information is correct, you're due to register yourself as unemployed later this morning. Do just that. One of Stoddart's cronies will probably contact you soon, and when that happens, let me know. You can reach me here or leave a message if I'm not available. What I don't want is you going on a one-man crusade. Just let the law take its course and we'll get the people responsible for the deaths of your father and brother in our own good time.'

The day was still young as Scott set out for the job centre. The thought of joining the queues of unemployed was distasteful after being his own boss for so long and he tried to concentrate instead on what the future might hold according to the prophecies of Haynes. The thought of ten thousand pounds for bringing Stoddart into the country pleased him; but even so, such a sum was no compensation for what had been taken from him and would by no means set him up in business in Spain.

Feeling the need to stretch his legs and walk while he thought things over, he parked his Citroen outside the flat, just off the Old Kent Road, which a friend was allowing him to use until his troubles were sorted out.

With his mind in a turmoil he walked the streets, oblivious to the crowds thronging the pavements and the almost stationary lines of vehicles which choked the busy lifeline to the City. In an effort to try to sort out how he really felt, and which course of action he should take, he tried to project his mind above himself, hoping to see things unaffected by the hot and cold passions of hate and vengeance. It was difficult considering his past losses of family, fortune and his dreams of the future. Yet, by the time he had joined the long, snaking queue of unemployed spilling onto the pavement outside the job centre, he felt he knew what he had to do. Glum and bored, he shuffled forward periodically as the front of the queue edged through the large plate glass doors.

There was a howl of laughter from a group of lads behind, and he turned to see why.

'Smoke?' asked a well-dressed stranger.

'Thanks,' said Scott, accepting one.

'Hope you have a light,' said the other, 'I seem to have lost my lighter.' As he reached forward, shielding the flame, Scott took the opportunity to study the man's face, which was good-looking, with blue eyes and rich, dark, well-groomed hair. The touch of his well-manicured hand, as he steadied the flame, was gentle. 'Thanks,' said the man, looking up. 'The name's Snow, Tony Snow.'

'James Scott. Looking at the way you're dressed it's not what I'd have expected to find standing in the dole queue. This is my first time. Have you any idea what the pay is for a single man?'

'Hard to say without knowing your circumstances as it can get a bit involved. For instance, if you're buying your own house and have a mortgage, they'll pay the interest for you. They'll also pay for bed and breakfast if you have nowhere to live.'

'I'm staying at a friend's flat,' said Scott, 'and I'm not paying any rent. My own place was stripped clean by burglars while I was on holiday. They didn't even leave me my bed.'

'In that case, you won't get much more than fifteen pounds a week. Don't you know anyone who'll give you a few days' casual work each week? You know the score, surely; fifteen to twenty cash in hand which you don't declare?'

'No chance,' lied Scott. 'I used to run my own water-sports business and that took all my time. I presume the

36

kind of people you're talking about are builders, taxi firms and market traders. I've never had the opportunity to mix with those kinds of people – at least, not well enough to ask that sort of favour. For all they know, I could just as easily be an inspector trying to catch them out in their fiddles.'

'That's tough,' Snow sympathized. 'You say you were into watersports and your face seems familiar. Where would I have seen you before, I wonder?'

'Probably on the television. A couple of races I won were televised and apart from that I did some television advertising to boost my sales.'

'What happened? Did you go bust?'

'No, business was beginning to boom. Those damn burglars cleaned me out, including the flat above the business premises. I wish I could get my hands on them. Losing my personal things and my stock was bad enough but what really creased me was losing my ski-cycle. I had it specially built and there isn't one to touch it in the racing world.'

'Now I know where I've seen you!' Snow declared triumphantly. 'You were interviewed on television after someone in a race complained that your engine fuel had been doctored to produce more power than anyone else's.'

'That's true,' admitted Scott, 'and they were right, too. But then, there's no rule to govern the type of fuel used; only the type of engine.'

'That's interesting. Maybe you have more going for you than the run-of-the-mill casual worker. I know quite a lot of people who could put your talent to good use, if you don't mind taking chances – and I'm not talking in terms of a few pounds. I'm talking thousands. Are you interested?'

Scott reached out to take a firm grip on Snow's arm. 'Try moving and I'll tear your arm off,' he smiled.

'Good,' said Snow, sighing with relief at getting over his first hurdle, 'but this isn't the place to discuss what I have in mind. You get signed on and wait for me here. I'll be through long before you, but I have some phone calls to make. If I'm not here you just hang around until I get back.'

'With the kind of wages you're talking about,' said Scott, 'I don't think I'll bother about signing on.'

'Take some well-intentioned advice,' advised Snow in a friendly tone. 'You go through the motions – I'm sure the experience will stand you in good stead in the near future if things get a little on the rough or sensitive side.'

Scott drew deeply on his cigarette and his eyes met Snow's before lowering to admire the quality and cut of his suit once again.

'For the sake of argument, let's just say that I place my life in your hands,' he replied by way of agreement.

'Good,' sighed Snow. 'As a matter of interest, what kind of speed can you get out of one of those ski-cycles?'

'The machine will give up to a hundred knots,' Scott told him with an ironic smile. 'The problem is that the water and weather conditions never allow that speed to be attained. I have managed seventy-five on one occasion, but that was pushing my luck.'

'Sounds fine,' said Snow, nodding his head in thoughtful approval.

'You're not thinking of using one yourself, are you?' asked Scott. 'Because if you are, be warned: those tiny little ripples of water you see the ski sliding over cause vibrations which can shake the hell out of you. It's akin to riding an ordinary motorbike over a newly-ploughed field at top speed.'

'I'll take your word for it,' said Snow readily, but when Scott asked just what it was he had to do, he replied coldly as they shuffled to the front of the queue: 'Be patient for an hour and you'll know all you need to know; then it's up to you.'

'Next,' called a male clerk in a flat, disinterested, gruff voice, and Scott turned in mild surprise before walking the few remaining paces to the desk where he sat down.

'Card,' grunted the clerk, reaching across.

'I don't have one,' said Scott. 'I haven't been here before.'

'Name?' sighed the clerk.

'Scott, James Scott.'

'Date of birth?'

'Twenty-sixth of the first, fifty-nine.'

'Age twenty-five,' mumbled the clerk as he filled in the form. 'Where and when did you last sign on?'

'I've never been out of work before. It's my first time.'

'Makes a change,' commented the clerk, eyeing him with curious interest. 'Most people who come here don't want work anyway. Scroungers and tea-leaves, the lot of them! What did you say your last job was?'

'I didn't. I ran my own watersports business. Thieves stole everything I had.'

'Parasites,' snarled the clerk, in an unexpected show of anger. 'Bloody parasites! Too damn lazy to work for their own benefit and more than happy to rob those who do. And I can't help you, more's the pity. Have you looked on the noticeboard for any vacant situations which might suit your needs?'

'No,' replied Scott. 'I didn't know there was one.'

'Over there,' the clerk pointed. 'If you find something of interest, come back and see me, don't queue up again. If not, you'll have to go to the Social Security to get benefit from them – although, unfortunately, if you've been self-employed, you can't collect any unemployment pay for six weeks. Best of luck,' he said, and raised his eyes to look beyond Scott and call: 'Next.'

Snow walked past Scott, giving him a broad wink and murmuring: 'Stick with it.' His knowing smile remained imprinted on Scott's memory as he walked towards the great noticeboard at the far side of the large office where several hundred small white cards were pinned up. Each bore the typewritten name and address of the prospective employer along with details of qualifications and pay. After studying a score of them in detail, Scott found it easy to believe why he alone bothered to look. Positions calling for little brainpower offered wages that would just about entice an idiot to apply, while those requiring special skills offered wages which were little more than an insult to a person's ego or intelligence.

'Anything of interest?' asked Snow, over his shoulder. Scott turned to face him.

'A man would have to be hard-pressed to take any of those,' he replied. 'The only job which pays well is removing blue asbestos lagging from Battersea power station. At my age I can do without that risk, no matter how small or how well-paid.'

'I heard the clerk telling you that you couldn't collect unemployment benefit for six weeks and that you need to apply to Social Security for a handout.'

'Sounds like the run-around treatment to me,' said Scott.

'Oh they'll give you something,' Snow assured him. 'Go through the motions,' he said again. 'The experience will work wonders for you later on. Take my word for that. I'm just off to make my telephone calls. See you outside.'

Together they walked out to the street, where Snow directed him to the Social Security department in the building next door. It was a cool, lofty room, some hundred feet square, with a single middle-aged be-spectacled female clerk sitting alone behind the long counter. A dozen people were scattered among long rows of bench seats and Scott noted that there seemed to be no particular order of their being attended to. It was more a question of watching to see when your turn came round. Suspecting that the lack of staff was probably due to the fact that it was time for afternoon tea, Scott noted those before him and sat down close to a young mother in the front row. After a while he grew bored and began to fidget as one by one the applicants approached the clerk and gave their sob stories, pleading poverty for cash hand-outs. To each she listened with the same bored non-chalance before handing them forms to fill in.

'I'm hungry,' declared a young flat voice, and Scott looked down to find two young children standing to one side of his seat looking up at him hopefully. The speaker was a dark-haired boy of about three, the other a girl a year older who gazed at him through large dark eyes.

'Sorry,' he said, 'but I don't have a thing to eat just now.'

'Jason! Mandy! Will you come here and sit down,' their young mother ordered in a harsh whisper and they turned obediently.

'But I'm hungry, Mum,' insisted the young lad.

'How many times do I have to tell you about not talking to strangers?' she began, but then a shuffling behind the long counter drew everyone's attention.

'Next!' called the new arrival, a young male assistant, at the same time as the other clerk dispensed with her client. The young mother and her two children made their way forward to her, leaving the male one to deal with Scott.

'What's your problem?' he asked.

'Basically I came here to register as unemployed in the hope of getting a job or unemployment pay,' Scott began, 'but as I was considered to be self-employed, the clerk next door sent me up here because the rules state that I can't claim from his department for the first six-week period.'

'What was the reason for the termination of your employment?' asked the clerk, placing a form on the counter.

'I ran my own business until thieves took everything I owned,' repeated Scott, as the clerk put pen to paper.

'I see.' He set the pen aside. 'Do you have any money in the bank, building societies, or any other savings?'

'I have about three thousand in my business account, but I owe at least double that amount to my main stockist.'

'Sorry. If you have more than twelve hundred in the bank there's no way you can claim.'

'But this isn't mine to spend,' explained Scott.

'Sorry,' repeated the clerk, 'but as long as you have it, that's all that counts. I would suggest that you let your creditors make you bankrupt and use the three thousand to live on until you qualify for unemployment benefit. Take this form to fill in – you can send it back when your funds are below the level stated.'

Despondently, Scott stood up and as he turned away his gaze fell upon the female clerk and the young family.

'The trouble with you,' retorted the mother, tears glistening on her cheeks, 'is that if you ever had children, you've forgotten what it was like and how quickly they grow out of their clothes and wear out their shoes. I spent the last I had on shoes for Jason before I came here. Now I have nothing left for food before my cheque comes through in tomorrow's post. Look, for Christ's sake, you can see for yourself that the shoes are new!'

'The trouble with people like you is that you expect the taxpayers to finance your inability to organize your own spending properly. Your rent is already being paid direct to the landlord because you kept spending it. Just fill in the form and we will re-assess your situation,' the clerk insisted.

'Go to hell!' snarled the young mother, tearing up the form again and again, adding unashamedly as she scattered the pieces over the clerk: 'You know I can't read or write. I'm staying right here until you give me some more money to buy food for my kids.'

Sympathizing with the young mother in her plight, Scott fully understood her anger and determination. Glancing back at the clerk who had interviewed him, he dropped the form he had been given.

'I guess I must have led a charmed life,' he said, as the document fluttered onto the desk. 'God forbid that I should ever be subjected to such an experience again – or worse, that I should be reduced to that young mother's present status. I feel nothing but shame.'

Looking up, the clerk fixed Scott with a direct stare and said calmly: 'Take your hate and multiply it one hundred-fold, then turn it into determination. If you succeed in that, you will never need to see this place again.' The words should somehow have come much better from a man of considerably more years and experience.

Still thinking of the young mother, Scott made his way outside to await Snow's return and half an hour later saw him weaving between the cars in the parking area opposite.

'Hi!' called Scott hopefully.

'Hi,' echoed Snow. 'How did you make out?'

'I didn't,' Scott said sombrely. 'How about you?'

'Great. If you're up to what I have in mind, the pay is ten thousand to transport a man across the Channel and take him back again at his convenience.'

'He must be desperate,' Scott declared.

'He is. His name is Max Stoddart and he's a gangland boss who ran foul of the law. Another gang is trying to take over his operation and he wants to get back quietly to stop them.'

'Max Stoddart?' echoed Scott, trying to fake surprise at hearing his name in connection with crime. 'I met him in Spain a few days ago. I had no idea who he was.'

'Well you do now,' said Snow. 'Are you game?'

'After what I went through in there, I am. I hope you realize I don't have a ski-cycle any more.'

'Don't worry, I'll organize everything,' promised Snow. 'You get the money up front on this occasion, and we go tonight. I'll pick you up at eight o'clock, if that suits you.'

'The sooner the better. I'll wait for you at my friend's flat – 29b Knights Place. It's just around the corner, off the Old Kent Road.'

'I'll be there. Right now I have some last minute details to take care of, so I'll see you later.'

'There is one question,' begged Scott. 'Is this going to be a one-off job?'

Inwardly Snow smiled. 'For Stoddart maybe, but I have lots of contacts with people who will pay well to be transported across the Channel. Some are criminals – not all of them British – wanting to come over from the Continent for one reason or another. Then there will be those wanting to go from England to the Continent to salt away their ill-gotten gains in European banks, where the tax man can't trace them. They won't necessarily be criminals as such. Many will be respected businessmen or couriers for them. They, of course, won't expect to pay as much for your services as a man on the run. Even so, I'm sure there's a lot of cash to be made.'

'What about you?' Scott enquired. 'Who pays you?'

'The customer. The money I give you will be after I've taken my cut for organizing things. If I'm too greedy and your fee is too small, we both lose out, because you won't accept. Agreed?'

'Common sense,' smiled Scott.

Prompted by morbid curiosity, Scott leaned against the wall waiting to see what might have become of the young mother with her two children. After lighting a cigarette, he followed Snow's progress between the multi-coloured rows of cars towards his own. Then, without at first realizing it, his eyes focused on another man, who also seemed to be taking an interest in Snow's movements. Could it be one of Haynes' colleagues, he wondered, keeping them under surveillance? Then he reflected that since Snow, according to Haynes, was close to Stoddart, who was also being hounded by a rival gang, it could also be one of them. Deciding not to take any chances, he walked to the kerbside to flag down Snow as he approached in his gleaming Porsche.

'I could be imagining things,' he warned him, 'but I think you're being followed.'

'Thanks,' said Snow. 'I won't stop. No point in drawing undue attention to you, but you'd better keep your eyes open in case our meeting has provoked any interest from one of my rivals. They can be rough if they think you know something that would be of interest to them,' and he pulled back into the traffic. Moments later, Scott glimpsed the face of the other man peering at him as he drove off in a brand new Jaguar.

Deciding to string Haynes along for the moment, Scott strolled back to his friend's flat and dialled Haynes' number. 'Stoddart's man made contact as you predicted,' he told him, 'and I'm supposed to be bringing Stoddart over tonight.'

'What do you mean, "supposed to be"?' asked Haynes.

'I'm waiting for Snow to pick me up now – beyond that, I don't know a damned thing. No time or place, or departure, pick-up point or destination.'

Haynes shook his head contemptuously. 'Mister,' he said, 'when you get to know that kind of detail in advance, you are one of three things: top of the pile, being set up, or dead. If you do manage to hear anything and get the chance, call me. Other than that, try to make yourself useful to Stoddart – get close if you can. If you put on a good show tonight I'm sure he'll realize that your special talent could be of use to him in running narcotics. Then I'll get my main man and you'll get yours.'

'I don't suppose you've found any of my gear yet, have you?' asked Scott.

Haynes thought quickly: if he told Scott that all his worldly goods were at the bottom of the River Thames by direct order of Stoddart, it could ensure that the man would never reach British shores alive; on the other hand, he realized that it might well fuel the fires of hatred sufficiently to drive Scott on.

'Answer me a question first,' invited Haynes. 'When you

44

eventually find the man responsible for the deaths of your father and brother, what would you choose? To see him rot in jail for twenty years or take the law into your own hands and kill him?'

Knowing that Stoddart wasn't that man, Scott could not see what bearing Haynes' question had on the answer to his own; but he answered it anyway. 'Given the chance,' he said icily, 'he will die a lingering death at my hands.'

'All of your possessions were stowed on board the houseboat you were renovating and the whole lot was sunk in the River Thames.'

An icy cold, tingling feeling, not unlike cramp, swept through Scotts body, leaving him in a cold sweat.

'I could get a hundred years in jail for what I'm thinking,' Scott replied, controlling himself. 'I'll be in touch, probably to tell you that Stoddart's bodily remains are on the bottom of the Thames along with my gear.'

Waiting for Snow, he was plagued by bitter thoughts. After several minutes of being sickened by the wild ramblings of his vengeful mind, he left the confines of the flat to walk in the fresh air outside.

'Boy, you look like a man holding the whole weight of the world on his shoulders!'

Scott lifted his downcast gaze to look at Snow, smiling at him cheerfully through the open window of the Porsche. He saw the handsome face but concentrated on the eyes, wondering what manner of man lurked behind the encouraging smile.

'I've seen better days,' he replied sulkily, settling into the passenger seat.

'You don't sound very eager,' observed Snow, putting the Porsche into motion.

'My day has been what many would refer to as a typical Monday. To be honest I feel so far down that there's only one way left to go – straight up.'

'Glad to hear it. You just stick with me and I'll make us both rich.'

'You have my undivided attention. What's on the agenda?'

'All in good time,' promised Snow. 'Everything has been arranged and providing the law or some of our rivals don't foul things up, your trip should be as simple as A-B-C. Why don't you relax? Play some tapes if you like.'

Taking Snow at his word, Scott selected a tape of fifty golden oldies of gunfighter ballads and reclined his seat a little. Leaning back, with his head on the comfortable rest and his eyes closed, scenes from classic movies came to mind, reflecting his mood. Slowly the tension eased from his body and he began to wander into the realms of sleep. When the tape ended, the steady drone of the Porsche's engine lulled him until Snow's angry retort to a careless driver brought him back to reality. Blinking, he opened his eyes to find that dusk had fallen and the windscreen wipers were brushing aside a fine, lazy drizzle.

'Have a good sleep?' asked Snow.

'I'm not sure,' admitted Scott. 'I was dreaming I was a drug smuggler.'

'That's interesting. Any trouble with the law?'

'No. As it happens, I was enjoying success beyond my wildest dreams and all because I'd realized in the early stages of my career that most smugglers got caught simply because they don't use their imagination – by which I mean that their methods of transporting the stuff, although ingenious, are basically the same.'

'I'm not sure what you mean,' said Snow, taking an interest.

Scott sat up in his seat, an idea beginning to form in the back of his mind.

'Simply this,' he began, noting from a road sign that they were travelling on a motorway towards Dover. 'The drug barons continue to move their consignments from A to B in the same old way. For instance, if we were picking up narcotics from a courier tonight, we'd have to bring it by road or rail. He would have already taken a risk by either travelling on one of the ferries or sneaking across the Channel on a private yacht where he could well have been picked up by radar. He would either abandon the yacht or use it again, which would increase his chances of getting caught the next time around.'

'And how did you get over the problem in your dream?' enquired Snow.

'One way, bearing in mind that in my dream I had the

specific task of moving large consignments of up to a tonne across the English Channel, was by using a relay method where no actual contact was made between the couriers. In effect, this eliminated the likelihood of their being tracked as suspicious by radar and intercepted by the authorities. The French connection would leave their coast and dump the cargo in the Channel while en route to another port where they could be searched without fear. Then a relay vessel would set out from an English port, pick up the goods and return to home waters. If that was picked up and tracked by radar the operators would probably shrug their shoulders and dismiss it as a joyrider or someone just travelling from one English port to another.'

'Sounds a bit haphazard to me,' said Snow, hoping that his criticism would elicit more details of what could prove to be a multi-million pound project. 'The street value of a tonne of narcotics would run close to one hundred million pounds. You don't just dump that kind of money in the busiest shipping lane in the world then trust to luck that you can pick it up again.'

'My first pick-up,' began Scott, giving considerable emphasis to the word 'first', 'was based on the method of picking up commandos at sea after they had been on a raid during the war. You may have seen it in films. The commandos swim out to a pre-set location, then a fast attack craft with a dinghy lashed alongside races along the line of men in the water, who are holding up strong rubber rings. These rings slip over the outstretched arm of a man lying in the dinghy and each man is whipped out of the water by sheer speed. Once that has been achieved, he is transferred to the mother ship.'

'Is this the kind of thing you would go in for, given the chance?' asked Snow.

'Why not? When you get right down to the nitty gritty of life, it's every man for himself. The power of the pound seems to be all that matters these days. Look at me and my past. I've worked as hard as I knew how, and where has it got me? My commitments outweigh my assets and all I have for my pains is the prospect of being charged with stealing my own stock in order to make a fraudulent claim

47

against the insurance company.'

'I know what you mean,' said Snow sympathetically. 'The trouble is that some people do these things so the law tars everyone else with the same brush until they can prove otherwise. Unfortunately, the likes of you get caught up in their intrigues and the insurance companies take advantage. Let's face it, a day's delay in paying out for your claim is money in the bank to them. If they can hang on for as long as two years, they'll have doubled your money in investments. That means when you do get paid out all you're really getting is the interest they have accumulated on your capital.'

'You make them sound like bigger crooks than crooks,' laughed Scott.

'They are, make no mistake about that. They're legal, too,' he added. 'Did anything else of interest come to mind during this dream of yours?'

'Only that I've just thought of two more ideas. I can't quite recall the details but one involved firing the stuff across or doing it in a big way by remote control. I remember talking to someone about the enormous expense of setting up the deal. The one aspect in my favour was that the method of transit was so unique that it was impossible to detect.'

'And you can't remember what it was?'

'No,' lied Scott. 'Maybe it will come back to me later.'

When darkness came, the continuous lines of red rear-lights ahead, combined with the bright headlights of on-coming traffic, began to strain Snow's eyes. His gaze flicked to his own rear view mirror. A vehicle with one bright headlight and one not quite as bright was still following some way behind. He ignored it, knowing that it was Rico Fernandez, Rodriguez' hatchetman. Minutes later, three soaring columns of large red lights loomed up ahead through the drizzle, resolving into the tall iron structure of a massive radio mast which acted as a landmark for the road leading to the small, sleepy town of Deal. Seconds after Snow had turned on to it, the Jaguar followed.

'We're heading for Deal?' asked Scott.

'We are. Have you been here before?'

48

'Not since I was a kid. My old man used to bring me down to fish off the pier,' said Scott reminiscently. 'We didn't have two halfpennies to rub together in those days, so coming down here was like a holiday. I used to love the night fishing best. My first catch was a twenty-four pound cod and from then on I was hooked on fishing.'

'Don't you go fishing nowadays?' asked Snow. 'It's supposed to be relaxing, they say.'

I've had the odd afternoon on the upper reaches of the Thames, but it's not the same. There's no chance of catching anything big up there.'

'Maybe you'll get more time to come down here if our little bit of business gets under way – at least, if you don't it won't be for the lack of time and finances.'

Reaching across, Snow opened the glove compartment to reveal a Colt 45 automatic resting on four packets of fifty pound notes, still in their banker's plastic wrappers. 'That's yours,' he continued, 'and as a show of good faith you can have it now. But let me give you a warning just in case you do happen to have any reservations. To make this little jaunt worthwhile it's a safe bet that Stoddart will be bringing in a quantity of narcotics.'

Scott reached out for the bundles of notes. Folding them double in his palm he flicked across the ends like a pack of playing cards. It took me a whole year of hard slogging to earn this much,' he said, with a touch of bitterness. 'If Stoddart, or anyone else, is willing to pay me this kind of money for a couple of hours' work, I don't give a damn what they carry with them.'

'That's good thinking,' smiled Snow, 'and we could improve on that considerably if you care to put that brain of yours to work. My guess is that this deal has opened a door in your mind that needs exploiting. I've a feeling that you're a natural for smuggling.'

'You won't hear any complaints from me,' promised Scott.

'Good. There's just one thing. Stoddart has all the contacts and he's going to be suspicious of anyone not connected with the game coming up with ideas. I know how it is when you have a good idea buzzing around inside your head. You get enthusiastic and you have to air your views – that's natural – but don't come on too strong with him. Where possible, let me do the talking.'

'You're the boss,' agreed Scott.

Snow had been casting frequent glances in the mirror and, since the Jaguar's headlights continued to shine through the rear window, Scott guessed his suspicions, although he did not appear to be worried. Fearing that Haynes was having them followed and might compromise him, he asked the obvious, saying casually: 'Is there something back there that I should know about?'

Snow automatically glanced in the rear view mirror again. 'It's the Jaguar you saw following me earlier today. Rico Fernandez, Rodriguez' hatchetman, is keeping tabs on us. After what I've been through in the past week his distant companionship comes as no surprise. Don't you worry about him. As far as tonight's run is concerned, I've taken care of every angle. However, if you come across him in the future, shoot first and ask questions later. He's an animal. If he thinks you know something he'd like to know himself, he'll stop at nothing to get it out of you – and by nothing I mean the extraction of fingernails and toenails with pincers, and the use of electrical charges to your more private parts.'

'What in hell's name have I let myself in for?'

'You're in the high-risk business now,' Snow warned. 'At a guess, I'd say your trip will consist of ninety minutes outward run and possibly a couple of hours on the return journey. At ten thousand a throw, that's good wages. Maybe you'd better take that Colt automatic, just in case. Keep it: it may come in handy. I have another taped under my seat.'

Scott took up the weapon with a certain amount of awe but when he felt it snuggled in his fist he was surprised at the strength and security it suggested.

'Have you ever used firearms before?' asked Snow.

'Yes, but not with the thought of using them to inflict injury on human beings. One of my sponsors in the early days was an arms dealer and I once went with him to a pistol club and the rifle range on another occasion.'

'Well, I shouldn't worry about it too much. Just having it handy often gives enough of an air of confidence to warn off the likes of Rico.'

'Let's hope so. When do I get to know the details of tonight's trip?' Scott enquired as they entered the quiet seafront town of Deal.

'In about twenty minutes,' Snow replied, pulling into the kerb some distance from the pier. 'This is where I leave you. There's a boat waiting for you behind the cafe at the end of the pier. You'll be met there by Andrew, a man in his fifties who has no right arm. He'll tell you all you need to know and see you on your way. I'll stay here to keep an eye on Rico and meet you on your return. Have a safe trip.'

Out of the car, Scott turned to see the dim shape of the Jaguar parked several hundred yards away. Patting his breast pocket to make sure that his fee was still there, he turned with head bowed against the heavy drizzle. Small, dark, eerie silhouettes of fishing boats lined the deserted pebbled beaches, bringing back memories of happy childhood days, but on the pier a great sadness swept over him and crystal-clear memories flooded back of his excitement as his father gave him encouragement and instructions in the landing of his first cod.

'Any luck?' he found himself asking a shadowy figure huddled in a hooded, waterproof coat.

'Catch mackerel with a bent pin tonight,' came the hushed reply. 'No sign of any cod. Too warm I guess.'

'Maybe the change of weather will bring them inshore,' said Scott encouragingly. 'My old dad always said: "The dirtier the weather, the better the catch".'

'Me too,' the stranger called over his shoulder. 'I only hope the cod believe it.'

With a smile Scott moved on. He passed many more patient, shadowy figures on his way to the cafe, where notices now banned fishing from the promenade deck surrounding it. That area, being the farthest from the shore and having deep water, had always been much sought after. Skirting the cafe, he emerged on the seaward side to look down into the black depths below.

'Looking for anything in particular?' asked a gruff voice.

Scott turned. The cafe was closed and only a single low-wattage bulb burned within. Menus and posters cluttered the windows, blocking out most of what little light escaped, and the man who stepped out from the shelter of a tall vending machine remained little more than a silhouette.

'The name's Scott,' he said, holding out a hand.

The man stepped forward, his right sleeve hanging loose, and replied gruffly: 'Andrew,' but made no move to offer his left hand to complete their meeting. 'Who sent you?'

'A man called Snow. We were followed, so he stayed in the car.'

Andrew nodded sullenly from within his hooded waterproof as he moved toward the safety rail, scrambled through and climbed down into his boat. Scott followed and stood for a moment to look around. Although the boat was obviously old, it was well kept, for the fine drizzle formed tiny globules on the smooth, shiny, painted surfaces. Twenty-five feet long, it was completely open with the diesel-powered engine situated in the rear. In the centre of the deck stood a large object shrouded with a tarpaulin, which Scott guessed was the ski-cycle.

'Is that my transport?' he enquired, nodding towards it.

'It is,' grunted Andrew. 'If you're ready, we'll get moving. I'll take you out and tell you all you need to know. Let go the moorings while I get the engine started.'

After attending to the forward end, Scott moved to the stern where a small rowing boat trailed in the deep shadows. He let the aft mooring go.

'Your wet suit is there,' said Andrew, nodding at a dim pile on the engine cover, 'and there's a watertight panier on your machine for your clothes. When you get afloat, you follow the pathfinder until you locate Mr Stoddart – he has a beacon signal which will guide you. When you reach him he'll dump it and Mr Snow will switch on another to guide you back home. Is that clear?'

'It might be if I knew what a pathfinder was,' replied Scott.

'It's a circular dial which picks up an illuminated signal. You just keep that fore and aft of you and you'll get where you're going. If the coastline gets in your path, or any shipping, just go round it. Any more questions?'

'Just one. At a guess I would say that the machine weighs close to three hundred pounds. Just how are we supposed to get it over the side?'

'We don't,' scowled Andrew. 'We pull the plug and sink my boat around it. Then you go on your merry way while I row myself back in the skiff.'

'Is that what's bothering you? The sinking of your boat?'

'It's been in my family since it was built before the war. We were at the Dunkirk evacuations. Lost my arm there in this very boat when I was just a lad. Now Stoddart says sink it. He thinks money can buy everything.'

'I'm sorry,' Scott apologized. 'I can't see me getting it over the side on my own, but I'll give it a go unless you have any other suggestions.'

'You must be a newcomer to Stoddart's organization,' commented Andrew, softening a little.

'We met just a few days ago.'

'Well, he's always treated me with respect and paid me well for my services,' Andrew explained. 'With what he's paying me for tonight I could buy a new boat to replace this old girl but the trouble is that we've come a long way together. Seen good times and bad. You don't just destroy something like that without feeling bad about it. It strikes me almost the same as putting a good friend down. I appreciate your offer anyway.'

A moody silence settled between them as they chugged quietly out to sea. When the bright lights along the shoreline dwindled to mere specks on the horizon, Andrew cut the engine and walked to where Scott sat astride the ski-cycle facing the stern. The sea was calm and a lazy drizzle lying over the water like a blanket kept the waves from forming.

'It's a smugglers' night tonight,' he remarked. 'You should have a good run on that machine of yours. Say hello to Stoddart for me and good luck. Better get your engine started.'

Squeezing both handgrips, Scott pushed the starter button with his right thumb and the engine fired into life then eased off to a steady throb. After satisfying himself that the pathfinder was working, Andrew stopped to unscrew the drainplug in the boat's bilges and, with seawater spouting in like a fountain, he walked to the stern and calmly climbed aboard the skiff. As the boat sank lower in the water, Scott stood watching him. Andrew stood at the smaller boat's stern with a single oar, which he swung from side to side like a veteran in order to get clear. Gradually the weight of the boat's heavy diesel engine dragged the hull beneath the waves and Scott made his departure.

Turning slowly, he scanned the horizon for shipping and with the machine and the pathfinder's signal aligned, he twisted the handgrips to boost his power. Spray began to whip up on either side as his speed increased, leaving only a thin white line of turbulence to mark his passing. A minute later he had reached full power and began to swing the machine to left and right in order to assess its capabilities and in case he needed speed for manoeuvres.

Satisfied, he resisted the impulse surging through his veins and concentrated on the other waterborne traffic. Cross-Channel ferries, hovercrafts, freighters and super-tankers formed a gauntlet and, where possible, he raced to use the undisturbed waters ahead of them rather than risk ploughing through the turbulence of their wake. He became aware of a feeling of recklessness which he'd often experienced before – although now the challenge was not another rider but the need to outwit the odds against him in order to obtain a more distant goal. Only now did he realize that he had placed himself as piggy-in-the-middle, with the law, whom he was supposed to be helping, on one side and Stoddart on the other. Neither, he suspected, would offer a helping hand should he fall foul of their opponent – unless, that is, he had something of value to trade. Once again he began to explore the possibilities of making himself useful to all parties concerned while at the same time manoeuvring towards his own goal.

After a while he noticed that the steady flow of luminous dots passing across the pathfinder's dial had speeded up, almost forming a solid line. This, he guessed, although he was still several miles from the French coast, meant that he was closing in on his destination. As a precaution he slowed down to concentrate on what lay in the sea close at hand. At sea-level visibility was poor and with the pathfinder's line solid he was even more cautious. Moving ahead at dead slow he picked out a brief flicker of light that died instantly. He stopped. Five seconds passed and it winked again, then there came the sound of an outboard motor from the same direction. Guessing that it must be Stoddart piloting the unlit craft, Scott eased the ski-cycle forward with the Colt automatic at the ready. The light winked again, giving him a bearing on a dark shape approaching low in the water which he identified as a small inflatable craft fitted with an outboard motor. A huddled figure sat in its rear shrouded in a hooded waterproof.

Pocketing the Colt he eased forward to make contact. 'It's me Mr Stoddart,' he called. 'It's James Scott.'

'Come alongside, bonny lad,' and as he did so, Stoddart shed the clumsy hooded waterproof to reveal a black wetsuit beneath. From his uncertain footing in the wobbly inflatable he reached over to place a well-wrapped package in the pannier, then scrambled astride the ski-cycle behind Scott. Almost as an afterthought, he held out the small black box which had emitted the guiding signal and threw it into the water close to the drifting inflatable.

'Welcome to my organization, bonny lad. Take me home,' he ordered.

'I can take you back to where I came from,' said Scott, 'but I was under the impression that I would receive guidance – and that our destination would be different from my place of departure.'

'Did Snow tell you that?'

'No, but we were followed to Deal from London, and he didn't seem too bothered. That, coupled with the path-finder to get me here and another signal to guide me back to where I've just come from doesn't really add up to returning to the same place.'

'You're smart, bonny lad,' said Stoddart approvingly. 'You're all right. Just cruise back the way you came until Snow starts sending a signal.'

'Don't you know our destination?' asked Scott, without thinking.

'There are several possible places,' Stoddart explained,

'but since my key men are being watched by the police or by members of a rival organization, it's a case of playing hide and seek. Snow is only one of many waiting for us. The others are decoys who will act if he can't.'

They had now drifted some way from the inflatable and after a few minutes an engine began to drone, louder than their own. With the ski-cycle idling quietly, Scott turned in a slow circle in an effort to locate it.

'There's a helicopter out there somewhere,' he warned. 'Judging by the noise we should have seen its lights by now, so it can't be the coastguard or a passenger flight.'

'Get out of here fast,' ordered Stoddart, but Scott thought that the poor visibility, coupled with the fact that they too showed no lights and made the minimum of noise, meant their chances were better if they remained stationary.

'No,' he argued, 'the whiteness of our wake will lead them to us like a beacon and they have more speed than us.'

'The only way anyone could have located us is if this machine of yours is bugged,' Stoddart rasped, producing a compact machine pistol which he rested on Scott's shoulder. The blood froze in Scott's veins as he caught a glimpse of the stubby barrel close to his cheek. 'Turn into the noise and we'll meet them head on,' said Stoddart, dispelling Scott's fears of being shot out of hand as a traitor.

The helicopter's dark, unlit, wasp-like shape came into view, crossing their path as they faced the French coast. Its course passed directly over Stoddart's abandoned dinghy some fifty yards away. Its outboard motor looked very much like a man sitting huddled in the stern. Swooping low the helicopter let out a long burst of lethal machine-gun fire that set a bright halo of light over the dismal sea below. The craft shuddered under the impact of bullets – the exploding of the fuel tank lighting up the seascape. Scott remained quite still, guessing that the brilliance of this explosion would impair the attacker's vision as it had their own.

'Don't shoot,' he rasped over his shoulder to Stoddart. 'They haven't realized that we're here.'

The helicopter had swung away but now it began to circle and Scott slowly manoeuvred to face it. Its occupants were evidently not satisfied, leading Stoddart to conclude that the ski-cycle had been tampered with and was emitting a signal which was being monitored. Drawing the Colt automatic, Scott held it steady at arm's length and when the helicopter's dark silhouette came into view, dead ahead, he whispered: 'Steady. We present a much smaller target for them than they do for us, and unless the helicopter itself is armed they'll have to come alongside before they can return our fire.'

Scott's outstretched arm remained rigid, with the helicopter dead ahead, and when it eventually veered slightly at a distance of one hundred yards, he started pulling the trigger as fast as he knew how. In seconds the Colt was empty but he knew that the bullets had struck home.

Stoddart's machine pistol chattered on. His onslaught obviously upset the aim of his adversary firing at them from the doorway or window, because none of the incoming missiles came close. The helicopter whisked past then suddenly nose-dived into the sea where it exploded with a brilliance that lit up the area for miles around. With his stomach feeling like jelly and his whole being trembling, Scott sat immobile and shocked.

'You must have got the pilot,' said Stoddart.

'Me?' croaked Scott in amazement.

'At that range a machine pistol is little better than useless but that Colt of yours would kill a man stone dead. We'd better get moving now before the coastguard arrives to investigate.'

Turning away from the burning wreckage, Scott looked down to find a steady signal pulsing across the pathfinder's dial. The sickness he felt over his first kill made him more cautious and, with Stoddart watching over his shoulder, he steered a little off course to avoid the cross-Channel hovercraft heading towards Dover. For a while they skirted the coast then the signal directed them towards a deserted sandy beach where the lone figure of Snow stood waiting.

'Welcome home,' he greeted them, offering his hand to

57

Stoddart as Scott beached the ski-cycle. 'Did you have a good trip?' Ignoring these overtures, Stoddart swung clear of the pillion seat to stand ankle-deep in the water.

'We had unwanted company,' he scowled, retrieving the package he had stored in the pannier. 'Scott here shot the hell out of the helicopter pilot and they crashed. My guess is that this contraption has been bugged and if it is one of our own who's responsible I want his head on a plate. In the meantime, leave it here. It may draw some more of our rivals to where we can dispose of them.'

'I can't imagine how anyone could possibly have got near it,' Snow said.

'It's too late to worry about the how of it,' snapped Stoddart. 'Just find out who and take care of it. In the meantime, get someone to keep an eye on this to see if it attracts any undue attention, then get rid of it and them.' He walked off up the sloping sandy beach and Snow, obviously hurt by his attitude, walked at his side with his head slightly bowed.

'Scott came up with some ideas that could be of great value to us,' he said, breaking the icy silence.

'Oh, he did, did he?' scowled Stoddart, his sideways glance at Scott reflecting his displeasure over being attacked. 'Well, maybe we can talk about that over a drink after we've changed.'

Topping the rise they found before them a large complex of mobile holiday homes, each about fifty feet long and with large picture windows facing the sea. Well-maintained, they had neat, open-plan gardens, and large concrete slabs provided off-road parking for one vehicle per unit. A few lights burned behind curtained windows, casting a little light on the otherwise unlit, deserted, narrow concrete road.

'Scott said you were followed down to Deal,' said Stoddart, breaking the stony silence again.

'It was Rico,' replied Snow. 'I left him watching my Porsche at the seafront. I'm certain it was bugged and as far as I know he's still there.'

'That's a shame,' he scowled. 'How did you get here?'

'I had a couple of the boys bring down some extra transport ahead of us – the way things have been going lately I didn't want to take any chances. There's a Range Rover waiting for you in the car park should you decide to travel up to the city alone and I also have an Escort there.'

They entered one of the mobile homes in the first row facing the sea. It was compact inside, with all furnishings fitted when it was built. The floors were carpeted, and all surfaces were of easy-to-clean polished wood, formica or glass. Stoddart, who had obviously frequented it in the past, made directly for the cocktail cabinet where he placed a package he had brought in from France. He reached for the three glasses and a bottle of whisky which he poured without asking.

'Despite any misgivings over the night's traumas,' he began, raising his glass, 'I do appreciate your efforts in getting me back home. Cheers!' As one they raised their glasses and drained them, Scott's face souring a little as the tangy liquid burned a passage down into the pit of his empty stomach. 'Do you know what this is, bonny lad?' asked Stoddart, nodding at the package as he refilled his glass.

The question hit Scott like a bombshell – did Stoddart know that Snow had told him what he'd be bringing in with him? His mouth sagged open and he lifted his shoulders a little as though to shrug as he looked beligerently at Snow for guidance.

'Well, I'll tell you,' Stoddart continued, 'and then I'll explain why. That,' he began, 'is cocaine. It weighs two kilos, or four and a half pounds. Add it to my weight and we are talking about a shade over two hundred pounds in all – and you just ferried it, and me, across the Channel for the princely sum of ten thousand pounds. Have you any idea what you could have earned if you had transported that same total weight across, instead of me?'

'Not a clue,' replied Scott nonchalantly.

'Ten per cent,' Stoddart threw at him. 'Ten per cent of an estimated street value of ten million.'

Much to the other men's surprise, Scott just stood there with the hint of a smile spreading over his face. Stoddart, looking him straight in the eyes, waited for a few seconds hoping for a reaction.

'Well,' he coaxed quietly, 'are you interested?'

59

Scott's eyes opened wide, his nervous thoughts beginning to become reality. A broad smile spread over his face as he shook his head. 'For my money, you're not thinking big enough,' he said. 'Boost your consignment so that my ten per cent becomes ten million and I'll explain how to move it in one hit. If we can reach a working agreement on that, I'll explain another plan which will enable you to move ten times that amount as often as you please with a minimal chance of being caught. The snag as far as I'm concerned is that I want my first ten million on delivery and in diamonds. The snag as far as you're concerned is that the profit from the first run will be required to finance my second idea. I hasten to add that once my second idea has been set up, you'll be in a position to transport narcotics across the Channel at will, with a minimum of expense and as often as you care to. And, as I said, there will be very little chance of losing any of your shipments.'

'Christ,' Stoddart whispered hoarsely, 'he's crazy. Nobody has ever moved that much stuff before without getting caught.'

'And why?' Scott challenged. 'I'll tell you why. It's because they don't think with a fresh mind. They try to find new hiding places but basically they are still using the same old means of transport. A private yacht or plane can be monitored by radar. If it's by container, freighter or a truck coming across on the ferry, the chances of large amounts getting through Customs are not worth talking about . . .'

Stoddart studied Scott's face, disbelief written all over his own. Then he glanced at Snow, whose expression remained blank, giving no indication as to his prior knowledge of the workings of Scott's mind. The appeal of making more millions than he had ever dreamed of mingled with the suspicion that he was being set up, for reasons he could not fathom. His mind raced back and forth at the speed of light, trying to find out the flaw. His first meeting with Scott in Spain had given cause for concern but Snow's investigation had shown the man to be nothing more than he claimed. Picking up the whisky bottle he walked to the dining room table and pulled out a

60

chair, feeling suddenly hot and clammy in the wet suit.

'Pull up a chair and convince me,' Stoddart invited, dragging the zip fastener down his throat to his navel.

'It's common knowledge that the biggest obstacle in moving drugs across the Channel in large quantities is that private yachts and suchlike are prone to being searched by the Customs and Excise men. Why not have the yacht leave its port of departure with the consignment, dump it in the Channel, then return to home port or wherever? When it leaves port over there I leave port over here and follow in its wake – but some distance behind – retrieve the consignment and return to home port. Since neither craft has actually crossed the Channel we should not – in theory – be subjected to a search on return, or give cause for suspicion if our movements have been monitored by radar.'

'In theory that sounds fine,' Stoddart agreed, 'but it does seem a bit harum-scarum to just dump millions of pounds worth of goods over the side in mid-Channel. Half of it could be lost – or have you given that aspect some careful thought?'

'I have,' Scott declared. 'Packaging is the secret. The narcotics are packed into buoys purpose-made for the job, with homing devices for easy location, and luminous grappling hooks fitted to the top for quick visual sighting and speedy recovery from the sea. As a precaution I would suggest an easy-to-operate plug, so that the buoys could be sunk instantly, if anything should go wrong. If the goods were packed with that in mind, the homing bugs would allow us to retrieve them at our convenience at a later date.'

Stoddart was impressed by the simplicity of the idea, despite the amount of preparation and co-ordination required. 'For the kind of millions involved, your idea does have a certain appeal,' he admitted. 'What had you in mind for the pick-up craft? That won't be easily done without stopping.'

'I thought a catamaran would do the job, with a bar fitted low down between the two hulls; so that you just run straight over the buoys until they are caught and can be hauled aboard. Weight-wise, for easy handling, I would suggest a fifty pound load to each buoy, with a maximum of twenty buoys; that gives you a thousand pound consignment.'

Stoddart refilled their glasses. 'Your idea is unique,' he admitted, 'and it does have a great deal of appeal, particularly the part about sinking and retrieving the goods. Moving or storing that kind of quantity could prove hazardous, so if it's tucked up on the sea bed it could be retrieved as requested, and would be reasonably safe.' Raising his glass he drank its contents in one go, and said: 'Tell me about the other idea.'

'My first idea developed from something I saw in a war film,' Scott admitted, 'and so did my second. It will cost millions to set up but I'm sure you'll appreciate its genius. It involves the use of torpedoes as transport for the narcotics.'

'Good God!' exclaimed Stoddart. 'Where in hell's name do you think we're going to get our hands on torpedoes, let alone the means of firing the damn things?'

Snow had been puzzling over what the transport might be, which had to be virtually undetectable, ever since Scott had told him about it. But knowing Stoddart's ways and stubbornness and seeing his reaction, he knew he would have to speak in order to get him to hear whatever else Scott's idea involved.

'Now just hold on,' he shouted, bringing Stoddart to a shocked silence. 'It's been just dandy for you these past weeks, living it up in Spain while I took all the flak. At times like this you should remember that I am basically your accountant and work for a percentage, and as far as that goes you can take my word for it that our days are numbered if you continue in the way you are. If you try to maintain your holdings and enterprises as they stand, the police are going to have a field day. They know as well as we do that Rodriguez is behind all the recent troubles, and they also know that if a gang war breaks out a weak link will come to light, sooner or later, and then where shall we be?

'If you try shooting Rodriguez, they'll nail you for sure,' he added. 'If you employ an army of hard men to protect your clubs, whorehouses, sex shops and video shops, you can bet they'll get a man in on the inside, in which case they'll know what you're thinking before you do. If ever a golden opportunity got up and bit a man, this has to be it. Even if you just sell the goods you already have enough to finance Scott's first idea and you'll make enough profit to set us all up in legitimate business out in Spain. If his second idea is only half as good and you decide to go for it, the profits will keep us in style for the rest of our lives without ever having to lift a finger again.'

'You just do as I tell you,' snarled Stoddart angrily. 'I'm going to nail that dago bastard for all the trouble he's caused me if it's the last thing I do; all our troubles will be over then.'

'No they won't,' Snow promised hotly. 'That will be when your real troubles begin. I wouldn't even be surprised to learn that the police are lying in wait under cover, just hoping you'll do that. Then he'll be dead, and you'll either be dead or a guest of Her Majesty's Government for the next twenty years, and they'll have a field day wrapping up both gangs. Can't you just imagine them revelling in the publicity and promotions?'

'That's as maybe,' Stoddart argued, softening a little as Snow's warnings rang a distant bell, 'but rather that than risk everything on a crackpot idea like he suggested. Who ever heard of using torpedoes to smuggle narcotics?'

'Just the three of us, so far,' Snow pointed out, his own defiance cooling, 'and that's why it's at least worth a hearing. If you don't go for it you've lost nothing, but I'll tell you this much: I'll guarantee that Rodriguez would.'

'Are you threatening me?' Stoddart flared afresh.

'For Christ's sake!' retorted Snow, throwing up his arms in exasperation. 'An ingenious idea has been born – if you don't grab it with both hands, someone else is going to.'

'Unless you intend killing me to keep me quiet,' put in Scott boldly.

Stoddart's angry glare immediately switched to him, and, as he silently damned him for his impudence, he realized that they both had a strong point.

'Okay, bonny lad,' he said, putting up his hands in mock surrender. 'Let's hear what you have to say.'

Retrieving the package of cocaine from the cocktail

cabinet, Scott dumped it contemptuously on the table in front of Stoddart. 'That,' he said coldly, 'is all you need risk. If you use that to manufacture the new drug called 'crack', you can treble your profits. That's the in-thing today. Those profits will finance my first idea, and the profits from that will pay for the second, if you feel inclined to take the chance.'

'The last thing I need from you is a lesson in finance,' growled Stoddart. 'Just get on with it.'

The rebuff was not entirely unexpected, but it aggravated Scott all the same. For a moment he was tempted to walk out leaving Stoddart to wonder about his idea and the millions he might have made from it.

'I have a friend who is an international arms dealer,' he began, 'so providing you're prepared to meet his price, I see no worry about the supply of torpedoes or the means to fire them. As for the type of torpedo, I would suggest using Marconi Spearfish. They can travel at up to sixty knots and have a range of almost twenty-nine miles. Each warhead carries a payload of two hundred and forty-nine kilos, or five hundred and fifty pounds of high explosives. I don't know how high explosives compare with narcotics in volume-for-weight, but I should think they're much the same. Apart from its carrying capability, the Spearfish is wire-guided, so it can be very precisely directed, and being powered by gas turbine engines, it can be re-fuelled for re-use. To take you one step further, imagine having a boat – or preferably a motorised barge – on either side of the Channel, chugging from one port to another but never making the crossing. Each fires torpedoes for the others to retrieve. I know that narcotics is a top-line proposition coming from the Continent, so all you need to do is find something worthwhile to smuggle from here to the other side and avoid sending empty warheads back for re-filling.'

Stoddart hated to admit it after his violent show of opposition but he was taken by Scott's idea. He pictured a small oil tanker of the type used on the River Thames – their decks were always awash when loaded and would attract no attention – with himself below deck, standing at the head of a line of ten purpose-made torpedo tubes. At intervals of five seconds he saw himself prod each button in turn, firing missiles which would travel unseen and undetected beneath the very noses of the authorities.

'How much do you think the operation would take to set up?' he asked.

'It's been a couple of years since I last heard mention of the price of a torpedo, and at that time they were four million apiece. Suitable boats are cheap; there are dozens moored up along the sides of rivers these days, rotting for the lack of work.'

'I must be getting old,' confessed Stoddart. 'My apologies to you both for my outbursts.'

'That's okay,' said Snow. 'Let's put it down to a severe dose of nerves. Things have been tough lately.'

'Does that mean "yes"?' asked Scott.

'It does, bonny lad,' said Stoddart, and turned to Snow. 'I want you to go back to London and start selling off all my properties and preparing to shut down all my operations there. I'll be staying here for a while to tidy up one or two loose ends. Try to keep things on a low profile and transfer all my cash out to Spain. As for you, bonny lad,' he continued, his attention once more on Scott, 'I want you to prepare for the first stage of our operation. If you need cash for the purchase of equipment just ask. I'll stay in touch to give the final details when I've organized things at my end. Now, since I feel the need to strike while the iron's hot, I'd appreciate you contacting your friend concerning the torpedoes and the equipment to fire them. If he is prepared to supply a suitable craft then so much the better. Obviously we don't want anything that's going to draw attention so get – or give – a description and a price. Personally, I'd prefer something along the lines of a steel barge with the means of towing or a small converted river re-fuelling tanker. Probably two, one for each side of the Channel, as you suggested. Any questions?'

'Not at the moment,' replied Scott.

'The same goes for me,' added Snow.

'Good,' said Stoddart, standing up. 'I have some serious thinking to do and I do that better while I'm taking a solitary stroll. Get yourselves back to London and keep in touch.'

Leaving Scott filled with anticipation over their prospective venture and Snow not daring to guess what was actually going on in his mind, Stoddart left, carrying his machine pistol and still wearing the wet suit. Outside the holiday home he stood in the shadows to see if there was anyone else about. The drizzle still persisted and the only sounds were the muffled voices coming from inside. Keeping low, he darted crab-wise to the brow of the sand dunes overlooking the sea where he lay completely flat. Through the gloom he saw two dark silhouettes inspecting the smaller, darker shape of the ski-cycle at the water's edge, confirming his suspicions that it had been bugged. A rumble of voices mingled with the gentle lapping of the waves and the squelching of feet in sodden shoes carried to him as he waited, wondering who the traitor had been.

After a fruitless search of the machine, the two turned towards him and began to follow the footprints in the sand. Stoddart cocked his machine pistol and waited. When they were but a dozen feet away, he whispered hoarsely: 'Hold it right there.'

They stopped, barely able to peer over the ridge. Then, recognizing the white face of Stoddart, they froze instantly and remained that way hoping that despite the lateness of the hour and the foulness of the weather, some innocent might come along to break his hold over them.

'Who are you?' asked one, while the other butted in: 'Are you hurt?' and leaned forward a little for a closer look.

'You can cut the crap,' advised Stoddart. 'We all know who we are and why we're here. You work for that dago Rodriguez and he sent you here to get me. What I want to know is the name of the informer in my organization.'

'Don't know what you're talking about, Mister,' declared one of the shadowy figures. 'We're from the holiday camp and came here especially for the night fishing. My name is Maxfield. Look, I'll show you my driver's licence,' and he reached inside his coat.

The flat, sharp crack of a single shot stayed the man's hand. 'Drop your weapon,' Stoddart ordered, but then immediately had a change of heart. 'Better still, drop your clothes both of you. Just dump them on the sand. One wrong move and it will be your last.'

They complied, knowing that even if they could draw a weapon, the chances of hitting Stoddart before he gunned them down were remote.

'Now, take ten backward paces,' he told them, swinging his body parallel with the shoreline and sliding down to where the two piles of clothing lay. 'Well now,' he mocked, retrieving a Browning automatic fitted with a silencer, 'I've heard of shooting fish in a barrel but never by fishermen.' He stood up. 'As I was saying, all I want is the name of the informer.'

'We don't know,' pleaded one man. 'Our orders were just to locate you and inform the police of your where-abouts. We don't know anything about any informers in your organization.'

'Well now, that's a crying shame,' goaded Stoddart. 'Maybe we should take a closer look at that ski-cycle contraption. Start walking!' and he waggled the silenced automatic. Shivering with fear they turned back towards the water's edge and walked to stand ankle-deep in the sea beside the machine.

'Have you ever ridden one of these things?' asked Stoddart. 'It's quite an experience. Get on and start the engine.' The men climbed on and, after some difficulty, managed to get it going. 'It distresses me to think of your embarrassment at being found naked on this,' Stoddart went on, 'but since you don't seem to have anything to bargain with I don't see why I should feel obliged to do you any favours. France is that way,' he added helpfully, using the automatic as a pointer. 'If you ever get to see Rodriguez again, tell him I said to keep looking over his shoulder. Now, take it real slow and easy when you pull away because in my nervous state I just might take fright and do something silly.'

Hardly believing they were to be set free, the two men edged backwards awkwardly, using their feet to steady the machine until it became buoyant. As they slowly set off, at an angle to the coastline and heading towards France, Stoddart waded out into the shallow water until he stood directly behind them. With the cold sea lapping at his calves he raised the Browning, sighted it on the back of the pillion rider's head and pulled the trigger. The head jerked and sagged forward giving him a clear shot at the driver, who followed suit.

'Do unto those as they would do unto you, bonny lad,' mumbled Stoddart to himself as the machine carried them on their last journey. 'Only do it first.'

Returning his gaze to the shoreline, he scanned it for signs of life. All was quiet. The unsilenced shot had disturbed no one.

4

It was midday before Scott finally gave up and climbed out of bed. The events of the previous twenty-four hours intruded continually on his peace of mind, reminding him of things he must do in the days to come, and making sleep impossible.

In an effort to sting his aching body back into physical awareness, and shock the relentless nagging of his brain into some sort of order, he languished in a cold shower until he shivered. Towelling himself vigorously, he dressed and sat by the telephone with a large glass of ice-cold orange juice.

'I'd like to speak to Chief Superintendent Haynes,' he said to the secretary.

'Who shall I say is calling?'

'Mr James Scott. I am enquiring as to whether any progress has been made regarding the burglary of my business premises and the flat above.'

'Haynes here,' said the familiar voice moments later. 'What have you got for me?'

'I did what I was supposed to do. I left Stoddart at the Greenacre Holiday Homes down on the south coast. It's a seaside holiday camp near Folkestone.'

'That follows,' remarked Haynes. 'It's one of his legitimate sidelines. He owns it. What else have you got? Did he discuss any future plans in your hearing? Did he mention any names or contacts?'

'None that I can think of. Was there one in particular you were hoping to hear about?'

'Frederick von Lichenburg, a Frenchman – his mother was French, his father was German. He's the man we're after.'

'Is he the drug baron you spoke about?'

'That's him – although to call him a baron would be belittling. He's the king of the whole damn slag heap.'

'In that case, I have something that may interest you. I'm talking about a couple of deals: one involves something like a thousand pounds in weight of cocaine and heroin, but the second may well involve an unlimited tonnage – and I'll lay odds that you'll never catch on to its means of getting across the Channel without my help.'

'Do I detect a note of self-interest in your tone?' asked Haynes.

'Let's just say that I have something to trade. First, I want the name of the man responsible for the deaths of my father and brother; then I want my insurance claim paid up in full without any further haggling – that shouldn't be a problem if you assure the insurance company and their assessors that I'm clean. I'm sure a man of your means could pull a few strings to see that my cheque is in the morning post.'

'That's an awful lot of assumption,' growled Haynes.

'In addition to that,' Scott continued, 'I want something from you in writing which will give me complete immunity if I get caught breaking the law during my dealings with you, or with the smuggling of drugs or anything else.'

'I think you are over-estimating my powers,' said Haynes after some thought. 'Supply me with some hard facts and I could have a word with my superiors with a view to enlisting you in the force as our undercover man. That would give you a certain amount of immunity – but there is no way that I could divulge the name of the man you seek. If anything untoward should happen to him it would reflect badly on the force as a whole and I would certainly lose my job. As for the insurance claim: well, I can only send in my report and then it's down to the company to decide when, and if, payment will be made. No doubt they would be much more sympathetic to your case if they were informed that you had joined us.'

Scott's ego crashed to the floor. He'd been so sure that Haynes would leap at the proposition. If he told him all he knew that should convince him. But then he would have nothing to bargain with if Haynes turned out to be using him, like Stoddart.

'I suppose that as an undercover agent any payments received during the course of performing my duties would also be forfeit?' asked Scott, hoping to use that as an easy get-out.

'I'm afraid so,' agreed Haynes. 'Those kind of perks are definitely not allowed.'

Holding the proceeds of his night's work in his hands, Scott flicked through the light wad of notes with his thumb and said thoughtfully, 'A bird in the hand is worth two in the bush. When I think I've got something that you might find worth trading for what I'm asking, I'll call you back.'

'You do that,' said Haynes, thinking that he held all the high cards. 'Are you expecting to see Stoddart again?'

'He said he'd be in touch,' replied Scott evasively. 'But then again, he might not bother now that he's got what he wanted from me.'

'I don't think you need worry about that,' Haynes assured him. 'Your little jaunt across the Channel must have been a real winner for him. If I'm any judge he'll be thinking that the two kilos of cocaine you brought in could just as easily have been two hundred – and when he gets into that league we'll both get what we're after. You just make sure that you're on call when he gets in touch with you.'

'Like I said, I want that name so badly I can taste it,' declared Scott convincingly and, still clasping the bank notes, he stabbed at the telephone rest to disconnect the call. His directory of addresses and telephone numbers had been stolen along with all his other possessions, but one number would always remain uppermost in his mind.

After a moment's thought he pressed the digits of Spiro Dieger's penthouse apartment in New York. Within seconds the single American ringing tone began to sound. He waited with bated breath, hoping that his friend and sponsor would be at home to answer his call rather than at some far-flung Arab outpost selling his wares.

'Hello?' replied the familiar, well-spoken voice.

'Hello, it's James Scott in London.'

71

'In, or from?' enquired Spiro, with an undisguised yawn.

'In – my apologies if I woke you up. I didn't dare hope to find you at home.'

'I flew in late last night,' confessed Spiro, 'and I planned on sleeping till lunchtime. Did you forget the time difference?' he drawled.

'To be honest, no,' admitted Scott. 'I'm afraid it's a case of necessity dictating the terms. I have a problem which only you can help me with.'

'Well, a statement like that doesn't sound like you need my sponsorship,' observed Spiro. 'Anyway, the last time I saw you you were doing well. While I'm on the subject, your ski-cycles provoked a good deal of interest with the Israelis. They plan to equip a commando-type unit with them. Some modifications will be needed on the engines as far as you're concerned, while I see to the framework so that machine-guns and rocket launchers can be fitted. I'll be coming over in a week or so and we can work on it then.'

'Sounds interesting.'

'That's settled then. Now, what's your problem?'

'It's a long story, but I need your help.'

'Fire away,' said the American encouragingly.

'My problem began a couple of weeks ago when I went to Spain, both for a holiday and to research the prospect of transferring my business out there. I had a bit of a mishap while hang-gliding and managed to land in the swimming pool of a luxury villa owned by a man named Max Stoddart. He turned out to be a fugitive gangland boss desperately wanting to get back to London without being caught. We talked about my business and the ski-cycle racing and he immediately saw it as a means of sneaking back across the Channel. At the time he didn't ask me to ferry him across. I can only assume that he wasn't prepared to take the chance on my refusing. So, to make sure I didn't, he had some of his henchmen strip me of everything I owned before I got home. He then made me an offer through Tony Snow, who was running Stoddart's business while he was in exile. What they didn't know was that the police had Stoddart's villa bugged, and

72

they knew everything.'

'Nasty,' grunted Spiro, expecting the worst.

'You haven't heard anything yet,' said Scott. 'A detective from the serious crime squad, called Haynes, obviously knew about my being robbed long before it happened and used it to make contact with me. At the moment he's holding the robbery over my head as a possible fraudulent insurance claim.'

'Doesn't it make you wonder who the criminals are?' interrupted Spiro.

'Doesn't it, though?' agreed Scott. 'Anyway, Haynes wasn't – or isn't – interested in Stoddart as such. Primarily he's after a man called Frederick von Lichenburg who lives in France and is apparently the big man supplying everyone with narcotics. As far as Haynes was concerned, my part was to bring Stoddart – who was transporting two kilos of cocaine valued at ten million – into the country. I was paid ten thousand for my trouble.'

'Ah,' sighed Spiro, 'the thin end of the wedge. The next step is for you to bring in a man's body weight of narcotics on your ski-cycle, giving Stoddart the opportunity to make a vast fortune while at the same time affording Haynes the opportunity to bag von Lichenburg.'

'That's right, but I put forward two more suggestions: the first, which I can handle, involves moving a possible thousand pounds in weight of narcotics. The second idea, which is where I hope you'll help me, has unlimited possibilities but I hasten to add will never get off the ground – or at least, that's not my intention.'

'Now you have lost me,' admitted Spiro, as the multitude of dollars per ounce of narcotics began to total tens of millions in his mind. 'Have you joined forces with the police?'

'No chance. From my experience they're no better than Stoddart, especially Haynes. He knows who caused the accident in which my father and brother were killed and the man's name is part of the price he's offering. What he doesn't realize is that he's made a mistake by telling me that if I stay close to Stoddart I'll eventually meet him anyway.'

'But will you know him when you do?'

'You can put money on it.'

'Maybe I will,' said Spiro thoughtfully. 'Tell me about this problem you have which involves me.'

'Did you ever do business with anyone who gave you the feeling that they'd do anything once you had served their purpose?'

'All too often,' replied Spiro ruefully. 'Usually after I've delivered the goods but before I've been paid.'

'Well I get that feeling with both Stoddart and Haynes and that's the reasoning behind my idea involving you. It's a little something to ensure my livelihood if Haynes fails to nail Stoddart and von Lichenburg on my next run.'

'Forgive my idle curiosity, but how much are you expecting to be paid for this run?' asked Spiro casually.

'Ten per cent of its street value. All I have to do is stay alive to collect.'

'Christ! You could retire to a life of luxury on those wages. Maybe you should forget your grievances, take the money and run. Settling old scores won't bring back your family.'

'I know. It's just one of those things I have to do. Since Haynes re-awakened the memory I can't think of anything else.'

'I understand, I guess. Carry on.'

'Well, the biggest problem with narcotics is getting them across the English Channel, and I've suggested to Stoddart that instead of bringing them over the water, he should think in terms of using torpedoes to carry them beneath – and that's where you come in.'

'That's brilliant!' Spiro exclaimed. 'How did he respond?'

'Not very well at first, but now he's all for it. What I'd like you to do is to go through the motions of selling him the torpedoes and the necessary equipment to launch them.'

'No problem. What kind of vessel had you in mind?'

'One suggestion is to convert a couple of small river refuelling tankers. They always sit low in the water when loaded so they wouldn't attract attention. The torpedoes and tubes could be housed in part of the holds with the rest being used as ballast tanks. The torpedoes could then

74

be launched back and forth at will and, since we intend using wire-guided missiles, retrieving them should be no problem.'

'And you don't want this to happen in actual fact?' asked Spiro.

'No. All I want you to do is keep the patter and promises going for a couple of weeks.'

'Glad to be of some help,' he replied. 'You can give Stoddart this number. There's always somebody here in the mornings. If not me, then one of my cleaners or the butler. I'll leave them instructions as to where I can be contacted.'

'Thanks a million,' sighed Scott. 'I'll cut you in for ten per cent of whatever I get out of my dealings.'

'That won't be necessary. I'll settle for a box of my favourite Havana cigars and a case of champagne. Can I get in touch with you at your shop, or have you moved?'

'I have moved and it looks as though I'll have to move again in case Haynes decides to have me watched. He might just think that putting me away would be better than nothing. From what I can make of things these days, all the police care about is their tally of arrests and prosecutions at the end of the week. I'll give you a call in a few days.' Replacing the receiver, Scott walked to the window.

The street was busy, but no more than usual. No one sat in the parked cars lining the roadside, nor did anyone lurk suspiciously where they might watch him to see when he left. Yet somehow he felt a foreboding like a dark cloud looming in the distance threatening to shed its deluge over him. Feeling the need to move, he retrieved his money and made for the door. Turning to take a last look around he muttered: 'I must be getting paranoid.' He knew that he would not return.

Outside, as the late afternoon sun beat down, the feeling persisted and he kept glancing behind him or stopping to browse in a window in order to survey the crowded pavements and traffic-choked road.

At last, turning to face the oncoming traffic, he hailed a taxi. 'The Anchor and Hope, Woolwich,' he said, handing the driver a fifty pound note. 'Keep your eyes open for anyone following and the change is yours.'

'My pleasure,' the young cabbie replied. 'If I spot anyone, do you want me to lose them or head for somewhere else?'

'Both.'

The taxi swung out into the traffic and the driver's eyes continually monitored the almost stationary line of vehicles behind them. After a few minutes he volunteered: 'It's hard to tell who is back there. I'll make a couple of detours to see what happens.'

'That's fine by me,' Scott agreed, and soon the driver took a left turn, away from the normal route to Scott's destination.

'I meet all kinds of people in this business,' remarked the driver. 'What's your line, if it's not too personal?'

'I was in the watersports business until some villain scuppered me. Now I'm on the dole and looking.'

'For what? A job or the villains?'

'The villains,' Scott admitted, and eyeing the No Smoking sticker on the dashboard, he asked, 'Do you mind if I smoke?'

'You go ahead, it doesn't bother me. It's the passengers coming after who complain but I've got some aerosol for the smell. Did you lose much?'

'Fifty thousand in stock, the same again in personal belongings and a houseboat I'd just finished renovating.'

'Christ! No luck with the police, I suppose?'

'No,' Scott lied.

'I don't know why the likes of us bother with them. When I got mugged for my takings last year they didn't seem all that bothered. So in the end I went looking myself – found the buggers, too.'

'What happened?'

'Me and half a dozen of the lads lay in wait for them coming out of a disco. If they do any more stealing they sure as hell won't do any more running afterwards. We stomped over them like a herd of crazy cows. Oddly enough, there's been quite a spate of taxi driver muggings but since then they've died down, so it looks as though we weren't far wrong with our victims.'

'Maybe I'll get lucky, too,' said Scott, thinking of

76

Stoddart.

'You never know,' agreed the driver. 'And if you'll take some good advice, see to the buggers yourself. The way the law deals with them these days they might as well not bother. A smacked hand and a twelve month prison sentence suspended is all they'll get for ruining your life. They'll be back on the streets doing exactly the same thing in eight months. It's enough to make you pig-sick. Any luck on your insurance?'

'Sure,' said Scott, cynically. 'From what I can make of it they're trying to pin it on me.'

'No disrespect, but there's plenty of that going on these days. Usually the stock disappears and the premises go up in flames to cover it up.'

'I was at least spared that. They left my place intact.'

'Can't say I've noticed anyone following,' said the driver.

'Keep looking anyway,' said Scott. 'I hoped I might have ruffled someone's feathers enough to make them show an interest.'

'Half an hour later, the taxi pulled into the kerb and Scott got out. Far away to the right he could see his own premises, but closer lay a small boating and yachting business owned by a friend and business colleague. The main building was two storeys high, its first floor, like his own premises, converted into living quarters with store-rooms for yachting accessories. The ground floor had also been a storeroom but was mainly dedicated to workshops and a trade counter. To the rear lay a solid concrete wharf and slipway where small craft could be hauled ashore for hull maintenance. A multitude of craft for sale were moored nearby in the murky waters of the River Thames. Feeling like a fugitive from the law, Scott walked down the wide entrance to the rear of the buildings where the trade counter was situated, eyes alert for any sign of Haynes or his colleagues. Reaching the waterfront he immediately looked for one craft in particular which was almost derelict.

'Hello there, sailor,' called a familiar voice, and Scott turned to see his friend standing on the open wheelhouse deck of a sea-angling boat.

'Hello, Charlie!' Scott cried, and was soon climbing the

77

narrow gangway.

'I thought you'd be living it up in Spain on the insurance money by now,' Charlie smiled, offering his hand.

'You and quite a few more,' replied Scott icily.

'Sorry. I guess that must be a sore point. How are you doing?'

'Bearing up under the strain, I guess.'

'That sounds like you know who. Can't the law do anything about it?'

'It's a long story which I'll tell you over a pint sometime when it's all over. Right now all I need is some equipment – which I can pay for in cash – and maybe a little help.'

'Name it and it's yours,' Charlie agreed, 'and if you can't see what you want I'll damn soon get hold of it for you.'

'The twin hulls of that old catamaran will do for a start. What's the asking price? I'll pay cash but I don't want any receipts or anything.'

Charlie glanced over at the twenty-five foot long hulls. 'They ain't worth much as they stand,' he admitted. 'How does a thousand sound to you?'

'Done! Next I want three powerful Hercules outboard motors and about fifty gallons of spare fuel in jerry-cans.'

'That thing was built to sail,' Charlie protested, 'not fly.'

'How much?' persisted Scott.

'The engines will cost you a thousand apiece and I'll throw in the fuel.'

'Done! Next is some fibreglass and a length of two-inch steel tube – ten or twelve feet should do.'

'How about a length of steel scaffold tube?' suggested Charlie.

'Fine. Now, apart from the use of your telephone, all I can think of are a few tools and possibly a place to stay until it gets dark. I'll head for my own place then. I can work under cover in the boathouse.'

'You can stay on board here or at my place,' offered Charlie. 'I'll get your gear together and it'll be ready to move when you are. Is there anything else?'

'I'd appreciate you keeping an eye open for anyone suspicious poking around. My telephones are still working so you can ring through.'

'Do you want to settle up now or come over to the

78

office?'

When Scott pointed out that he'd need to come over to the office anyway to use the telephone, Charlie's hand went straight to the belt of his boiler suit.

'Damn,' he muttered. 'I got myself one of those portable things for when I'm working out here but I keep leaving it all over the place,' and he went off to find it.

Scott had his money ready by the time he returned and while Charlie checked it and stuffed it into his pocket, Scott tapped out the digits of Snow's number.

'I'll be getting your gear together,' said Charlie. 'If there's anything else you need, use the phone. Just dial nine.'

'A sleeping bag wouldn't go amiss,' Scott called after him, 'and maybe something to eat and drink.' Then, turning his attention to Snow, he asked: 'Have you got a piece of paper and a pen handy?'

'Sure.'

'The name of the man to contact for the torpedoes is Spiro Dieger. He lives in New York and can be contacted on this number, preferably in the morning. I've already spoken to him and he's expecting to be contacted by you or Mr Stoddart.'

'I'll let Stoddart deal with that,' said Snow. 'How are things going with the other project?'

'I'll be starting on the boat in a couple of hours and should have it ready by the morning. From then on, it's all down to you.'

'Where are you?'

'As soon as it gets dark I'll be going to my boat shed behind my old business premises – should be safe from prying eyes there. If you need me you can use the telephone. I'll remove the one from the office and use the one in the boat shed. If you want to see me down here you'll have to come by boat.'

'Why all the cloak-and-dagger stuff?' asked Snow suspiciously. 'Nobody's looking for you.'

Realizing that Snow was unaware of the intrigue surrounding him, and thus the danger, Scott explained: 'The police think that I robbed myself and sold everything so that I can make a fraudulent insurance claim. If they see you visiting me and relate you to Stoddart the whole bunch of us will be under surveillance before you can bat an eyelid.'

'Okay,' Snow agreed. 'Stoddart is keeping on the move so I can't contact him. I'm expecting him to call any time now so I'll pass your information on and get back to you when I have something for you.'

Scott watched as one of Charlie's helpers hauled the twin catamaran hulls towards the jetty and where the engines lay waiting. Minutes later, one had been fitted to the rear span of the decking between the twin hulls. Not wishing to be seen, Scott sat down inside the covered inner wheelhouse leaving Charlie and his hired help to take care of his needs. Suddenly he felt tired and his eyes heavy, so feeling reasonably safe he allowed himself to doze.

An hour later the boat rocked gently, bringing him back to a state of semi-consciousness, and the smell of hot food teasing his nostrils brought him back to full awareness.

'It's only canned Scotch broth,' said Charlie, peering down at him, 'but it'll keep you going for a while.'

'Smells like heaven,' replied Scott, taking the shiny brown dish. 'Just what the doctor ordered.'

'I was talking to Fred – he's my helper-cum-storeman, and he tells me that there were a couple of city gents nosing around yesterday, asking questions about you. All he could say was that he knew you by sight and what you were doing for a living. He thought they were insurance people or possibly the Old Bill making enquiries. I told him that if he wants to continue working for me he'd better start acting dumb where you're concerned.'

'Thanks, Charlie,' said Scott sincerely. 'Maybe I'll be able to do you a good turn some day.'

'Let's hope I don't need one,' Charlie replied. 'I chucked in a few things I thought you might need, just in case. Fred will be going soon and it will be dark in half an hour.' And with a promise to leave his yard lights out and keep the dogs in until he saw that Scott had gone, Charlie wished him luck and departed.

The broth satisfied Scott's hunger and sent a warm glow radiating from his stomach that chased away the chills brought on by inactivity. When darkness came, he boarded the catamaran and started the outboard motor. Traffic on the river was light and with nothing moving in the shadows his only enemy seemed to be the moon, casting a bright glow from a clear sky onto slightly rippled water. Scott moved slowly, keeping the engine noise at a minimum until he reached the large, thirty foot high roller door facing the river. There he pulled alongside to operate the hidden outer controls. As the great door rumbled upward he manoeuvred to come about, stern first, into the dock. He cut the engine, grabbed a mooring line and jumped ashore to make the carft fast before closing the outer door again. A minute later the deep, hollow rumbling stopped with an ominous clang which echoed through his brain long after it had died away.

Fearing that Haynes might have taken the precaution of posting a man outside, Scott padded through the gloomy interior to what had once been the main showroom at the front. A single ray of light penetrated the glass which had been sprayed with black paint by the thieves to hide their activities from the public, and which now afforded Scott the same protection. Seeing nothing suspicious he turned to survey all that remained of his former livelihood. The floor was strewn with glossy literature and lifesize posters still hung on the walls, bringing back memories of happier times before he'd met Stoddart and encountered the topsy-turvy world of intrigue, death and paranoia. With a bitter taste in his mouth he turned to his office and scooped up a telephone from the floor. The only other item to remain was the heavy safe. He'd thought it secure, but now it stood empty with its door yawning.

As he closed the door between the showroom and the boathouse, returning the way he had come, a loose board creaked and reminded him of one of the irritating jobs he had promised to do a thousand times. With his back to the door he tried to visualize the scene before the thieves had struck.

The balcony on which he stood was fifteen feet above the U-shaped concrete dock and the water just three feet below that. Directly ahead was the guard-rail made to look like the heavy wooden bulwarks of a sailing ship and spanning fifteen feet to either side. The highly-polished wooden helm of a ship had stood proudly between two gleaming ship's telegraphs and at either end of the mock bridge, wide steps with ranch-type handrails led down to the dock. The walls between the storage shelves and benches were brightened by large, hand-painted murals of watersport scenes. More sporting activities such as hot air ballooning, hang-gliding and microlight flying were depicted on the upper corrugated sides of the roof. With a deep sigh of frustration Scott thought of the many long days and nights he had spent making the place look attractive to encourage customers to talk about his business to their friends. Still clutching the telephone he reached out to turn on the lights before returning to the catamaran.

'You have a lot to answer for,' he mumbled, his thoughts returning to the evil Stoddart. More from anger than necessity he began to work on the catamaran and was soon cursing Stoddart's henchmen afresh for taking his tools. Making two holes above the waterline in the fibreglass hulls without the aid of an electric drill proved difficult but at least Charlie, in his wisdom, had packed a hammer, chisel, hacksaw with spare blades and a fibreglass repair kit plus a large tube of Superglue. The food he had packed gave an insight to the lonely bachelor life Charlie led – several tins of broth, soup and beans, a loaf of sliced bread and a packet of butter. Yet although he had re-membered a tin opener and spoon, he had neglected to in-clude a knife with which to spread the butter.

With care, Scott began to tackle the most arduous task first: cutting the decks of the twin hulls to make safe stowage for his expected contraband cargo and forming lids with the pieces he had cut out to keep the sea at bay in rough weather. He carefully chiselled a small hole then wound his handkerchief round the spare hacksaw blade and started his first cut. His brow began to glisten with sweat and his fingers grew stiff from gripping the makeshift handle. An hour dragged by painfully before the first section was complete and he realized that to cut ten holes in each of the hulls for the expected twenty canisters would take too long. As he looked along the length of the craft, cursing himself for not asking his friend for the loan of an electric jigsaw, he decided not to persevere but to cut one large, elongated hatch in each hull. For three more hours he laboured, dreaming of a frosty pint glass filled with ice-cold lager in his favourite local public house, until at last the first hatch was complete.

Taking time off to have something to eat and a leisurely smoke, Scott added another to his growing list of reasons to hate Stoddart and his henchmen – they had even taken his cooking stove and he had to eat the tin of beans cold.

At two in the morning he started work on the second hull and by half past four it, too, was complete. With time an unknown factor he began to work on fitting a catch-bar low between the two hulls. An hour later it was in place with the first of the crude fibreglass repairs made.

The more Scott thought about Haynes, the more he convinced himself that the man was being too clever for his own good. Either Haynes had picked up Stoddart's trail and was having him watched in order to catch Lichenburg; or he had Lichenburg under surveillance through Interpol and would close in to make the arrests from that end, following through from the sources of supply right down the line to the street pushers.

Standing on the balcony looking down at the catamaran, Scott's mind explored the possibilities of Haynes having the premises wired for sound so that he would be able to monitor his return. He gazed up at the steel-framed girder-work supporting the roof and knew there were a thousand places where a small electronic listening device could be hidden. The thought became an obsession which he knew would plague his mind later when he ought to be asleep; so he climbed the iron-runged ladder, which was formerly used to service a long-departed overhead crane for inspecting the girders, coated now with an un-disturbed layer of dust.

Suddenly the telephone began to ring, its bell shattering the quiet and echoing through the emptiness. Heart pounding, Scott scampered down to the dockside where he had plugged in the instrument and then, his hand on the point of picking it up, he froze, allowing it to ring until at last it stopped. Holding down the rest with one finger he removed the handset and positioned the hacksaw on the rest to keep the contact breakers open. Very cautiously he unscrewed the ear and mouthpiece to find a tiny micro-transmitter inside.

'You're not so green as you're grass-looking,' he muttered to himself as he carefully removed it. Then, satisfied that he had laid the ghost which had stalked his restless mind, he shook out the sleeping bag and crawled inside. Sleep came quickly and throughout the day the sun beat down on the corrugated roof warming the interior and giving him comfort as his tired body restored the energies lost during the past sleepless days.

At six that evening the telephone bell again echoed in the emptiness, jolting him back to awareness.

'Hello.'

'Scott?' It was Snow.

'Yes.'

'It's on for tonight, if you're ready,' said Snow.

'I'm not, but I can be. What's the form?'

'Not over the telephone. I'll come down and see you later. Shall we say around eight o'clock?'

'Suits me. I'll keep an eye out for you. Has Stoddart made any contact with Dieger yet?'

'This morning. He's flying over in a couple of days' time just to work out a deal. We shall have unloaded tonight's consignment by then so we'll have cash in hand to start the real business moving. Has there been any sign of anyone poking around at your end?'

'No,' Scott lied. 'Did you have any particular reason for asking?'

'I'm not sure. Rodriguez has been asking why I've been selling off Stoddart's business interests. Just keep your eyes peeled,' he said. 'The word is out that something is going down and there are those who'd like to get in on the act after we've done all the dirty work. That includes the police.'

'I'll be careful,' Scott promised. 'See you later.'

With the appetizing aroma of tinned Scotch broth filling the air, Scott washed, shaved and reflected as he regarded himself in the mirror that the life of intrigue demanded a man's total attention. Why, he wondered, should Dieger

84

want to make a special trip to see Stoddart? Since Dieger dealt in death anyway he would presumably have no qualms about making some easy millions via narcotics – which meant that by opening his heart to Dieger he had now put himself in the firing line. And if that were so, who would be the man detailed to eliminate him, he wondered? And when? Dieger had always been a trusted friend and so would be the perfect person to lure him, unsuspecting, to a convenient place of execution. But then Scott discounted him on the grounds that he had too much to lose by getting entangled in petty murder when he probably had contacts to do that sort of thing for him. Snow was probably capable of many devious acts but murder would not be among them, he thought. Stoddart, on the other hand, had killed already and for no more reason than catching someone spying on his activities.

Plumping for Stoddart, Scott turned to the question of timing. It would not happen before making his cross-Channel run. However, once he had delivered the precious cargo he could be dispensed with, making the additional saving of his commission. That meant he'd better take some extra precautions.

He sat down and began to sip his broth while deliberating. Eventually he telephoned Haynes, who asked: 'What can I do for you?'

'Somebody bugged my telephone,' Scott said flatly. 'I want a straight answer. Was it you or one of your colleagues?'

'Why should I do that?' Haynes hedged.

'At a rough guess I'd say that I have less than twenty-four hours to live. A straight answer from you could make a great deal of difference to both of us.'

Haynes thought about it and tried to make judgement on Scott's tone of voice. 'It was one of my lads,' he admitted, 'although if it comes to court I'll deny it.'

'It won't,' promised Scott. 'The problem is that I've started a ball rolling which I think is about to roll right over me and leave me looking like a pancake. I have enough cash to make a run for it but even if I did get away I don't suppose I'd achieve much for long. Not to put too fine a point on it, I need your help.'

'Tell me about it,' invited Haynes.

'I put two propositions to Stoddart, one of which involves bringing in a thousand pounds of narcotics and goes down sometime before dawn.'

'So?' replied Haynes casually.

Highly suspicious, Scott remarked: 'I've got the sneakiest feeling that my news is not news to you.'

'To be honest, it isn't,' admitted Haynes, 'but carry on. I don't know everything – your suspected demise, for instance.'

'Do you have any knowledge of my second idea – using torpedoes to transport narcotics across the Channel?'

'Broadly speaking, yes. An ingenious idea I thought, and I intend letting it go to some extent.'

'You seem to be well informed,' remarked Scott drily, wondering whether Haynes had bugged Stoddart's mobile home.

'Not as well informed as I'd like to be. We can't have dead bodies left all over the place now, can we? Suppose you tell me about it.'

'Thinking that Dieger was a friend, I called him to ask if he would string Stoddart along with the torpedo idea. I told him I was setting up Stoddart to get even with him for wrecking my business. Now I suspect that they've got together behind my back.'

'Which means that Dieger has probably spilled your story to Stoddart,' Haynes cut in.

'Exactly,' agreed Scott. 'If he hasn't yet, it's only a matter of time before he does.'

'Have you given any more thought to joining our force?' asked Haynes, his brain racing to solve Scott's problem while at the same time solving a nasty one of his own.

'No thanks,' said Scott emphatically. 'I've had enough intrigue in the last few days to last me a lifetime. I just want what's mine and then I'm departing for pastures new.'

'Okay,' said Haynes, 'I'll put my cards on the table. The wife and child of one of my undercover men have been kidnapped by a rival of Stoddart's. If my people handle it, it will probably blow my man's cover. That will not only put his life at risk at a very crucial time but blow the three years' hard work we've all put in on this case. On top of that there's no guarantee of a successful outcome, for the man who has them is the one responsible for the deaths of your father and brother. Am I provoking any interest?'

'Yes. But I still don't see how I can help, or how the situation helps me.'

'You will shortly. What I am about to reveal will cost lives if you talk and yours will be accountable to me. Do you understand what I'm saying?'

'I guess I do.'

'Good. Now, Tony Snow is due to meet you soon. He is my man and its his wife and child who have been kidnapped. I'll be contacting him shortly and any instructions from me will come through him. Is that understood?'

'Sure,' agreed Scott, astonished. 'But are you aware that since the ski-cycle was found to be bugged, Stoddart has been suspicious of Snow? He didn't make any specific accusations but his thoughts were pretty plain.'

'He didn't say,' Haynes admitted. 'Rodriguez – that's the man you're after – used Snow's family to force him to sell Stoddart out. The sooner we put them all away, the better I'll like it.'

'Am I to assume that you want me to rescue Snow's family?' asked Scott.

'Possibly. He doesn't know your face yet so you could get quite close. I'll work something out and instruct Snow. Now if you don't mind, I have some intricate thinking to do before Snow starts out to meet you. Just keep a cool head and don't worry.'

Replacing the telephone, Scott sat for a moment in amazement thinking about Snow being an undercover detective. 'How in hell's name can a man like me get himself into such a bloody mess?' he moaned as he prepared more fibreglass compound. 'I'm beginning to wish I'd never heard of sunny Spain – absolutely nothing has gone right since I went there.'

Carefully applying the stodgy compound around the rough repair he wondered about Dieger and whether he had done him a serious injustice. But then, even if he had, Dieger would do nothing contrary to the law to warrant his arrest or prosecution. Even if he found out that Scott had gone to Haynes out of fear for his life then surely Dieger would at least understand why, even though he might feel slandered. Eventually the ringing of the telephone stopped the worrisome meanderings of his mind.

'Hello,' he said apprehensively.

'It's Snow. I'll be with you in ten minutes.'

'I'll roll up the door.'

Moving along the dock, Scott flicked the switch on the door control then stationed himself at the entrance on the down side so that he could look up river. He stood recalling the comings and goings of powerboats he had repaired and the variety of craft he had sold – his favourite the high-powered, manoeuvrable ski-cycle. Staring into the night at the twinkling of distant lights across the river, his eyes lost their focus. Then his memories turned sour as he recalled the night of the tragedy when his loved ones had been taken from him. Old hatred returned, filling him with a cold resolve which he knew he could not now set aside – not now that this opportunity had presented itself.

Like an omen, a tugboat drifted by ghost-like on the calm waters, the noise of its powerful engines lost in the distance. Suddenly its horn blasted, bringing him back to awareness in time to see Snow's solitary figure piloting a small motorboat into view. Out of curiosity he remained in the shadows of the now unlit interior and, as expected, with the charade now over between them, Snow brought his boat in without any need for guidance. As he reached the point of no return directly beneath the high roller door Scott flicked the control. His movement, combined with the sudden deep rumble of the roller door moving in its greasy runners, startled Snow, who let the boat drift into the side with the engines cut. When Scott turned on the lights only his head showed above the bulwarks. His face was haggard, his stony eyes stared at Scott over the uncaring sight of a machine pistol.

'That's a bit Draconian,' Scott remarked with a strange smile. 'I thought the use of firearms by our police was virtually forbidden?'

'Being Stoddart's right-hand man does have its compensations,' growled Snow, 'and don't ever make the mistake of forgetting that. Lives are at risk – yours included, I hear.'

'I take it that you've been talking to Haynes,' said Scott, hoping to clear the air.

'Nobody talks to Haynes,' said Snow sourly. 'He gives the orders and the rest of us start jumping. Don't be fooled by his good nature when he's being friendly or his nastiness when he's not. He's the best there is as far as I know. Without exception, anyone who works for him has the greatest respect for his ability, even if he is a bit despotic.'

'I'll try to remember that,' said Scott, all too aware of his own experience of the man.

Snow secured his mooring and walked along the dock-side to look at the catamaran, his face reflecting his cynicism. Stepping aboard, he walked the length of the deck spanning the twin hulls, pausing only to glance at the jerry-cans of spare fuel and the two additional outboard motors still lying untried on the deck.

'Time is running short,' he said at last, placing his machine pistol on the deck while he inspected the one engine already fitted. 'Can you make it to Dover by three am? If not, I'll have to call Stoddart and get him to hold off for twenty-four hours.'

'Those two extra engines will give me all the speed I need once they're fitted,' Scott assured him.

'Good. We'll unload the stuff I've brought for you, then I'll give you a hand. I'll relay your instructions as we go.'

'Suits me,' shrugged Scott, looking into Snow's boat. 'Why the aqualung and wet suit?'

'Your cargo isn't coming ashore,' explained Snow. 'Stoddart is worried about rivals homing in when it's landed. As it happens, he's found an American buyer who'll take the whole bundle off his hands in one hit. Your job is to pick the stuff up, head for the holiday camp, then sink it with the catamaran about a thousand yards offshore. When Stoddart's contact has raised the cash you'll be the one to retrieve it for him. There shouldn't be a problem: he owns a damn great ocean-going yacht which will anchor on site.'

'His name wouldn't be Dieger, would it?'

'Not this time,' said Snow, turning to meet his enquiring gaze with a knowing smile. 'That would be a little too convenient now, wouldn't it? Just in case anything goes wrong and the authorities butt in or you get bothered by any of our modern-day pirates here are a couple of devices to make you disappear in a nice big puff of smoke. I would suggest putting one in the forward end of each hull. Here,' he said, offering Scott a small electronic detonator, 'is the means of setting them off. Just flick the switch and push the button. Next is your pathfinder which you'll switch on when you come abreast of Broadstairs. It's accompanied by a micro-transmitter whose signal will be picked up by Lichenburg's private hydrofoil called Paris Two.

'When they pick up the signal they'll start transmitting back to your pathfinder. But don't follow its course immediately because they won't leave their point of departure – Dunkirk – until contact is made. When it is they will steer a course down the Straits of Dover into the Channel, dropping off the loaded buoys en route. You'll have their wake, the pathfinder, and the electronic bug fitted to each buoy to guide you to them. When you have all twenty accounted for, knock out your transmitter. They will stop receiving your signal and also stop transmitting. I shall be monitoring you both so that when they stop I shall start. It's just a precaution to eliminate foul-ups, like you getting lost or bad weather closing in. Any questions so far?'

'Just one. I thought one of your main objectives was to get the skids under Lichenburg?'

'We already did. At the moment he's helping Interpol with their enquiries in the hope of getting his sentence reduced. He'll be piloting the hydrofoil as planned but under heavy armed guard. Anything else?'

'What about the American buyer? Surely you're not going to allow him to get away with all that cocaine?'

'No chance. That haul of cocaine is going to be our honeypot and every greedy little bee who tries to get his grasping hands on it is going to find himself tangled up in a spider's web from which there's no escape. All we have to

90

do is keep our wits about us and we'll end up with every gang boss within a hundred miles of London in the slammer.'

'What about your wife and baby? Haynes seemed to think that I could be of some help in that department.'

Snow's face hardened. 'All in good time,' he said icily. 'When Stoddart is taken care of, Rodriguez will be our next target. Now let's get this lot onto the catamaran and I'll give you a hand to get those outboard motors fitted and tanked up. I see you have around fifty gallons of fuel – I hope that's going to be enough. We don't want you running dry halfway through, do we?'

'More than enough,' said Scott confidently, picking up one of the cardboard boxes. As they boarded the catamaran his curiosity got the better of him and, although he guessed that his question would remind Snow of his own problems, he found himself saying: 'This Rodriguez, what's he like?'

'You'd better get into that wet suit while I make a start on the engine,' growled Snow. 'It's going to be a cold night sitting on the open deck in those clothes.'

Shrugging off the effects of the wall of ice Snow had thrown between them, Scott stripped off in silence and as he stooped to retrieve the insulated wet suit he heard a footfall on the loose floorboard leading from the showroom to the balcony above the dock. He froze, swivelling his eyes in their sockets to see if Snow had heard. The man's back was to him as he fitted the second outboard motor and gave no indication that he had. Scott's eyes looked down at the machine pistol which lay in easy reach and partially covered by his own discarded clothes.

'Well now, what have we here?' sneered Rico Fernandez. He stepped into full view, accompanied by his colleague known as The Turk.

'What are you doing here?' snarled Snow.

'Not disturbing anything,' leered The Turk. 'I wonder what your wife would make of this? Come to think of it,' he said, eyeing Scott's naked body, 'I wouldn't mind some of him myself.'

'Hold it, Turk,' Rico ordered. 'There'll be time enough for that if they don't play ball.'

'We had an agreement,' Snow retorted. 'You were supposed to leave us alone until the stuff was landed.'

'Sure we did,' agreed Rico, 'but the boss got to thinking that an estimated hundred million pounds worth of cocaine is a shade too much to trust anyone with. For that kind of money you might decide to forget that you're a family man, especially since your wife has decided that she's had enough of you,' he boasted.

'You're a liar,' snarled Snow. 'She wouldn't have anything to do with the likes of Rodriguez.'

'The trouble with you is that when you taught her the difference between right and wrong you forgot to tell her that one year of the lifestyle provided by the likes of Rodriguez is worth a whole lifetime with you – copper,' he sneered.

The heavy emphasis on the last word was like the announcement of a death sentence to Snow, and he knew it. Scott still knelt before him. The machine pistol was at his fingertips, partially covered by his trousers, and his hand rested on the deck for support. Snow's own weapon hung snug in its holster under his arm. He knew that if he reached for it, Rico or The Turk would separate his body from his soul before he could even clasp the butt.

'Copper,' he echoed, feigning ignorance. 'What's that supposed to mean?'

'It means that your wife is playing footsie with Rodriguez and that your brat has let the cat out of the bag.'

'She's only two-years-old, for Christ's sake,' argued Snow.

At the slight movement of Scott's head he glanced downwards and in that moment knew that Scott was about to make a move which would result in Rico and The Turk opening fire. He also knew that there was little he could do except create a diversion. Feigning a move to his right he snarled to Scott: 'Go for it!' and cartwheeled over the side into the water to his left.

As Rico and The Turk fired instinctively, Scott dived forward and flattened himself on the deck. More detonations boomed in the emptiness as their guns pumped bullets. Scott quickly brought the machine pistol to bear on The Turk. For a moment the weapon chattered in his hands and The Turk threw up his arms. His face was a mixture of shocked disbelief and horror as he staggered back under the impact to stand stiff-legged, boggle-eyed, open-mouthed – and quite dead.

Rico reacted with a hasty shot before ducking behind the wooden balustrade of the balcony. Marking his position, Scott hauled back on the trigger. As the bullets smashed a passage through their target, Rico's tortured being rose above the balustrade, his right hand reaching out with gun pointing, his left clutching his blood-soaked chest. Rooted to the spot, Scott looked up into the black, hypnotic eye of the gun barrel and knew that when it spat flame his fate would be sealed.

Snow broke the surface between the two hulls forward of the catamaran, drawing Rico's attention. Then, as the man leaned forward as if in a dream to re-sight his weapon he over-balanced and splashed into the water close to Snow.

White-faced and trembling, Scott moved forward to kneel above Snow, who hung by one hand in the bloodstained water, clutching Rico with the other.

'He's still alive,' gasped Snow. 'Haul him up first.'

Reaching down, Scott took a firm hold on Rico's shoulders and hauled his limp body onto the deck while Snow scrambled up and knelt at his side.

'Come on, you bastard, wake up,' he urged, patting Rico's face with the flat of his hand. After a while, Rico began to regain consciousness and Snow demanded harshly: 'Where are you holding my wife and daughter?'

'Go to hell,' rasped Rico weakly.

'Maybe some of your own medicine will prise your tongue loose,' Snow threatened. 'You answer my questions or I'm going to shove my fingeres in those bullet holes. You can scream the place down if you like; no one but us is going to hear,' and he purposefully drew back his clenched fist with his index finger thrusting forward. Rico's eyes flickered to Scott's face which remained impassive and showed no sign of the horror he felt at having to witness such an act.

'Your wounds are fatal, Rico,' said Scott quietly, hoping to forestall Snow. 'Why don't you do everyone a favour and make a clean breast of things?'

'If it wasn't for you and your whizz-kid ideas, I wouldn't be lying here waiting to die,' accused Rico.

'And if your good buddy Rodriguez hadn't set Stoddart up and started what is rapidly turning into gang war, none of us would be,' Snow fired back. 'All Scott wanted to do was move his business out of this rat race. For what it's worth, until a week ago he was just an innocent, hard-working nobody and now look at him: he hasn't got a pot to piss in. On top of that, he has two killings to live with for the rest of his life. That may not bother the likes of you and me, but he's not like us.'

Rico's gaze swung back to Snow. He coughed, his hand automatically clasping his bullet-torn chest. When he had finished coughing he raised his blood-soaked hand to view it, then let it fall again, asking: 'How long have I got?'

'Minutes,' replied Snow.

'Okay. I'll tell you what you want to know. But there's a price. I've got a wife and kid of my own. Me and The Turk were going to escort you both to make the pick-up and then do a runner with it. Rodriguez didn't know a thing about our coming here. I doubt if he'll take his spite out on them if he finds out as there wouldn't be much point in it. What I would like is for my wife and kid to be sent home with a little something to get them started in a new life.'

'I can't make promises like that,' said Snow, but Scott interrupted him.

'Maybe not,' he said, 'but I can. If I ever get paid for my services to Stoddart I'll take care of them for you. That's a promise.'

'Okay,' sighed Rico. 'What do you want to know from me?'

'First I want to know where Rodriguez is holding my wife and daughter,' said Snow.

'They're at the Zulu Club. His story about them being split up was just a lie to keep you from trying to rescue them. He figured that if you thought rescuing one would mean losing the other, you wouldn't try anything at all.'

'Does he know that I'm an undercover man?'

'No, I found that out by accident when I was detailed to

94

look after your kid for an hour. She was looking at some picture book and said: "That's my Daddy. He used to dress up like that." It was a picture of a uniformed cop. I put two and two together and figured that the law was about to close in. Then I thought about your deal with Rodriguez and figured that me and The Turk could jump you and your friend and do a runner with the stuff before anyone realized what was up. It just goes to show what they say about the best-laid plans of mice and men. I thought I'd be a multi-millionaire by tomorrow night; now it looks as though I won't need to worry about it. You don't happen to have a bottle of Scotch around, do you? I feel frozen to the bone.'

'Sorry,' said Scott. 'When Stoddart's men cleaned me out they took everything but the posters on the wall.'

'Too bad.'

'My wife,' interrupted Snow. 'Is she being treated all right?'

'Sure,' said Rico weakly, 'but don't leave her with Rodriguez too long. She's beautiful − too good for the likes of you or him. I wouldn't put it past him to give her the needle so's he can have his way with her. No offence.'

'None taken,' lied Snow. 'I'll call my governor to get you moved out of here.'

'Sure. No rush.'

Snow walked over to the telephone leaving Scott to play nurse. Rico faded as Snow returned. 'We'll leave him on the quay side. Haynes is sending someone along to clean up. In the meantime we'd better get moving or you'll be late for the collection.'

'What about your wife? Is he going to send someone to rescue her?'

'I didn't mention anything about her,' Snow admitted. 'When he goes down it's going to be for more than an abduction. We'll talk some more about that after your run tonight.'

As Scott began to put on his wet suit, Snow fitted a fresh magazine to the machine pistol. 'That was pretty good shooting,' he remarked, glancing at the tiny dark holes in The Turk's forehead. 'Those bullets came so close to parting his hair they almost missed.'

95

'It wasn't intended,' Scott admitted. 'I thought to put him down with a body shot which was a more certain target, but seeing the size of him I can see how lucky I was. It looks as if it would have taken a cannon shot in the chest to kill him.'

'Maybe you have a guardian angel,' mused Snow. 'One thing's for sure, I'll be needing one if I'm going to get through these next few days.'

'I thought you and Haynes had it pretty well wrapped up?'

'So did I,' agreed Snow, 'but I don't put much trust in Rico's deathbed confession. He's just mean enough to hide the fact that Rodriguez knows about my being on the force. He could also be lying about my wife and daughter being held in the same building, hoping that I – or Haynes – will go in and make a right cock-up of rescuing them. On top of that, there's always the possibility of Rodriguez doing a deal with Stoddart by trading the information for a cut in the profits from tonight's caper. It would only take a situation like this to unite them. If that happens a good many years of hard work will go down the tubes – me included.'

At a loss for words, Scott started the third outboard motor which Snow had just fitted and fuelled. Exhaust smoke billowed lazily on the still air as it roared into life.

'You'd better get moving,' Snow shouted above the noise. 'Is there anything you're not sure of before you go?'

Shaking his head in reply, Scott held out his hand, which Snow grasped firmly, holding his gaze solemnly for a few moments. Then, with a wink, he let his hand go free and boarded his own boat.

Minutes later, Scott eased the catamaran out through the yawning boathouse door with all three outboard motors idling. Manoeuvring to head downstream, he glanced at Snow as he set off upstream against a fast, outgoing tide, and wondered if he would ever see him again.

Still pondering on the intrigue, Scott increased power to begin his journey. The night was crystal clear and the moon shed a bright coldness on the smooth, tranquil waters from the star-studded heavens above. Behind him, the city lights projected a great red domed glow. Long lines of streetlights stretched away to each side marking the tracts of concrete and tarmac roads with their commercial and domestic buildings of all kinds.

These scenes soon gave way to the less populated suburbs and the heavy commercial factories: the Blue Circle cement works, the paper mills, the power stations which lined the banks of the lower Thames at Purfleet, Northfleet and Gravesend. Beyond lay the eerie quietness of the marshlands where only a few lights twinkled from remote villages in the darkness and the river traffic was non-existent.

Putting all three engines at full power and the helm on auto-pilot, Scott began to build a barricade from the jerry-cans to shield himself against the breeze caused by the speed of the catamaran. He then assembled the gadgetry Snow had provided from within its shelter. Huddled down at the stern, Scott was barely aware of passing such familiar landmarks as the massive fuel tank farms belonging to the refineries and the wreck of the Montgomery, an American munitions ship sunk by the German bombers during the Second World War.

Abreast of the seaside town of Sheerness, at the gateway to the North Sea lanes, he picked out the distant glow heralding Margate and navigated his way to the North Foreland beyond which lay the Straits of Dover. The weather conditions were still favourable for his pick-up although not entirely in his favour as far as being spotted by the authorities was concerned. Off Broadstairs he switched on the first of Snow's gadgets.

The first signs of life were the lights of cross-Channel ferries in the distance that ran from Dunkirk and Calais to Ramsgate. As they crossed his bow, heading into port, he began to pick up a signal from the hydrofoil Paris and at once put the catamaran on a course due east for ten minutes at full power. He then turned south-west to achieve an exact course alignment with the hydrofoil. In a matter of minutes Scott spotted her lights half a mile ahead and hit the freshly churned waters of her wake. Almost immediately he picked up the signal of the homing bug in the first container and cut power by half to give himself more time to spot, collect and stow each one.

The first illuminated grappling hook danced into view a hundred yards away and he piloted the twin hulls astride it until the two crude devices made contact with a dull, metallic clunk. Switching instantly to auto-pilot, he quickly retrieved and stowed the pear-shaped buoy and its precious contents in the modified hulls. From the moment he'd sighted the first buoy he counted aloud, hoping to be able to judge the distance between them. It took one minute. The second container clunked home and he repeated the operation, stowing it in the other hull in order to maintain an even keel. In the minutes that followed, his earlier deep-down coldness was overcome by a heart-pounding warmth which brough beads of sweat to his brow. The twin hulls gradually sank lower in the water and soon the hydrofoil's superior speed increased the distance between the two craft until its light was like a distant star on the dark horizon.

Suddenly, even though he had been alone before, Scott felt a different kind of loneliness and realized how much at risk he was with a king's ransom of drugs at his fingertips. He refuelled and settled down at full power to follow the pathfinder's signal for home.

Before long, the cold began to creep into his bones, boredom set in and his mind began to wander. His first thoughts were of what he wanted to do after he had claimed his fee from Stoddart for bringing home the contraband cargo. From here he moved on to his fears of being cheated and then back to his earlier fears of being betrayed by his former sponsor, Dieger. This, in turn, led him back to the containers, the plugs he had to remove in order to settle them on the sea bed, and the electronic bugs for re-locating them at a later date.

Reverting to auto-pilot, Scott retrieved one of the containers for inspection. It was shaped like a pear-drop, stood three feet tall and was made of a shiny alloy which blended with the sea in the cold light of the moon. The grappling hook at the top unscrewed to allow an easy exit of air when the screw plug in the bottom was removed. Its body was completely smooth. There were no rivet joints or seams to be seen, nothing to indicate how it had been

98

constructed, or how it might be emptied without being cut. Knowing that the hook and the bottom plug were throw-away parts, Scott could only guess that the homing bugs had been sealed inside at the time of packing.

He replaced the first container and began to prepare the rest, working methodically along the line in first one hull, then the other. Disheartened, he dragged the twentieth container on to the open deck. He knelt beside it and took the grappling hook in his left hand. Holding it steady he gave one of the four arched hooks a sharp jab with the palm of his right hand. Unlike the others, the screw thread remained fast, so he took a firmer grip and tried again. Still the hook refused to budge. In an effort to gain more purchase he eased the container forward to an angle of forty-five degrees, crouched astride it, held it firm with his left hand and struck hard with the right. It still remained stuck.

Determined not to be beaten he took a firmer grip with his knees and, thinking that the screw thread might have been strained when fitted, held the hook with his right hand and struck with his left. To his astonishment the hook moved as though it had been machined with a left-handed thread. Easing his weight further forward until the container was horizontal, Scott studied the upper part in the moonlight while slowly turning the hook clockwise. A fine, highly-precisioned joint appeared several inches down from the top. Obviously it was necessary to have some means of opening for the purpose of packing and unpacking – but why one requiring such highly-precisioned workmanship that it was almost impossible to detect? He proceeded with caution.

When it came free, he carefully moved it away from the main body, checked for wired booby-traps or pressure points, and turned it towards the moonlight for inspection. The cone proved to be just that but with a homing bug stuck in the interior just below the grappling hook's base thread. This Scott squeezed with his fingers to render it useless. Turning back to the main body, he manoeuvred its open mouth up towards the light so that he could see inside and was at once struck by the heavy gauge of the walls. He judged them to be at least an inch thick and the container as a whole too light for them to be solid. He tapped gently with a knuckle. It sounded neither solid nor hollow, and he concluded that a layer of cork had been inserted between the two skins for protection.

Looking further within, he could see that a sealed perforated tube had been fitted between the open top and the plug hole at the bottom, presumably to allow sea water to enter quickly, and to keep the precious, vacuum-packed packets of cocaine safe from damage by the sea or its creatures during their short stay on the sea bed.

He replaced the grappling hook top, stowed the container away and then proceeded to damage the homing bugs in the rest so that only he would know of their exact location after leaving them on the sea bed.

Back at the helm he checked his bearings visually by noting the haloes of light over the distant towns of Dover and Folkestone, before checking the pathfinder – which had developed a fault since he had last looked. He altered course to head due west, calculating that this would take him to his destination. The flickering line of luminous dots on the pathfinder's scope swung to a line directly fore and aft, giving credence to his decision. Out of curiosity Scott tapped the pathfinder's glass dial. To his surprise the flickering stopped. For a time he sat huddled, watching the coastline loom up through the darkness. Then, buttocks aching from the hardness of the cold deck, he came to full alertness as the pathfinder began to flicker again.

In his solemn loneliness he had been pondering on the next stage of his mission: the sinking of the catamaran. His mind had wandered on to ships and distress calls in morse code which was what the pathfinder's flickering dial proved to be telling him. 'SOS' it read again, again and again. Guessing that Snow was using the transmitter to warn him, Scott checked the magazine in the machine pistol and, with dawn barely an hour away, sank the catamaran a thousand yards offshore. He swam down to settle it on the sea bed before striking out for the beach.

Once he had reached the shallows he stopped to survey the beach. The lines of neat mobile homes were hidden behind the rise of golden sandy beach and two dark silhouettes stood motionless below the skyline close to the water's edge. In an effort to identify them, Scott raised his face mask and peered across the gently lapping waters. Both wore dark, hooded jackets to keep them warm during their lonely vigil and it was impossible to see their faces. Scott waited patiently in the hope that they would move or speak to give some indication as to their identity.

'He's not going to show,' a quiet voice predicted. 'I'll lay odds that he's done a bunk with the stuff.'

Scott concentrated all his senses on the reply. Even though he could not understand the words he knew that neither man was Snow or Stoddart. Replacing his mask he ducked below the surface and swam along the shoreline to a point two hundred yards away where a wooden surf breaker reached down to the water's edge. He crawled ashore and circled behind the two men on the beach to view them from the grassy verge above. Only one of the mobile houses was showing a light and he recognized it as the one used on his previous visit.

As dawn began to break, the two figures below grew restless. Lying flat on his belly, Scott compared each man's shape, stance and bearing with those of Snow and Stoddart. Even without seeing their faces or hearing their voices clearly he knew that he'd never seen them close up before. Scott swung around to lean on one elbow and wondered what course to take. The sky was becoming brighter by the minute and he knew that it was only a matter of time before the men gave up their vigil. If his assumptions were correct they would return to the mobile home where he guessed Snow was being held. The SOS suggested that although the operator was held captive he was not under direct supervision.

His eyes strayed from the lonely light shining through the curtained window to the machine pistol. It had been completely submerged when Scott swam down to sink the catamaran and now he wasn't sure whether it was safe to use – or even usable. Deciding that his best chances lay with the men on the beach, he huddled down on his belly to await their return.

Daylight came swiftly and the two men, knowing that the time for any surreptitious landing was long past, turned and began to retrace their footprints. As their slightly bowed heads came into view over the rise, Scott raised his own torso to rest on his elbows.

'Just freeze!'

The men came to an abrupt halt and lifted their startled faces to peer at Scott. He presented an awesome target, his face mask reflecting the light as it rested on his forehead while he menaced them with the machine pistol.

'Don't even think about it,' he warned as the eyes of one suggested that he might be contemplating a dive to one side. 'I'll cut you in half before you hit the deck.'

'What do you want?'

'Drop your weapon in front of you, take three paces back, then strip down to your skin. If you behave yourselves you might just get away with an early morning swim.'

'And if we don't?'

'If you're counting on my not shooting because of disturbing anyone, forget it. You'll be dead and I'll be lost beneath the waves before your souls have had time to leave your bodies.'

Without further argument the first speaker gingerly opened his hooded anorak, removed a hand-gun from a shoulder holster and tossed it into the sand between them. When his companion had sullenly done the same, the pair began to strip naked. Scott watched their every move.

'Now, who sent you?' he demanded as they stood meekly before him.

'Rodriguez.'

'Where is Snow?'

'He's in the holiday home behind you. The one with the light showing at the window.'

'Who else is with him?'

'No one. Rico and The Turk were supposed to meet us down here but they didn't show. We didn't fancy splitting up so we tied Snow up and came down here to wait for you.'

'For what it's worth,' Scott said, 'they tried to do a runner with the stuff I was bringing in. They're both dead now and unless I get some straight answers and co-operation I'm going to tell Rodriguez that you were in

102

with them. You can start by telling me where Snow's wife and daughter are being held.'

'He's holding them at the Zulu Club,' replied the spokesman.

'Exactly where?' Scott persisted. 'Describe the club and its interior.'

'It's in St Martin's Road – the usual sleazy tourist rip-off joint. You know what I mean: a chat-up type of commissionaire outside, touting for custom; good-looking birds wearing next-to-nothing inside who'll entertain the punters until the money stops flowing; and there are rooms upstairs if a particular hostess takes your fancy and you can afford her price.'

'Never mind that!' snapped Scott irritably. 'Supposing I went in. What would I see once I got through the front door?'

'A large, expensive-looking foyer, usually with a bouncer in a monkey suit hanging around in case of trouble. Since it's supposed to be a members-only club there's always a sexy come-on hostess there ready to sign you in for a membership fee. From there, the punters are taken into the main clubroom where they can buy drinks for themselves and the hostesses. If they want to they can take a hostess upstairs for a romp in bed or to watch hard porn videos.'

'How do you get upstairs?'

'There's a door behind some heavy drape curtains.'

'Is there any other entrance?'

'Only at the back of the club.'

'And where precisely are Snow's wife and daughter being held?'

'In the basement flat – that's Rodriguez' private quarters, or, at least, it's where he stays when he has a mind to – usually when he's breaking in a new hostess. Rumour has it that all his girls sleep with him first, before they're taken on. Some say that he's not above using dope to force the girls to go on the game for him.'

'Tell me about the flat. How do you get in? Has it got a rear entrance? And what's the layout?'

'There are two entrances at the front – one through the basement door, the other through a door to the left in the foyer. There's also a back entrance. Beyond that I can't tell you anything – I've never been there.'

Scott quickly looked around. The sun was just creeping over the horizon and soon holidaymakers would be up and about, which suited his original plan. However, the thought of shepherding his captives naked into the sea had lost its appeal. A simple plea to almost any unsuspecting bather would gain them a towel to cover their private parts, after which a single telephone call would be enough to warn Rodriguez about his interest in the club and in Snow's wife and daughter.

'Just back-pedal a few more paces,' he ordered, stooping down to gather up their weapons and clothes. He wrapped them all in one of the anoraks with the exception of the ageing Luger. 'I hope you were telling me the truth about there being no one guarding Snow,' he said. 'Now, move ahead of me,' and he stood aside to let them pass under the threat of the Luger's pointing barrel.

Noting the direct look thrown at him by the tall man who had acted as the spokesman, Scott immediately became suspicious and hung back a few paces. He watched as they negotiated the slope.

'What are your names?' he asked, hoping to divert their minds from exploring the possibilities of escape.

'I am Simmons,' said the spokesman, 'and he's called Callan.'

'Does he talk?'

'Not much. He suffers from a speech impediment which makes him embarrassed in front of strangers.'

From the rear, wearing only their socks they looked quite comical as they trudged up the soft sandy slope. But no secret smile touched Scott's grim, tired face as he watched for the inevitable.

The warning came when Callan glanced to one side, his eyes turned hard in their sockets in order to locate Scott's exact position. Suddenly the man bent forward, his legs spread wide, and began to scoop sand between them at high speed like a hound dog digging a hole. Almost simultaneously, Simmons turned sharply to pounce on Scott, whom he expected to be stunned by the hail of fine sand thrown into his face. With all his weight on his right foot, Simmons swung round at a crouch, ready to launch himself down the gentle slope at his captor. Then, his grimace of determination turned to sheer horror. He froze, perched on one leg while the other hung in mid-air, his arms raised outward from hunched shoulders, for Scott had taken a swift side-step to avoid the sand and was crouching low, aiming the Luger at Simmons' private parts.

'You've got some balls,' said Scott coldly, watching as Simmons struggled to keep his balance. Simmons' glance swung from the whiteness of Scott's index finger as it curled around the trigger, to the stony look in his eyes – a sure indicator that he would not hesitate to inflict the cruellest of injuries at the slightest provocation.

Slowly Callan turned, looking from Simmons to Scott as he did so. When he could see both men quite clearly, Scott swung the Luger to point at Callan's penis.

'O-O-Okay,' stammered Callan, lowering his hands to clutch his genitals protectively. 'Y-Y-You win.'

Without a word, Scott began to unwrap the bundles of clothing and took out the hooded anoraks. He emptied the pockets, threw the anoraks to the ground at their feet and said: 'Stick your legs through the armholes. Keep the backs of them behind you and don't pull the sleeves above your knees. If that doesn't slow you down, nothing will.'

While they carried out this order, Scott rummaged about for what he believed to be the door key of the mobile home. A minute later they moved off again, the captives waddling like a pair of penguins. Relieved – but sceptical – Scott ushered them the two hundred yards to the mobile home and he inserted the key in the lock.

'Now,' he said. 'Is there anything you want to tell me before I open the door? Because if I find any surprises in there I'm going to start shooting in your direction first. Do I make myself clear?'

'There's a guard dog,' Simmons blurted out when the Luger's barrel lowered again to threaten his masculinity. 'It's a Rottweiler and it'll tear you to peices.'

'So,' said Scott.

'B-B-B-Brandy,' called Callan.

The home vibrated slightly as the beast inside padded

towards the door and began to cry for its master.

'H-H-He w-w-won't b-b-bite if I go first,' declared Callan.

'Better let him,' Simmons advised. 'If you hurt that dog he'll go berserk and that Luger won't do you any good at all. He loves that dog more than anything on God's green earth.'

'Then you'd better make sure you both behave yourselves,' growled Scott.

Turning the key, Callan pushed the door and let it swing open. Just inside, a muscular black and tan Rottweiler stood obediently and wagged its stumpy tail. Moving closer, Callan touched the dog's shoulders with the tip of his fingers and the animal bounded forward to rest its front paws on his shoulders. At once, Callan cradled the animal's head affectionately against his own. 'Easy, boy,' he said, without a trace of a stammer.

'Get him shut up in one of the rooms,' said Scott, and Callan gently lowered the dog and clapped his hands, equally playfully, but in such a way as to be well-placed should the order be given to leap forward.

'Fetch,' ordered Callan, and the dog scampered inside.

Hobbling awkwardly up the two steps, the two men led the way into the spacious living room where, by the time Scott had entered, Brandy had returned with an enormous bone clamped between his jaws. He dropped it at Callan's feet and then stood back, wagging his stump expectantly. When Callan picked it up and threw it through an open bedroom door the beast bounded after it and Callan drew the door closed behind him.

'It's a smart man who knows his limitations,' observed Scott. 'Now, where's Snow?'.

'Tied up in the bath,' replied Simmons sullenly.

Once again the look on the man's face and his manner gave cause for concern and, guessing that this was what lay behind the bathroom door, Scott glanced around for something with which to render his captives harmless while he investigated.

'Take the covers off those scatter cushions,' he said, indicating two which lay on a large sofa. Simmons held back, leaving Callan to carry out the order. 'Now, sit on

106

the sofa,' said Scott, looking specifically at Simmons. 'Put one of those over his head,' indicating Callan, 'and zip it up as far as you can. Then put the other one over your own head.'

When this had been done Scott dumped all the clothes in an untidy heap on the floor and removed the leather belts from their trousers.

'Get yourselves face down on the floor with your hands behind your backs,' he said. The men leant forward, fell awkwardly to their knees and eventually lay prostrate on the carpet. Still wary of Simmons, Scott stepped astride him first. He pressed the gun barrel hard against the back of Simmons' head, fastened the trouser belt tightly around his upper arms and repeated the operation on Callan.

Satisfied that neither man now presented a danger, he opened the bathroom door to find the reason for Simmons' agitation. Snow lay exhausted over the side of the bathtub with his hands tied securely to the taps. The bath was filled with bloody water and his shirt and trousers were torn to shreds. His body was bruised, and blood-stained wounds bore testament to a mauling by the dog.

'Jesus Christ!' muttered Scott angrily. 'What in hell's name have they done to you?'

First he removed the necktie securing Snow's hands to the taps and then the wadded flannelette gag from his mouth. As he eased him out on to the floor he spotted a box-like pathfinder transmitter hidden between the toilet pan and the bath.

'I guess I owe you,' he said quietly.

Snow opened his eyes and managed a weak smile. 'I could use a drink,' he croaked weakly. 'The bastards put salt in the bath.'

Scott eased Snow down to sit with his back against the bath panel, filled a coloured plastic beaker with water and held it to his lips. Snow drank deeply, emptying it, and then, with his head back and his eyes closed, he raised his right hand as though to keep Scott at a distance.

Guessing what was coming, Scott raised the toilet seat. 'Easy, now,' he said softly, hauling Snow carefully to his knees and holding his head over the toilet pan. Moments later, Snow's pain-racked body heaved as his stomach rejected the strong, salty water he had been forced to swallow.

'God,' he rasped, 'I hope you shot the hell out of them because if you didn't I'll not be responsible for my actions if I ever get my hands on them. How did you get past the dog?'

'Never mind that now,' Scott hedged. 'Your right arm and leg seem to be useless. Do you feel as if you've any broken bones?'

'Right now they all feel broken. Christ, they gave me some pounding,' he admitted. 'Just let me rest here for a few minutes.'

'Sure,' Scott agreed, 'take your time. How about a brandy or something?'

'Make it long and straight.'

Making his way back into the lounge, Scott poured out a large brandy and returned to find Snow still sagging over the toilet pan. He stood astride him and reached down to take him by the shoulders.

'Come on,' he urged quietly. 'Kneel upright and get this down you.'

Slowly, with Scott's help, Snow eased himself up and gulped down the amber liquid – which his stomach rejected almost immediately.

'Thank Christ I haven't got a dose of the runs to go with this,' he gasped, when at last he drew away from the toilet pan.

Ignoring his half-hearted jest, Scott reached out for a face flannel from the vanity unit and wiped the perspiration from Snow's face.

'That feels good,' said Snow. 'Nice and cool.'

'Do you feel like trying to move yet?'

'No. Give me a few more minutes and I'll be okay.'

'Sure – take your time.'

'Did you get my SOS?'

'Indeed I did. How did you manage to send it?'

'With difficulty. I managed to sit astride the side of the bath and tap it out with my foot. After a while I got cramp and had to get back in again. Apart from that my wrists were so tightly tied that hanging over there made matters worse and cut off my circulation.'

'How come they didn't take the pathfinder transmitter?' asked Scott.

'They didn't know what it was. Once they had the receiver for the homing bugs in the containers they thought they had it made. They didn't realize that we never intended landing the stuff anyway. The one thing that kept me sane through all the pain was the thought of them sitting out on the beach waiting for something that wasn't coming. My only fear was that they might grab you and torture you as they did me.'

'I didn't know you cared,' jibed Scott.

'You know what I mean. Apart from seeing you hurt, a lot of people have gone to a lot of trouble to nail . . .'

'Come on, up you get,' Scott cut in to quell his explanation. 'I've got a nice big surprise for you in the lounge.'

'Easy,' scowled Snow.

Any hope that Snow's condition was not as bad as he thought was soon dispelled. As Scott hauled him to his feet his right leg hung limp as did his right arm.

'Are you sure they're not broken?' he asked.

'No, although that was some kind of kicking they gave me. With them using me for football practice and that damned dog trying to tear me limb from limb, I'm surprised there's anything left of me that still works.'

As they reached the doorway to the lounge, Snow's left arm hanging round Scott's neck for support, he jerked with surprise at seeing the prostrate, hooded figures on the floor.

'Take it easy,' growled Scott, as Snow tried to bear his weight on his injured leg. 'I know how you feel but returning their hospitality won't do you any good in your condition.'

'No, you don't know how I feel,' argued Snow. 'Give me a gun and I'll make sure they never do it to anyone else.'

'Killing them might solve the problem of what to do with them but I want no part of it,' snapped Scott.

'Murder?' Snow laughed sadistically. 'Maybe – but I was thinking more of blasting their knees and elbows away – and that's just for starters.'

Trying to understand his anger, Scott guided him to the sofa and made him comfortable. 'You ought to have a doctor to take a look at those bites,' he said with concern, inspecting Snow's torn right arm.

'Never mind that,' snarled Snow. 'Just get me another drink. Maybe I'll cool down in a minute.'

As Scott tilted the bottle towards the tumbler, he turned and saw Snow retrieving a gun from between the sofa cushions.

'Don't even think about it,' warned Snow, aiming the weapon at a point between Scott's eyes. 'You say you know how I feel. Well, I'll tell you something: you know sweet FA. These bastards came so close to drowning me I lost count of how many times. And what kind of animals kick a man when he's down and set a dog on him? Well, mister, now it's my turn. As grateful as I am to you, I'll put you down if you come between me and those two bastards.'

Scott stood rigid. He shifted his gaze from the hypnotic eye of the gun to Snow's hate-filled glare and realized that perhaps he was right. He didn't know how much Snow had been made to suffer or whether Snow would indeed shoot him if he tried to disarm him in order to protect the captives. All he knew was that the look in Snow's eyes was not to be ignored.

'Maybe you ought to take those hoods off first,' he advised. 'Be a shame to shoot the wrong men.'

Snow looked down. 'That's them all right,' he snarled, turning the gun to pistol-whip each hooded head in turn. 'How does it feel?' he goaded when their cries of pain had died away. 'Can you remember how much you enjoyed torturing me? Well, now it's my turn and I'm going to enjoy myself – you can take my word for that.' As he spoke he stroked one of the hooded heads with the gun barrel until its tip traced an ear. Then, taking careful aim, he brought it chillingly back to full cock.

'F-F-F-For Christ's s-s-s-sake,' stammered Callan, shaking with fear. He had heard the venom in Snow's voice when he referred to the atrocities committed against him and he had no doubt that he was about to be made to suffer. As the weapon slid down to lie flat against the side of his head he knew that his ear was about to be shot off and that the bullet would continue its downward thrust to shatter his collar bone and enter his chest.

'Don't lower yourself to their level,' pleaded Scott.

'Why not?' argued Snow. 'It's all they understand.'

'I'll t-t-trade my life for information,' Callan blurted out.

'Shut up!' shouted Simmons hoarsely. 'He won't hurt you. It's more than he dare do.'

This statement aroused Scott's suspicions at once but Snow was too hell bent on his quest for vengeance to notice, and at once swung the gun to take a quick shot at Simmons, who howled in pain as he writhed on the floor with a lump missing from his right heel.

'For Christ's sake,' yelled Scott. 'Have you gone stark, raving mad? You'll have the whole campsite alerted.'

'It'll be worth it!'

'Think of what Simmons has just said and then listen to what Callan might have to say.'

'What do you mean?' asked Snow, with a questioning look.

'He said that you wouldn't dare shoot.'

'Well, now he knows different!'

'You're missing the point. What information does he have which would lead him to make a statement like that?'

All the pain they had inflicted on him suddenly ceased to bother Snow as the words, like the carriages of a train, moved along his lines of thought and came to an abrupt halt. As an officer of the law, his actions of the past few minutes were inexcusable under any circumstances. Rico, now deceased, had claimed that only he knew that snippet of information but now Simmons' declaration strongly suggested that he also knew his secret. How had he come to know? Had Rico lied? Did Rodriguez know that Snow was working undercover? And if he did, how would that effect Snow, his daughter and his wife?

'Take him into the bathroom and question him,' he told Scott. 'I'll question Simmons out here and we'll compare their stories later.'

'You'll get nothing out of me,' declared Simmons.

'I'm not so sure that's a good idea,' Scott challenged. 'Apart from the fact that you're in no physical state to handle him if he should get the upper hand, I don't fancy you being out of sight in your present mental state.'

'What you really mean is that you're afraid I'll shoot him,' said Snow, the ghost of a sardonic smile teasing his battered face.

'Yes,' admitted Scott. 'A little bit at a time.'

Snow struggled to his feet and, using the furniture for support, limped into the kitchen – the pain showing plainly on his face. In the lounge they could hear cupboards and drawers being opened and closed as he rummaged through them. Eventually he reappeared clutching a small tube. He eased himself down on to his knees, via the sofa, and shuffled painfully to Simmons' side.

'You move a muscle without my say-so,' he threatened, 'and I'm going to blow your ears off.'

Sweat began to break out on Simmons' face beneath the hood as he felt Snow's hands fumbling with the belt that secured his arms behind his back. Realizing that he was being untied, he began to explore the possibilities of taking advantage of his freedom but decided to wait in case the hood was removed and he could see. First one hand was lifted and he felt a light, cold, feather-like touch on each fingertip. A moment later this was repeated on the other hand. Then both hands were gently placed, palm-inwards, on to his buttocks and held there for a moment. Only when he tried to move them did the truth dawn on him: his hands had been superglued to his behind.

'That should hold him,' Snow declared, turning back to Scott, and offering him the gun added: 'If it bothers you so much, you can take this.'

Scott met his hard-eyed stare and tried to reach beyond it to fathom what was going on inside Snow's head. But all that registered were the stony, unrevealing eyes and the weapon he held out.

'You'd better hang on to it, just in case,' he sighed defeatedly, and hauling Callan to his feet guided him into the bathroom.

Simmons heard the door close then a shuffling noise as Snow moved and he wondered what he was doing. A match scratched on the gritty surface of its box and he heard it flare into life. Then the strong smell of cigar smoke awoke his craving for a cigarette. Snow's shuffling movements drew closer and Simmons could hear his stifled groans of pain as he reached down to unfasten and remove the hood. Expecting a burning cigar to touch his bare skin, Simmons flinched when Snow's cold hand hooked under his belly to roll him over on to his back. The unexpected manoeuvre caused his injured heel to hit the floor and his face screwed up in agony as he jerked it up and then lowered it gently to rest across his other shin.

There was a pause of several seconds while Snow savoured his cigar – the only sound was the faint murmur of Callan's voice from behind the closed door of the bathroom. Hardly knowing what to expect as Snow puckered his lips to blow out a steady stream of blue smoke, Simmons tried to move his hands. He hoped that by some fluke they might break free but Snow saw him wince against the pain when they would not. He smiled down casually at Simmons and swung his injured right leg upward then twisted his body in a toy soldier-like movement until he stood astride him. Then he painfully lowered himself to kneel on Simmons' shoulders, pinning him to the floor. With deliberation Snow drew on the cigar until its end glowed bright red.

'I suppose you thought you had the monopoly on inflicting pain,' he said quietly, tapping the cigar so that ash drifted down into Simmons' face. Simmons closed his eyes and turned his head away. 'Well now it's my turn,' continued Snow, 'and to be perfectly honest I don't give a damn if you don't talk. Your friend Callan will tell us all we want to know.'

When Simmons opened his eyes again the cigar was only inches away from them, although he couldn't quite feel the heat of its smouldering end. Suddenly Snow's free hand gripped his jaw like a vice, steadying himself against the thrust of Simmons' heaving belly as he tried to unseat him. The manoeuvre proved futile and, as he settled, ash from the cigar again fluttered down into his eyes. Simmons screwed them up against the pain.

'If I talk I'll be hunted down like a dog and shot,' he

admitted, tears welling up in his stinging eyes.

'That's tough,' Snow admitted. 'No doubt if Callan talks you'll be able to convince Rodriguez that it was him and not you. If he believes you I'm sure it will give you a great amount of comfort while you're learning to read Braille. If he doesn't believe you,' he continued, lowering the cigar to where Simmons could feel its warmth on his eyelids, 'I'm sure that your blindness will serve as a blessing in disguise. You won't be able to run and you won't be able to see him coming. Your end will come more quickly.'

'You bastard,' Simmons snarled.

'Not me,' replied Snow quietly. 'I didn't ask you to come down here and torture me. Neither did I invite you to enjoy it.'

'Supposing I talk? What are you offering in return?'

'Depends on the information. Until I know, I can't say.'

'Okay. Since I don't have any choice, I'll trust you to give me a good deal. Rodriguez sent us down here but he isn't the real boss. The man behind him is into everything and steadily wiping out the other gangs or controlling their activities through people like Rodriguez. He controls the pimps, the pushers, the madams and their whorehouses. If there's a bank or bullion job you can bet he's in the background somewhere taking his cut. If a member of a gang gets caught he sees that he doesn't talk – by threats of beating, execution or, in some cases, breaking them out of jail. He has eyes everywhere. He even has access to police files and computers.'

'Give me a name,' Snow persisted.

Simmons looked him in the eye. Beads of perspiration were forming on his brow and fear was written all over his face as he mustered the courage to whisper the name which could mean certain death.

'Give me the name,' urged Snow.

'Haynes,' said Simmons at last, 'your boss. He's the one masterminding crime in London these days.'

'Haynes!' in utter shock, Snow's bewildered brain began to sift through the seemingly insignificant things that had happened in the past. All at once they made sense if Haynes was, in fact, masterminding London's under-world. Even the abduction of his own wife and daughter

114

made more sense and explained how Rodriguez had found out he was married and where his wife lived, since his private address and visits home to see them were kept strictly secret from his undercover life. It also explained Haynes' plausible excuses for not sending a squad to rescue them.

The million dollar question was, how far had the rot spread? And who could he turn to for help?

The bathroom door opened, disrupting his thoughts, and he turned, white-faced, to meet Scott's bland stare as he stood in the doorway. 'What did you get?' he asked.

'The business. That smooth-talking, conniving bastard Haynes has stitched us all up and I'm wondering how involved he was with Rodriguez when my father and brother died. He was with the river police in those days and he told me it was Rodriguez who had caused the accident that killed them. Rodriguez was in the process of picking up a consignment of illegal narcotics at the time.'

'Maybe that's where it all started,' mused Snow. 'What's bothering me is where, and how, it ends. My first instinct is to get my wife and daughter out of Rodriguez' clutches and away to a place of safety.'

'What about us?' asked Simmons.

'What about you?' Snow turned back to face him. 'If we let you go free, you'll make a beeline back to Rodriguez or Haynes to spill your guts in the hope of redeeming yourself at our expense.'

'And either one would repay us with a bullet in the back of the head,' Simmons shot back. 'Speaking for myself, all I ask is a safe place to hide until you've done what you have to do.'

'M-M-M-Me too,' stammered Callan.

Snow eased himself off Simmons' chest to sit on the sofa. 'Stoddart owns this site,' he said, 'and there are a couple more holiday homes kept vacant at all times just in case he needs them for his own use. You can stay in one of those for the time being. The problem is going to be finding someone to make sure you stay there.'

'I'd say that's you,' suggested Scott. 'You're in no condition to travel so you may as well stay here and do something useful.'

'That may be so, but I'm heading back to London to collect my wife and daughter and nothing is going to stop me.'

'Talk sense, for Christ's sake,' flared Scott. 'Your face is known. The minute they see you they'll be on the alert, especially in the state you're in.'

'Then what do you suggest?'

'That I go after your wife – my face isn't known. Your wife and daughter are being held at the Zulu Club, so I'll go there as a customer. I have a score to settle with Rodriguez on my own account anyway.'

'No,' said Snow, shaking his head. 'You haven't had any experience in this sort of thing or with these sort of people.'

'Maybe not, but the last few days have been an education. Let's face it, it's going to be at least a couple of days before you're even halfway fit to do yourself any good. If I don't succeed, you can go in later.'

Snow thought about it for a moment. Scott was right about his state of health hampering any efforts of his own, but delay meant more time for Rodriguez to find out what had happened to his men. Even now he must be waiting for news from them about the cargo of narcotics he had sent them to steal.

'You don't look so hot yourself,' he said at last. 'A good meal and a few hours sleep might do you some good before you go.'

'I'll take a train and a taxi and grab some sleep on the way,' promised Scott. 'Right now I think it's a case of striking while the iron's hot – don't you?'

'What are you going to do about Haynes?' asked Simmons.

'For the time being we'll let him think he's in the clear,' said Snow. 'The worst possible medicine we can dish out is to have him caught with his hands firmly wedged in the cookie jar.'

5

Being back on the busy streets of London gave Scott a special feeling and he stopped to view his image in a shop window. In a flashy sports jacket and trousers, with an expensive camera hanging in its shiny leather case, he looked every inch an American tourist. He turned a little to his left; good, no sign of a bulge beneath his right arm to give away the presence of the Luger.

It was just midday, sunny and warm, the road crammed with vehicles and the pavements with people from all walks of life. There were Mr and Mrs Average enjoying their lunchbreaks. There were the young, clinging to-gether in happy groups, wearing bright, trendy, clothes and sporting outrageous hairdos to impress each other. There were also tourists dressed like himself, and a few unaccompanied males who seemed to be interested in the sex shops and displays; the girls with their favours for sale and the prospect of enjoying London's twenty-four hour night-life.

Further up the street was the unlit neon sign of the Zulu Club. As he approached, he sensed the alert eyes of the hustling, tout-like commissionaire watching him. Main-taining the air of a shy, sly pervert, he slowly advanced towards him.

'My god,' exclaimed the commissionaire in friendly surprise, 'if ever a man looked as though he needed cheering up, you do.'

As Scott turned, a trendy young woman of about twenty came from behind the tout and passed between them. She smiled at Scott as he admired her brightly-coloured hair and exquisitely made-up face. He turned to admire her

117

voluptuous, denim-clad figure from the rear and the commissionaire observed: 'Now that is nothing more than a put-on. She'll tease you until you go half-crazy with lust and then take you for every penny you've got. She'll have the shirt right off your back.'

'She'd be welcome to it if there was anything left of her after I'd finished with her,' drooled Scott in an American accent. 'Did you ever see a woman with a wiggle like that before?'

'She sure is something,' agreed the commissionaire. 'Simone, that's her name. Never forget a face. She used to work here, but the boss fired her because she didn't always have the customer's interests at heart, if you know what I mean.'

'Not exactly,' pleaded Scott.

'Well, let me put it like this,' he began to explain, as though Scott were a little slow on the uptake. 'We've got girls in there,' he said, indicating the club. 'They're employed because they're beautiful and that's what the tourists come here for: to have a nice, quiet drink with them without the wife crowding their play. Now being red-blooded as I'm sure you are, you just might take a fancy to one of those hostesses. But if the lady of your choice isn't forthcoming after you've treated her right, you go away feeling that the club has let you down. Now we can't have the club getting a bad name like that, can we? So we only employ the girls who have the customers' well-being at heart. Like the notice says over the bar: if you don't see it – ask for it.'

'You mean that you have girls in the club who look like her and will do anything a man asked?' beamed Scott with an air of innocence.

'Sure they will,' promised the commissionaire. 'Why don't you step right inside and find out for yourself?'

'I don't know,' said Scott sheepishly, raising his hand nervously to scratch a non-existent itch on the back of his neck. 'To be honest, I'm kind of shy in the company of ladies. I sort of – well – you know, I can't talk to them.'

'Can't talk to them?' echoed the commissionaire.

'Jesus! You don't have to worry about that with our girls. They're professionals – they do all the talking, if they

118

feel the need. In fact, they'll fulfil your needs without you even saying a word if that's what you want. You want a few drinks before taking one of them somewhere a bit more private? Just say the word and I'll take you inside and smooth the way for you. How are you fixed for cash to get things moving in the right direction? It's a con I know, but to get into a club like this you have to be a member.'

'Okay, I guess,' said Scott, pulling a wad of fifty pound notes from his pocket. 'I haven't quite got the hang of your money yet. This is my first visit to England.'

Seeing so many notes of such high denomination, the commissionaire's eyes lit up and he reached out to take two.

'Mister,' he said, taking Scott by the arm, 'you just leave everything to me. I'll see to it that you get the best the house has to offer. What takes your fancy? A nice English girl? An Indian? A West Indian? Chinese? How about a beauty from the Emerald Isle? A green-eyed, flame-haired Irish colleen with the body of a goddess.'

Allowing the man to usher him inside, Scott found himself in a large foyer adorned with rich maroon drapes and tall, exotic plants in tubs. To his right were a pair of heavy, wooden, highly-polished doors with ornate brass fittings, with a burly bouncer alongside in a black tuxedo suit, talking to a beautiful hostess.

Her flame-coloured hair, shining from much brushing, reached down to the small of her back, while the green dress, which barely held her ample breasts in place, was so short that it scarcely concealed her panties as she stood erect. Deliberately turning his head away as though too shy to meet their eyes, Scott glanced to his left to locate the interior door which Simmons had said led down to the basement flat where Rodriguez was hiding Snow's wife and daughter. While his head was turned, the commissionaire raised his free hand to rub his fingers against his thumb – indicating to the bouncer that Scott was carrying a lot of money. In response, the bouncer inclined his head and the hostess' face brightened into a beaming smile.

'He's a little on the shy side,' explained the commission-aire.

'Now, who'd have thought a handsome hulk like you would be shy?' marvelled the hostess in an enchanting Irish brogue, advancing to slip her arm through his.

Scott turned to look into her bright green eyes and deliberately let her see him glance down for an instant to take a sly look at her ample breasts. 'I guess that's what comes of living out in the wild with only my Pa for company,' he drawled. 'Unless you call a couple of thousand cows and some cowboys company.'

'You'll have to join the club,' the bouncer cut in. 'I'm afraid it's members only.'

'Just give him a card,' scowled the commissionaire. 'He's paid his membership fee to me – I'll sort that out with you later, when our friend has settled in.'

'What's your name, honey?' asked the hostess. 'Mine's Anna.'

'Scott.'

'Scott,' she echoed, as though the name had some special appeal. 'Well, Scott honey, we can go into the main bar through there if you like. It's quiet now but as the day wears on there will be other girls and members coming in. If you'd rather, we can go upstairs to my room and have a few drinks in private.'

'I don't get to be alone with girls like you where I come from,' began Scott, 'but then, the day is young yet. I think I'd like to hang around down here for a while and have a few drinks while I enjoy what the house has to offer.'

'Anything you say, honey,' she smiled.

Scott's slight attack of nerves as he approached the club had diminished as his act with the commissionaire progressed. Now, as the immaculate bouncer turned to open the doors to the club proper, he realized that he was fast approaching the point of no return. In just a few minutes he would have to face the real curtain call – or cut and run like a scared chicken – and knowing that he could not face Snow with a lie to cover his failure, he stepped through the doorway with pulses pounding so hard that he was now almost shaking.

'Come on, honey,' coaxed Anna, 'the place is empty, so there's no need to feel embarrassed.'

He remained standing just inside the door and heard it

close behind him. The bouncer remained on the other side. Scott's main concern was how many people were in the club and his attention was immediately drawn to the bright lights of the bar where the barman was replenishing stocks depleted by customers the previous night. From there his eyes wandered to scan the rest of the club. Long, heavy drapes hung beside open windows, indicating that it was still a little early for customers. Yet tables and chairs were neatly set out and the cleaners had obviously completed their daily chores.

'You're early, darlings,' a barman greeted them in a very effeminate voice. 'What can I get you, handsome?'

Looking along the shelves behind the bar, Scott said: 'I'll have a large Grouse whisky with water and ice. Anna?' he asked, turning towards her questioningly.

'Champagne, darling,' the barman cut in. 'That will be exactly eight pounds.'

Scott peeled off a fifty pound note and tossed it on to the bar as if it was nothing, bringing a smile of interest to the barman's face as he turned to give Anna one of those 'Is this another sucker?' looks. She responded by brushing an imaginary itch at the tip of her nose with her index finger. Avoiding Scott's eyes, the barman reached towards a silver ice bucket and his open palm came to rest on the cork of an unopened champagne bottle which he rolled around in the chipped ice before removing it.

'Seems kind of quiet,' ventured Scott. 'Do you have any music?'

The champagne cork came out with a loud pop. 'Sure,' smiled the barman. 'There's only the juke box at this time of day but there's a video with it. You'll need some tokens to make it work. They're five pounds each.'

Scott scowled. 'Even with my limited knowledge of your currency, that sounds pricey!'

'You won't think so when you get an eyeful of our videos,' the barman assured him with a wink, pushing a drink towards Anna. A moment later he put the token on the counter and Scott picked it up. Sliding from the bar stool, he reached out and gently touched Anna's shoulder as he passed behind her. As she sat on the stool she suspected nothing, merely gave a mental sigh, expecting

121

his hands to caress her shapely bottom or to reach under her arms to hold the weight of her ample breast in his cupped hand.

Instead, Scott's left hand gently caressed the curve of her waist and he whispered in her ear: 'Now, we're not going to make any silly noises, are we?' As he spoke his right hand came to rest on her right shoulder and from the corner of her eye she could see the shape of the Luger. She froze, her clear skin breaking out into a cold sweat, and her eyes swung to the barman's back as he raised a glass to the whisky optic. Seeing her and Scott reflected in the mirrors behind the shelves, he froze as well, and their eyes met. Scott's were ice-cold as the Luger moved to point at the back of the barman's head.

'You've got my undivided attention, sweetie,' said the man. 'I just work here for a wage and that doesn't include getting my brains blown out.'

'Glad to hear it,' said Scott quietly. 'Just freeze the way you are for a moment and no one will get hurt. Lay your hands palms upwards on the bar,' he said to Anna, moving the Luger to point into her ear. When she obeyed, he reached around her with his left hand to squeeze a single droplet of Superglue on to each fingertip. Then he told her to turn her hands over and press down hard which she did. The barman was told to turn around without altering the position of his hands and he complied like a toy soldier, the glass of whisky held high. Covering him with the Luger, Scott reached across for the glass saying: 'Stand directly in front of her and put your hands palm upwards on the bar.' Carefully he repeated the operation, glueing the barman's hands to the bar as well.

Gulping down his whisky, Scott placed the empty glass on the bar. 'I've got no quarrel with you, it's Rodriguez I'm after – or, to be more precise, the wife and daughter of a friend who he saw fit to kidnap. According to my information they're being held in the basement flat.'

The barman gave a shrug which could have meant anything and Scott looked beyond him to meet Anna's reflected gaze in the mirrors.

'I don't owe him a damned thing,' she said vehemently. 'She's there and so is the kid.'

'That's good. Who else is down there?'

'He picked up a runaway last night,' Anna replied. 'She's with him.'

'A runaway?'

'A young girl who had run away from home to find fame and fortune in the big city. He'll have charmed the pants off her by now – she'll be on the streets in a week. If he hasn't used drugs on her yet, he soon will.'

'Why should he want to do that.'

'To keep her dependent on him. That's how most of us get started in this game. For what it's worth, I hate his guts. You'll get no trouble from me.'

'That goes for me, too,' added the barman.

'Sorry,' apologized Scott, 'but I can't take your word for that. Pucker your lips as if you were going to kiss her,' he said to the barman and Scott then proceeded to smear Superglue on them. 'Now,' he said, 'reach over and give the lady a nice big kiss.'

Mentally applauding Snow for his idea of using Superglue as a quick method of securing his victims, Scott moved back the way he had come and opened the door to the main foyer. The bouncer stood talking to another scantily-clad hostess but there was no one else in sight.

'Excuse me,' said Scott apologetically, 'we seem to have a problem getting the video working.' Both looked down as he brought the Luger into view. 'You know what they say,' he continued, raising the weapon to aim at a spot between the bouncer's eyes. 'The bigger you are, the harder you fall. Now get down and crawl in there on your hands and knees – and keep in mind that you'll get no medals for any heroics just a bullet in the back of the head. Ladies first.'

Working quickly, he soon had them both stuck and kissing across one of the tables. Satisfied, he moved at the double to the front door and called the commissionaire over.

'What's the problem, guv?' he enquired.

'Quick, come into the bar. There's been some trouble between the big chap and the barman. The girls are trying to calm them down but blood's going to flow soon.'

'Jesus Christ! I've told that meat-head a thousand times,'

the commissionaire began angrily. 'Never mind,' and he pushed past Scott.

Flicking the door shut with his heel, Scott brought the Luger down hard on the back of the man's head. He fell like a stone, and as his sprawling body came to rest Scott reached down to grasp his limp arms.

Scott dumped him with the others, returned to the foyer and went straight to the door leading down to the flat. He could hear a children's cartoon show on the television, somewhere below, and with the Luger pointing the way he crept down to a long hallway which ran through the rear of the building. Stealthily moving forward, he peeped inside the room where the television was. It was a luxuriously furnished lounge and a young girl sat with her eyes fixed on the colourful screen. Opposite was the kitchen and he crossed the hall to peer through its open door. Another door led from the kitchen to the dining room which also had a door giving access to the hallway further along.

Passing through this he came to the bathroom and toilet, which left two remaining doors, one each side of the passageway. One of them had to be the master bedroom. Suddenly there came a woman's muffled cries, chilling the blood in his veins, and he froze where he stood with the Luger pointing at the door. The cries grew louder by the second and the truth dawned. The ice melted in his veins and the blood began to boil for the woman was obviously having an orgasm. Whether her cries were of sweet pain he neither knew nor cared. All he could see was the look of disgust on Snow's face when he asked about Rodriguez and, jumping to the conclusion that Rodriguez had used drugs on Snow's wife to subdue her while he forced himself upon her, he shouldered the door open.

The pair making love on the bed were oblivious to him as he charged across the room. 'You dirty bastard!' he snarled, jamming the Luger hard into Rodriguez' ear.

Rodriguez turned, his passion dying as his handsome, swarthy, tanned face blanched. His mouth sagged open as though to speak but he said nothing as Scott turned his attentions to the woman whom he recognized as Snow's wife from his description of her.

124

'Take it easy,' he said. 'I'm a friend of your husband.'

She remained silent, her wide-eyed expression telling him that she was afraid – too afraid, he thought, to face the reality of her embarrassment at being found naked, spread-eagled on a bed with her limbs tied to its four corners.

His eyes boring into those of Rodriguez, Scott's mind flashed back to their first meeting, several years before, and his first reaction was to take his revenge. He even began to squeeze the trigger but restrained himself thinking that such an act of brutality at close quarters would drive Snow's wife beyond her limits of endurance.

Instead he snarled at Rodriguez: 'Put your hands behind your back, palms facing outwards.'

Releasing his grip on her shoulders, Rodriguez withdrew his hands from beneath her arms and Scott increased the Luger's pressure on Rodriguez' ear as a painful reminder to be on his best behaviour. He spread the Superglue lavishly over the man's palms before pressing them firmly against his bare buttocks.

'Now roll over towards me until you hit the floor,' he rasped, 'and stay belly down.'

'What are you going to do to me?' asked Rodriguez.

'I'm still thinking about it,' Scott snapped. 'Just do as I say or I might make up my mind to blow your brains out.'

Rodriguez rolled clear and bumped heavily on to the floor, leaving Scott to free Snow's wife unhindered. Her eyes followed him in disbelief as he released each arm in turn. She sat up as he moved to the foot of the bed to untie her feet. He could feel her eyes staring at him and he raised his head.

'You like looking at my body,' she said in a quiet lustful, husky tone, lifting her hands to caress a perfectly formed breast and then raising herself to kneel. 'You're not afraid to take me, are you?' she taunted, lowering her right hand to sensually touch the pubic hair between her thighs.

Scott swallowed hard, taken aback by this unexpected turn of events.

'I like men who are men,' she continued. 'I like a man who isn't afraid. I like them to treat me like a woman, a woman with a physical desire. I don't want to be placed on a pedestal like some queen or goddess where I can't be touched.'

She began to shuffle towards him on her knees as he stood there, dumbfounded. 'I wasn't being raped,' she went on. 'We've been lovers for a long time now. He wanted me like that and I loved every precious second of it. You can tell my husband that when you see him. Tell him to find himself another virgin ice-queen because I'm a slut and enjoying what he could never give me. And if he tries to come and get me back, or hurt Mannie in order to get me back, tell him I've written some letters which certain people would find very interesting. One of them is addressed to his own boss, Stoddart. Now, why don't you get out?'

'Hold on,' cut in Rodriguez. 'You must be this new whizz-kid of Stoddart's. Scott, isn't it?'

For a brief moment, Scott glanced down at Rodriguez then back to Snow's wife. His brain was having difficulty in absorbing the situation. There were questions he wanted to ask: like had she told Rodriguez that her husband was working undercover for the police? And, if she had not, what the hell did she think she was doing striking up a relationship with a man her husband must surely some day play a part in sending to prison for a very long time? But knowing that asking such questions might prove to be disastrous, Scott took a deep breath and asked one he felt safe with.

'I came here, at no small risk to myself, believing that you and your daughter had been kidnapped,' he said. 'Under the circumstances I think the least you can do is to reassure me that this is not the case and that you are free to come and go, as you please.'

'Kidnapped?' she laughed scornfully. 'I can't imagine how my husband got that idea into his head. I told him I was leaving him a week before I actually walked out. As you have already witnessed, I'm keen on bondage sex — and he insisted on treating me like a nun.'

'Did you tell him who you were leaving him for?'

'I didn't consider that to be any of his damned business!'

The heat of her passion had begun to cool and she turned to Rodriguez in search of an answer. 'What do you

126

know about this kidnapping business? When you insisted I was to stay indoors for a few days with someone to protect me at all times, you said it was because you feared your rivals might try to use me to blackmail you.'

'And that's the truth, so help me,' Rodriguez blurted out.

'You're a bloody liar,' said Scott. 'You used her to blackmail her husband into giving you information which would help you wipe out Stoddart and later to try to get your hands on the narcotics I brought in for him.'

'Okay, I admit that,' he said, looking at Snow's wife, 'but that happened after she left him. It had nothing to do with the way I felt – or still feel – about her.'

As he pleaded his case, naked and helpless on the floor, he rolled from his belly on to his side where he could see better. The sight of him lying there helpless began to trigger her craving for sex and she shuffled towards the edge of the bed on her knees.

'You're a liar,' she accused him, her eyes flashing – 'and you', she flared at Scott, 'can either get the hell out of here, or stay, as you please. Tell my loving husband what you have seen – tell him that this is what I call being alive.'

Making a great show of her intentions, she flicked one leg from beneath her and stepped sensually over Rodriguez' inert body to place her foot firmly on the floor beyond him. 'Now it's my turn,' she threatened huskily.

Scott stood completely agog. He was holding the Luger and feeling about as welcome as a clown at a funeral. Ignoring him, she raised herself as tall as she could while bearing her weight on one knee and one foot.

'Jesus,' muttered Rodriguez harshly, his eyes glued to the tiny triangle between her thighs.

She stretched, placing her other foot on the floor so that she stood astride him with her firm breasts standing proud from her lithe body. Looking up expectantly, he rolled on to his back and ogled her supreme nakedness.

'If you want to do a deal for the cocaine, give me a call,' he said briefly, without taking his eyes off her. 'You stitch Stoddart up and we'll split the proceeds sixty-forty. Cash on delivery.'

Oblivious to his bargaining, Snow's wife arched her

back, raising her hands slightly. She formed her slender fingers, with their long manicured nails, into claws, and Rodriguez realized for the first time that he was the one to be the bonded slave; that the passion in her eyes, combined with her clawed hands, represented much pain. Scott stood riveted to the spot, hardly knowing what to do for the best. The threat of the Luger evidently meant nothing. By using her body and her craving for bondage sex she had rendered him completely useless. Lowering herself, oblivious to his presence, she knelt astride Rodriguez' midriff, her clawed fingers reaching for his chest. They made contact and as she drew them down, she manoeuvred her stomach forward so that the lips of her vagina slid along the length of his penis. Rodriguez' face screwed up in pain as her fingernails drew blood and when his eyes opened they rolled back in order to see Scott.

'For Christ's sake, get her off me,' he pleaded. 'She's going to tear me to pieces.'

'It's what you wanted,' said Scott quietly, turning away. 'You pays your money and you takes your choice.'

When he reached the street he hailed a taxi to Victoria Station and tried to make some sense out of what had happened at the club. Like a man in a dream, he boarded the train to Dover and wondered how he was going to explain it to Snow. He stared out of the window until his eyelids drooped under the steady flashing of passing scenery and he slept.

The beauty of Snow's naked wife entered his dreams. Her long, jet-black shiny hair hung down like a mane to the small of her back and her large, dark brown eyes beckoned him to her bed. The train swayed – the clatter of the iron wheels over an intersection bringing him back to a state of limbo. The vision of her beauty faded for a moment but returned as he strove to recapture and enjoy the dream of her nymphomania. He awoke at Dover and joined the bustling throng, still not knowing what to tell Snow. He reluctantly boarded another taxi to take him to the holiday campsite.

Scott felt a desperate need to delay the inevitable, as he looked along the neat rows of mobile homes to the only brick building on the site – its own much-used super-market.

'Are you feeling okay?' asked the driver as he paid his fare.

'I get car sick – I'll be fine in a couple of minutes. Keep the change.'

With a smile, the man nodded his thanks and drove off. Scott turned towards the supermarket and suddenly the last thing he wanted was to join a crowd of shoppers. He decided to face Snow with as much of the truth as he deemed necessary and headed for the mobile home called Pasadena where he had left Snow guarding Simmons and Callan. Scott gave the door a single sharp rap before letting himself in. The lounge was empty and no sound came from any of the other rooms. A search revealed no sign of life or of a struggle yet he felt a deep sense of foreboding. Snow had been in no condition to travel very far and it was most unlikely that he'd have been able to hold his captives under proper supervision, if he had.

After checking the Luger, Scott made his way to the Rhondo, the first of the mobile homes, where again he gave a single sharp knock before letting himself in. Closing the door, he sensed he was not alone and suddenly Stoddart pounced into view, a Colt automatic pointed at Scott.

'So, you came back to the scene of the crime, bonny lad,' he accused angrily. 'Lean against the wall and spread your arms and legs.'

'What the hell are you talking about?' asked Scott, raising his hands.

'Just do it,' Stoddart snarled, arms outstretched, aiming the Colt at his head.

It was no idle threat. Stoddart's eyes had a wild look about them and Scott reached for the wall, saying: 'Just take it easy with that thing.' Stoddart moved closer and pressed the Colt against the back of Scott's head while he searched him.

He stuffed the Luger into his waistband, and rasped: 'Okay. So, what have you done with the shipment? And what have you done with Snow?'

'The shipment should be on the seabed where I left it,

and Snow moved to the Pasadena just before I left. A couple of Rodriguez' men paid us a visit while we were making the run last night. He was beaten up pretty bad and moved there for safety,' said Scott.

'If the shipment is out there, how come I'm getting no signals from the bugging devices?'

'Probably because some prick didn't put the right ones in the containers. The seawater will put them out of action.'

'And how do you explain the bloodstains all over the place?' asked Stoddart.

'Like I said, Rodriguez' pals beat Snow up. They set a Rottweiler on him too. They hadn't a clue what the pathfinder transmitter was and Snow managed to use it to warn me. I sneaked ashore and caught them waiting for me.'

'Well,' said Stoddart, 'I'll believe you when I see Snow. We're going to take a walk to the Pasadena. Don't think you can escape just because there are people out there. One wrong move and it'll be your last.'

'Snow isn't there. Neither are Simmons or Callan. I checked before I came here.'

'Simmons, Callan and a Rottweiler?' he said, softening a little. 'I know that trio. What did they call the dog?'

'Brandy.'

'Are you willing to take me out to see the shipment for myself?' he asked, as if Scott had a choice.

'I'll take you down and bring it up for you, if you like,' offered Scott. 'It's all there – twenty canisters of it. And I'd say there is considerably more than I agreed to bring in.'

'You were being well paid,' Stoddart pointed out, 'and I guess you're telling the truth so you can relax.'

Lowering his arms, Scott turned to face him. 'I could use a drink and a smoke,' he said. 'My nerves were in tatters before I got here and your reception hasn't exactly helped.'

'I wonder where Snow has gone,' Stoddart pondered aloud. 'It's not like him to wander off without letting me know.'

Scott lit his cigarette and inhaled deeply. It was strange

130

that Stoddart had neglected to ask where he had been – but he was glad.

'In my opinion, Snow wasn't in any condition to go wandering anywhere further than the bathroom,' he told him. 'He took one hell of a beating from those two and as for them, unless someone happened to have Superglue solvent in their pocket, I can't imagine them getting very far. They were pretty well glued up when I left them.'

'Maybe Rodriguez sent someone else down to rescue them,' suggested Stoddart. 'I'll check when I go back into town later. He didn't say anything to you that might give us a lead?'

'Not that I can think of. Is there anywhere else on the campsite he might have gone?'

'I've looked. There's no sign of him anywhere. The way things have been going lately, it might be a good idea if you checked the shipment to make sure that Rodriguez hasn't found some way to make Snow tell him where it is. They could even have done a deal together.'

'If he did – and I wouldn't bet on it – I'd say that Rodriguez is in for a big disappointment. Without my knowledge of its precise location it would take a month of Sundays to find it with those transmitters out of action.'

'I guess you're right, bonny lad,' Stoddart agreed amiably, but catching Scott looking at him it didn't strike him as the kind of look one man gives another during the course of a conversation. It was direct, as if Scott was trying to search beyond his eyes to uncover a guilty secret. 'I need a drink,' he sighed, turning away with a deep sense of guilt, and asked in an effort to change the subject: 'Have you had any more bright ideas?'

'About what?'

'Like last night's job and your idea of using torpedoes.'

'A couple, as it happens. One I shall keep to myself for the time being; the other should be right up your street. The only problem is the timing.'

While he was speaking, Stoddart turned towards him, raising his glass to his lips, and in that instant Scott saw death in his eyes. There was no doubt in his mind that Stoddart had murdered Snow, Simmons and Callan, although he'd no idea whether he had uncovered the links between Rodriguez and Snow or found out that Snow was an undercover agent. Thinking back to when Stoddart had confronted him with the Colt, he decided it was all an act. If Scott had wanted to steal the cocaine he could have done so without ever coming ashore to meet Snow and if that was his plan there'd have been no reason to kill him. His blood ran cold at the thought of Stoddart and Dieger getting together behind his back. If they had already, he knew that he was marked for death the moment he outlived his usefulness.

'Timing,' said Stoddart now, 'what's wrong with our timing?'

'Snow said that you had a buyer for the shipment and that you were moving it tonight.'

'That's correct. So what?'

'Since you didn't ask where I'd been this morning, I'll tell you,' began Scott. 'Some years ago I suffered a personal tragedy and I've been looking for the man who caused it ever since. I saw him briefly when it happened and I saw him again today. His name is Rodriguez.'

'And how does that fit in with my plans?'

'I'd say that he's caused you more than his share of trouble just lately and I think he would give just about anything to get his hands on that shipment – mostly because it belongs to you. What I'm suggesting is that I pretend to double-cross you and offer him the cocaine at a price he can just about afford, but can't refuse.'

'How do you propose to do that without him realizing that you want revenge?'

'He doesn't know that I know it was him,' said Scott.

Stoddart pondered for a moment on the prospects of avenging himself. Then, as his mind raced on to explore the more devious aspects of causing Rodriguez more lasting pain, a cold, calculating smile spread over his face. 'Why don't you forget this crap about going to Spain and setting up your own watersports business and stick with me? You'll live like royalty. Nothing but the best will be good enough for you – and if you have enough money, believe me, nothing is out of reach. There's nothing on God's green earth that the almighty dollar can't buy.'

Like a drowning man grasping at a straw, Scott realized

132

that if the offer was genuine and he accepted it, Stoddart would feel secure from any repercussions following his dealings with Haynes – if Dieger had related them to him, as he strongly suspected.

'I'm bound to admit that although your offer has a lot of appeal it's not the way I envisage my future – yet my brain just seems to have a natural aptitude for this sort of thing. I didn't set out to have these ideas, they just come into my head of their own accord. Standing here, thinking about the millions of pounds I could make with very little effort and virtually no risk, I realize that to turn down your offer would be plain stupid. With one reservation, you've got yourself a deal.'

'Spit it out, bonny lad,' said Stoddart encouragingly. 'Put your cards on the table so that we all know where we stand.'

'I've been looking for Rodriguez for a long time, so I'm not going to let him off the hook now – not at any price,' said Scott emphatically. 'If I tell you my next idea, you may feel that my vendetta and your own would put our future plans in jeopardy if we carried it through.'

Realizing that he had given him the excuse to urge him to reveal his idea without seeming to be forceful, Stoddart hedged. 'Being cautious is second nature to me. I want that bastard so bad I can taste it but I can't allay your reservations unless I know what you're talking about. Why don't you speak up and trust my judgement? After all, I've been around for a long time and so far I've survived everything life has thrown at me.'

With an inward smile, Scott allowed his face to reflect a few moments' hesitant brooding. 'Okay,' he said at last, 'I suppose it's common sense to start as we mean to go on. As I see it, when this torpedo run across the Channel gets under way, it'll only be a matter of time before the market here is saturated. Admittedly by that time we'll have made a billion pounds or so which could be invested for a good return.' He'd kept a watchful eye on Stoddart's face as he spoke and could almost see his brain ticking over – a saturated market registered as a slump in prices, violent gang wars, treachery, and the enlistment of a flood of investigators to stop the flow of drugs across the Channel.

'My alternative is to go international,' he continued, 'by investing the profits from the cross-Channel venture in a fast attack craft which I'm sure my friend Dieger could supply. The one I had in mind was a SØLØVEN Class, built for the Danish navy. It has a top speed of fifty-four knots and is just short of a hundred feet long, which makes it suitable for ocean-going voyages. Its range of four hundred and sixty nautical miles can be increased by substituting the bulk of its armaments for additional fuel tanks. Obviously this will be carried out while converting the craft into a luxury yacht, leaving only its torpedo tubes intact – camouflaged, of course. The goods would again be delivered by torpedo, only this time long-range and controlled by computer. I've heard that there's one with a range of sixty-eight miles, which puts the mother ship beyond any coastguard patrol vessels, and in many cases, in international waters, out of reach of the authorities. If I'm wrong about that, any approaching vessels considered suspect would be picked up on the radar and outrun with the attack craft's superior speed. We could run along the coast, say of the USA, delivering our shipments at will without ever needing to go closer than sixty miles.'

As he spoke, Stoddart's mind turned his words into pictures as he considered the problem of getting fresh supplies to the converted attack craft as it travelled the world like a wartime surface raider. They could use innocent-looking supply ships, he thought, and for the first time began to see himself as an international drugs baron with none to equal him. Not even the gnomes of Zurich, or fabulously rich oil sheikhs would be able to command more finance – or the power that went with it. He imagined a single torpedo warhead packed with two hundred and fifty kilos of cocaine – valued at two hundred thousand pounds per kilo at street level – speeding unhindered and undetected to its destination ashore. He thought of the tens of thousands of miles of shoreline belonging to the United States alone, and the heavily populated cities with their countless addicts, pushers and barons to keep supplied. His mind boggled at the possibilities.

'Brilliant,' he said enthusiastically. 'Your idea is nothing short of brilliance. I'm amazed that no one has thought of it before. Secrecy is going to be essential. If organizations like the Mafia were to get wind of such a scheme they'd stop at nothing to take over before we could get it off the ground.'

'Agreed,' said Scott, 'but what about our friend Rodriguez? Must I live with the burden of knowing that he's to be spared my vengeance so as not to jeopardize our future plans?'

'I think not,' said Stoddart, after a moment's thought. 'Like you, bonny lad, I find that his continued presence dominates my every thought. He's there when I close my eyes to go to sleep and he turns up in my dreams. What I suggest is that my arrangements for the sale of the cocaine go ahead, but there will only be nineteen containers. I shall call my buyer and tell him that one container was lost during last night's operation.

'You can get in touch with Rodriguez. Tell him that you've cheated me out of one container by convincing me that it was lost at sea and it's his for two million in cash. Its retail value is five but he'll try to beat you down to one because that will be all he can raise in a hurry. Give him a hard time but accept his bid and make it quite plain that you will only deal with him in person. He'll try to dictate the place of exchange – partly because he won't trust you but mostly because you're a nobody, and he wants to try and get the cocaine without paying for it. Demand that he meets you here, offshore in a launch, during the late evening when there are few people about. Tell him that you'll mark the place with a boat left at anchor but don't show yourself until he arrives on the scene.

'You can use an aqualung to stay out of sight. Stack some of your cylinders up on the sea bed in case you need them. It might be a good idea to arm yourself with one of those evil-looking spear guns, just in case he comes prepared with divers himself. Once you have everything set up you simply inform the law about the deal, so that he gets caught with the goods in his possession. He should go down for a good long stretch. It doesn't matter whether or not he pays, just so long as he gets caught red-handed. However it goes, once the trade is made you head for the

135

sea bed and out of harm's way. Even if the law tries to bag you, out of spite, they'll have their work cut out finding you at night. And with more oxygen available you should be able to put a lot of unexpected distance between you and them. Don't come back here when it's over, go to the King's Head Hotel in Deal. Ask for Ruben, the manager, and tell him your name: nothing more. He'll be expecting you and will look after you until I come back from my trip to Europe.'

'Sounds fine to me,' agreed Scott. 'What's the form for tonight?'

'An ocean-going luxury yacht is due to anchor offshore this evening. As a matter of trust, you will accompany me because I wish you to see for yourself that to close this deal as a bulk order I've had to drop my price considerably. That will cut down your percentage by a third. I know this is disappointing but it does save us the time and risks involved in seeing it through to street level where we would reap the maximum benefits.

'I'm doing it this way to get a quick turnover so that I can begin financing the cross-Channel torpedo venture without further delay. If we progress to our latest idea of becoming international barons, this will become a normal situation. We must allow our clients to make a reasonable return of profit on their investments and I don't really feel inclined to set up our own worldwide street distribution points at this time. That is unless, of course, you have any brilliant ideas on that?'

'No,' admitted Scott, 'but I'll give it some thought. In the meantime I'll go along with you for a quick turnover until we get established.'

'That's good, bonny lad. Now I suggest we get some rest. I feel as though I've just run in the London Marathon – and, if you don't mind me saying so, you look ready to drop.'

'I couldn't sleep if I tried. My brain is pounding like a high speed diesel locomotive. I think I'll go for a good long swim to tire myself out then maybe I'll grab a couple of hours' sleep.'

'Why don't you see to those oxygen cylinders while you're about it? There's a watersports section in the

136

supermarket. Just tell the manager that you work for me and sign for anything you need.'

6

The sun was high, bright and unusually warm as Scott picked his way through the crowds of sunbathers lying in the warm, soft sand on the beach. Dogs barked as they bounded after sticks thrown by their owners and children splashed happily in the warm shallows. Further out were swimmers enjoying themselves – from teenagers to old age pensioners – and among them and beyond were craft ranging from inflatable dinghies fitted with outboard motors to high-speed powerboats. Many a head wearing goggles and snorkel probed the inshore depths, while occasionally a figure clad in wet suit and aqualung harness, like himself, surfaced for a few moments before disappearing again.

Apart from the two extra oxygen tanks he was carrying, Scott blended in with the rest. As he waded in, chest deep, no one paid him any attention. He began to wonder if he'd been right not to take a boat to make his task easier but it would also have acted as a marker for his dive. Shuddering at the very thought of being under surveillance, he ducked beneath the waves and began swimming steadily out to sea. Timing himself, he surfaced to get his bearings after about twenty minutes, but the distance seemed vastly different in the bright daylight. Thankful for the opportunity to locate the haul before its planned collection, he began a systematic search of the sea bed. Using small piles of rocks as markers, he moved in an ever-widening half-circle, far beyond the merrymakers.

Soon the sea bed began to show more growth of seaweed and the scanty rocks were much larger than before. Carefully he searched, until what looked like an orange football stood out amid the long, dark, drifting kelp which marked the spot where he had sunk the catamaran. Everything was much as he had left it except that now the current had trailed the kelp over the decks, where it hung lazily around the three outboard motors.

In an effort to get a reasonable bearing, Scott struck out for the surface and as he suspected, found he was further from the shore than he had intended. Some three hundred yards away, towards the shore, a powerboat raced parallel to it. The closest life to the boat was at least another five hundred yards off and, satisfied that the site was well off the beaten track, Scott returned to the depths and paid out more line so that the marker buoy hung some ten feet below the surface.

He knelt down in his tranquil world and wound the buoy's nylon cord around a cleat screwed to the catamaran's deck. Suddenly, for no reason that he could explain, he felt as though alien eyes were watching his every move. His muscles stiffened, his heart pounded and he began to tremble. His skin tingled as a hot flush swept over his entire body, then moments later he felt as cold as ice.

He remained on one knee with the kelp drifting lazily, reaching out to embrace him, and turned slowly to peer through the still water. The only sound was the escaping spent air as it rose in a mass of sparkling bubbles through the penetrating sunlight to the surface, some forty feet above. A three hundred and sixty degree sweep produced no similar sign to indicate the presence of other human life yet the feeling persisted.

Certain that he was in no immediate danger, Scott stood upright and, facing the shore, began a second slow sweep to his right and stopped. Through the wall of water, almost at the edge of his vision, was a blurred shape. Even before his feet left the catamaran's deck, a choking lump rose in his throat and every stroke of his flippered feet increased the feeling of nausea that began to ferment in the pit of his stomach.

A few feet away he stopped again, kneeling in the waving arms of kelp and making the sign of the cross on his chest. For there, standing solemn-faced, with eyes closed and heads bowed, their hands still glued to their

buttocks, stood Simmons and Callan. Snow stood alongside, his eyes defiantly wide open, his arms floating lazily
with elbows bent. His fingers were interwoven into a
double-handed fist just inches away from his mouth as if
in prayer – or as though, even in death, he was pleading
to be avenged.

Stunned, Scott's feet swung down into the drifting kelp
until it swirled around his chest. Stoddart's name echoed
through his numbed brain and he was unable to take his
eyes off the shiny steel handcuffs around Snow's wrists.
He felt in some strange way that even in death Snow was
still trying to tell him something. Haynes' name came to
mind and he tried to fathom how he could be implicated.
After the allegations made by Simmons and Callan, Snow
would hardly turn to him for help. He could only assume
that Haynes must have had Snow under surveillance or
that he was making use of bugging devices to keep abreast
of what was going on.

The awesome, pleading figure of Snow held a strange
fascination for him and he began to wade through the
kelp towards him. His foot came into contact with
something heavy and, stooping to push the kelp aside, he
found a fourth body. It was Rodriguez and while the
others had no visible wounds to indicate their cause of
death, other than drowning, he had been shot in the
forehead. Kneeling down, Scott searched Rodriguez and
found that his pockets had been stripped of all personal
belongings and identification. Only a loose end of small-
gauge anchor chain trailed close by, the remainder being
wrapped around Snow's feet to keep him anchored to the
sea bed.

His search of the other bodies proved equally fruitless
and Scott turned towards the shore again, passing the
catamaran with its precious cargo en route. Two names
ran through his mind, Stoddart and Haynes. If Stoddart
had been the assassin there would have been no point in
agreeing to hold back on one of the containers as bait for
Rodriguez. That left Haynes. If he had Stoddart's holiday
hideaway bugged, as he claimed, then he would have up
to-the-minute information on Stoddart's plan. He would
also have known that Simmons and Callan had disclosed

140

his treachery to Snow and himself. This in turn would mean that he would have to eliminate all those concerned, except himself and Stoddart – if he was, in fact, after the cocaine.

Scott paused for a moment to consider that point. He had to keep himself alive because he was the only one with the exact knowledge of the cocaine's location. But in which case, why was Stoddart so important? 'Because someone has to order the salvage of it,' the voice of his conscience scowled back from within. 'If Haynes is the crook you think him to be, and he killed Stoddart in the hope of forcing you to tell him where the stuff is, he might find that you would rather die than talk. More so, since it's obvious that he would have to kill you anyway.'

The dark, weed-strewn sea bed gave way to fine sand as he approached the shore and he began to hear the distant noises of growling engines and gleeful holiday-makers. When he submerged, his conscience continued to bombard him with questions over how Rodriguez managed to get himself murdered and dumped in the sea so quickly? Scott shrugged this off with the only answer he could think of – Haynes was not working alone. With an effort he blocked off that avenue and turned to thoughts of the future. The first question requiring an immediate answer was whether he should disappear with the proceeds of his cross-Channel trip. Although the idea had a lot of appeal, it led to other questions. Would Stoddart search him out and take his revenge? Would Haynes use his authority and knowledge to proclaim Scott a criminal and have him hunted down, in the hope of recovering the cocaine – either for his own enrichment, or for the prestige of his capture?

Brooding, Scott left the water and trudged up the beach, oblivious to the noisy activities of those around him. The soft sand gave way to a neatly mown grass and before he knew it he was reaching for the door of the holiday home. He froze with his hand hovering, reflecting on the choices he faced. To enter would mean great wealth, a life of comparative, if not extreme, luxury. If his ideas were to become reality, money would spout as though from an everlasting fountain, with foreign travel a normal part of life. The price would be the ever-present prospect of capture by the law and the risk of death through his unlawful dealings or treachery.

Once again he contemplated turning back but he knew that if he tried to act honourably, by reporting it all to another member of the police force, Haynes would move heaven and earth to implicate him.

Taking a deep breath, he entered, dreading the confrontation to come. All was quiet. He guessed that Stoddart was still sleeping and gave out a deep sigh of relief for the stay of execution. He made his way to the bathroom, stripped in preparation for a shower and felt, for the first time in his life, naked beyond the point of being undressed. Gazing around in search of those hidden ears, his skin began to crawl at the thought of being secretly observed. So with a mixture of anger and distrust, he stepped into the perspex cubicle and closed the sliding door behind him. He turned his back to the hot spray and allowed the rivulets of water to trickle down his shoulders and chest before setting to work with a sponge and lathering his body with the sweet-smelling soap. With the silky, liquid warmth easing the tension from his aching muscles, he spent several minutes in pleasurable contemplation of using those secret ears as a means of setting a trap to ensnare Haynes in a web of his own intrigue.

'Hell, man, it's like a sauna in here,' complained Stoddart, disrupting his thoughts.

'Sorry, the trip was longer than I expected. I ached from head to foot by the time I got back.'

'Did you locate the shipment?'

Scott turned off the shower and stepped out of the cubicle. 'Sure,' he said, moving towards the mirror set into the wall tiles above the handbasin. 'It's all there – just as I left it.'

Reaching out, he wrote in the condensation on the mirror, 'This place is bugged,' and Stoddart's face blanched, his face a stony mask.

'The hell you say,' he said quietly as his Adam's apple rose and fell.

'I surely do,' Scott confirmed, adding with a broad wink: 'One hundred millon quids' worth. It's a pity the pubs are closed. I feel like celebrating, don't you?'

Stoddart looked him straight in the eyes. 'No, I damn well don't,' he scowled. 'I'm as hungry as a bear – can you cook?'

'Eggs, beans and chips are my limit,' said Scott. 'Don't you have a restaurant round here?'

'Sure we do, but mostly they serve egg, bacon, beans and chips.'

'Thank Christ for that,' said Scott. 'It's got to be better than my cooking.'

Scott's revelations about the bugging had thrown Stoddart completely off balance. The implications had sent his mind reeling and he answered Scott's questions with the first thought that came into his head. As the truth began to dawn, his first reaction was to put as much distance between himself and the holiday home as he could, at once. Unwashed, unshaven and wearing only a pair of underpants, he turned to leave the bathroom. When Scott continued speaking as though nothing was wrong, he turned back in amazement.

'I've finished in here,' said Scott, touching his nose meaningfully with his index finger. 'Don't forget to shave. You look like some old dosser with that stubble. The chances of our getting served with you looking like that are minimal I should think.'

Thinking that Scott had something he wanted to discuss while the razor was buzzing, Stoddart reached out for it but to his surprise, Scott opened the door and began to walk through.

'Where are you going?' he asked.

'To get dressed. I'll brew some coffee while I'm waiting for you. Take your time, though. I'm not so hungry that I can't wait for you to get cleaned up.'

Stoddart opened his mouth to reply and raised his hand in an effort to give some emphasis to his words, but Scott had already gone. Realizing that if Scott was right, anything he said might be overheard, he lowered his hand, closed his mouth and shook his head with a despondent sigh. He turned towards the shower with arms outstretched in a gesture of futility, palms upward, casting his glance at the ceiling and whispering in

143

exasperation: 'May the saints give me strength.'

Yet Scott was so confident; he must be quite sure about something. Turning on the shower as hot as it would go, Stoddart slowly rotated, allowing its heat to soak into his tense body. Gradually he began to relax. As his brain began to function without panic, he realized that if Scott was right about the bugging then any sign of hasty departure would be picked up and might force the listeners to react prematurely. His line of thought shifted to Scott as a person; likeable enough, he thought sceptically, but there had been times when he'd thought him naive and lacking the instinct of self-preservation at any cost, even to the point of murder when the stakes were high. Yet the man had other qualities. His ideas were original on a grand scale and he'd shown no sign of flashiness so far. If anything, he was quiet and unassuming.

'I think maybe I've done you an injustice, my bonny lad,' he said to himself. 'What's more, I think you and I are going to get on real fine in the future.'

He stepped out of the shower. Water dripped on to the floor from contempt rather than carelessness as he reached for a towel. Drying his face, he wiped the steam from the mirror, threw the towel over his shoulder, picked up the electric razor and began to peer at his image as he removed the stubble from his face. Time had taken its toll, he thought, looking at his balding head and the beginnings of the crow's feet around his eyes.

Returning the razor to its holder, he poured a generous puddle of aftershave in his palm and wiped the fiery liquid around his cheeks – and was struck by a thought. Retrieving the razor, he removed the rotary head as if for cleaning and found that it was not quite as it had been the last time he'd opened it. This one had been designed as a hi-tech electronic listening device which drew its power from the rechargeable battery unit inside the casing. 'It could be that your arrival on the scene was providential, bonny lad,' he thought.

Entering the bedroom, he half expected to find signs of hidden panic in Scott – for he'd had a fleeting thought of him leaving the bathroom to pack everything required for a speedy exit. It came as no surprise that the only change was the aroma of percolated coffee and, curious as to the workings of Scott's mind, Stoddart dressed quickly.

Scott sat in an armchair, sipping a mug of coffee and reading a magazine. The only sign of his having taken any interest in Stoddart's movements was a second mug of coffee on the table. Stoddart picked it up by the handle, caressing its body with his other hand, and when its heat instantly stung his fingers he knew that Scott was not the disinterested person he pretended to be. In fact Scott had watched him with a bland expression from the moment he entered the lounge.

Stoddart raised his mug to his lips and noted a secretive mocking quality about Scott's eyes which he found irksome.

'Something wrong?' he asked sharply.

Scott stood up, smiling broadly. 'I was just wondering what my cut is going to be now that you've done a bulk deal for the cocaine.'

Stoddart looked at him, his first thought returning to the fact that anything he said could be overheard. Realizing that Scott must also have considered this aspect, and that his answer could not possibly be of any additional help to the eavesdroppers, Stoddart deduced that he was up to something.

'I'm letting the consignment go for sixty million,' he said. 'Your percentage remains the same – ten per cent. That gives you six million.'

'That's a lot of cash to be carrying around,' remarked Scott.

Smiling, Stoddart said: 'You could be right,' and drew a diamond on the table's polished surface with his index finger. 'Is that a problem for you?'

'No,' said Scott, watching him. 'I was just wondering about the next stage. Am I to be a partner or shall I still be working on a percentage?'

This line of question aggravated Stoddart. It seemed to him that Scott was taking advantage. 'I haven't given the partnership details much thought,' he hedged, 'but since you ask, you put your share from this deal and we'll split everything sixty-forty. That leaves me supplying the main bulk of the finance and the contacts while you keep the ideas coming.'

'I could use some of the proceeds from this deal to live on,' Scott pointed out.

'No problem,' agreed Stoddart reluctantly. 'How does a straight million sound to you?'

'Done.' Scott smiled. He placed the magazine on the table and wetting his index finger, began turning the pages until he came to a picture. It showed an American ship undergoing repairs at sea in a purpose-built floating dry dock, which was itself a ship. He flicked more pages over and there were pictures showing how the mother ship could take on ballast to partially sink it and how the great doors fitted to the stern opened to allow a stricken vessel to enter.

Stoddart knew that Scott had solved the problem of keeping a fast attack craft supplied for long journeys. The mother ship, carrying everything including the fast attack craft, could remain hundreds of miles outside a country's territorial waters. The smaller craft could speed away from it, fire its torpedoes loaded with drugs and wait for their return before moving off to the next rendezvous.

Stoddart's raised head showed a beaming smile. 'A picture is sometimes better than a thousand words, bonny lad. Shall we go and eat?'

The grass was soft underfoot as they walked along the ridge above the beach. It was six o'clock and although still bright and warm, many of the families on holiday had left to go back and eat. Scott's own stomach began to rumble at the thought of food, but Stoddart made no move towards the restaurant.

'How did you come to the conclusion that the place was bugged?'

'I found Snow, Simmons and Callan – Rodriguez was there, too,' replied Scott, looking down at his feet as he walked. 'They're all dead out there.'

'Jesus Christ! Why? How?' Stoddart stammered.

'To answer that I think we're both going to have to bare our souls. A few minutes ago, I gave you the final piece of the jigsaw. I did that for a good reason. If you choose, you can carry on without me now. I have deliberately become surplus to your requirements.'

Stoddart nodded thoughtfully, yet guessed that Scott was not talking just for the sake of enlightening him. 'That's true enough,' he agreed, 'but it doesn't explain your belief about the bugging – and so far you haven't produced any evidence about that?' he concluded, keeping his own discovery a secret.

'Go back to our first meeting,' said Scott, 'when I landed in your swimming pool. I hadn't a clue who you were and all I knew about crime or criminals was what I'd read in the newspapers. Whether you believe that when I have finished talking is up to you. Anyway, as you know, because you arranged it, when I returned home everything I owned had been stolen.' Scott gave Stoddart a sly glance and saw his Adam's apple rise and fall compulsively, but made no comment.

'That was followed by Snow making me a very generous offer to smuggle you back into the country,' he continued. 'What you didn't know was that, meanwhile, I was summoned to be interviewed by the police about the robbery. They basically threatened to lumber me with having arranged it myself while I was out of the country unless I helped them. If I agreed, they promised to clear me of suspicion so that I could collect the hundred thousand pounds insurance claim. In addition, I was to be told the name of the man who had caused the deaths of two of my family – who, incidentally, proved to Rodriguez.' Scott went on to relate the events that followed, leaving nothing out, Stoddart listening carefully and weighing up the pros and cons as the intrique unfurled.

When he had finished, Stoddart remained solemn and quiet. For a moment he thought of the many deaths that Scott had been involved in, by way of participation or as an accessory after the fact, for a man unused to being a party to such atrocities. Since their first meeting his life must have been a nightmare and Stoddart thought this was probably the reason for Scott's mind dwelling on methods of smuggling, and why his ideas were unique. He probably turned to such thoughts in an effort to shut out those he'd rather not dwell on. His revelation that Snow was working undercover for Haynes shook Stoddart to the core but the Haynes' intrique astounded him. As Haynes' part in the affair was revealed, Stoddart thought that here was a person who would always get his man or achieve his goal in life, whether it be for promotion or to preserve the law for the law-abiding. Then Scott described the last sighting of Snow, chained in handcuffs. Law officers just didn't go around murdering their own men.

'Questions, questions, questions,' he sighed in exasperation, shaking his head. 'I guess all of this has turned your world topsy-turvy, bonny lad.'

'To put it mildly.'

'If it's any consolation, although you have put forward some great ideas, you've turned my world upside down, too. That cocaine represents just about everything I could beg, borrow or steal. I can see now that Dieger is giving me the run around to get you off the hook, and on top of that it sounds as though Haynes has abandoned his ambitions of controlling London's twilight world and is going for the big time. What's bothering me is Claude Durac; the captain of the hydrofoil. He's given me no hint that there are any problems which poses some questions. If Haynes is behind the bugging, will he pull the rug from under our feet tonight if we go ahead? Will he try to take the cocaine from us and the sixty million in diamonds, or will he try to cut himself in on the deal and our future plans?'

'Perhaps the answer lies in considering the alternative,' suggested Scott. 'We could leave the stuff where it is and return for it at a later date. That would at least make Haynes look silly if he has taken control of the Sea Queen. If we don't show, her owner will be in the clear – if there are no drugs, he can't be charged.'

'True, but if Haynes doesn't react as we think I shall have lost credibility with my American contacts and then what am I supposed to do with the shipment? Haynes, in his official capacity, will make sure that I never again set foot on British soil to sell it and, with the American market dubious, that leaves me with only Europe. With my contacts over there I could buy a whole mountain of the stuff but selling it is another story. I'd be dead in a week if I tried to horn in on their market.'

148

'Let's try another tack,' suggested Scott. 'We both know that to be convicted you have to be caught in possession and we're also fairly certain that Haynes is after the shipment in part or as a whole – not to mention the diamonds, of course. There's no way that he's going to try anything until the shipment is landed. That in itself gives us two elements of surprise: one, we're pretty sure that he's going to be there, and two, there's no way that he's going to make a move until at least one of those containers has been landed and tested.'

Stoddart turned towards Scott, wagging a finger at him as though in reprimand for some misdemeanour. 'Ah,' he said, his eyes almost twinkling, 'now I see where you're heading. We'll go ahead as planned only you won't be coming on board with me as I had intended. You will leave a few minutes after me, wearing the diving gear. Head for the shipment and await my signal before you bring anything up. I'll use a flashlight – one continuous beam for all clear. If I flash on and off several times, come in close and get me the hell out of there. In the meantime I'll call Poldark and get him to stand by to pick us up in a fast boat.'

Satisfied with their arrangements, they strolled to the restaurant where Scott took a seat by the window while Stoddart used the public telephone outside.

'Would you like to order?' asked the young waitress, and Scott looked up from the grubby tablecloth to meet her gaze.

'Two coffees, please,' he replied. 'White, with no sugar.'

'Sugar is on the table,' she pointed out.

'I'll have two poached eggs on two toast. My friend will order in a minute.'

'Your friend?' She gave him an odd look.

'He's using the telephone outside.'

'Oh. Would you like a sweet?'

Scott looked at the single page menu, propped up against an outsize salt and pepper pot.

'Deep-dish apple pie with fresh cream,' he said, as Stoddart joined him.

'Would you care to order?' asked the girl.

Glancing down at the menu, Stoddart's expression

turned to disappointment and disgust and Scott smiled at what he must be thinking of the typical 'chips with everything' fare. Shaking his head in disbelief, Stoddart said: 'Better make it a couple of poached eggs on two toast. I don't think my stomach could handle anything else and I'll have an apple pie with cream to follow.'

'Snap,' grinned Scott. 'They say that great minds think alike.'

'So they say, bonny lad.' Sitting with his back to the window, Scott glanced at the faces of the many customers, a reasonable cross-section of any average holiday community – giggling teenage girls and their pink-faced boyfriends; a group of louts in their late teens who were a little on the boisterous side; and three families of mother, father and children.

'Do you have any sons or daughters?' asked Scott.

'A daughter,' replied Stoddart. 'You're not married, are you?'

'No, I'm still waiting to be swept off my feet. I tried living with a girlfriend but it was doomed before we'd begun. When I get up in the morning I like to be quiet and preferably alone for an hour or so but she liked to have all the latest pop music blaring. It drove me crazy.'

'And you wanted to start a business in Spain?' asked Stoddart drily. 'From what I've seen it's all discos. At night you can hear them for miles and mostly they go on well into the early hours.'

'I can cope with that,' said Scott. 'It's when it's in the same room that it gets me.'

'Tell me something,' Stoddart asked seriously. 'Why didn't you opt for taking your dues and getting out of this game?'

'I keep asking myself the same question,' he admitted. 'I guess it's the thought of finding out at first hand if my idea works. There's a challenge to it. If anyone has ever tried using torpedoes before, I sure as hell haven't heard about it. Why do you do it?'

'I'm a rebel, bonny lad. I have to beat the system. Crime to me is like alcohol to the alcoholic. When I get an idea into my head, nothing will erase it until I've tried my luck. This one of yours, for instance, is an inspiration. Can you imagine what it will be like if we can get it off the ground.?'

'Sure,' grinned Scott, 'but I was just remembering your reaction when I first suggested it. You thought I was stark, raving mad.'

'I did, and that's a fact. I suppose it was because the idea itself is bold, untried and ridiculously expensive to set up. To do the job properly will need something like a military operation, and secrecy is going to be essential. I'm just hoping that your friend Dieger doesn't let us down.'

'He might not have been bothered about selling a few torpedoes,' said Scott, 'but this is a whole new ball game. If we go the whole hog, his sales will total hundreds of millions. It might be worth giving some thought to offering him a partnership.'

'You're joking!' scoffed Stoddart. 'This is going to be the biggest money-spinner ever; you just don't give away things like that.'

'I wasn't thinking of giving anything away,' retorted Scott. 'I was concentrating on the possible problems of supply and demand. If he was a partner you could order anything you wanted and have it delivered where you required without any fuss or bother – and, let's face it, he has contacts all over the world.'

Stoddart thoughtfully chewed the last of his poached egg before swallowing it, and raised his fork to shake it gently at Scott. 'You could be right at that,' he said. 'I could also save a great deal of outlay.'

'I wouldn't put it to him quite like that,' advised Scott. 'It suggests that you might be expecting him to supply everything on the prospect of him getting his share of the profits if we're successful. Why not offer him a share in the profits, based on his meeting your demands of supplies and equipment?'

'That sounds a bit like succumbing to blackmail before the threat has been made,' argued Stoddart.

Scott smiled. 'No, it's making sure you get what you want where you want it, in preference to other customers. And on the scale of profit margin you're talking about, what's a couple of million here or there?'

Stoddart thought for a while before breaking into a smile reflecting some depth of emotion. 'You remind me of my daughter in some respects,' he said. 'A couple of years ago she pestered me and the missus to take her to see the Blackpool lights, and the first night, when we'd walked along the golden mile to see the sights, I took them for a drink in the Queen's Hotel – that's a big public house and hotel, just a few yards off the sea front. They have pop groups singing there and other acts and it was packed to capacity. While I was battling to get served at the bar, my daughter went off to powder her nose and within minutes of her returning, one of the waitresses beckoned us to an empty table. It seemed odd, but I thought no more about it. The following night we went back there, having enjoyed ourselves so much. Sure enough it was packed again, only this time Margaret, the waitress, spotted us right off and beckoned us to a reserved table. It transpired that my bonny lass had given her a twenty pound tip to see that we had a steady supply of drinks. On top of that, she'd told her that I was a talent scout from London. You're beginning to make me feel like she did. I'm not taking you anywhere, am I, bonny lad? I may be holding the reins but you're doing all the leading.'

'If that be the case,' said Scott, with a hint of sarcasm and a large measure of sincerity, 'I do hope that in a couple of years you will look back on this luxurious dinner and dance with some fond emotions.'

Stoddart looked down at the apple pie and nonchalantly spooned the runny cream over it. 'One thing's for sure,' he reflected, 'when you get this low down there's only one way left to go and that's straight up. Even the glasshouse wasn't this bad.'

'The glasshouse?'

Stoddart smiled at his youthful ignorance. 'That's an old army prison where discipline is spelled out with a mammoth sized "D". They guarantee to set you free in one of three different states of well-being; a highly disciplined soldier, a nutcase, or dead.'

'Dare I ask which of the obvious two categories you put yourself in?'

'Highly disciplined, but very much opposed to authority,' replied Stoddart sombrely. 'And now, my bonny lad, I think it's high time we took up the gauntlet and challenged some of that authority which doesn't appear to be practising what it preaches.'

Evening was closing in when they left the restaurant. The throng of holidaymakers had thinned considerably, and the beach was almost deserted. Out at sea was a large, white luxury yacht, cruising majestically towards them from Dover.

'That will be the Sea Queen,' said Stoddart. 'They'll be sending a launch in about an hour, I should think.' Scott made no reply; he was remembering his last sighting of Snow.

On entering the holiday home, Stoddart made straight for the drinks cabinet, saying cheerfully as he held a large bottle of dry ginger: 'I suppose we ought to celebrate in anticipation of making our first step towards a billion pounds. I'm for a large whisky – how about you?'

Looking from the bottle to Stoddart's face, Scott guessed that he wanted to create an atmosphere of expectancy to delude any eavesdroppers. His eyes flicked to a tin of orange juice. 'Ain't you got no beer?' he mimicked, and Stoddart took his cue with a wry smile.

'Cigar?'

'Why not?' said Scott. 'Might as well get used to the good life.'

Stoddart opened the large picture window and watched as the Sea Queen dropped anchor half a mile offshore. 'I'm going to get myself a yacht like that some day,' he called to Scott, who had gone into the bedroom to change into his wet suit.

'You should be so lucky,' he replied. 'If I'm not mistaken, the time to enjoy luxury is going to be your problem. This operation is going to take a lot of personal dedication.'

Stoddart began to reminisce. 'It reminds me of the old days. When you have the time you can't afford to spend the money and when you do have the cash to spare, the workload is such that you can't spare the time.'

'You could make a super killing and get out while you're ahead,' suggested Scott.

'Super killing. Did you have anything particular in mind?' he asked, taking a long pull at his cigar.

'Nothing special. I'd put everything into the cross-Channel venture, landing consignments from Lands End to as far up as Great Yarmouth. The profits could be invested to equip and supply a venture running from,' he paused to think, 'let's say Miami. It's a well-known hot spot for drugs, right up the north Atlantic coastline of the USA, into Canada and as far as Newfoundland. Having achieved that, I'd head for Greenland with the spoils and fly from there to wherever the fancy took me.'

'Greenland?' Stoddart challenged haughtily. 'Bermuda would be more my choice.'

'As it would be to any outsiders who happened to take a calculated guess at your plans,' Scott pointed out emphatically. 'If you flood the USA with drugs, you can bet your bottom dollar that you'll provoke some keen interest from the big-time syndicates – not to mention the Mafia. What do you think they're likely to do, knowing that you're out there with a billion dollars plus in diamonds and cash?'

'Who do you think we'll be dealing with, if not the big-time syndicates and the Mafia?'

'Is that what you had in mind?' asked Scott when he returned to the lounge in his wet suit.

'They have the distribution outlets already set up and hungry for supplies,' Stoddart pointed out. 'And they have the kind of cash we're talking about to pay for the shipments.'

'I guess you're right, although I wouldn't accept cash. You could get palmed off with a load of counterfeit bills and it's too bulky.'

'I had planned on sticking to diamonds,' Stoddart assured him, 'but you could have a point about getting mugged at the end of the line by the very people we've been supplying.'

'Have you given any thought to how payment is going to be made bearing in mind, of course, they'll be on the shore and we'll be at sea? You can't just fire torpedoes ashore at a pre-determined location and expect Charlie, on the receiving end, to send the dollars out to us.'

'Hardly,' Stoddart grinned, 'but don't worry about that side of things now,' and he prodded his ear to indicate

154

that he did not wish to enlighten their eavesdroppers.

'There's a launch coming ashore,' said Scott, nodding in the direction of the sea.

'Time to go then. It'll be dark in an hour or so. Will you be able to locate the shipment without any problems?'

'I don't anticipate any. The yacht's a fair distance away from the site, though maybe they could move closer when you're satisfied with everything on board.'

With a wry grin, Stoddart turned to pick up the telephone. Scott could imagine the sarcastic reply Stoddart might have given had it not been for his comments being overheard.

'It's time to go,' said Stoddart, matter-of-factly into the mouthpiece before replacing it. Replying to Scott's look of enquiry with a bland silence, Stoddart just nodded his goodbyes, smiled and left.

Outside he took a deep breath, filling his lungs to capacity while looking up at the clear blue sky. Night was coming in fast now and the yacht would soon be a blaze of lights from stem to stern. He let his breath go in a lingering sigh through puckered lips, thrust his hands into his trouser pockets and made his way to the beach. As he topped the rise of grass leading down to the sands, he was joined by an elderly man who was several inches shorter than himself, with a roly-poly figure. Stoddart turned towards him, nodding a greeting.

The man glanced at him over a pair of bi-focals. 'Nice to see you again, Max,' he said. 'It's been a long time.'

They fell in step and began to walk slowly down to the water's edge where a launch had beached.

'Isaac,' Stoddart began, 'we've done a fair bit of business over the years. We could hardly claim to be bosom pals but I'd like to think that at least we could call ourselves good, trusting friends.' The old man nodded. 'The truth of the matter is that I'm expecting trouble on the yacht,' Stoddart went on, and his companion looked up from the soft sand at his feet to the launch awaiting them.

'What kind of trouble?' he asked.

'There's a copper by the name of Haynes. He's had my place bugged and has apparently been dogging my footsteps for some considerable time. My information is that he's bent and it's my guess that he's not on board officially. I think he's after the diamonds, as well as the shipment, for himself.'

'Under those circumstances it would seem foolhardy to continue,' the old man remarked.

'Not necessarily so. If Haynes is as bent as I think he is, neither he nor any of his henchmen will make a move until the shipment is on board. It's worth more at street level than the diamonds. What I'm asking you to do is to carry on as agreed and do the valuation for me – you'll not be breaking any law. When it's done you come ashore, leaving me to carry on. I've made my own arrangements if there's any trouble after that.'

'Seems that my part of the business remains the same. My fee has been paid in advance and all I have to do now is earn it.'

'You're a good man, Isaac. If this deal comes off, I have even bigger ones in mind. A lot of travelling is involved but it will be worth millions to you in valuation fees.'

'I'm an old man,' Isaac shrugged. 'I don't travel well these days and I don't need the money any more. Now, my son is trustworthy and ambitious – why not let me approach him on your behalf?'

'Sure, why not? It's all in the family.'

'Are you Stoddart?' asked the boatman in an American drawl as they waded out to the launch. Looking at him, Stoddart did not recognize him as a member of the crew from his previous visits to the Sea Queen.

'I am,' replied Max, turning aside to help the old man aboard.

'I was told to bring you and a diver,' said the boatman, making no move to aid the old man.

'Bonny lad,' said Stoddart, fixing him with a suspicious, hostile glare, 'you can take us on board, or leave us where we stand – it makes no difference to either of us: whatever pleases you just tickles me to death.'

At this the boldness left the boatman's face and he glanced over at the Sea Queen. 'Okay, okay,' he said, 'take my hand and I'll give you a hoist aboard.'

With an effort, and a boost from behind by Stoddart, the old man scrambled over the side and squelched to the stern seat where he sat down. Stoddart waded to the bow and pushed his full weight against it. When the craft became buoyant, he hauled himself aboard and made his way aft to sit with the old man. For a minute, the boatman manoeuvred astern, looking over their heads in the direction of the Sea Queen, and clearing the shallows he turned his attention to the controls, giving the engine a burst of power in forward motion. The stern sank deeper as the propeller grasped hungrily beneath the surface for more water to reject in a mass of swirling white foam. Stoddart took no notice of his recklessness, aware of the man's contempt over his rebuff. Captain Titus Duval's intense dislike of smoking in his presence prompted Stoddart to sit back and relax with a cigar for the few minutes it would take to reach the yacht.

'She's a lovely boat,' ventured the old man. 'It must be nice to be so rich that you can afford such luxuries.'

Stoddart shot him a sideways glance. 'Come on, Isaac,' he scoffed, 'even you could afford a yacht like that if you chose to.'

'I suppose you're right,' he nodded with a smile. 'My Jewish blood wouldn't allow it, though – at least not unless there were large profits to be made.'

Stoddart laughed. 'There's no fool like an old fool,' he scoffed. 'You're looking so green already, I swear you'll puke if you don't get on board pretty soon.'

The old man raised his hand and brought it down on Stoddart's knee. 'You're right, of course,' he laughed. 'I'm just an old fool with envious dreams which I wouldn't fulfil no matter how rich I was, or how young. I have three gods: the one I pray to, my family whom I worship, and my greed for gold, which I hope will guard me and mine against the poverties of this earthly existence. For myself I ask none of the luxuries of life: just to grow old gracefully with my few home comforts.'

'And with a host of happy grandchildren screeching their heads off while you try to take a well-earned afternoon nap in your favourite armchair.'

The old man's pale blue eyes looked beyond the physical things before him and he nodded as though in approval, as the happy faces of his many children and grandchildren came to mind.

'I guess a man's wealth is only judged by the houses, cars and yachts he owns, if he deems it so,' he said at last. 'Until now, I've never really given any thought to how my life affects those close to me – not deep thought, anyway. Now that I have, I'm beginning to realize the depth of family love and life. The funny thing is that I should gain such wisdom in circumstances like these.' He began to look around, scanning as much of the horizon as he could see without turning in his seat.

'Hey now,' said Stoddart reproachfully, 'you can cut that out. I know what you're thinking and you can forget it. In an hour you'll be back on terra firma: fit as a fiddle and on your way back to your family.'

'God willing,' said the old man, turning away with a tear rolling down his cheek.

As if heralding the coming darkness, the Sea Queen's deck lights came on. The launch's engine slowed to a purr and they gently nudged the landing platform which had wide steps leading upward.

A moment later, the boatman stepped nimbly over to secure the launch. 'Welcome aboard the Sea Queen,' he said, offering his hand, though without much enthusiasm. The old man stepped cautiously on to the platform, followed by Stoddart, and they proceeded up the steps. The boatman coughed irritably as Stoddart raised the cigar to his mouth and, taking the hint, tossed it over the side after one last puff. At the top of the gangway, a seaman stood on watch and the tension eased a little when Stoddart recognized his smiling face.

'The Captain sends his compliments and requests that you join him in his private quarters, sir,' beamed the man.

'Thanks,' Stoddart replied, noting how quiet it was. 'No parties tonight?'

'No sir. The Captain has ordered a quiet ship tonight. After eight bells it's shore leave for all but the duty roster.'

'Well, that must include you.'

'Yes sir, in two minutes' time I shall be relieved.'

An icy finger ran the length of Stoddart's spine as the boatman lead them to the Captain's suite. Pushing open the door, he politely bade them enter, his smile almost a sneer. 'Mr Stoddart and friend, sir,' he called, as they stepped over the threshold. In an instant Stoddart's nose set the alarm bells ringing, for there was the sweet tang of cigarette smoke.

His attention immediately focused on Captain Titus, who was struggling out of a deep leather armchair.

'My dear Max,' he said beaming. 'My apologies for not piping you on board personally, but, as you see, I have had a mishap and can just about hobble with the aid of a crutch.'

Stoddart advanced towards him. 'Please don't,' he pleaded, offering his hand. 'There's no need to trouble yourself on my account. This is my friend and business colleague who has agreed to value the diamonds for me. Captain Titus, this is Mr Yitzhak Isaac. Isaac, meet Captain Titus.'

'My pleasure,' said the old man courteously.

'Please make yourself comfortable,' Titus invited. 'Can I get you a drink?'

'A glass of cold milk?' replied the old man, almost apologetically. 'If it's no trouble, of course.'

'Don't even think such a thing – I drink it all the time. I keep a fine cellar but that's strictly for guests. Max here has a liking for my brandy.'

'Under the circumstances, perhaps I had better do the honours,' offered Stoddart.

'No, I'll buzz my steward. That's what I pay him for.'

While he did so, Stoddart took the opportunity to look around. The lounge was exactly as he recalled it from previous visits in Hamburg. The window ports were locked and the air conditioning purred quietly. All the doors leading to the adjoining rooms stood silently ajar, but not enough to see into them; and Stoddart grew suspicious, wondering why.

Suddenly something moved and he turned to look through the window port, but only the darkness stared back at him. 'You're getting jumpy,' he told himself, but he continued to search for something solid to prove that his fears were justified.

The thick, pale blue carpet bore no sign of bloodstains which might have indicated that the Captain's leg had

159

been injured during a savage beating. None of the four brown leather armchairs showed any sign of damage indicative of a violent scene. The large, matching sofa against one bulkhead suggested nothing more than that a body might rest there in complete comfort.

A light rap on the door behind him broke his concentration and Captain Titus looked past him at the uniformed steward, his face registering shock.

'You rang, sir?' asked the man in a well-spoken accent.

An icy chill zipped from the base of Stoddart's neck to the small of his back, for the Captain's steward on his previous visit had been a Frenchman aged around thirty. Glancing at the Captain's face he detected a flush of dislike in his eyes as he asked: 'Could you get us two glasses of milk and a large brandy for Mr Stoddart, please?'

'Certainly, sir, I'll get the milk from the galley first,' and when Titus pointed out that there was plenty in the cold cabinet, the steward replied, in a manner suggesting that he was less conversant with the Captain's requirements than he should be: 'I forgot.'

In their previous meetings Stoddart had noticed many things about the Captain: he never drank alcohol, smoked, or allowed anyone to smoke in his private suite, and only drank milk or mineral water, which was kept in a special cold compartment of the cocktail cabinet. This was a large, highly-polished wooden piece of furniture, with legs that swept down from each corner to run diagonally across the floor, joining like a cross in the middle. When the front was pulled down to form a serving platform, part of the flat top slid back to give access to a selection of spirits, wines and glasses. The lower half of the front, fashioned from small pieces of finely interlocking slatted wood whose joints were almost impossible to discern, slid sideways to reveal the cold cabinet.

His suspicions aroused by the steward's obvious lack of knowledge, Stoddart turned to the man. He stood six feet tall and was handsome by any standards, with a swarthy, broad face, blue eyes and rich, dark hair. From Scott's description he was almost sure it was Haynes and his appearance in the cabin gave credence to Stoddart's suspicions of being observed through the window port, minutes earlier. In Scott's absence there was little chance of the man being recognized.

'I'm feeling a little on the peptic side myself,' said Stoddart as the steward crossed the room. 'I think perhaps I'll join the Captain in a glass of milk.'

Not being familiar with the cold cabinet, the man faltered, but Titus quickly came to his aid. 'The lower section just slides to one side,' he explained, pointing; then he turned to Stoddart and said, to cover his embarrassment: 'He hasn't had time to get used to things yet. I had to let Rene go home – he had some domestic problems.'

Stoddart nodded and smiled politely. He felt like drawing attention to the suspicious bulge beneath the steward's armpit, but settled for replying lightly: 'Don't we all.'

Titus was growing more nervous by the second, and when Haynes approached with their drinks he decided to try to cover his foolhardy and premature appearance.

'I'm sorry,' he began, as Haynes stooped to pass him the glass of milk, 'it was foolish of me to try to deceive you. This is my bodyguard.' Haynes' startled face at once calmed, and inwardly he sighed with relief as Titus went on: 'Buying sixty million pounds' worth of diamonds in Hamburg had its drawbacks. Word must have got out, because we had prowlers – that's how my leg got injured. De La Tour, my contact in Hamburg, suggested a minder. This is Chandler.'

'Hello,' said Stoddart, with a strained smile. 'Now, since our business appears to be no secret to him, might I suggest that we make a start? My man is out there by now, waiting to recover the shipment.'

Titus agreed, placing his untouched milk on the long, low, gold and blue map-of-the-world coffee table, around which they sat. Pain showed on his pale, sallow, hook-nosed face as he struggled to his feet. As his tall, gaunt frame hobbled to an adjoining room, Stoddart tried to fathom his reasons for living. He neither smoked nor drank, and although he loved to have a bevy of half-naked young beauties of the fair sex around, no one had ever known him to go to bed with them. He travelled the world

161

on his luxury yacht but apparently never went ashore, all business being transacted on board or not at all. His only vice seemed to be his greed, with no levels to which he would not stoop in order to satisfy his lust for wealth.

The door stood slightly ajar and Stoddart stared through the gap, straining his ears suspiciously. Within two minutes, Titus returned, carrying a small, highly-polished leather valise which he placed on the table before Isaac.

'There we are,' he said. 'Three hundred and eighty quality gems, all told, complete with a bona fide bill of sale and individual valuations.'

'We shall we see,' said the old man cynically as he opened the bag. He polished his eyepiece and reached into his pocket for a notebook which he placed on the table. Then he took out the first of several chamois leather pouches which he emptied on to the table. Stoddart's heart began to pound when he saw the contents, but the old man just prodded them nonchalantly with an index finger for a few moments. Without taking his eyes off them, he reached into his pocket again for a polished wooden box, about as large as a king size cigarette packet and with the greatest of care he removed the dissembled parts of a miniature set of gem scales. Using miniature weights to satisfy himself that they were correct, he selected a gem, checked its quality through his eyeglass, weighed it, and then recorded his estimate of the value on the notepad.

'These are fine stones,' he ventured, without breaking his concentration. 'Your prowler would have done well had he managed to get his hands on these.'

Titus' hand strayed involuntarily to his injured leg. 'Absolutely,' he agreed.

Stoddart sipped his milk in anticipation as the list on the notepad grew longer, and the total at the bottom of each page acquired more and more digits. After an hour, the milk tasted sour in his mouth and he longed for a cigarette. The merest hint of tobacco smoke teased his nostrils again, and both Chandler and Titus showed signs of detecting it too.

'Might I beg the use of your bathroom?' asked Chandler

162

politely, and Stoddart looked at Titus with interest, knowing that another of his eccentricities was never to allow anyone in there.

'But, of course,' he almost beamed in relief. 'It's the door on your left as you cross the bedroom.'

Titus pretended to treat Chandler's exit to the bathroom with a bland disinterest, but Stoddart noticed that he could hardly wait for him to get out of the room before hissing: 'He's from the police and he knows everything.'

'Naughty, naughty,' mocked Chandler from the doorway, and Titus almost suffered a heart attack as he jerked round in shocked surprise. Isaac and Stoddart saw his mouth sag open and his eyes bulge in their sockets. And as they glanced round at Chandler, their blood chilled. He was standing with arms outstretched, holding a hand-gun fitted with a silencer. Without another word he pulled the trigger and Titus jerked sharply back in his chair as the bullet smashed through his brow and out through the back of his head.

'Was that necessary?' Stoddart flared angrily. 'You could have taken the diamonds and been a million miles away before anyone could do anything about it.'

Chandler lowered the gun and came towards them. A second man appeared in the doorway leading to the bedroom. Sensing him, Chandler turned to shoot him dead without warning. 'That's for fouling up,' he snarled before turning back to Stoddart. 'Need I elaborate on what will happen to you if I don't get what I want?'

'I think you've made your point,' admitted Stoddart. 'Just what do you want?'

'I had figured on cutting myself in on your little business venture,' said Chandler, 'but I think the time for that has passed. There are too many ifs and buts and no bond of trust. I've no doubt that if I don't cut and run now I shall end up like them.'

Stoddart, wanting to know for sure who he was dealing with and how much he knew, asked: 'What business venture is that?'

'The one you've been cooking up with Scott. Torpedoes, fast attack craft, and so on. For a man with no criminal background whatsoever, he certainly has a natural aptitude for it.'

'He's brilliant, make no mistake about that,' declared Stoddart.

'Doesn't it make you wonder about him, though?' asked Chandler with a secretive smile.

'Not particularly – should it?'

'It might, if you moved in the informed circles that I do. Rumour has it that some governments have formed a special force to combat the big crime syndicates, particularly those running drugs. Apparently they are called the G Force, or the gunners, mainly because when they go gunning for someone, they don't stop until they succeed.'

'I hardly think they'll have wasted their time on the likes of me,' said Stoddart. 'Up until a week ago I was just a big fish in a small pond compared with the international syndicates.'

'It could be that you're the means to an end,' Chandler pointed out. 'An avenue through which they might achieve their objectives.'

'I had Scott thoroughly checked out and he proved to be no more than he said he was,' Stoddart argued.

'So did I, but it still doesn't stop me from being suspicious.'

'You've been in the force too long,' said Stoddart. 'You're Haynes, aren't you?'

'Does it matter who I am?'

'Not particularly. So, where do we go from here?'

'You,' said Haynes to the old man, who was looking frail and white-faced, 'put the diamonds back into the bag with your notes. And you,' he continued, threatening Stoddart with the gun, 'are going to order Scott to haul that shipment of cocaine in for me. If things go well I shall leave you all tied up on board while I depart for parts unknown. The alternative is a bullet between the eyes – and I'll settle for the diamonds.'

'I guess I don't really have much choice,' admitted Stoddart. 'I only hope that Scott hasn't given up: I wasn't expecting the valuation to take this long.'

7

Scott watched as Stoddart fell into step with the old man and headed for the beach. He wondered who the old man was and why Stoddart had not seen fit to mention their meeting; but when they dropped from sight below the ridge his misgivings suddenly evaporated. There was much to do and soon he was following in Stoddart's footsteps. Pausing just long enough on the grassy verge above the beach to let the launch reach the yacht, he then continued down to the water's edge.

Submerged in the lonely tranquillity of the depths, his agitated mind began to worry about all the things that might happen. There was no way that he could accept that Haynes would not misuse his authority in order to get on board the Sea Queen, and then vanish with the diamonds. It was a good prize but then again, Haynes, having his identity well documented, would not settle for half measures. Not only was it not his style but he would need the power those extra millions would give in order to avoid prosecution from the law.

Like a guiding light, the glow of the yacht brightened the dark grey gloom ahead and within minutes the long, cigar-shaped hull hung above him like an avenging angel. Scott turned to lie on his back and looked up at it. He was fighting a silent battle with his conscience over whether to locate the cocaine haul or board the Sea Queen first and assess the situation. Scott guessed that if there was trouble, Stoddart would need an aqualung in order to elude pursuit, so he pressed on until he located the catamaran. Everything was exactly as he had left it, yet somehow a voice in the depths of his subconscious nagged at him and he knelt on the deck to take stock.

With all the containers accounted for, he began to check the incidentals. All three outboard motors were still secure, which did nothing to ease his mind. There were still two full jerry-cans containing five gallons of petrol secured to the deck – he had discarded the empty cans during the journey. The detonators were accountably used and the smoke canisters were where he had left them. Like a puzzle the pieces came together. He needed to create a diversion to aid him in an escape if the need arose. The jerry-cans he ruled out because of their weight and the problem of ignition in the present circumstances.

He surfaced, feeling that time was slipping by. Armed with a single smoke canister and the standard knife carried by most divers, he began a steady breaststroke in the direction of the yacht. By the time he reached the outer rim of its bright halo of light, there had still been no signal from Stoddart. He trod water for several minutes and kept his eyes on the activity on board. With her brightly-lit, deserted decks, the Sea Queen was like a ghost ship, so much so that he began to suspect that perhaps Haynes had put everyone on board to sleep before making off with the diamonds.

Unable to contain his anguished curiosity any longer he dived beneath the hull and surfaced beyond the rim of light on the lee side. The launch still lazed at its mooring at the bottom of the gangway while on deck the duty watch stood motionless, leaning against a bulkhead. For a moment Scott considered calling from the darkness in order to provoke some sign of life but opted instead for a more positive course of action. He moved to a point just forward of the yacht and located the anchor chain where he had left his aqualung and the spare he had brought along for Stoddart. Hauling himself upward, the climb proved easy until he came to a metal disc fitted to the chain just below the bow, which was designed to stop rats from getting on board. All he could do was manoeuvre himself until he was actually lying with the chain supporting his torso from beneath. Then, with the greatest care, he used the disc for support while he clambered over. Panting, he climbed over the side on to the fo'c'sle deck where he crouched to survey the scene for any sign of life.

The decks were brightly lit. But with the exception of a brief flicker of light, which he assumed was someone lighting a cigarette, all the window ports and portholes facing on to the forward deck were dark. For a full minute he remained motionless, watching the bridge window. A dim glow of light showed from within. It was probably an officer on watch having a smoke to while away the time.

Taking a chance, he raced along the seaward side to a companionway amidships. He pulled back the rubber hood of his wet suit and cautiously crept up the stairs, straining his ears for any alien sound. All was quiet on deck but the lights showed through some of the window ports which he checked. Another set of steps gave access to the bridge and the Captain's suite. Knowing that the bridge was occupied he crept up to peer through the window ports of the latter.

In that instant his heart started to pound, for there was Haynes coming out of the Captain's bedroom, pointing a gun. His hand jerked under the weapon's recoil and, fearing that Stoddart was the target, Scott moved further aft out of Haynes' line of view so that he could see through to the forward part of the cabin where Stoddart sat. For an instant their eyes met before Scott's gaze came to rest on the newly-deceased Captain Titus. Shaking with shock and feeling vulnerable on the open deck armed with only a knife, Scott searched for a place to hide – but there was nowhere. Even the stairs leading to the boat deck above were open-plan.

The deck on which he stood was open to the elements, while the boat deck was set inside with launches suspended on davits for lowering them into the water. An idea began to form as Scott ran upwards. Knowing that Stoddart had seen him through the window, he knew that whatever happened he would come out on to the deck to give him the desired signal. His mind still racing, he clambered on board one of the launches to check its means of propulsion, which proved to be petrol. He felt better by the second as he ripped off the upholstered seat cushions in the open stern sections to find the fuel tanks.

But there were no jerry-cans of spare fuel. This proved to be no more than a minor setback. Removing the glass-fronted face mask from around his neck, he broke the flexible fuel feed pipes which supplied the engines and began sucking out the spirit, spitting it into the face mask until it was full.

Voices drifted up from the deck below. 'Just remember,' warned Haynes, 'any tricks and you'll be fiddling in hell before you know it.'

Scott peered over the side of the launch as Haynes spoke and Stoddart, who, guessing that he would be hiding above since there was no cover below, spotted him.

'Didn't I give you my word?' he replied to Haynes. 'Didn't I promise to do as you asked in return for my life and leaving the old man out of it?'

'Okay, okay,' Haynes said irritably, 'just give the damned signal.'

'Hadn't we better get a launch overboard first? The shipment is several hundred yards further out. There's no way he's going to cart it this far.'

'What do you mean, several hundred yards further out? You never mentioned that before,' Haynes snarled.

'You didn't exactly give me a chance, did you?' argued Stoddart.

'Hell! If you're playing some kind of game, you'll pray for a quick death before I'm through with you.'

Scott felt a momentary panic. There was provision for four launches: one was missing and a second had been moored at the gangway, which left just two on the seaward side. Even if Haynes chose not to risk passing the duty watch at the gangway, it was still a 50-50 chance that he would choose the launch closest to the stair head as Scott had done.

But fortune was smiling. Haynes, following Stoddart with a gun at his back, never queried his suggestion, and a minute later Scott heard their voices a mere three feet away.

'Do you know how to operate one of these things?' asked Haynes.

'No,' admitted Stoddart, giving Scott a bearing on where he stood, 'but it shouldn't be too difficult to work out.

They're supposed to be made simple in case novices like me have to operate them during an emergency.'

Scott was on edge, visualizing the launch being lowered. First it would swing out several feet on its davits to clear the deck below where, under normal circumstances, the crew and passengers could board in comfort before continuing down into the water. Knowing that the first manoeuvre would put him out of Haynes' reach, he steeled himself to do what he must. He reassured himself as to where he thought Haynes stood, sprang up and hurled the mask full of petrol at him.

Haynes was fully alert, and even as Scott began to move he brought the gun to bear, firing at virtual point-blank range. The petrol was ignited in flight and as fiery rain showered over him Haynes dropped the gun and the diamonds and screamed in terror while trying to beat out the flames. In a blind panic he ran towards the ship's side, crashed into the safety rail, dementedly clambered over and jumped, but failed to clear the deck below. One sharp crack, signifying a broken leg, was followed by another as he rolled head first into the solid bulwarks of the yacht's side.

His cries fell silent when mercifully he fell unconscious to the deck, the flames still burning. Hardened as he was, Stoddart stood shaking for several seconds as he rubbed his flash-burned eyes. A picture of Scott being jerked to his full height under the impact of the bullet burned into his mind. Through blurred vision he found the side of the launch and scrambled aboard to find Scott sprawling on its deck with blood oozing from a chest wound.

'Can you hear me, bonny lad?' Stoddart cried, but Scott heard nothing, his head lolling from side to side oblivious of his presence.

'Jesus Christ!' called a voice from below, and Stoddart looked down to see the duty watch crewman standing aghast at the sight of Haynes.

'Never mind him!' he shouted. 'There's a man up here with a gunshot wound in the chest. If you have a medic on board get him up here on the double. If not, get this damn boat lowered so that I can take him ashore.'

The launch rocked slightly and Stoddart turned to see

an officer in tropical white uniform looking over the side at Scott. Suddenly he disappeared, but his footsteps indicated that he had only gone as far as the boat deck guard-rail.

'Get on the radio,' he ordered the crewman below. 'Tell HQ that we require a surgeon for a patient with a gunshot wound to the chest. He looks to be in a bad way. Move, sailor! I'll get him into the Captain's cabin.'

Stoddart tried to think quickly. If he remained on board all would soon be laid bare. Although Haynes' finger-prints on the weapon would clear him of the two murders committed in the Captain's cabin, there would still be a great deal to answer for.

'No!' he shouted, thinking that if he could get the boat to sea, Poldark could pick them up and take them to Deal. There he could get friendly medical help for Scott. 'We're police officers,' he explained. 'Get this damn launch lowered into the sea and I'll take him ashore.'

Ignoring him, the officer climbed into the launch and took out a sealed first aid package from the survival kit. 'Don't give me a hard time, mister,' he said sharply, breaking open the tin. 'Grab one of those dressings while I cut away his suit.'

Picking up the dressing, Stoddart started to protest, but the officer said angrily: 'The name is Spiro Dieger. I'm a G Force agent and this yacht is part and parcel of our operation. Everything that happened in the Captain's cabin is on video tape, so now shut up and do as you're told.'

Stoddart pulled back his hand from Scott's wound as if he'd been electrocuted, staring at Dieger with bulging eyes as he thought of Scott betraying him.

'No, he isn't one of us,' snarled Dieger, forcing his hand into position to staunch the flow of blood. 'Just keep it in mind that he got in this condition by saving you from getting shot. Now, hold that against the wound good and tight while I lower the boat to where we can get him out without too much movement – and don't try making a break for it, because you won't make it.'

Stoddart was a frightened man. His only consolation was the fact that Scott had not deliberately plotted his

170

downfall, and that Haynes had received his just deserts. In a matter of seconds, the launch hung stationary above the deck below and Scott was gently placed on a stretcher by two crewmen, who carried him off to the Captain's cabin. Dieger took Stoddart by the arm and, hesitating for a moment to spit contemptuously over Haynes' charred remains, led him to the Captain's cabin. The bodies of Titus and Haynes' partner in crime had been removed to a guest room.

Now, for the first time, Stoddart studied Dieger, who spoke with a well-bred, rich American accent and was in his mid-forties. He stood six feet two inches tall and had slate-grey eyes, a full head of dark, wavy hair and a physique like a Greek god, which made Stoddart feel like a balding dumpling.

One of the stretcher bearers came out of the Captain's cabin shaking his head.

'How is he?' asked Stoddart.

'Not good. The bullet went clean through, smashing a rib front and back. He's lost a lot of blood, too, but he's not coughing any up so there doesn't appear to be any lung damage.'

'What about the medical team?' asked Dieger.

'They should arrive in a few minutes – they're coming in by helicopter. I'll check on the radio.'

'Good.' Dieger turned to Stoddart. 'You look like a stiff brandy wouldn't go amiss,' he said, and without waiting or worrying about what Stoddart might do while his back was turned, he poured two large brandies from the deceased Captain's stock. When he turned to re-cross the cabin Stoddart could see that despite his casualness, Dieger was thinking hard.

'So, where do we go from here?' he asked.

'That rather depends on you,' Dieger replied. 'You can either go to jail or carry on exactly as you are under the guidance of G Force.'

Stoddart gaped: he'd been taken over by a multinational organization. 'You're joking,' he stammered. 'You're no better than Haynes.'

'Quite the opposite, in fact,' declared Dieger. 'Haynes was an officer of the law who chose to use his authority to

171

further his own criminal activities. The G Force is comprised largely of reformed criminals who vow to devote their lives, time and resources to wiping out at least some of the scourges plaguing this earth.'

'That's some statement to swallow,' protested Stoddart, 'knowing that you must have stood by while Haynes shot Titus as well as his own man, and did nothing about it.'

'There was nothing we could do,' argued Dieger defiantly. 'The shootings were unforeseen, provoked by Haynes' man smoking when he knew it would alert you. As it transpired the shootings have brought things to a head that much quicker than we expected. Now at least we can put our cards on the table and get on with the job. All it requires is a "yes" from you.'

'A "yes" to what?'

'I can't tell you that until you give me the answer. All I can say is that the knowledge you already have is enough to ensure that if your answer is "no", you will be placed where the security is so strict that you'll never be able to communicate it to another person for as long as the G Force is in existence.'

'Solitary confinement for life,' scoffed Stoddart. 'Under British law you'll never achieve that.'

'Not in prison, perhaps,' he agreed, 'but we shall in an institution for the criminally insane.'

He wasn't bluffing and Stoddart's flesh crawled at the thought of spending his remaining years in such an institution. Scenes from documentary films came to mind and he knew that even the sanest of men could be broken after being made a part of it for a long period.

'I don't seem to have much choice,' he said at last. 'What about Scott? I'd like to see him get a fair crack of the whip. But for my intervention into his life he'd be setting up business in Spain now and apart from that, I owe him for saving my life. Nobody ever did a thing like that for me before.'

'But for him, the G Force would still be struggling in ten years' time to achieve what we now hope to achieve in a year,' Dieger admitted. 'As he knows nothing of the G Force he'll have little to tell; but since he has started things moving in the right direction I'm inclined to persuade him to stick with us by more gentle means.'

'In other words you mean "no".'

'I mean exactly what I said. Maybe when you realize just what you two have set in motion you'll understand the gravity of . . .'

But before he could finish there was a commotion from the Captain's bedroom and a crewman appeared in the doorway, his face showing deep concern over Scott's well-being.

'He's very low but he won't settle down until he sees someone called Max. I've given him morphine but he's fighting it all the way.'

'You'd better set his mind at rest,' advised Dieger. 'When he sees that you're okay he'll probably settle down.'

Stoddart moved to Scott's side, followed by Dieger. Scott was pale from loss of blood, the skin around his eyes tinged with blue as death hovered. Sensing their approach, Scott opened his eyes slightly, then opened them wider as he recognized Dieger. He tried to raise himself.

'Easy,' soothed Stoddart. 'Take it easy. You'll only make things worse.'

From weakness Scott fell back, but the panic remained in his eyes as he groped to bring Stoddart closer to him. 'You don't understand,' he said feebly. 'You've got to stop.'

'Why? Tell me why.'

'I died,' Scott explained. 'I just floated away but I could still see you. My mother must have died too, because she met me and we went to heaven together. My father and brother were waiting for us. There were lots of family and friends, but they wouldn't let me in. They said I had done bad things and that I was to go back to hell until I'd put things right. My mother cried when I left, just like she used to do when I was a kid.'

Stoddart recalled stories of similar experiences and he himself believed that there was a heaven and a hell. Heaven was where everybody believed it to be, but hell was here on earth.

'If you should see your family and friends again,' he said, 'tell them that you refuse to do as they ask. Make them send you back because your friend Dieger here has

173

work for us to do.'

Scott's hand rested on his shoulder in an effort to push him aside so that he could speak to Dieger. 'Stop now,' he begged, 'before it's too late.'

'Things are not what they appear to be,' said Dieger. 'We have a big job to do. Its honest work. You must rest and when you're better you can help us put together the biggest coup ever undertaken against crime.' Scott looked from Dieger to Stoddart.

'You'll never know the truth if you don't fight to stay alive,' said Dieger. 'And only then, if you decide to stick with us.'

'I'll fight,' promised Scott. 'How bad am I? I feel as though I've been hit by a cannon ball.'

Stoddart opted for frivolity in the hope of raising Scott's spirits. He peered down, pretending to pull down the dressing. 'Nar,' he said, mimicking a cockney accent, 'it ain't such a big hole. In fact, the last one I seen like that had hair round it.'

Scott smiled weakly. As they turned to leave a crewman entered and said: 'The helicopter's just coming in to land. I've ordered a launch to be taken round to the seaward side, ready to ferry the surgeon over.'

Dieger nodded his approval. 'Get that mess on deck prepared for transporting, along with the two in the guest room – they can go back to HQ with the helicopter. Better also send a copy of the video and the murder weapon, preferably with the fingerprints intact.'

The crewman left and Dieger followed with Stoddart as far as the lounge. 'Take a seat,' Dieger told him, motioning towards the coffee table. 'You wanted to know what you're getting into,' he went on, perching on the very edge of a seat. 'Here we have a map of the world. There are thousands of cities and every one of them a target for the syndicates pushing drugs. As you well know, if we wipe out one, two more will pop up to take its place to supply the ever-increasing demand. Our task is to lure these syndicates into dealing with us. By using Scott's idea we can not only guarantee delivery, but also guarantee any increase in demand. While all this is going on, I hope to increase our demands to such an extent that the producers will only be able to guarantee our supplies – likely to be tens of thousands of kilos – by allowing us to collect it direct from their strongholds. When and if we achieve that aim, we go in with highly-trained mercenary forces to wipe them out.'

'Killing them?' challenged Stoddart.

'I see no alternative where the producers are concerned,' admitted Dieger. 'As for the syndicates and their distribution networks, we'll settle for handing over any personal dossiers of incriminating evidence to the appropriate authorities so that they can be dealt with by the law.'

'And what about us?' asked Stoddart. 'We'll be worse than those we're trying to stop. We'll be responsible for shipping hundreds of tons of the stuff to the very people you say we are hoping to stop. If ever there was a paradox, this has to take the biscuit.'

'To a large extent I agree,' said Dieger. 'But apart from the end justifying the means, we shan't be passing all of the increased demand. A lot of our vast profits will pay for the dumping of a great deal of it, and more will be kept off the streets by our own network of informants passing information on to the authorities. This tactic will also serve to force up prices. Not only will this put it out of many people's reach, but it will also finance more dumping.'

'I'll say one thing for you Yanks: when you do something, you do it in style,' said Stoddart, admiringly. 'It sure beats the hell out of a country boy like me.'

'You do yourself an injustice. As I recall, you and Scott are the ones who drew up the blueprints. Us Yanks just touched them up a little and set them to their best advantage.'

'That sounds just like the English: plenty of good ideas and inventions but ailing when it comes to the courage and the cash,' said Stoddart. 'That brandy, for instance. Now that just has to be a British product,' he mocked. 'Did you know that British brandy is so weak it needs a lot of extra help getting out of the bottle and into the glass? You actually have to tip the bottle upside down.'

Dieger grinned but took the hint. As he was pouring, a crewman ushered in the surgeon and two assistants. The surgeon stopped beside Dieger and relieved him of the bottle.

'You're becoming a bad habit,' said the surgeon briskly. 'This,' and he held the bottle aloft, 'should be for medicinal purposes only and we are sick – sick to death of having our otherwise busy lives disrupted by you.' He raised the bottle and drank before passing it to one of his assistants, who was so heavily laden that he could not accept it. 'Never mind,' he grumbled, strutting towards the bedroom, 'it'll keep.'

'Nice chap,' observed Stoddart cynically. 'I hope his problem doesn't affect his work.'

'It won't, that was just bravado. Now I suppose you'll want to know what you're getting out of all this?'

'Dare I ask?'

'It won't be the multi-millions you planned on making, that I can guarantee. However, neither will the risks be so high with the G Force behind you. During your term of office all expenses are paid. Naturally you are expected to play the part so there's no limit in your particular case. Wherever you go, your lifestyle will be observed – as much by those you deal with as by the G Force whose job it will be to keep you safe. If you're invalided out, you will receive a minimum pension of not less than one million pounds sterling. But if you complete your term and we gain our objective, you'll be given a lump sum of ten million.'

'Big deal,' Stoddart scoffed. 'I stood to make four times that tonight if you hadn't conned me.'

'Ah, but I did, and if Haynes had been backed by one of the bigger syndicates you would be where he is right now.'

'There's a point you could clarify,' said Stoddart. 'Scott said that Haynes had Claude Durac in his pocket. Is that true?'

'Partly. Durac is one of us, so the reverse would be closer to the truth.'

Stoddart shook his head in bewilderment. 'It's getting like a man can't believe his shadow is his own any more.'

'That's a fact,' agreed Dieger. 'For you, this morning's crime did not pay. This evening, with me, I hope it will.'

'Dare I ask the fate of those who prove only to have

176

pretended to join you?'

'The last man to try it had a thing about being hung,' smiled Dieger cynically. 'Mind you, he was a real villain. We had him transported to Malaysia where smuggling drugs is an automatic hanging offence. After two years in what they call prison they cured him of his fear: they hung him. Need I say more?'

'No,' said Stoddart hollowly, thinking of his own fear of drowning. Changing the subject, he asked: 'Would you do me a favour? Could you find out if Scott's mother has really died? He's sure to ask when he comes round.'

Guessing that the information was as much to satisfy Stoddart's curiosity as to allay Scott's fears, Dieger nodded. 'That shouldn't be too difficult,' he said, standing up. 'Did you know that her grief at losing her son and husband drove her insane?'

'No.'

'Oddly enough, their deaths were caused by a couple of villains who were attempting to pick up a consignment of drugs. They both drowned in the River Thames,' he said meaningfully. 'How does the thought of your remains drifting on some remote ocean bed grab you? With all those crabs, lobsters and shrimps nibbling at your flesh.'

Stoddart realized that somehow Dieger knew of his fear and was giving him fair warning. 'One thing's for sure,' he began, in the hope of hiding it, 'no matter what you say, you'll never put me off eating shellfish.'

At that point the bedroom door opened and one of the surgeon's assistants entered. 'We need more plasma,' he said. 'Can you send someone back to the helicopter for some?'

Dieger promised to take care of it at once and added, turning back to Stoddart, 'I'll radio ashore for information about his mother while I'm about it. Help yourself to a drink while I'm gone – you look as though you could use one.'

With that he was gone and Stoddart asked the surgeon's assistant about Scott.

'Just about hanging on. By rights he should be in an intensive care unit, but moving him would be fatal. What kind of weapon was he shot with?'

'A Walter P K Special. How do you rate his chances?'

'Let's put it this way: this is one long-shot that I wouldn't put my shirt on.'

He returned to the bedroom and Stoddart helped himself to a large brandy, but found that the alcohol and the lack of company depressed him. After ten long minutes he could no longer stand being cooped up with nothing to occupy his mind but his worries. He refilled his glass, went out on deck and stood gazing out to sea. For a moment his eyes searched the dark blue, cloudless sky before coming to rest on the helicopter, floating unlit a hundred yards off. The sea was calm but showed signs of recent disturbance by a passing craft. The only sound was a launch, probably returning from the helicopter with the life-saving plasma and approaching the gangway on the yacht's landward side. Moments later footsteps approached. It was Dieger.

'Any news?' he asked.

'No. And you?'

'She died two hours ago,' said Dieger. Stoddart remained silent and drained his glass before throwing it into the sea in a gesture of contempt.

'Maybe there is more to life than we have here,' said Dieger reflectively.

'Maybe, but I wouldn't bank on my becoming a holy Joe on the strength of it.'

'If I saw it, I wouldn't believe it,' admitted Dieger. 'In fact, I'd get downright suspicious of you.'

'Somebody, somewhere along the line must wonder about you,' remarked Stoddart. 'That is, unless you're getting more out of this than you're giving the likes of me.'

'Maybe,' responded Dieger non-committally.

'How did you come to get hooked, anyway?' persisted Stoddart. 'I'd have thought a man of your stature, wealth and international contacts would be untouchable.'

Dieger stared out to sea, smiling a secret smile as he recalled how he had first begun his quest. 'I was a sergeant in Vietnam,' he said at last. 'Tens of thousands of brave Americans lost their lives out there, a good many of them because they were let down by their own comrades. There are many ways to win wars, you know. You take the gooks, for instance: one of their tricks was to get as many military personnel as possible hooked on drugs, which had a dual effect on those in the field of conflict. When they were high they didn't know what the hell they were doing and when they were down they couldn't give a damn. A good many personnel at the bases trafficked in the stuff for their own personal gain. Millions of dollars' worth of weapons and equipment were bartered for it – information too, if it comes to that. I was sent out there specifically to break it up.

'Basically, I did there what I'm doing here. I became a part of the operation so that it could be smashed from the inside – or at least, with the bona fide information I supplied. As a consequence of my work there my government encouraged me to become an international arms dealer, travelling the world doing shady deals with anyone in order to gain contacts, or information that might be of use to the United States.

'Then one day the American government realized that the drug problem was getting out of hand. It began as a witch hunt against the Russians, for some people believed that they were aiding the smugglers and producers for propaganda and demoralization purposes. I was on the trail of one of the high-ranking KGB agents – a woman – when I first became aware of Scott's existence. She loved to gamble on him when he raced on the ski-cycles, and once she flew from the United States to England just to see him. Being curious, I approached him with a sponsorship proposition, hoping to find out if they were working together. He even supplied me with some odds and ends for my customers.

'Then came the big break. He called me on your behalf and we put everyone in contact with him, and their contacts, under surveillance. As it transpired, we were in contact with some of them anyway.' Dieger turned to look at Stoddart before continuing. 'At the end of the day, I can't help wondering if we will find evidence of communist backing behind the producers.'

'Somehow I get the feeling that you're not just telling me this to pass the time of day,' observed Stoddart. 'You wouldn't by any chance have a specific assignment in

179

mind, would you?'

'Perhaps,' said Dieger, indifferently. 'Perhaps.'

'What's going to happen to my shipment out there?' asked Stoddart, nodding towards the open sea.

'While I was on the radio I called headquarters to inform them of the situation. They're sending a team of divers down to locate it, while other members of the G Force research possible buyers.'

8

While negotiations for his previous shipment of cocaine continued, Stoddart remained a guest on the Sea Queen under the protection of the G Force. A week had passed before Scott regained full consciousness and was fit enough to be told of Dieger's true quest in life. This gave him new heart, and he had plenty of time to consider it while lying in bed, building up his strength.

Since the seventy million asking price was more than any single British dealer could raise alone – and Dieger refused to either reduce it or split up the shipment because that would defeat his objective – the dealers begged for more time to raise the funds. To make sure of the sale, Dieger created a situation that had dealers begging. The authorities, assured by G Force that large amounts of illegal drugs were about to flood into Britain, operated a clamp-down which netted many smugglers and frightened off a good few more. This not only made supplies scarce, forcing up prices on the street, but also led to a great slump in the bulk-buying market abroad. When the clamp-down had been in operation for two weeks, prices rose so high that Dieger, using Stoddart as a front man, threatened to increase the price by another ten million.

McNalty, who had fought shy of financing the whole deal because it meant putting up everything he owned as security, kept himself well informed. When street prices had almost doubled, the prospect of such a high yield of profit broke down his resistance, and everything was going according to plan until he stopped to gloat over the mounting piles of bank notes, gems and precious artefacts stored in the strong room at his country mansion. Nagged by the ever-present thought of losing it all, he considered making a fraudulent claim, but realized this was out of the question. For how could he explain such a haul to an insurance company? He hit on the idea of going ahead with a financing deal and then hijacking the buyers, the sellers and the cocaine, and retaking his own millions at the same time.

Manpower would be no problem, as he knew from his many years of dealing with the criminal fraternity. And since he was providing most of the finance he was in a prime position to make demands of the buyers in order to protect his interests.

After mulling over the finer points and the possible dangers of the plan, he secured the strong-room and entered his favourite room: the spacious library. At the touch of a button the book-lined shelves closed behind him to conceal the heavy steel doors from view, and cheered by the thought of making the coup of his life, he helped himself to a Havana before picking up the telephone.

Drawing hard on his cigar while waiting for a reply, he casually viewed its long, brown shape and sent a slow, steady stream of blue smoke through puckered lips. A full minute passed by as the number continued to ring. Prepared to wait a little longer, he sat on the corner of his desk looking at the rows of books with their titles picked out in gold leaf, and thought contentedly of what lay behind them in the strong-room. From here his thoughts turned to the fate of anyone who tried to steal the contents from within.

He smiled, realizing how he could achieve his aim without the aid of anyone else at the scene of the exchange; and if his terms were acceptable to all concerned, there would be little chance of interference by the authorities and no bodies to bear witness against him afterwards. At last he depressed the telephone rest and immediately dialled another number. While waiting for an answer his eyes roved to a portrait of himself which hid a wall-safe from view, and he smiled, for it was simply a lure to fool burglars and contained only some token valuables to keep them satisfied.

He looked again to the book shelves beyond which lay the strong-room. Only a villain of the most brutal type – or an informed one – could ever make him tell of its existence. His smile turned to stone at the thought of being forced to open it . . . for a secret number added to the combination would activate a pressure plate just inside the door. That, in turn, would trigger the release of toxic gas rendering the intruders unconscious in seconds and the door would automatically close. If he were forced to enter first, all he'd have to do would be to drop to the floor where a ventilator blowing oxygen had been installed, and inhale while the toxic gas cleared. If he were kept outside, under guard, the same facilities had been installed in the library.

The ringing tone stopped as the telephone was lifted at the other end, but no voice spoke in answer.

'McNalty here,' he said. 'I would like to talk to Mr Warburton, Mr C J Warburton.'

'C J speaking. Have you raised the cash yet?'

'Sixty million, as agreed. Have you raised your ten million?'

'Just. I'll call Stoddart and set up the deal. When can I collect?'

'You can't. I've decided to come along on this deal. I'll bring it with me.'

'You're crazy, man. Have you any idea how touchy these deals can be? Everyone is just waiting for one party to try and grab all the goodies. On top of that, we'll be half-expecting problems with the law.'

'Haven't you given that aspect any thought?' asked McNalty bluntly.

'You're crazy, man. We're dealing with big-time people on this one. Cross them and there's no place to hide.'

'Stoddart's not big-time,' scoffed McNalty.

'Leave it out,' retorted C J. He's fronting for someone with a lot more clout. A week ago he couldn't show his face on the street; now suddenly he can. On top of that, he's on the business end of the biggest deal we've ever seen in this country. What's more, he reckons that this one is just the tip of the iceberg.'

'That could be most profitable for the likes of us,' McNalty remarked. 'I insist on coming along. Where do I meet you?'

'That depends on Stoddart. I'll call him and we'll haggle until we agree on a location that suits all parties concerned.'

'Might I make two suggestions? Here, at my place, or on board my yacht, The Saracen. In fact, I would deem the choice of either a great favour. The pollen count is high and it's playing hell with my hay fever.'

'There's no way they're going to agree to a meeting place on your home ground, for any kind of reason,' C J declared flatly. 'Christ, that's almost as bad as them inviting us on board their yacht to do the deal.'

'Is their yacht air-conditioned?'

'How the hell should I know? I don't even know if they have one,' he scowled. 'I was just speaking figuratively.'

'Well, I should ask,' suggested McNalty, 'because if we both take our yachts and make the trade at sea, not only will it help my hay fever, but it will also eliminate the element of surprise by outside parties.'

'Agreed,' said C J, 'but it would put us at serious risk if Stoddart decided to pull a fast one.'

'C J, Stoddart is looking for customers who can meet his demands. Now, how many people or syndicates do you know who can raise that kind of stake?'

'None,' he admitted.

'So, if he screws up, his whole UK operation goes down the tubes. So, what is he going to do the next time around?'

'With seventy million of our money in his pocket, I doubt if he'll give a damn,' said C J wryly.

'Rubbish,' growled McNalty. 'Stoddart is only a front, you said so yourself. There's no way he's going to cross the people he's working for. Even with seventy million, there's no place for him to run to where they won't find him. Just make the call; let him see that we're prepared to trust him in order to maintain a regular business relationship, and then call me back.'

'Am I to assume that you will withdraw your backing if I don't?'

'You are. There's a great deal more at stake here than a one-off deal and I, for one, don't intend passing up the opportunity of being part of what could end up as a monopoly of the UK narcotics market.'

Knowing that when it came to making a fortune, McNalty was a shrewd judge of men, C J reluctantly agreed and the line went dead.

McNalty smiled. Completing the transaction in the confines of his mansion would have made life easy; but completing it on his yacht, which as a result of his phobia of being kidnapped or robbed had been fitted with similar safeguards, would be perfect. Completing it elsewhere would have its drawbacks, but if all else failed he knew that he could set aside his greed for the whole cake and be satisfied with his original share.

The ringing tone sounded again in his ear until a young, female voice replied: 'Home, Industrial and Personal Security Services. Can I help you?'

'My name is McNalty. I would like to speak to Mr Forbes O'Mally.'

'I'll put you through, sir.'

'Forbes O'Mally,' replied a male voice. 'How can I be of service?'

'Your company fitted a security system to my home about three years ago, and a similar system to my yacht, The Saracen.'

'Ah, that Mr McNalty,' O'Mally beamed. 'No problems, I hope?'

'No, everything is just fine. If you recall, at the time of our discussions about the installation of the security system on my yacht, you mentioned something about a bullet-proof vest.'

'Yes – you thought it something of a joke,' said O'Mally reproachfully. 'Have you changed your mind?'

'Not entirely, but I would like one delivered to my home immediately – by which I mean now.'

Stoddart soon realized that once Dieger set his mind on a goal, nothing would deter him from achieving it. From the word go, all prospective buyers and financiers had had their telephones tapped and, as the field narrowed, those who remained in the running were kept under twenty-four hour surveillance. Prices were monitored and financial resources researched in order to maintain a good balance between the parties concerned, and all appeared to be going to plan until the Sea Queen's radio operator requested their presence in the radio room to hear recorded telephone calls made by McNalty.

'He's up to something,' said Stoddart confidently. 'In twenty years he has never been known to personally cross the line between the legal and the illegal.'

'Well, he's about to cross it now,' said Dieger thoughtfully. 'I wonder why? The bullet-proof vest suggests that he expects trouble – which in itself should be enough to deter him from coming, if not withdrawing his financial support altogether.'

'There was nothing to suggest that Warburton might make a grab for the whole kitty,' said Stoddart, 'which leads me to two possible conclusions. Either McNalty is playing it safe, which I doubt, or he has somehow put together a plan to make a grab for the kitty itself – and I'd have thought that completely out of character for him.'

'Maybe this Forbes O'Mally of Home, Industrial and Personal Security Services could shed some light on the situation,' suggested the radio officer.

'It's a possibility, I suppose,' agreed Dieger, and asked Stoddart: 'Do you know anything about the company?'

A distant bell was ringing in Stoddart's mind as he recalled a court case involving a thief sueing his intended victim. He smiled, but there was no warmth in his eyes.

'Play that tape again,' he said. The radio operator rewound the tape and set it in motion once again, with Stoddart listening, eyes closed to savour every syllable.

'There,' he said in a harsh whisper, and the radio operator stopped the tape.

'What?' queried Dieger.

'He suggested clinching the deal either at his mansion or on board his yacht. Let the tape run some more,' he said, adding almost impatiently: 'It's got to be that.'

'What has?' growled Dieger.

'Did you know that one of our crazy laws dictates that if you have a burglar alarm fitted, it has to make a noise of some description? In other words it must warn not only anyone within the vicinity, but also the burglar.'

'And what bearing does that have here?' asked Dieger.

'A few years ago the HIPSS were fitting systems that would put thieves to sleep after they had triggered the alarm, and in this case they were in the process of robbing a vault filled with art treasures. Now, supposing McNalty has had these systems fitted to his home and his yacht? We all meet; we have the cocaine. Warburton and his henchmen bring everything they can raise and so does McNalty. Then McNalty releases the gas and we all go to sleep, leaving him to get rid of us at his leisure before making off with the lot.'

'And what, may I ask, prevents McNalty from being put to sleep with the rest of us?' asked Dieger.

'I'm not sure,' he admitted. 'Maybe he'll bring something that looks like an aid for his supposed hay fever, which will render him immune. There could be something incorporated in the bullet-proof vest – that's feasible if the HIPSS had intended selling their systems to companies who have guards for their vaults. The guards could just stand obediently to one side while the villains did their thing.'

'Okay,' said Dieger. 'Let's assume you're right. We set sail and rendezvous with McNalty, Warburton and co. We'll assume that all parties will be armed, or none at all. Considering the bulk involved, we send a party over to their yacht to check the cash, and they do the same to check the cocaine. Subject to everything being acceptable on both sides, we make the trade, but somewhere in this sequence of events McNalty has to make his move. Any suggestions?'

Stoddart threw up his hands. 'Beats the hell out of me. All I can say is that I think he will.'

'What about the gas?' asked the radio officer.

'Maybe he has some spare supplies,' suggested Dieger, 'or perhaps he plans to use the supply he already has fitted to his safe. Give HQ a buzz and inform them of the situation – see if they can confirm whether or not McNalty had these systems installed. That at least will give us a lead to the validity of Max's fears. If Warburton makes contact, tell him that Max has gone ashore and you don't know when he'll be back.'

'See if you can find out if McNalty suffers from hay fever, too,' added Stoddart.

'Such gloomy faces,' scoffed Scott from his perch on the yacht's bulwarks when they joined him, leaning over the rail to look out at the sea. They smiled.

'How are you feeling today, bonny lad?' asked Stoddart.

'Bored,' he admitted. 'Why the gloomy faces?'

'It's a long story,' said Dieger.

'Well, I don't have a trouble in the world to mar my otherwise inactive brain, so how about giving me something to chew on for a change?'

Stoddart caught Dieger's eye and when he nodded his approval he began to explain what had happened. As he finished none of them were any the wiser, but Scott broke into a secretive, knowing smile which both Stoddart and Dieger found irksome.

'What's so funny?' asked Stoddart.

'Come into my parlour, said the spider to the fly,' he quoted. 'Your tale of woe reminds me of a rather vulgar story about a hungry tramp, a ready-to-eat duck, a sexy maid, her equally sex-starved mistress and her daughter. In order to get food, the tramp had to seduce the maid, but the mistress's daughter caught him leaving the premises afterwards with the duck and threatened to call the police. In desperation he confessed all, but she refused to believe him and demanded that he return the duck and seduce her as the price of her silence. He obliged, but the mistress caught them in the act; the daughter was packed off to bed, leaving the tramp to explain. Seeing how well endowed he was, and how well he performed, the mistress was inspired and she, in turn, promised that he could keep the duck if he obliged her. What none of them knew was that the master had caught a dose of venereal disease and unwittingly passed it on to the maid. To cover his sins he bribed the tramp to go on begging for food at his home, knowing what was likely to happen.'

'Entertaining though your story is, I fail to see the connection between it and us in our present predicament,' observed Dieger.

'Firstly,' said Scott, 'if you play your cards right it will be you who ends up with the cocaine and the money, instead of McNalty. To that end, it might be a good idea to bribe O'Mally into telling you everything he knows about McNalty's burglar alarm systems. If you find that he is planning to make a killing at everyone else's expense, then do unto him as he would do unto you – only do it first; but make it look as though he did. If he survives the wrath of Warburton he'll never finance another deal, even if he has a nest egg tucked away somewhere. Warburton is likely either to be ruined, or wanted for murdering McNalty. All you need do is find another buyer for the shipment. Whether you could set up a similar deal up north is in the lap of the gods.'

'Your idea has a villainous appeal about it,' agreed Dieger. 'We could use the shipment to cause the biggest purge ever mounted in Europe by the authorites.'

'Come again?' asked Stoddart, who was thinking of his percentage.

'We could plant two-kilo parcels of cocaine in dead letter-boxes in airports, sea ports and border crossings throughout Europe; then leak the information to Customs. There'd be such a purge as to stagnate normal trafficking. We might be able to set up a deal for a shipment direct from the producers in Pakistan and China, and if the G Force agents can achieve similar goals back home in the USA and Canada, we'll be in Colombia before you know it.'

Stoddart swallowed hard at the thought of it. 'We have to catch our cat before we skin it,' he scowled, 'and how does that affect our percentage of dumping, if we skin McNalty?'

'You get paid twice, I guess,' grinned Dieger.

'Well, that's something,' growled Stoddart grudgingly.

'I thought that might appeal to your better nature,' said Dieger. 'And now, if you will excuse me, I think I'll go and see if I can hustle things along in the radio room.'

'You're still not keen on those raids, are you?' asked Scott when Dieger was out of earshot.

'If I want to get shot to hell and gone, I can do that here,' Stoddart grumbled.

'Why don't you look on the bright side? Maybe McNalty

will get lucky. I'll see to it that you get shot after he's gassed us, if that's what it takes to please you.'

'Thanks a bundle, bonny lad,' said Stoddart sourly. 'A man could live his whole life through and never know a friend like you.'

'We can but try,' he grinned. 'Fancy a spot of fishing to pass the time? The mackerel are running and you can catch them with a bent pin and a piece of string.'

'Not for me. I wouldn't mind a run ashore, though. Boats are all right, but they have their limitations when it comes to keeping one's mind occupied.'

'I wouldn't advise it, under the circumstances,' Scott warned. 'I've got the sneakiest feeling that things are going to start popping soon.'

Stoddart agreed. 'I know what you mean. How long is it since you were last ashore?'

'I wouldn't exactly call my last trip ashore "a trip ashore",' replied Scott amiably. 'A helicopter trip to the hospital for a check-up and X-rays hardly constitutes a day out.'

'Don't you miss the ladies?'

'Only when I see them running half-naked on the beach, or flaunting it on some of the speed boats as they pass by,' he admitted. 'I've never been much of a ladies' man. Give me a speed machine to play with any day.'

'From my experience they both have one thing in common: they call it instant death, and for my money I'll take the ones with the long legs and big boobs.'

'So you're a sucker for a big pair of boobs, are you?' grinned Scott. 'Maybe we should see Spiro about arranging a party on board. According to the crew they used to invite nurses from local hospitals in Captain Titus' day.'

'Some chance,' he scoffed. 'He's dedicated to what he's doing and nothing more counts.'

'I sometimes get the feeling that he's motivated by some personal tragedy,' Scott admitted. 'Have you noticed that he never talks about his personal life? I've never heard mention of a wife and family – or even a lady friend, if it comes to that.'

'Maybe you should study his face when he talks about Sahara Sediki,' suggested Stoddart.

'How do you mean?'

'The venom he professes when he talks about her is in his eyes, too; I get the feeling that it's inspired by a rejection.'

'I can't say I've noticed,' Scott admitted. 'Let's hope you're wrong, though, because that kind of relationship can be dangerous.'

Dieger's approaching footsteps put a stop to any further speculation.

'Any news?' asked Stoddart.

'Some, but not about the gas. It appears that McNalty married a certain Magdalene Leone around twenty-five years ago, who died two years back. There were two sons: Leonardo, now aged twenty-four, who lives in the USA, and Vincent, twenty-three, who lives in Bessina, Sicily. There's a daughter, Cora, studying here in Oxford, but she's of no interest to us at the moment.'

'The name Cora Leone rings a bell,' mused Stoddart.

'Like Mafia,' put in Scott.

'Precisely,' said Dieger, 'which means that we want McNalty in our pockets, not dead or in jail, so if he is planning something special it will be much to our advantage if it takes place here, on board, where we'll have more control over events and be in a position to video him in action. Assuming that all goes according to plan, Scott will fly out to Malta on the first available flight, while Max and McNalty will head for Sicily. I'm staying here.'

'Now, just you hold on there,' protested Stoddart. 'You're going to send me and McNalty to Sicily, and presumably you're going to use a video of him committing a crime in this country as a guarantee for his good behaviour in Sicily.'

'Not quite. The video will be shown to his daughter. Her passport will be confiscated and she'll be put under our protection in case Warburton decides to use her to get back at him.'

'You are one evil bastard,' remarked Stoddart. 'So, what do I do in Sicily?'

'You'll be introduced to McNalty's son and his brother-in-law, Francisco Leone, who incidentally is a Mafia don who used to live in the USA and now lives in exile, although he still has powerful connections there. Between you, you are to set up a deal for us to deliver one hundred tons of cocaine to major cities around the USA. You are to demand payment in diamonds – which we believe they will find unacceptable, owing to the amount. In fact, I doubt if they could raise that amount of currency in any event. What we're after is part-ownership of some of their enterprises so that the US government can get their own men on the inside.'

'And you think they're going to accept a tupenny ha'penny country boy like me as the mastermind behind all this?' argued Stoddart.

'If they try pulling your file from Scotland Yard or Interpol, they will,' said Dieger confidently.

'What about me?' asked Scott. 'What am I supposed to do in Malta?' But before Dieger could reply, the radio officer approached with a typewritten message which he read silently, not enlightening them as to its contents.

'You will begin to set up our supply lines,' he continued, turning to Scott. 'I shall join you as soon as my work here is finished. A ski-cycle has been provided to get things moving – and from what I'm told, it's the most powerful thing you are ever likely to straddle. Sneider will be there.'

Scott felt a momentary surge of adrenalin. Deep down, Sneider was a nice guy, a champion rider, even to the point of being a good loser in the races in which they had both competed. It was his attitude during the build-up to the race that Scott found aggravating. He continually sneered and taunted his opponents until they were so infuriated that many took chances which cost them their victory.

'During your rides for pleasure,' Dieger went on, 'he will taunt you and challenge you to a race, but you'll hold off until it raises enough interest. When it has, you'll do your usual practice runs to create interest on an international scale. By then I should be with you, to guide you through the next phase of the operation.'

'Sounds fine to me,' agreed Scott, guessing that he was being used as bait to draw Sahara Sediki out into the open.

'Why Malta, of all places?' asked Stoddart. 'Christ, the island's only about nine miles wide by eighteen long. It hardly seems the place to achieve what I think you're after.'

'It's smack in the middle of the territory I frequent as an international arms dealer, for a start,' explained Dieger. 'It's flanked by all the Arab states where my dealings are well known. So anything I do, although provoking interest, won't be viewed with undue suspicion. When I start moving arms by the shipload, nobody is going to dream of my real purpose. Secondly, Pakistan is not so far away. When Sahara arrives on the scene and we allow her to find out what we're up to, she's going to start pushing for us to buy Colombian cocaine rather than Pakistani heroin – which is just what I want. If she takes the bait, we'll proceed as planned in order to get to grips with the Mafia and put her off her guard. The second time around will wipe her out. Any questions?'

'No, but supposing we have when you're not around?' asked Stoddart.

'You'll have to use your own initiative for on-the-spot decisions. Apart from that, a G Force agent won't be too far away. You'll be provided with a shadow at all times.'

'A shadow, or baby-sitter?' asked Stoddart sourly.

'A minder-cum-adviser. We wouldn't want anything to happen to you before you collect your percentage of a two-billion pound deal, would we? Now, may we get back to the business in hand? The good news is that we now know about McNalty's burglar alarm system; the bad news is that we may have to suffer a small amount of discomfort in order to nail him.'

'Something tells me this isn't going to be one of my better days,' sighed Stoddart.'

'As you said, the alarms were banned in this country by law, and the company installing them were ordered to stop. They were also told to make available the names of all customers they had supplied, who in turn were supposed to have them replaced. McNalty had his removed, but since he'd paid cash for it he demanded that all the materials were his, and he kept them. After the inspectors had cleared him, he paid the workmen to come back and refit them. The gas cylinder is easily removed for replacement. It's about as big as two U2 torch batteries

193

and is very potent. One whiff disorientates you, the second will put you out for at least twelve hours. Recovery is always accompanied by a king-sized hangover.

'The bullet-proof vest ordered by McNalty was originally one of the items supplied with the system, for use by the guards. Apart from protecting its wearer, it, too, was fitted with an oxygen supply and a small mouthpiece which tucks out of sight just below the neckline. When the gas is released, the guard, if he hasn't already been made to lie down, hits the deck and holds his breath for as long as it takes to get the mouthpiece in place. We shan't elaborate on what happens if the villains tie up the guards, shall we?' he concluded sarcastically, looking at Stoddart. 'Any questions?'

'How and when?' asked Stoddart.

'At ten o'clock tonight we head due south for ten miles and wait. McNalty will be meeting us there in his own yacht, The Saracen. Only a minimal crew will be present on each side, in our case Kolme, my chief engineer, Pike, my first officer, and the three of us. The same number will crew The Saracen.'

'That's cutting it a bit fine,' remarked Stoddart.

'Not for what we have to do.'

'What about those bullet-proof vests?' asked Scott.

'They're being sent down by express motorcyclist. They should be here in plenty of time.'

'What does this McNalty look like?' asked Scott.

'I suppose you could say he's a youngish-looking fifty,' said Stoddart. 'Bald as a coot, and the last time I saw him he looked as fit as a fiddle. He's a sporty type, but a shrewd man to do business with. Loves horses and young ladies, but not fast cars: he's more of a Rolls-Royce type – the city gent, in fact, but don't be fooled. He's a self-made man and as hard as they come. This fetish he has about security is only his way of keeping what he's got; not because he's running scared. He's about five foot eight and weighs one hundred and eighty pounds. That may not seem like anything special to be afraid of, but in his younger days he was some kind of animal in a fist fight what you would call a hungry fighter; the kind of man who trains his mind to shut out his own pain while meting out a goodly share himself. He may have softened with age, but I wouldn't count on it.'

'There's nothing on his criminal record to show that he has a history of violence,' Dieger pointed out.

'That's probably because no one ever reported him – but then they wouldn't, would they?'

'Why not?' asked Dieger.

'If he financed you in some shady deal and then had to lean on you to get his money back, you'd hardly go running to the law because you got your legs blown off, would you?'

'I suppose not. Has he ever been known to carry firearms?'

'Hardly,' smiled Stoddart. 'Men like him don't take that kind of risk. They pay others to do it for them.'

'You're wanted on the radio, sir,' called the operator from the bridge, 'and there's a launch coming alongside.'

'I'll be right there,' Dieger called back, and politely excusing himself he turned away.

'Have you ever wondered about him, bonny lad?' asked Stoddart when he'd gone.

'How do you mean?'

'Well, he's recruited us to help him, but so far we've nothing in writing to prove it. He could be taking us all for a ride, for all we know. So far, he's got my shipment of cocaine and the Captain's sixty million in diamonds, and he'll soon have McNalty's seventy million.'

'Leave it out,' laughed Scott.

'You may well scoff, but you just think about it: in a few hours' time we'll rendezvous with The Saracen just out of sight of land, with both vessels manned by a skeleton crew. A smart operator would take the lot and do a runner, leaving the dead on a sinking yacht.'

'Just so long as that man isn't you,' argued Scott suspiciously.

'Me?' he laughed in all innocence. 'I wouldn't know how to begin piloting one of those things.'

'No,' Scott pointed out, 'but I would.'

'I'm sorry I spoke,' said Stoddart, 'but don't just pooh-pooh the idea and forget it. Keep your wits about you, because when you're looking down the wrong end of a gun barrel it will be too late,' and allowing his annoyance to show, Stoddart turned to leave.

'At a guess, I'd say that by normal standards you have had a fair crack of the whip where life is concerned,' observed Scott.

Stoddart turned back sharply, his eyes drawn to the angry red scar left by Haynes' bullet.

'Fair crack of the whip?' he flared without thinking. 'Let me tell you something; everything I have, I worked for. Nobody ever gave me a damned thing; I took it and the risks that went with it.' He wanted to go, to rid himself of his sudden anger, but somehow the sight of Scott's chest stopped him.

'Maybe it's time to give something back,' suggested Scott quietly. 'I can make an educated guess at what's eating you. I can even understand how it must be alien to your nature,' he added, in an effort to explain his feelings. 'I just wish that you could feel the deep-down emotions that I feel when I do something good.'

Stoddart filled his lungs with air, his chest heaving, and when he let it out in a deep sigh his body seemed to sag in defeat.

'You should have been a bloody preacher,' he said. 'I'm sorry for blowing my top: I guess the waiting and being cooped up on this damn yacht is getting on my nerves.'

'I'll make a deal with you,' offered Scott. 'I'll stick around so that when you wake up and realize the truth of all the millions that you've let slip through your fingers, because of me, you'll have someone to kick.'

Stoddart smiled. 'It's a deal. Now, how about joining me in a drink?'

'Better make it wine – the dinner gong sounded just a couple of minutes ago.'

'And that's another bloody wind-up,' Stoddart growled. 'With the amount of catering staff on this yacht, you'd think that they might serve the meals at more reasonable times. Take breakfast, for instance: all right, so the duty watch have to have theirs before they go on at eight o'clock – but surely they don't have to ring those damn bells to wake everybody else up.'

'That's the way ships are.'

196

'And they do the same thing at eleven-thirty,' Stoddart went on. 'Christ! You're just about coming to terms with the day ahead, and they're serving a damn great lunch at a time when a couple of eggs and bacon would go down a treat.'

Scott tried to explain: 'Seven bells meals are for the duty watch. Ours is from twelve until one.'

'And dinner is at six,' he growled, ignoring Scott. 'Six! How the hell is a man supposed to function properly at a time of day when he really needs to be on the ball, if he's bloated out and half asleep with a belly full of food?'

'Easy. All you have to do is get yourself a nine-to-five job.'

'The hell I will – at least, not unless it's pm to am.'

Parting company in order to adhere to another of the yacht's strict rules, they went to their respective cabins. Slipping out of shorts, Scott had a quick shower before dressing for dinner, his mind plagued by the thoughts provoked by their conversation and Stoddart's obvious state of mind. He tried to understand the man's natural instinct to make the killing of the century, but the multi-millions of pounds began to total beyond his comprehension. By the time he left his cabin he was convinced that Stoddart's only possible motive could be super-greed or an insatiable desire to beat the odds at any cost. The question was: would he be satisfied to achieve those goals as part of the G Force team, or would he try to beat the odds alone?

Leaving his luxury guest suite, aft of the bridge and beneath the boat deck, Scott glanced towards the beach, where sun-worshippers were still abroad, and Stoddart's holiday site still thronged with people. It seemed strange that only a curious few had ventured as far as the Sea Queen and he wondered if there was something alien which they could see but he could not.

High-stepping over the raised storm step, he went down to the companionway two decks below his own, which ran athwartships with the doors facing forward, giving access to the deck officers' cabins. To his left, amidships, was a plate glass double door with brass furniture and a hardwood surround, all gleaming from much polishing. He pushed it open and entered, letting it swing shut behind him.

Greeting the three engineer officers on his left, and the deck officers on his right, he moved towards the Captain's table, at whose head sat Dieger. To his right sat the first officer, a stocky, barrel-chested man in his late forties with dark, beady, close-set eyes, who had served with the American marines. A shiver ran down Scott's spine as their eyes met and when he nodded a curt hello, the movement of the man's muscular chest threatened to burst the seams of his tight-fitting, bum-freezer white jacket. Across from him sat the chief engineer, whose manner and physique were entirely different; being Vietnamese he was short and slightly built, with soft dark eyes, and he trained in the martial arts each day with his countrymen subordinates on the boat deck. Stoddart sat opposite Dieger at the foot of the table, his back to the door.

'Evening all,' said Scott cheerfully, taking his seat. 'What exotic delights has our esteemed chef provided to tease our palates this evening?'

'Good evening,' Dieger greeted him, as though they had only just met after a long absence. 'With an effort I've managed to persuade Max to try a dozen fresh oysters, followed by clam chowder. You would be well advised to try it – it's more of an experience than a delight.'

Turning to look up at the expectant steward, Scott smiled, saying: 'Who am I to argue?'

Breaking off a piece from a crusty roll, Stoddart complained: 'I reckon they must be diving for the oysters – I ordered mine ten minutes ago,' and stuffed it into his mouth.

'You must forgive Max,' said Dieger. 'He doesn't seem to be quite himself today.'

Scott met Dieger's gaze and saw a hint of guile hidden in the faint smile that teased his eyes. 'I think he's missing the bright lights and hustle and bustle of the big city,' he replied in Stoddart's defence. 'All this lazing around doesn't fit too well with men of action.'

'Ah,' Dieger smiled. 'He also serves who sits and waits.'

'And that's a fact,' Stoddart grumbled on. 'Much more of this and I'll have to join chief Kolme's martial arts class, just for the exercise.'

'You'll be most welcome,' invited the chief engineer. 'First, we must cleanse the mind and you must rid yourself of all material things.'

'I wasn't thinking of becoming a monk,' he groaned, 'although I might just as well. I can't remember the last time I got laid: talk about having plenty of lead in your pencil and no one to write to!'

Scott laughed as the steward placed before them a large plate of oysters in the whole shell, and said: 'Maybe we should send someone ashore to get you one of those life-size rubber dolls.'

'If you mean one of those sex-aid things that you have to blow up yourself,' said Stoddart as he attempted to open the first oyster, 'it would probably mug me, the way my luck's running these days.' The blunt, flat knife slipped, and the oyster spun in his hand. 'Any decent restaurant would serve these on the half-shell,' he complained.

'Ah, but who's to know if your oyster might have been the one with a pearl in it?' smiled Dieger.

'I'll consider myself lucky to get an oyster, let alone a pearl,' he moaned.

Somehow, Scott knew that Dieger was playing a game with Max, and that the oyster would have a pearl inside. As his own shell parted, his eyes were glued on Stoddart's hands. The shell came open in his palm but it was obscured from general view, and with a bland look on his face Stoddart carefully laid the upper half of the shell on the plate before prizing the oyster loose from the remaining half with his knife.

'I'm damned if I can figure out why they go crazy over these things,' he said, raising it to his mouth, 'but here goes.' Tilting back his head, he let the oyster slide in, twirling it round his mouth with his tongue before swallowing. 'Not bad,' he said, turning to Scott. 'Try one yourself.'

Scott looked down and his eyes opened wide. 'Christ!' he beamed. 'I've got a pearl!'

'Thank Christ for that,' said Stoddart, spitting out one in his palm. 'I thought my teeth were falling out.'

Dieger's face creased into a smile. 'You had me worried

for a minute,' he said, as Stoddart held the tiny orb to the light between his finger and thumb.

'I'm going to make myself a little bet,' he said, studying the gem. 'I'm going to bet that there's a pearl in each of our oysters, and that you had them put there. The only thing that bothers me is why.'

'On troubled waters we pour oil,' explained Dieger. 'When the minds of men are troubled, we temper them with wine, women and wealth. Those pearls are worth a cool fifty thousand pounds each – consider them as a down payment for your efforts on behalf of the G Force so far. If all goes well tonight, there will be more to come.'

Stoddart opened another shell and removed the pearl before swallowing the oyster. Scott reached over to place his pearls on the Irish linen tablecloth in front of Stoddart.

'One good thing about these,' he said, 'is that considering their value, they're easy to carry. As far as I'm concerned, you're the money man; I wouldn't know how to begin selling them, let alone how to invest the money.'

Stoddart was shaken by Scott's gesture, but he wasn't fooled: Scott was simply prepared to give up his pearls in order to prevent Stoddart from trying to outwit Dieger and McNalty, and for some reason he could not explain, he felt that if anyone could make him an honest man, it would be Scott.

'Sometimes I wonder about you,' he smiled, 'although I think the best place for these is the Captain's safe. When the time comes for making decisions on what to do with our spoils, we'll make them together.'

As the tiny circle of gems grew, Dieger felt the tension ease out of Stoddart, and he tried to understand Scott's evident attempt to give away his pearls in order to keep Stoddart loyal to the G Force. Curiosity soon got the better of him, and when his personal steward approached to serve coffee he scribbled a note on the back of a menu and instructed him to give it to the radio officer without delay.

'What did you do before getting involved in all this?' Stoddart asked Kolme.

'Many things. I began as a simple fisherman on my father's boat in Vietnam. When that was stolen by escaping Cong prisoners, I managed to get a job as a

200

mechanic on one of their air bases. Towards the end I volunteered for special assignments, behind enemy lines.'

'Is that where you met Spiro?'

'You could say that. I was taken prisoner by the Cong and thrown into a submerged, rat-infested cage in the river. Spiro had already been there for a week, and had devised a plan to break out. All he needed was a guide to get him through the jungle, or a pilot to fly the helicopter which came to collect prisoners of importance. At his suggestion I bargained my freedom for betraying his true identity, and when the helicopter gun-ship came to collect him, I killed the crew and decimated the camp with its vast weaponry. At the same time another patrol was coming in from the jungle, with two crew of a downed American helicopter as prisoners. Their fire drew mine in retaliation, and when the killing was done they flew us back to our own lines in the helicopter. We've been together ever since.'

'When you get right down to it, the big cities with all their high-powered criminals are nothing but dirty little-bitty puddles filled with piranha,' said Dieger. 'Everything's the same. The commodities vary as time goes by, but the stakes, the risks, the intrigue and treason don't. When I think back over the assignments I've been involved in, it brings back one particular memory. My father was just about to paddle the tar out of my backside for taking a couple of dollars out of my mother's purse. "Son," he said, "when you get to be our age you'll find that there ain't a damned thing you can do that we didn't try sometime during our lives".'

'You sound as though you're speaking from a great deal of personal experience,' remarked Stoddart.

A cold smile gave an underlying credence to Dieger's reply. 'You may have spent a lifetime pitting your wits against all-comers in your dirty little puddle. I've been doing the same thing for more than twenty years in a swamp that covers three-quarters of the globe; the only difference between us is that I, generally speaking, deal with crime on a grander scale.'

Dieger's steward approached again with a pot of boiling coffee and hot milk, which he placed on the table before giving Dieger a note, waiting while he read it.

'That will be all, thank you,' said Dieger. 'Get cleared away and I'll see you tomorrow. Mr Pike,' he continued, turning to the first officer, 'see that all hands are ashore before joining me in my cabin. Chief, double-check the engine room and then give Mr Pike a hand to secure the gangway.' Turning to Scott and Stoddart, he invited them for a drink in his quarters and as they moved towards the door, Pike walked back to the galley.

'Move it,' his deep voice rumbled.

'He doesn't strike me as being the friendliest of people,' ventured Stoddart when they reached the open decks.

'Who?' asked Scott.

'Pike. Have you ever managed to get him into conversation?'

'To be honest, he never gave me the feeling that he wanted to. He can just about manage a casual "hello", and that's it.'

'Have you ever noticed how the crew react when he gives an order? Man, do they jump!'

'He's a good man to have around in a tight spot,' put in Dieger without turning back. 'Don't ever make the mistake of judging him by his looks. He's anything but the mule-brained bruiser he pretends to be.'

'I had a mind to ask him about his past at dinner,' remarked Stoddart. 'I wonder what he would have said?'

Dieger pushed open the door to what had been Captain Titus' suite. 'I'll tell you,' he said. 'Quote: "all you need know about me is that I was born, and some day, God willing, I shall die. The only unknown factors are when and how, and how many scum I shall have sent to hell before me", unquote.' They followed him in and he asked what they would like to drink.

'An ice-cold beer would be appreciated,' said Stoddart.

'Me too,' said Scott.

Dieger walked towards the cocktail cabinet. 'A man's personal life is his own affair,' he concluded, 'and Pike is entitled to his privacy as much as any man; but I'll tell you enough to make you wary. He's half Puerto Rican and was born on the wrong side of the tracks in Miami. His mother, father and brothers pushed drugs and his three

202

sisters were prostitutes. To get away from that he joined the army as a boy soldier and enlisted in the marines. We first met in Vietnam while on special assignments, and one day he received a letter telling him that they had all been wiped out by a rival family. They burst into their home with machine guns and left their trademark: the males holding bundles of bank notes, and more bundles between the females' thighs. Well, Pike held his emotions under wraps, but when his unit ran into trouble on his next assignment he went missing in action. During his absence there were all kinds of enquiries from back home as to his whereabouts. The story goes that an unknown person eliminated the rival family, but one at a time to achieve maximum fear. Even when they were found in groups, only one was killed; the others were made to lie belly down. They were all gutted with a knife.

'Six months after Pike went missing he returned, emerging from the jungle claiming that he'd been taken prisoner by the Cong. There was no evidence of him making the return trip from Vietnam to the States, but as his story couldn't be disproved, he couldn't be charged; yet there's no doubt in a lot of people's minds that he did it, myself included.'

'He sounds like a bundle of fun,' remarked Stoddart.

Dieger handed them their drinks, and said: 'I wouldn't care to give him good reason to come after me.'

Feeling that the story had been a deliberate warning to himself, Stoddart raised his glass to his lips and said: 'Cheers.' As he was gulping down half its contents, Kolme arrived with Pike.

'Well, gentlemen,' began Dieger. 'Are we ready to go?'

'Yes, sir,' said Kolme, but Pike just nodded.

'Good. Your bullet-proof vests are on the table. Help yourselves, they're all the same. Now, since nothing other than the rendezvous and manpower were discussed, we all have to play our parts by ear. When we come alongside The Saracen I want you, Kolme, to head for the boat deck to act as our cover man. They will presumably send a party aboard to check out the quality and quantity of the cocaine, in which case we're likely to be invited on board to check their money. If McNalty is going to make a move it will be some time after he has checked the cocaine – probably when we've sent a party to check his seventy million. It's my guess that he's propositioned his team into making a killing at our expense, and then he'll wipe them out after they've done his dirty work.

'The only clue we have as to how it will be done is the use of gas and his admission to being a hay fever sufferer, suggesting that the gas will be hidden in some sort of aid for that particular ailment, so be ready to use the breathing apparatus fitted to your vests – and remember: one whiff of that gas will disorientate you, so just hold your breath for as long as it takes to insert the mouthpiece – or breathe out. The carrying of arms is not forbidden, but I imagine all parties will be searched before negotiations even get started.'

Looking at Stoddart and Scott, he added: 'Since Pike, Kolme and myself are well-trained veterans, that could be to our advantage. Any questions?'

'Just one,' said Stoddart. 'Up until now you've taken care of all the negotiations in my name; when it comes to the crunch, who's going to do the talking?'

'Why, you, of course.'

'In that case, someone had better tell me where the cocaine is, because I haven't seen hide nor hair of it since it was brought on board.'

Dieger smiled. 'If you remove the linen tablecloths and look at the corners of each side of the dining tables, you'll find a snug-fitting, hardwood dowel rod. Just give it a tap at the side and it will slide out. When you lift off the surface shell you'll find that the table base beneath is constructed like a large tray, about four inches deep, and that's where the shipment is hidden. You and Scott can remove it now, while we head to our rendezvous. There should be several large plastic bread trays in the galley, so I suggest that you pack it in those. You'd better come up on the bridge when you're finished.'

'Suits me,' said Stoddart, adding as he turned to Scott, 'shall we get to it?' Scott picked up the first two vests that came to hand and followed him.

Telling Pike to weigh anchor, and then join him on the bridge, Dieger nonetheless reached out a hand to restrain him until Scott and Stoddart had left. 'Not so fast,' he said quietly, and picking up one of the vests, he began to inspect the breathing apparatus. Carefully he pulled the mouthpiece, which was attached to a small-bore flexible tube, from just inside the neck, and let it hang outside. Turning to Pike and Kolme, he bent it double and just at the base, where the soft plastic tube did not run over the hard plastic insert of the mouthpiece, a ring of tiny holes appeared. 'Some of that gum you're so fond of chewing would come in handy to seal these,' he said to Pike.

An evil glint appeared in Pike's eyes as he dug into his pocket. 'You're obviously up to something,' he grinned, passing him some gum.

'Just a precaution. Whatever happens, I don't want them harmed. Is that understood?'

'Anything you say,' Pike agreed.

'And now, gentlemen, if you'll excuse me, I'll get into this damned thing,' said Dieger. 'We weigh anchor in ten minutes.'

Popping the stick of gum into his mouth, Dieger began to chew while stripping down to the waist. When the gum was pliable he wet his finger and thumb, removed it from his mouth and moulded it around the doctored pipe. When he had dressed again, he removed a large diary from his safe and began to write:

August 29th, 1986. Time 20.45 hours. Paid Scott and Stoddart commission in pearls as stated earlier. Surprised when Scott gave his to Stoddart for safe-keeping and possible investment. Considering past deeds of Stoddart in relation to Scott, I have taken the precaution of having my steward tamper with their breathing apparatus. If all goes well I shall question both men while they're under the influence of Scopolomene, in the hope of finding Scott's motives.

My reasons for doing this are as follows:

By any normal standards I would have judged Scott unlikely to waive any thoughts of revenge for Stoddart's wrongdoings, but after a great deal of research into his past, and getting to know him quite well during his stay on the Sea Queen, I would not judge him to be normal. He has a fine brain, as past deeds will testify, and he is not of an outwardly malicious nature. My worry is that he may be building Stoddart up so that he can take his revenge at a time when he feels it will have the most devastating effect. Such an action could reflect, of course, on the reputation and lives of members of the G Force: needless to say, precautions must be taken to ensure that this does not happen.

Signed – Dieger.

Satisfied that he had put his records in order, he returned the journal to the safe and made his way up on to the bridge. Checking that Scott and Stoddart were well-occupied via the video monitoring system inside the radio room, he then scanned the fo'c'sle for Pike.

'Winch it up,' he called through the intercom, then pushed the telegraph to Stand By to alert Kolme. When Kolme responded, he ordered: 'Slow ahead.' Moments later the deck beneath his feet began to vibrate slightly, and turning the helm he brought the Sea Queen around to face the open sea. It was calm and the bright, moonlit sky sparkled with a myriad stars. Seeing Pike leave the winch, he moved the telegraph to one third ahead.

'It's not exactly the kind of night I'd choose for this sort of thing,' declared Pike, coming on to the bridge.

'There's nothing to worry about,' Dieger assured him. 'Even if the coastguard monitor our movements on radar, there's nothing clandestine in two yachts from home ports running alongside each other for a while.'

'It's times like this when I wish we could have some immunity,' said Pike.

'Getting that kind of protection would blow our cover quicker than anything. As you well know, even the officials are not above taking bribes for passing on information to interested parties. I dread to think how much McNalty or Warburton would be prepared to pay in order to find out what they're walking into tonight.'

'Yeah,' grinned Pike. 'Are they going to crap their pants when the curtain goes up!'

'If they don't, we sure as hell will,' observed Dieger. 'Take a peek in the radio room to see how Scott and Stoddart are doing, and make sure you secure the door after you.'

While he was gone, Dieger spotted the bright bunting stringer lights of a distant yacht, which would eventually cross their path at a point five miles ahead. 'Pike,' he called, 'there's a yacht approaching on the starboard quarter. Get the Aldis lamp and ask who they are.'

Pike brought the lamp out of the radio room and stood at the bridge window, saying as he worked it: 'Stoddart's face looks as though it's been carved out of granite. Do you think he might make a play for it?'

'I gave it some serious thought,' Dieger admitted, 'but I doubt it – not just yet, and certainly not without help. There's too much for one man to move, and he's hopeless with boats.'

'They're flashing back Saracen.'

'Flash back Sea Queen,' said Dieger, altering course.

'I somehow get the feeling that Scott wouldn't go against you,' Pike offered.

'I know he wouldn't under normal circumstances, but there's something there that triggers off those alarm bells. I just can't put my finger on it.'

'Well, it can't be greed or he wouldn't have handed over those pearls the way he did.'

'That's what finally made me suspicious of him.'

The opening of the bridge door brought their conversation to an end.

'Everything's ready,' said Stoddart. 'Is that McNalty now?'

'It is,' said Dieger.

'Life doesn't appear to have treated him too harshly,' commented Scott. 'His yacht must be much the same size as this one, and they don't fall off Christmas trees.'

'If he thinks we fell off one, he's in for a shock,' said Dieger tartly. 'Take the wheel, Pike, while I go out on to the wing with Max.'

Quietly they stood on deck in the light breeze, watching The Saracen come up from astern and run alongside them.

'Are you prepared to heave-to and come alongside?' called McNalty.

'Tell him we are,' said Dieger to Stoddart, before giving Pike the order to stop engines and stand by. To Scott he said: 'Go below and throw them a line. Put the spring fenders over and make the line fast.'

'Nice to see you again,' called McNalty. 'You've moved up in the world, too, by the looks of you.'

'You'll hear no complaints from me,' Stoddart replied. 'Can you send a man over to check the merchandise when you're ready? If you're satisfied with his report, we'll come and check your finances before making the trade.'

McNalty had guessed what Stoddart's moves were likely to be, and they didn't coincide with his own plans to get as many of the two crews together in the same place at the same time.

'Surely we can cut all that crap, Max?' he said lightly. 'The way the law is clamping down, shipments are going to get scarce, so I shall want to know that any future supplies are guaranteed. Why don't we get our relationship on to a good footing from the start, based on trust? We'll bring the cash over straight away; then when everyone is happy with the deal, your chaps can help us transfer the shipment over here. How does that sound?'

'Take it,' rasped Dieger.

Stoddart called back: 'Suits me fine!'

'Pike,' said Dieger as the two craft gently nudged each other, 'secure the helm and come with us. Their helmsman can stand watch for both of us. Better take a line astern before we get too wrapped up with the business in hand.'

It was obvious that McNalty had given a great deal of thought to the proceedings. By the time they had reached the lower deck, he, Warburton and Warburton's partner, Ramsay, were waiting with the two large chests.

'To save a lot of what I believe to be unnecessary aggravation, I have persuaded my group not to carry any firearms,' McNalty declared. 'Naturally, we would appreciate your doing likewise.'

'None of us are carrying weapons, anyway,' said Stoddart. 'We came to the conclusion that arms would only hamper negotiations, and the last thing we need out here is delay.'

A tear-drop provoked by the use of glycerine welled up in McNalty's eye and spilled over to run down his cheek.

208

'Damned hay fever,' he sniffed, wiping it away with his handkerchief. 'We'll lift these chests up on to the side – can you haul them over from there?'

'Sure,' agreed Stoddart, 'but take it easy. We don't want to lose any at this stage of the game.'

Soon the two chests had been transferred and were quickly followed by McNalty, Warburton and Ramsay.

'The shipment is in the dining saloon,' said Stoddart, stooping down to grasp one end of a chest, Scott taking the opposite end. When McNalty raised a handkerchief and noisily blew his nose, his partners in crime took the hint and stooped to retrieve the second chest. McNalty's eagerness continued: when Dieger moved ahead to open the doors, he followed, and reaching the dining saloon invited the bearers to place the chests against the dresser-like cupboards where cutlery and condiments were kept.

Turning, his gaze came to rest on the neatly-packed bread trays. 'Now, isn't that a sight for sore eyes?' he smiled. 'If you have no objections, Ramsey can select a couple of packets at random and make his test while you check your money.'

'The sooner the better,' agreed Stoddart.

'Good,' said McNalty. 'I'll unlock the chests for you,' and he reached into his pocket for the keys. 'Damn hay fever,' he sniffed again, retrieving his handkerchief at the same time. Turning his back, he unlocked the first chest and lifted its lid to expose the piles of bank notes. 'Be my guest,' he said, inviting them, with a wave of his hand, to inspect the contents. With Scott and Stoddart thus occupied he turned his attention to the second chest, Dieger watching his every move even though his back was to him. McNalty's sniffing caused a stinging sensation high up in the bridge of his nose and provoked a sneezing fit, under cover of which he contrived to expose the mouth-piece of his breathing apparatus, before stooping to turn the key in the chest's right-hand lock.

'Don't stifle it or you'll blow your brains out,' joked Stoddart as McNalty straightened up with his hand-kerchief covering his throat. Drawing a lungful of air in readiness to sneeze, his head came back and then jerked forward into the hand holding the handkerchief.

'Excuse me,' he apologized, inserting the key into the left-hand lock and, as it turned, his head turned too, so that his face could not be seen clearly by Scott or Stoddart. As he lifted the lid with one hand, the other, holding the handkerchief, darted inside for the small cylinder of gas. Making a grab for his mouthpiece Scott managed to lose his balance, which upset Stoddart and both tumbled to the deck as McNalty sprayed them. A single large stride took him within reach of Warburton and Ramsay, whose startled, wide-eyed looks of horror turned to grimaces of bewilderment as their first breath of gas disorientated them. Leaving them to fall where they might, McNalty continued his sweep to find Dieger, who had been about four steps behind him.

When their eyes met, panic surged through him and with the stakes uppermost in his mind, he lunged forward, spraying the gas into Dieger's face while grabbing for his mouthpiece with his free hand. Dieger side-stepped, leaving him to stagger past and sprawl headlong on top of one of the dining tables. Desperately he twisted, swinging his legs clear of the chairs surrounding it before making a mad dash for the door to the galley. It opened before he reached it and, as Pike's burly frame blocked his passage, he came to a sliding halt. For several seconds no one moved or spoke; the only sound apart from the steady humming of the air conditioning was made by the gas cylinder falling from his limp fingers. When McNalty finally turned to face Dieger, he was standing by the open exit door, calmly motioning him towards it.

McNalty stood for a few moments more looking from the prize he had hoped to gain, to the inert bodies lying on the deck. As he moved forward, followed by Pike, he contemplated the folly of his ways and certain death. Dieger's face as he passed him gave no encouragement, and his gruff orders to Pike when he joined them in the companionway offered McNalty no hope, even if his life was to be spared.

'Get Kolme and bring any crew left on board The Saracen over here,' he said. 'Then signal our crew out in the launches to come aboard. We'll take The Saracen back to our anchorage for the time being. When the crew arrive, detail someone to put Scott, Stoddart and the other two into bed. They'll be taken care of, in good time.'

'What are you going to do about me?' bleated McNalty. 'You've got everything I own now.'

'Not quite,' Dieger corrected him. 'If you would care to accompany me to the bridge, we'll get the real business of the day underway.'

'What do you mean, "the real business of the day"?'

'All in good time.'

Walking along with Dieger lightly holding him by the elbow, McNalty's mind flashed back to how he had planned to make his killing and then, to cover his crime, to sink the Sea Queen with all hands, along with his own colleagues and crew. Now he felt devastated, to a point where death seemed to be a better option than living. Since Dieger had shown no intention of taking lives, it was safe to assume that, in addition to his financial ruin, he would also spend the rest of his life wondering what devious arrangement Warburton and Ramsay might have in store for him.

'Are you the police?' he asked.

'No,' replied Dieger coldly. 'If we were, you'd have been read your rights by now.'

'If you were, or are, criminals,' persisted McNalty, 'I'd have expected you to have eliminated us all and sunk me with my crew.'

'There's still time,' Dieger pointed out. 'First, I have a proposition to put to you which will make tonight's fiasco look like a robbery of the poor box at a Sunday school.'

'You could have discussed a deal with me without going to all this trouble.'

'Sure I could, but this way I've got you by the balls.'

McNalty swallowed hard. 'What makes you so sure that I won't turn the tables, the first chance I get?' he asked meekly.

'Sometimes living can be more traumatic than death,' Dieger warned him ominously. 'You have a daughter living in this country, for instance.'

'Leave her out of this!' snarled McNalty in a surprising show of temper.

'I wouldn't dream of harming a single hair on her pretty

little head – in fact, you are going to call her to explain why it's become necessary for her to go into hiding, with bodyguards to keep her safe. It wouldn't do for Warburton or Ramsay to find her if they escaped, now would it?'

'You bastard!'

'It was you who brought this about,' Dieger pointed out; no one else.'

'I'd love to know just how you managed to set me up so neatly,' said McNalty bitterly. 'It couldn't have been Warburton or Ramsay because they didn't know about the gas. You obviously did, to be ready for it.'

'It just goes to show that it's getting to a point where a man can't even trust his own shadow,' Dieger mocked. 'Just keep that in mind for the future: it could save you a lot of grief.'

He steered McNalty into the radio room, where he turned on the video monitors, rewound the tapes and then replayed them to show him that he could produce hard, indisputable evidence with which to blackmail him, if he chose.

'The plot was perfect and so was your performance,' said Dieger, complimenting him, 'but I doubt if your daughter would appreciate finding out what her father is really capable of.'

'Okay, so you've got me by the balls,' he agreed. 'What do you want from me?'

'First of all, let us discuss what I'm prepared to do for you if you agree to my terms. Firstly, your daughter will be kept safe and will never get to know the truth about you from anyone involved with me – that includes silencing Warburton and Ramsay and your crew. Secondly, I shall repay the loan you took out on your home, and hold it in trust. I'll also deposit ten million pounds in a Swiss bank for you – although that won't be available to you until our business is concluded. Thirdly, from now until that time, all expenses will be paid by me; and, last of all, any commission you make along the way will be yours to keep.'

'You must want something real bad to have gone to all this trouble setting me up. What is it?'

'I want you to help me to set up the biggest world-wide

212

narcotics network ever undertaken, or ever likely to be. My operation involves the movement of hundreds of tons at a time, with guaranteed deliveries.'

'You're crazy! Nobody could move that amount of stuff without detection; and if they did they'd have hell's own job marketing it. Apart from that, there'd be gang wars everywhere: the local barons wouldn't wear it, and God only knows what the Mafia would do. It would wipe out one of their biggest earners overnight. No thanks; you're too crazy for words.'

'Am I? You just hit the nail right on the head. I can move the stuff, but I don't have the distribution network; the Mafia does. What's more, they have the muscle to keep the other barons in line.'

Sweating profusely, McNalty strove to comprehend what Dieger had in mind. Absently he reached into his pocket for his cigars, and after offering one to Dieger, lit them both.

'I have got a brother,' he began, but stopped in mid-sentence. There was a long pause. 'You're some kind of son-of-a-bitch,' he continued vehemently. 'You've set up this whole operation just to make a connection running from you to me, to my brother-in-law in Sicily, and from him, smack into the heart of the Mafia network.'

'Go to the top of the class,' said Dieger with a grim smile.

'If you'd approached me this morning with such a scheme I'd have thought you were putting me on. How will you transport that much stuff?'

'Now, that's the multi-billion dollar question,' smiled Dieger. 'If you knew the answer to that, I'd be out of business, wouldn't I?'

In McNalty's own estimation, Dieger was nobody's fool, despite his failure to make a killing. One aspect of Dieger's deal held out a promise of notoriety amongst the wealthiest men in the world, and as part of such an organization McNalty could acquire more wealth in one year than during his whole lifetime so far. And if he could uncover the secrets of the transportation, he could relay it to his brother-in-law's Mafia friends so they could cut Dieger out. That would repay him in kind, and earn McNalty a fat percentage as a commission for all shipments involved.

'Count me in,' he said at last. 'Where do we go from here?' But Dieger, reaching out to shake his hand, wasn't fooled.

'For the moment you stay on board the Sea Queen. When Stoddart gets back on his feet you put your affairs in order, and then go with him to set up the deal with your brother-in-law.'

'What about Warburton and Ramsay? It's going to take something drastic to keep them from coming after me.'

'They are part of my insurance to keep you loyal,' Dieger threatened. 'As long as you play the game, I'll guarantee to keep you safe from them, but be warned: one wrong move and they'll be furnished with everything they need to track you down, and that includes your daughter.'

'You have my word,' lied McNalty.

'Then you don't have a thing to worry about, do you?'

'We're ready when you are, sir,' said Pike from the doorway.

Dieger stood up. 'Perhaps you'd care to see our guest to a spare cabin until I'm ready for him,' he said. 'Post a guard, but see to it that he has everything he wants. Have you re-stowed the shipment and put the cash in the strong room?'

'It's being done now, sir.'

'Good. I'm expecting a particular guest some time after we drop anchor. Show him up to my cabin the minute he arrives. If I'm not there, find me.'

The telegraph rang and as the Sea Queen's engines began to throb, Dieger stood at the wheel, reflecting on the night's work. Everything had gone according to plan, with the results turning out better than expected – particularly regarding Scott and Stoddart, in as much as he would not have to explain why their apparatus had been faulty.

'Mr Pike sends his compliments and asks if you would like to be relieved,' called a voice from the bridge door. The duty-watch helmsman stood outside on the wing, looking almost afraid to intrude.

'Get us both some coffee first,' he replied.

214

In the next few minutes the lights along the shore grew larger in size, but fewer in number as the population retired for the night. When the helmsman had taken over, Dieger stood alone out on the bridge's wing until Pike's rough voice broke into his thoughts; moving back inside he set the engine room telegraph to Stop Engines. As they approached their former anchorage he switched on the intercom and gave the order to drop anchor, telling the helmsman: 'There's a launch on its way. With any luck there'll be a Dr Mann on board; ask Mr Pike to show him to Scott's cabin, and tell him I'm on my way there now.'

Without waiting for an answer, he left the bridge and made his way down to where Scott lay sleeping peacefully on his bunk. For a long time he stood there in the semi-darkness, looking down at Scott's face and wondering what dark secrets lay behind its serenity.

Soon the doctor arrived; a tall, thin, gaunt man, who enquired in a deep voice: 'How long has he been out?'

'About an hour,' said Dieger. 'Does that make a difference?'

'No, but it's better to know these things, just in case anything goes wrong. Scopolomene has been known to have fatal reactions when administered in conjunction with other drugs.'

'If there's the slightest doubt in your mind, forget it,' said Dieger. 'He's a good man and I don't want to lose him.'

'If I had any doubts I wouldn't be here. I'll check him out, just the same.'

For all his lank gauntness, Mann moved with ease when handling a patient, and finding Scott still wearing the bullet-proof vest, he slid his palm beneath his shoulders and hauled him to a sitting position before stripping him down to the waist.

'Nasty,' he commented, looking at the scar on his chest. 'Lucky, too.' Easing him back into the bunk, he proceeded to check Scott's pulse, heart, blood pressure, temperature and reflexes. 'Sound as a bell,' he declared at last. 'Got himself quite a physique, too: must train a lot.'

'He's the sporty type,' explained Dieger. 'Used to own his own watersports business before he got mixed up with

215

our lot.'

'What's the problem, then?'

'He got dragged into crime by your next patient, and there's something I don't quite understand going on between them.'

'Homosexual?'

'Even if it were that simple, I wouldn't consider it to be any of my business.'

'Well, I'll give him a shot and we'll see. Give him a minute before you start with the questions.' The hypodermic needle slipped into Scott's arm and the syringe-plunger forced the Scopolomene into his bloodstream. After a minute, Mann said quietly: 'He's all yours.'

'Scott, can you hear me?' asked Dieger.

'Yes,' he replied in a faint, ghostly voice.

'Who am I?'

'Spiro Dieger.'

'Do you trust me?'

After a long pause, Scott said: 'Yes.'

'You don't sound so sure about that.'

'I think that you will do anything in order to achieve your objectives. Even hurt or sacrifice a friend.'

'That's an interesting point. Would you do something like that?'

'Not pre-meditated,' said Scott.

'What about Stoddart? After the way he ruined you, I'd have thought you wouldn't care too much what happened to him.'

'Maybe some day he'll give me no choice.'

'If you feel like that about him, why did you give him your pearls? Was it to make him feel secure, or to gain his confidence?'

'Yes.'

'Can you explain why you think you have to go to those lengths in order to gain his confidence?'

'He was in the launch with Rodriguez when my father and brother were killed, but I didn't know that until I was shot. It was the way the light struck his face when Haynes' gun ignited the petrol.'

'And you still don't want revenge, after finding that out?'

216

'I did at the time, but after you told me about your work, I changed my mind. If I can keep him on the straight and narrow for as long as it takes for you to succeed, I shall have achieved more than if I'd murdered him.'

'Does our success mean that much to you?' asked Dieger.

'Yes,' he replied flatly. 'My only misgiving is that when it's all over, someone else might start the ball rolling again.'

'Tell me about your relationship with Sahara,' invited Dieger. 'You met her a few times: what did you talk about?'

'Racing, mostly.'

'Surely you must have chatted about other things?'

'She seemed interested in my business – she asked a lot of questions about the ins and outs of it. As I recall, she seemed surprised when I told her that you were my sponsor.'

'Did she ask any questions about me which would make you suspicious of her, knowing what you know now?'

Scott remained silent for several seconds. 'Not really. She asked what I did for you in return, since it obviously wasn't advertising. I told her that you dealt in all kinds of machinery and that I sometimes carried out modifications on ski-cycles for you.'

'Did she ask you to be specific about the modifications?'

'Yes, but I told her that I couldn't tell her anything more than that because I didn't think you'd like me to.'

'How did she react to that?'

'She laughed and started pulling my leg about international intrigue – she knew all about you being an international arms dealer.'

'Did she ever ask you to do anything for her?'

'Not exactly. Once she invited me to a party with some friends after I'd won a race, and introduced me to a Frenchman who she said could put some highly paid work my way, if I was interested. I got the feeling that it was smuggling and turned it down by telling him that I had more work than I could cope with already, running my business.'

217

'Can you remember his name?'
'Jules St Just.'

9

Even though Dieger was out of sight, Scott was always aware of his presence. At Gatwick airport he met Sneider, who baited him into an argument over cheating in ski-cycle races. The argument developed into a fist fight, drawing the attention of some news reporters who just happened to be there – courtesy of Dieger. On the flight from Gatwick to Luqa, Malta's air terminal, Sneider had flared up again, and more pictures were taken as two in-flight security men hauled them apart; they had to keep them apart for the remainder of the flight. At Luqa, Sneider had shown signs of becoming aggressive again, but the security officers kept him in order with threats of deportation. From there Sneider had gone his own way, leaving Scott to be chauffeured to his destination, and once again Dieger's power and presence became evident.

The Atlantic Mirage was not the luxury yacht that Scott had assumed it to be, but by classification an ageing Thomaston class landing ship dock, five hundred and ten feet long, with a beam of eighty-four feet. During the day it was a noisy hive of activity, with tradesmen modernizing and refurbishing it, but it was in any case an odd-looking craft. Unlike traditional ships, the bridge and accommodation were well forward, leaving three-quarters of the after deck space clear. Part of this enormous area had been converted so that it could be opened, with large, hydraulic rams operating giant flap-like doors, while another section served as a helicopter landing pad. It was beneath this deck that most of the refurbishing was being carried out. The docking well, three hundred and ninety-one feet long by forty-eight wide, was flanked on either side by seven open galleries which were filled with all manner of tools and equipment. One prominent modification was a storage conveyor for amphibious landing craft, which looked like a giant vertical ladder with clamped cradle arms reaching out instead of rungs.

There had been no sight of a fast-attack craft, but everything had been tried and tested. Scott had stood in awe when the stern doors were opened and the ballast tanks flooded to increase the vessel's draught, and when the docking well was flooded to simulate the docking of a stricken ship, he joined the tradesmen in a private dip in jubilant celebration. The following day his powerful new ski-cycle arrived, and he named it the Meteor, after the trailing flames stencilled on its black cowlings. Much to his disgust, Dieger gave the order that he was forbidden to ride it out in the open until he had taken at least seven days' holiday to see the sights.

During those seven days Scott came into contact with many Maltese people and found them to be among the friendliest he had ever known. He visited the museum known as the Malta Experience, to learn of the island's great fight during the Second World War, and saw much of the splendour and beauty of the churches, the tiny historic cities and the old fortresses.

On the morning of the seventh day he borrowed one of the Atlantic Mirage's small launches and set out to tour the entire Maltese coastline. Unhurriedly he piloted his way through the deep, crystal-clear waters of Sliema Creek, which looked nothing like its name suggested. Here were no muddy banks covered with lush marsh grasses or trees, but hard, flat rocks where the sun worshippers lay and from which swimmers dived. In the marina, and the busy inland flank of the city of Sliema itself, there were hundreds of yachts.

After coming abreast of the massive ancient fortifications of St Elmo, which stood guard over the harbour's entrance, he turned north-west to skirt the seaward side of Sliema, where the ground rose to some thirty feet above sea level in places. Holidaymakers swarmed everywhere and the island's main coast road was well used. There were few yachts here, and no pleasure boats, and such beach as there was consisted of slabs of rock with a generous smattering of large, natural pools filled with deep, crystal-clear water, for those who chose not to venture into the open sea. Here, too, could be found the island's only gambling casino. Standing high up and proud, it allowed its patrons a grand view of ships travelling the busy sea lanes during the hours of darkness, their lights sparkling on the horizon.

Pressing on, he followed the coast to Qawra, where he crossed St Paul's Bay and passed between the two islands of St Paul – where, according to legend, the saint was shipwrecked – before entering the yawning mouth of Melliema Bay. All was quiet here, with no ships or people to mar the tranquillity.

During the crossing, Scott began to reflect on what had happened since he had lost his business. He reached Anrax Point, at the island's northerly tip, almost without noticing it; his mind had meandered on in an effort to justify what he had become, and he was trying to visualize the conclusion of Dieger's quest. The infiltration, black-mail and destruction of the Mafia in the United States flashed before his unseeing eyes without misgivings, but the thought of raiding Sahara Sediki's stronghold in order to stem the flow of narcotics at its source made his skin crawl.

He imagined having to trek through steamy, humid jungles alive with tigers and poisonous snakes, stagnant, leech-filled waterways and all manner of unspeakable creepy-crawlies, and visualized being fired upon by Sediki's guardians and compelled to crawl through the thick undergrowth in order to reach their destination. Obviously, once there, a full-scale war would break out; bodies, even friends, would be shot, maimed and mutilated in the name of justice.

Hardly aware of it, he crossed the open sea, passing the small island of Comino, and as he was circling Gozo, Malta's second largest island, an idea began to form in his mind that brought a smile to his face – even though it made him itch all over.

Suddenly he wanted to return to the Atlantic Mirage to await Dieger, whenever that might be, and increasing power he completed his circuit and retraced his passage. After sighting Marfa Point he plodded on down the coast, paying scant attention to the rugged cliffs, large caves and other scenic landmarks. Not even the tourist attractions such as the ramshackle weatherboard village where the film Popeye had been made, the enormous concrete gun emplacements from The Guns of Navarone, or the Blue Grotto, could slow him down.

He was passing across Pretty Bay towards Delimara Point at the island's southern tip when he spotted a dark shape speeding towards it and judged that their paths would cross. As they closed the distance between them, the hunched figure in a black wet suit and crash helmet on a powerful ski-cycle became more distinct. Believing it to be Sneider and not wanting to get involved, he slowed down, hoping that the man would sweep out to sea and then return behind after circling his position.

As predicted, the rider crossed his bow two hundred yards off with just a glance in his direction, but all Scott could see was the bulk of the helmet and the tinted glass of the visor. The rider continued for another few hundred yards before making a tight, dramatic turn, sending out a great white sheet of spray, and slowing for a few seconds to study him. He surged forward again as though to come at the launch on a collision course, and Scott, imagining Sneider's grim features behind the visor, guessed that he was about to take the opportunity to test his courage. With the machine speeding towards him, Scott continued on his course, expecting the rider either to go behind or, at worst, to skim past his bow close enough to touch.

At fifty yards he knew that this was not to be, and his heart began to pound in contemplation of the prospect. If he cut the engine and the rider swept behind, a collision would be inevitable; yet if he continued and the rider misjudged him, the result would be the same.

At thirty yards the rider's buttocks came away from the seat and his shoulders hunched forward; but they were too close now for manoeuvres and the speed was too great. The hunched stance could mean only one thing: as Scott bent at the waist, the rider jerked sharply upwards only fifteen feet away, hauling the ski-cycle's handlebars with him. Scott watched in horror as if seeing it in slow motion: the curved ski runner left the water and a moment later the whole machine was airborne. When it arced overhead with engines screaming, like a Stuka dive-bomber, Scott turned to follow its progress, despite the sea water raining back down on him. Standing high on the footrest with legs bent and body at ease to absorb the impact of landing, the rider splashed expertly down.

In those moments Scott knew that the rider was not Sneider, for the wet suit evidently clung to the shapely bottom of a woman. Fifty yards further on she slowed down and turned broadside on to view him, and though she never uncovered her face and only gave a friendly wave before speeding away again, Scott knew that it was Sahara.

It was a great relief when at last he was crossing the yawning mouth of the Grand Harbour, heading for Fort St Elmo, and when he re-entered Sliema Creek minutes later, where the Sea Queen lay alongside the Atlantic Mirage, the tension just floated away.

'How have you been keeping?' called Dieger from the Sea Queen's deck.

'Great,' beamed Scott, mooring the launch at the lowered gangway.

'You're looking fit. What have you been up to?'

'Seeing the sights, mostly,' he replied, shaking Dieger's hand, 'although today's outing was partially in preparation for the race. I did a complete tour of the islands to get an idea of what to expect, and Stoddart was quite right about them being small. Under racing conditions, the complete circuit shouldn't take more than a couple of hours. I can't wait to do a practice run on the ski-cycle.'

'I'm afraid I have some bad news on that score,' Dieger told him sombrely. 'Sneider's body was fished out of the Grand Harbour a few days' ago. It's said that he'd been tortured.'

'Christ! He was a bit of a pain, but I wouldn't have wished that on him.'

'That's one of the risks we take, I'm sad to say. As a precaution I'm going to assign a bodyguard to you. One of Kolme's men should do.'

'Have you any idea why he was tortured?' enquired Scott. 'Or is that asking the obvious?'

'It is,' Dieger admitted. 'Fortunately, he didn't know enough to do us any harm – and if Sahara was behind it his death may well have saved us a great deal of trouble because now she'll know exactly what we wanted her to know. No doubt we'll soon find out the truth of it all; her next step will be to make an approach to do a deal, if I'm not mistaken.'

'Speaking of which,' said Scott, 'while I was crossing Pretty Bay just now a rider – who I took to be Sneider – jumped right over the launch. When I turned to see how well he made the landing I was surprised to find that it looked like a women. She stopped about fifty yards away, just long enough to give a friendly wave, and then took off again. I couldn't see her face because she was wearing a crash helmet.'

'That's interesting,' Dieger said. 'Have you thought you were being followed at all, since arriving here?'

'No, but then it wouldn't be too difficult to follow anyone without their realizing it. There are so many tourists here at the moment.'

'Well, you'd better keep a weather eye open in future, just in case. In the meantime, I suggest that we be seen together, having a good time. How does an evening at the Casino grab you?'

'What you really mean is that you want to make yourself available,' said Scott reproachfully.

'Us,' Dieger corrected him. 'It's my guess that Sahara will approach me through you – and since she's a rich lady who just loves to gamble, the Casino is a good place to be.'

'Bucking the tiger has never been one of my failings,' said Scott. 'I'd like to come along to watch, though.'

'Good. Have you eaten today? Dinner is about to be served, if you're hungry.'

'I'd better take a raincheck on that,' Scott replied, looking down at his grubby shirt and shorts. 'By the time I get changed, dinner will be over.'

Dieger smiled. 'Oh, I think we can make an exception in your case.'

As expected, Scott's appearance drew veiled looks of

surprise from the Sea Queen's officers, some going so far as to raise their faces in obvious disbelief when Dieger bade him sit at his right hand at the table.

'I'll just have the seafood platter,' he said, as Dieger's personal steward approached, then coloured with embarrassment at making such a mistake.

Dieger grinned, but nodded his approval, saying: 'I'll have the same. Make sure there's plenty of coffee on the hotplate and then get yourself ashore – and mind my orders are obeyed: no one is to travel alone, for any reason. Should any of the crew feel the need to get romantic, tell them I'm expecting to be ashore all night and any female company is to be back there before breakfast.'

'Are you that worried?' asked Scott.

'A little. Apart from that, it will give Sahara the opportunity to get someone aboard to nose around.'

'Sounds as though you want her to find out what you're up to.'

'Up to a point,' Dieger admitted, 'but she can really only get confirmation of anything she may have learned from Sneider. Apart from that, it may stop her resorting to more extreme methods to get what she wants – not that that would amount to much. What do you think of the Atlantic Mirage by the way?'

'She looks a bit of a wreck at the moment. If Sahara does send someone on board hoping to discover what you're planning, she'll be on a loser. There's bits and pieces of machinery all over the place, most of which looks like junk to me.'

'It is,' agreed Dieger. 'It all came with the ship, and I had it left on board in the hope of confusing the enemy. We'll dump it when we get to sea.'

'Speaking of confusion, have you any idea how Sahara managed to get wind of what's going on?'

'Our dead letter-box operation has been a huge success. The authorities in Britain and throughout Europe have really cracked down, which has not only forced up street prices to an all-time record, it has also caused a great slump for the producers. The barons are just too scared to touch it, which is understandably worrying to other

225

governments, such as my own, fearful that the slump in Europe will cause a flood elsewhere. Suppliers like Sahara naturally want to know what's going on, and are desperate to secure new outlets, and I think she's desperate enough to kill off any opposition if it means she'll secure a customer with an order such as ours. All we have to do is keep her interested, without letting her find out the method of delivery.'

'Have you any other suppliers tendering for the order?' asked Scott.

'We shall be meeting one at the Casino tonight; an Indian gentleman by the name of Mohammed Ranjit Singh. Somehow I don't think he'll ever see his native land again, once Sahara gets her hands on him.'

'I suppose that's one way of getting rid of them,' Scott remarked. 'All you have to worry about is that it doesn't start a war that leaves us in the lurch.'

'I don't think we need worry ourselves about Sahara's safety,' said Dieger confidently. 'She's a born survivor.'

'Speaking of which,' said Scott, 'how is Max progressing?'

'The Leone family welcomed our offer like a gift from the Gods. After checking Stoddart out, Vincent called his brother, Leonardo, in the USA and within twenty-four hours Stoddart had advised me to proceed as planned. The only stumbling block appears to be the price and the demand for payment in diamonds and guarantees of delivery; but the way our tactics have bled the market dry and forced up the street prices, I can't see them haggling for much longer. In the present climate, the longer they haggle the higher the price is going to be.'

'Aren't you afraid that this may have an effect on our buying price? It could ricochet down the line to such an extent that the likes of Sahara will take advantage. If she does decide to eliminate any prospective suppliers, you'll be faced with either paying her price or being embarrassed over not being able to meet your own deliveries.'

With Scott knowing Sahara as well as he did, his logic was a matter of plain common sense, and Dieger remarked: 'What is it you English say? "You're not so green as you're grass-looking",' he quoted. 'Do you realize,' he

226

added in mock anger, 'that I shall now be forced to protect one of the very people we're trying to eliminate?'

'Sorry about that,' grinned Scott. 'We also have a saying that it is sometimes difficult to see the wood for the trees.'

'Very apt, in this instance. You don't happen to have any more bright ideas, while you're on the subject?'

'Considering that she must know of as many producers as you do, I'd be inclined to let her believe that some of them, at least, have representatives here. The fact that they're not means that she can't get at them, which will restrain her from using her full bargaining powers.'

'The more I see of you,' remarked Dieger, 'the more I'm inclined to think that you missed your true calling, somewhere along the way.'

'Maybe that's because nobody called until you came along,' replied Scott sombrely.

'Perhaps,' he agreed thoughtfully. 'As it happens, there's one aspect of our quest which I'm having serious reservations about. Perhaps you'd care to give it some thought.'

'I'm all ears.'

'When we've concluded the first stage of our business with Sahara and made our deliveries to the Mafia, we're due to return to Colombia to wipe out both her and her operating base. If we go in with a mercenary force through the jungle, her guard outpost might spot us, which will mean a long drawn out battle costing many lives on both sides. If we use helicopters and supporting gunships we could provoke an international incident, with serious repercussions if any of our men are identified as American, or in the employ of America.'

'What you need are soldiers who are completely at home in that particular environment,' said Scott. 'I would suggest the Eciton Carnivorous. They're specialists in carnage, reputed to be virtually indestructible and guaranteed to instil the most profound fear into the staunchest of enemies.'

Scott's casual blandness had Dieger fooled, and believing that his good nature was being taken advantage of, Dieger looked at him enquiringly, while digesting his words. Scott stared back, with the hint of a mocking smile in his eyes, as the names of the most feared tribal Indians, natives and pygmy races bombarded Dieger's brain. Embarrassed, Dieger raised his hand to scratch at an itch at the crown of his head; then as the truth of Scott's words dawned, his thoughtful frown became a smile and he visualized his enemies suffering under the fearsome onslaught of his newly-found legions. Scott grinned in recognition and Dieger shook his head in fits of uncontrollable laughter that drew enquiring looks from the other officers.

'Mister,' he said at last, 'I would hate to have you as an enemy.'

'I wouldn't hurt a fly,' protested Scott.

'Of course you wouldn't,' agreed Dieger, still shaking his head. 'Can I get you some more coffee?'

'No thanks. If there's time, though, I'd like to take a nap before going ashore to the Casino.'

'Make time,' insisted Dieger. 'I want to have a look at how things are progressing on the Atlantic Mirage anyway. Then I'd better make some arrangements for Sahara to be kept on tenterhooks. Shall we say nine o'clock in my quarters? We can have cocktails before we make our way there.'

'Surely you're not going to take the Sea Queen?' he scoffed. 'It's only ten minutes by taxi, and a quarter of the distance.'

'Yes,' Dieger smiled, 'but it wouldn't do to deprive Sahara of the opportunity to send her spies on board the Atlantic Mirage now, would it?'

'Well, they won't see much, will they?' Scott argued. 'Just a load of junk and tradesmen working. If anyone can figure out what you're up to from that, they'll have to be psychic.'

'That's the general idea. As long as they can't figure out our method of delivery, they can't compete.'

'At the moment I can just imagine her thinking that you intend using ski-cycles to convey the stuff ashore – and in the quantities you're talking about, that would not only be hazardous in bad weather, it would also take for ever. The losses might prove to be a financial disaster.'

'And the coastguard would soon become suspicious of

any ship close enough to carry out such an operation,' Dieger pointed out.

Finishing off the last of their coffee, they left the luxury of the Sea Queen for the Atlantic Mirage where they parted company.

In his cabin – a large, single berth room with adjoining bathroom, which he guessed had originally been allocated to an officer – Scott lay down on his bunk, which was large and comfortable with a polished wooden side to keep the occupant safe within its bounds in heavy seas. There was no air conditioning, but a fan fixed high in one corner could cover the bed and a writing desk fitted beside it at the head. The fitted wardrobes, also of highly polished wood, spanned the full height between the deck and the deckhead.

Slowly his eyes closed as he nestled into the warm, soft comfort of the pillow, and in the darkness of his meandering mind he imagined what caused the various distant noises vibrating through the ship's hull. The generators gave out a steady low rumble, which was broken every once in a while by the harsh, rapid chatter of a powered metal chipping tool, used by the fitters to remove old, obsolete iron brackets, or unwanted metal standing proud from flat surfaces. Sometimes there was a heavy, rhythmic clang, followed by an echo, which he judged to be a fitter driving home one of the enormous engine nuts with a sledgehammer and the flogging spanner tailor-made for the purpose.

As he was drifting off to sleep, visions returned of the island's beauty spots, such as the Blue Grotto, the Popeye village and the beach at Golden Sands, with the happy, smiling faces of the tourists. Suddenly the people parted to allow a clear view of the sea, where the solitary figure of a woman waded ashore towards him, water glistening on her long, shapely legs. Slowly he raised his eyes, appreciating the beauty of her body, and she stopped for a few moments to turn with arms lifted so that he could view the flat of her stomach and her perfectly shaped bottom.

When she had turned full circle, the top of her scanty bikini had disappeared to reveal voluptuous breasts, and he tried to move forward to meet her as she advanced, but could not. Then she was standing before him and he studied her face, the mouth full and sensuous, the lips inviting. She smiled, her head tilting forward slightly, setting off her high cheekbones and dark blue laughing eyes to their best advantage.

'Sahara,' he heard himself say, bringing him back to awareness. It was still daylight, so even though he sensed a change, there was no reason to panic. For a few moments he lay there listening, eyes closed in an effort to recapture the vision of Sahara before realization dawned. All activity on board had ceased, leaving only the generators to emit their steady throb. Knowing that it was unusual for the workforce to stop before ten o'clock, he swung out of his bunk to look through the porthole. Not a soul was to be seen working out on deck, and guessing that Dieger had ordered all personnel ashore early, in order to allow Sahara's spies to check out the Atlantic Mirage un-hindered, he showered and put on a dark suit, white shirt and black bow tie. When he left his cabin it was just five minutes to nine and, dressed as he was and in such circumstances, he felt out of place. Picking his way through the cables, hoses and coiled hawsers littering the deck, he made his way down to the Sea Queen.

'You're looking quite the city gentleman,' remarked Dieger.

Scott smiled as he admired Dieger's choice of white tailored shirt and jacket, highlighted by a black bow tie, trousers and shoes. 'James Bond, I presume,' he smirked. 'I wouldn't mind feeling as comfortable as you look.'

'I don't think I've ever seen you wearing a suit before,' admitted Dieger. Then, recalling the pain Scott had felt at not being allowed to go to his mother's funeral, despite ordering the suit for that particular occasion, he added quickly: 'Have you ever been inside a casino?'

'No. The nearest I ever got was seeing them on films or television.'

'A man can get through quite a lot of cash in those places,' said Dieger casually. 'How are you fixed?'

'I have about a hundred pounds.'

'That won't do,' he scoffed. 'Since tonight is business I'll advance you five thousand Maltese pounds. There'll be

230

more if you need it.'

'You're joking!' said Scott, swallowing hard. 'That's half a year's wages.'

'Was,' corrected Dieger. 'Tonight you have to play the part of a flamboyant young spendthrift whose motto is: easy come, easy go. Maybe a few drinks will help loosen you up.'

'In that case I'll have a gin and tonic with plenty of ice and lemon,' said Scott, and Dieger gave him a sly grin before picking up a tall lager glass which he quarter-filled with gin. After adding ice to bring it to the halfway mark, he topped it up with tonic.

'Try that,' he invited.

Scott sipped it. 'That's fine.'

'Would you care to join me on deck? We'll be passing the old fort at St Elmo in a few minutes and it has a special fascination for me.'

'Glad to,' Scott agreed.

Up on deck they leaned against the side, gazing at the shore as they sipped their drinks.

'I wonder how the Maltese people feel about the horrors of nuclear warfare,' mused Scott as they passed beneath the ancient cannon, which had once spat fire and iron at the enemy.

'Pleased, mostly, I should think,' replied Dieger. 'These islands have next to no strategic value since the coming of the nuclear bomb – which in itself should mean that they'll never again be caught in the middle of someone else's conflict as they were in the Second World War. With the twenty-one thousand tons of bombs supposed to have been dropped here, I'm surprised anyone survived – in fact, I'm surprised that the island itself survived.'

'Maybe there's a lesson to be learned from it, after all,' suggested Scott thoughtfully.

'Such as?'

'No matter how big, bad and powerful you are, in the finish you end up like Hitler and his Third Reich: dead, but not forgotten.'

After passing St Elmo, to starboard, they altered course north-west, putting the busy city of Sliema out of sight behind their super-structure to leave them staring out into the empty Mediterranean.

'It must have been something to see when the Turks invaded,' reflected Dieger. 'Can you imagine the awesome spectacle of waking up to find more than two hundred sailing ships sitting out on your doorstep, packed with a good forty thousand fighting men?'

'I wonder why we do it,' Scott mused quietly.

'Do what?'

'Fight.'

'The obvious answer is because we like it – although I'm damned if I can see how.'

'What brings you to that conclusion?'

'Because we never stop. You put a name to it and we'll fight for it or over it. Power, politics and religion are the worst; then, when we give them a rest, we turn to greed, sex and anything else that comes to mind. Sometimes I wonder if war isn't a part of some great super-natural plan to cull the human race every now and then. Can you imagine how many we'd be by now, for instance, if the Second World War had never happened?'

'Probably standing on each other's shoulders, ready to cut someone's throat for a crust of bread.'

'Which proves my point: if someone didn't lead us into war by the nose, we'd end up doing it out of desperation.'

'So,' Scott finished for him, 'we might as well take up arms and enjoy it.'

At first Dieger thought he was being sarcastic. Scott's mood had turned sullen, and he seemed reluctant to continue their philosophical conversation. It was only after several minutes of silence that the truth dawned, by which time the jingling telegraph on the bridge had signalled Stop Engines.

The grating rattle of the anchor chain and the splash of the great barbed hook plunging into the water, drew Scott from his thoughtful mood.

'If you're so sure that Sahara is keeping a close watch on our operation,' he began, 'aren't you worried about her spying on us when the torpedoes are loaded on to the Atlantic Mirage? Even if they're packed in unidentifiable crates, it's a racing certainty that she'll bribe someone to find out what you're carrying.'

232

'You worry too much,' said Dieger. 'Even if I wanted to load up here, the government wouldn't allow it. And by the time she finds out what we're up to, it will be too late. Now, shall we go and see what lady luck has in store for us?'

They made their way to where the deck officer was organizing the lowering of the gangway. 'Your launch will be ready in a few moments, sir,' he volunteered.

Dieger nodded his thanks while Scott continued to air his fears: 'Supposing she has me kidnapped, and tortures me like she did Sneider?'

'Oh, I don't think you need worry on that score,' said Dieger confidently. 'I've already taken precautions against it. Just think: you could be lucky enough to have her seduce you to try to get you to talk.'

'I'm not so sure about the "lucky" part. She always struck me as being a bit of a tigress between the sheets,' he grinned. 'She'd probably tear me to pieces.'

'I know many a man who would pay good money for the privilege.'

Scott remained silent, preoccupied with the thought of seeing Sahara as they were ferried across the casino's private marina to the docking area, carved out of the natural rock a good thirty feet below. There was also a private swimming pool and a large patio, complete with an outside bar and barbecue. A fancy dress party was in full swing, adding to the colour and gaiety of the evening. Four chefs dressed as headhunters busied themselves amid clouds of blue-grey smoke, striving to satisfy the hunger of the guests. On one side there was an abundance of prime cuts of steak, sausages, kebabs and cutlets, while the other was set out with fresh salad, trout, salmon and all manner of shellfish, including oysters. The crowning glory was an enormous stone urn of caviar, set in an ornamental silver bowl.

Although the night was warm, a few guests suffered the discomfort of cumbersome Victorian attire, while a smattering limited themselves to loin cloths and grass skirts.

There were pirates and soldiers, vicars and highwaymen, while outstanding on the female side was a stunning mermaid accompanied by her Neptune, a daring Queen of Hearts, whose playing card barely covered her charms, and a particularly feline black cat. Drinks were served free of charge from a bar set in the mouth of a large cave in the rockface, directly beneath the casino.

Carefully edging round a crowd of holidaymakers who were dancing to an Hawaiian tune, Scott and Dieger mounted the stone steps leading to the casino. At the top, Scott stopped for a moment to look down on the happy, colourful scene. The aroma of barbecued meat hung lazily in the night air, teasing his appetite despite his recent meal. Through the haze he saw two upturned faces which appeared to be paying him and Dieger undue attention.

One was dressed as a headhunter, the whites of his dark eyes matched by the whiteness of the bone protruding from each side of his nose and his even, brilliant white teeth. His companion presented herself as an Amazon, with long golden hair spreading like a fan across her back and partially covering her shapely bottom; she wore only a chamois leather loin cloth and brassiere. In addition to the large knives which they each wore at the waist, he wielded a large, very real looking axe, while she sported a longbow and a quiver of arrows, hooked over her shoulder so that the leather thongs gave emphasis to her ample cleavage.

Scott's eyes swept uneasily over the crowd and beyond, scrutinizing the many small yachts and powerboats to see if anyone else was overtly interested in them.

'Something bothering you?' asked Dieger.

Scott turned a little but did not immediately meet Dieger's eyes. On the far side of the casino, which was a good hundred and fifty yards from the busy main road around the seaward side of Sliema, the buildings were a blaze of light. Amongst the traffic, which was constant, plied the occasional horse-drawn carriage favoured by the tourists for seeing the sights. As far as the eye could see, the wide pavements along the shoreline were alive with pedestrians, out for a stroll in the cool of the evening. Only a narrow road leading to the car park lay between, leaving the casino almost isolated.

'Is there anything special going on here tonight?' asked Scott.

'Not that I'm aware of. The fancy dress barbecue isn't

out of the ordinary; there are dozens of them going on all over the islands, every night of the week. It's part of the tourist itinerary. Why do you ask?'

'I must be getting paranoid,' said Scott, shaking his head. 'Take no notice.'

But Dieger persisted. 'What did you see that bothered you so much?'

'Just a couple of people in fancy dress, looking at us.'

'They were probably our bodyguards,' Dieger smiled. 'There'll be more inside. I'm known quite well in this part of the world as an arms dealer, which makes me an ideal target for extremists who have a grudge, or feel inclined to hold me to ransom for a cargo of arms.'

'Oh, that makes me feel great,' said Scott. 'I'll be looking over my shoulder all night long, now.'

The commissionaire opened the door for them with a polite 'good evening'. Inside, the semi-circular foyer was noticeably cooler, and the only sound in the quiet luxurious setting was the low humming of the air conditioning. Dominating the centre of the foyer was a miniature desert oasis with a fountain, surrounded by a model Arab caravan in the shade of dwarf palm trees. There were more exotic plants between all the doors, and by the main doors to the casino where a uniformed attendant stood. He opened the door to let them pass through, unchallenged. The sweet aroma of cigars tainted the air inside, but the air conditioning drew out the offending smoke long before its presence could foul the atmosphere.

Both men and women indulged at the tables, but the night was still young and people were not yet crowding around to play. By-passing the cashier's cage, which was on their immediate left as they entered, Dieger headed straight for the bar at the far end, where he ordered a bourbon on the rocks before turning to Scott, who said: 'I'll stick to gin and tonic with plenty of ice and lemon,' and leaned back on the bar so that he could watch the players while surveying the casino's interior. Two roulette games were in progress, with maybe a dozen players between them. One table played by the American rules, the other by the French, and elsewhere baccarat, black jack and buelle were being played.

'You don't seem too impressed,' remarked Dieger.

'It's not exactly my scene,' Scott pointed out, 'although I did expect to see a hive of activity in here.'

'It's early yet, and this isn't where the real games are played. This stuff is strictly for the tourists – and a front to keep the authorities happy, for the big-time games are played in private rooms. A man has to be on the ball to play in those games, though; you never know exactly who you're playing against – unless you've been around – and many a good man has been fleeced by international hustlers.'

'I wouldn't have thought it worth their trouble. Hotels and travel must be costly, and when you consider the possibility of two or more persons involved in fleecing a few thousand out of one, it hardly seems profitable.'

'Don't you believe it. A great many millionaires bring their yachts here just to get away from the European hotspots for a while. A syndicate of around four people will finance one of their group to latch on to an un-suspecting prey; then, when he comes to a place like Malta for a break, the sucker is enticed into a private game where all the other players are members of the syndicate. They'll pop something into his drink while he's on a winning streak, to get the stakes boosted, and then, when he's feeling on top of the world, they take him to the cleaners. Many a man has woken up to find that he's signed cheques or IOUs to the tune of hundreds of thousands of pounds.'

'Supposing he realizes what's happened and refuses to honour his debts?'

'Sometimes the threat of physical violence persuades them to cough up; more often than not, there's a woman involved and I'm sure I don't need to paint pictures to explain what that means.'

As they chatted on, more guests arrived to play the tables, some in fancy dress. One was dark-skinned and dressed in the rich, silken finery of an Indian sultan.

'May the blessings of the prophets be upon you,' he greeted them mockingly, touching his forehead and chest with his fingertips as he bowed slightly.

'And may he see fit to share his wisdom with such lowly mortals as us,' smiled Dieger in reply. 'Can I get you a drink?'

'Just an orange juice, thank you,' he begged. 'As you are aware, my religion forbids the drinking of alcohol.'

'Of course,' said Dieger, and when he'd ordered he explained to Scott: 'This is a business associate of mine. Mohammed, this is James Scott.'

'A great pleasure,' beamed Mohammed, offering his hand.

'How do you do,' replied Scott sheepishly.

'We have business to discuss,' said Mohammed. 'Where can we meet?'

Dieger hedged. 'That depends – there are other suppliers involved. Firstly I need to know quantity, quality, price and delivery dates. At the moment I'm toying with a firm order of not less than one hundred metric tonnes.'

'Toying?' choked Mohammed. 'Never has such a quantity been moved. The risks will be enormous. Surely you must be joking?'

Although no name had been put to the commodity in question in such a public place, Scott's blood turned to ice at the thought of Dieger speaking of it so openly. He turned away to hide his shocked embarrassment, only to find the reason for Dieger's openness. There, close by, stood the lady he had seen earlier, dressed as a black cat. Despite the hooded mask and whiskers, her smile was unmistakable, and when she spoke her soft seductive 'hello' blotted out Dieger's reply from Scott's mind.

'You're a long way from home,' she remarked, moving to his side and slipping her arm through his. 'Are you on holiday?'

'Not exactly,' he stammered. 'More of a business trip. These are some friends of mine. This is Spiro Dieger, and . . .'

'I know,' she cooed, cutting him off in mid-sentence. 'Our paths have crossed from time to time.' She smiled seductively and asked: 'Would you mind if I stole him from you for a few minutes?'

'Be my guest,' he smiled, adding to Scott: 'But mind, her

claws are sharp. Big cats are sometimes called panthers, and they are quite partial to human flesh, so I'm told.'

'Oh, I won't eat him,' she promised, and steered Scott towards the balcony overlooking the large patio where the fancy dress party was still in full swing.

Since she had made her wishes quite plain, Scott hauled open one of the large patio doors and stepped out on to the balcony, closing it behind them. The evening had cooled considerably. Offshore lay the Sea Queen at anchor, her lights ablaze, and the noise of a party on board mingled with that of the musicians below.

'It looks as though everyone is hell-bent on having a good time tonight,' remarked Scott, in an effort to get the conversation going, but she replied quite seriously.

'Can we dispense with the small talk? We both know why you're here and there doesn't seem to be a great deal of time left for me to put in my bid.'

'To the best of my knowledge,' he replied, 'the bidding has been taken care of. The only problem would seem to be how to supply the quotas required at a rendezvous acceptable to both parties. As you can appreciate, moving a hundred tonnes of heroin from Gartoc in Tibet, across India to Lahore in Pakistan, and down to Karachi, where it is acceptable to us, does have its drawbacks.'

She had removed her cat mask while he was speaking and now stood facing him, her eyes riveted on his, following his slightest movement without breaking contact.

Now she came closer, placing her hands on his hips. 'You intrigue me,' she whispered, moving in to kiss him.

Her first kiss was gentle and designed to test his reaction. When he responded, her arms encircled his neck and she gave him a foretaste of the passion within. While inwardly wary, he responded by letting his hunger show.

'My,' she sighed, clinging to him, 'you're full of surprises. I used to think you were so sweet and innocent. Now I find that you're not only involved in the biggest narcotics operation ever undertaken, you have a hunger which I suspect will take a great deal of satisfying.'

'It just goes to show that things are not always as they seem,' he replied lightly.

'Like you working for Dieger, for instance – that was a shock. Were you working for him when I introduced you to Jules St Just?' she asked casually.

'I often used to bring shipments in for him from the continent,' he lied. 'That's why I gave your friend the cold shoulder. A man can't work for two bosses in this game.'

She released her hold on him, withdrew a few inches to where she could see his face and asked huskily: 'Did you use your ski-cycle to transport it?'

His hands still rested gently on her trim waist, so that the slightest movement of her lithe body was transmitted to him. Once again her eyes searched his, the dark pupils following his every movement, making him feel as though she clung to his every word.

'Always,' he continued to lie. 'It was quick and virtually impossible to be detected or monitored by radar – and apart from that, I could out-run anything that floated.'

'I understand that he's negotiating a contract with the Mafia to supply every major city in the USA and Canada.'

'So the story goes,' he hedged.

'My contacts also tell me that he's devised a foolproof method of transporting it.'

'At one time I thought he intended using a mother ship and a whole squadron of trained ski-cyclists,' he lied. 'Now I'm not so sure.'

'It's feasible, though,' she urged, searching the inner depths of his eyes.

'Oh sure, although the risks are a great deal higher than just a short trip across the Channel. The loss of shipments could be greater than usual, too.'

'Oh?' she cooed in surprise. 'Why?'

'You just don't go out and buy yourself a ship the size of the Atlantic Mirage and then go globe-trotting as you please. They have to be registered,' he explained. 'All departures, cargoes and destinations have to be declared to the authorities.'

She knew about the Lloyd's List, a newspaper on sale all over the world which gave details of shipping departures and arrivals, but failed to see its significance regarding Dieger's operation as she believed it to be. 'So how does that complicate things?' she asked. 'A legitimate cargo can be carried as cover, and dummy companies could be set up to handle cargoes, if need be. Since the real reason for the trip would no longer be on board at the time of docking, I fail to see the need to worry.'

'The cruel sea is why,' he explained. 'Ships may plough through the heaviest of seas or ride out the worst storms, but not a squadron of ski-cyclists. Even a moderate sea could be enough to ground them, or lose them a shipment, but you could hardly wait around for days at a time until the weather changed. A voyage designed to make twenty separate deliveries could be prolonged by as much as a month, and even if the authorities didn't get suspicious, the insurers would certainly question the vessel's seaworthiness after such obvious delays. And if the schedule was adhered to, at the risk of failing to make its deliveries, I imagine Dieger would lose his credibility with his Mafia friends. The only alternative would be to take a chance on losing men and machines in unsuitable weather.'

As she moved her foot, shifting her weight a little, her thigh moved suggestively between his, and the soft firmness of her breast pressed gently against his chest. 'Will you help me persuade Dieger to give me the contract to supply him?' she asked, leaning back slightly so that her hips pressed provocatively against his. 'I can supply all the cocaine he requires, deliver without any difficulty, my base of operation is close to the sea and I have the local police in my pocket.'

'The only problem I can see is that he's wanting to buy heroin.'

'So I've heard, but the way the major powers have clamped down recently, I should think his Mafia contacts would be glad to get their hands on anything, provided the quality is good.'

'Under the circumstances I can't see any problems – from what I can gather Mohammed won't be able to meet Dieger's demands so easily. Why don't you stay out here while I go and get us a drink? I'll see if I can get his attention while I'm about it.'

Wrapping herself around him, her body promising heaven, her passionate kiss leaving no doubt in his mind as to how far she was prepared to go in order to achieve her goal, she purred: 'I would consider it a great favour. Perhaps we could get together so that I can show my appreciation?'

His hands slid downward to the top of her thighs before sweeping slowly back upwards to caress her shapely body. 'I sometimes wonder what it is about a woman's body that drives a man crazy,' he replied. 'Is it the actual feel of it – or the mystery of not knowing how she will react?'

She kissed him again with increased passion, her clawed fingers drawing down the length of his back inside his coat. He reeled against her with the sweet pain of it, which only served to add more fuel to her already mounting needs.

'Go,' she panted huskily, 'or we shall end up making a spectacle of ourselves out here.'

'I'm not so sure I dare,' he grinned, pressing his pelvis against her.

'Dieger was right,' she smiled, zeroing in on his eyes again. 'I could eat you.'

That particular way she had of looking at him lingered in his mind as he broke loose and turned away, saying: 'Make it for breakfast after the night before.'

In the casino, which was so packed that it was impossible to move about freely, Scott shuffled towards Dieger at the bar, scanning the heads to see what had become of Mohammed. There was no sign of him anywhere and when he asked: 'How did it go with Mohammed?' a broad smile spread over Dieger's face as he inhaled deeply.

'Mister,' he grinned, 'you smell like a whore's boudoir.'

'I'm not surprised,' Scott smiled back. 'She damn near seduced me on the spot. I think she might have, if I'd held out a little longer.'

'Well, for what it's worth, Mohammed will be on the first plane out of here. We've done the deal, the only unanswerable question is when. The shipment is to be collected at Pakta, a remote Tibetan village close to their base, just across the Pakistan border. How about you?'

'She's aching to do a deal. I guess the clamp-down is hurting her pretty badly. All you have to do is go out there and talk to the lady.'

'That is no lady,' retorted Dieger. 'She's one hell of a woman, though. Did she try to find out how the delivery is going to be made, by any chance?'

'She did, but didn't press the subject when I denied any knowledge. She definitely knew that you were going to use a new method, though. Maybe she'll give you the heat treatment in the hope of finding out. Either way, she wants to see you outside so that she can make her bid.'

'There's only one way to find out,' Dieger agreed, 'although I doubt if she'll press her luck with me. If all else fails, she'll bide her time until we've made our first run; then she'll bank on having another go at you, or approaching one of our crew.'

'Do you think she could set up an operation like ours?'

'Probably not. There are not too many arms dealers around who can lay their hands on the necessary equipment. Apart from keeping everyone guessing, it's more a case of making sure that no one else gets the chance of using your idea in the future. It's impossible to calculate what the big organizations can accomplish when the stakes are so high. Anyway, I think we've allowed Sahara to sweat it out long enough. Why don't you get yourself some chips and try your luck at the tables?'

'I'm not so sure about that,' said Scott. 'I can't say I'm inspired by what I've seen so far. I think I'll just hang on at the bar with a drink, for a while.'

'Suit yourself,' agreed Dieger solemnly, 'but try to think of your image: you're supposed to be one of the jet-set now.'

Dieger's frown of displeasure remained imprinted on Scott's mind long after he'd gone, and it dulled his own mood. After leaning back on the bar watching the players for some time, he approached the cashier's cage to purchase some chips. At the blackjack table the game seemed slow and did nothing to fire his imagination, but nevertheless, when a seat became vacant he stepped in and placed a blue chip on the table as his bet. The dealer, sensing that he was not familiar with the game, reached out to turn the chip over so that the hundred pound marking would be face up. No one else seemed to notice his presence. Scott lifted the corner of his first card to

242

peek at it: the ace of diamonds, and his second card was the ace of hearts.

'Split them and double your stake,' advised a female voice behind him and he turned, half expecting to find Sahara; but to his amazement he found the tall, golden-haired Amazon lady standing there.

Dropping his gaze to ponder on the delights of her breasts, which were barely contained in the soft beige chamois leather brassiere, he said provocatively: 'Seems a shame. They look perfect as a pair.' She smiled, revealing beautifully white teeth, and her eyes mirrored her appreciation of what she took to be a compliment. Turning back, he parted the aces without a word and placed a second blue chip on the table.

The dealer flicked a second card face up on each: the king of diamonds followed by the king of hearts. Looking up at Scott, he said: 'I can't ever recall turning up a pair of red kings on their own aces before,' adding casually: 'Many a superstitious gambler would take that as a sign to ride his luck.'

But Scott retrieved his winnings, saying: 'I'm neither a gambler nor superstitious. Where I come from they call it beginner's luck.' The double win had failed to inspire him to continue in such a slow game, and nodding his thanks, he withdrew to the bar and ordered another drink.

'You're not an easy person to get acquainted with,' said a soft voice in reproach. He turned to find the young Amazon standing at his side.

'Sorry, I guess I'm not at my best tonight. The name is James Scott. Can I get you a drink?'

'Sonia Blessed,' she smiled back. 'A chilled white wine will be fine. Do you mind if I call you Scott? It has a friendlier ring to it than James, and Jim or Jimmy sound boyish.'

'Scott suits me fine.'

'Are you here on holiday?'

'Partly. I'm involved in the modifications being carried out on the Atlantic Mirage, which is moored at Manoul Island in Sliema Creek.'

'Is your work interesting?'

'Sometimes, but things are pretty routine at the moment. I guess that's why I'm not on good form. In truth, I'm just plain bored.'

'Your form seemed better than average a few minutes' ago,' she contradicted. 'Why don't you try your luck at the roulette table?'

'You wouldn't be one of those beautiful ladies the casino employs to encourage people to play at the tables and preferably lose their money?' he asked directly, adding with a smile: 'No offence intended, of course.'

'The answer is no, and none taken,' she replied pleasantly. 'I'm a police woman, plain clothes.'

'There's nothing plain about what you're wearing now,' he mocked, 'and you should know better than to walk around like that. The sight of you is enough to drive a man crazy with lust.'

'But not you?'

'Showing my feelings is not one of my failings. What are you doing here, anyway? You're obviously on duty,' he challenged in an effort to find out why she had struck up an acquaintance at that particular time.

'Oh?' she said in surprise. 'And what brings you to that conclusion?'

'Being nothing more than a country boy, I couldn't even guess,' he smiled, taking a sip of his drink. 'Would you care to give me the benefit of your experience at the roulette table?'

'Of course,' she smiled.

Taking Dieger at his word, but wanting to capitalize on his country-boy image in the hope of prising more information from his new-found friend, Scott placed the two blue chips he had won squarely on the number thirty-six, whereupon everyone at the table turned in surprise to see who had made such a foolhardy wager. There were two croupiers, both of whom gave a 'here's another sucker' grin and promptly turned to their mediator with a knowing wink. He gave them a curt nod to continue.

Horrified at Scott's apparent ignorance, Sonia reached out to retrieve the wager, saying: 'You shouldn't bet like that.'

Scott restrained her hand. 'Another saying where I come from is "Change your mind and you change your

244

luck".'

'But it's not a wise bet,' she protested. 'There are several ways to . . .' but his grip on her wrist held her firm.

'That's my choice,' he insisted. 'As I see it, all I can lose is what I won in the first place. It's not as though it's my own money.'

'But thirty-six was the last number to win,' she persisted. 'Have you any idea what the odds are against it coming up again?'

'No – but it would be interesting to calculate the odds against my predicted luck.'

'One thousand, three hundred and sixty-eight to one against,' she said emphatically.

Scott grinned. 'It's easy to see why you're not out on the street directing traffic,' he said as the ivory ball began to click around the spinning wheel of fortune, and something in his secretive smile told her that he was aware of the fact that she had acquainted herself with him for reasons other than friendship.

Gasps of surprise from the other players brought his soul-searching look from her back to the game.

'Number thirty-six wins,' declared the croupier, speaking as though he had a frog in his throat.

'Bingo!' shouted Scott, throwing his arms around her. 'How much have I won?'

'Seven thousand pounds, plus your stake,' she beamed. 'Your luck is unbelievable.'

'Well done, young man,' cried an elderly, well-dressed, well-spoken Englishman further along the table. 'It makes a pleasant change to see someone riding the tiger without falling off. Take some good advice: either ride your luck or get out while you're ahead – by which I mean play your own game in your own way. No offence, my dear,' he concluded, with a friendly smile to Sonia.

'I'll do just that,' promised Scott as he scooped up his winnings.

'Are you going to quit?' asked Sonia, seeing him hold back while the other players placed their bets.

'No,' he replied, 'I'm just thinking. Every fibre of my body is screaming for me to back thirty-six again.'

'That's absolutely ludicrous! You might just as well

throw your money away. The wager is against all possible odds. I couldn't even begin to calculate them.' But he was already reaching out to place a neat stack of ten blue chips on number thirty-six.

'That's why most people come here, isn't it?' he remarked. 'To play the odds. To challenge fate to take what they have or bestow on them riches beyond their wildest dreams.'

'Easy come, easy go,' she sighed in exasperation.

'No wonder people look upon the English as being half-crazy.'

'Only half?' he taunted, for the elderly man was reaching out to match his bet.

'Young man,' he volunteered as the other players gaped, 'somehow you inspire me to ride along with you.' And one by one they each placed a chip of varying denominations with his.

'We're all pulling for you,' said another. 'Good luck.'

The croupier swallowed hard. Knowing that the casino stood to lose close to a hundred thousand pounds if Scott's luck held, he turned to the mediator for advice; but their wagers were within the casino's limits, and he gave a curt nod to continue. When the croupier delved into his pocket for a handkerchief to wipe the perspiration from his brow and palms, the further delay incensed the crowd which had gathered round the table. Their silent vigil progressed into uneasy mutterings, increasing the tension. Patrons from further afield, sensing this, moved closer.

'Spin it,' someone growled, and as the croupier's hand reached out to spin the wheel, everyone kept one eye on him and one on the ivory ball. Gradually the blur of colour slowed and the numbers became more distinct. The clicking of the ball as it flicked in and out seemed very loud in the expectant silence.

When people at the rear used the shoulders of those in front for support as they craned their heads to see, there were mutterings of complaint, and when, finally, the ball came to rest, the crowd erupted.

Sonia threw her arms around Scott's neck, forcing him back, off balance, into the wall of bodies. 'You did it,' she cried, and guessing that if anything would draw Dieger and Sahara in from the balcony, it was the jubilant cries of the crowd, Scott planned his next move.

'We surely did!' he shouted, lifting her in a bear-hug. While gleeful pats of congratulation rained down on his back from those who had followed his lead, he spotted the elderly gentleman shouldering his way towards him.

'Congratulations and well done, my lad,' he beamed. 'I knew you would do it, the moment I laid eyes on you.'

'Thanks,' Scott smiled, shaking his hand. 'I guess it's my lucky day.'

'Have you any idea of the odds against such a wager?'

'No, I couldn't count that high,' Scott confessed, adding, as he spotted Dieger coming in from the balcony: 'You'll have to excuse me. All this excitement has brought on a call of nature.'

'But you can't break off now,' enthused the man. 'You're standing on the threshold of a phenomenon which anyone would consider himself lucky to witness, let alone be part of.'

'I wouldn't know much about that, not being an habitual gambler,' Scott confessed, 'and breaking the bank of Malta's only casino isn't my idea of having a good time. Being rich just doesn't mean that much to me. Now, if you will excuse me, I have to pay a visit.'

'Then pick out some numbers and let your young lady play for you while you're away,' the man persisted. Surveying the expectant faces around him, Scott could see that they believed every word of the elderly gambler's prediction. They were hungry: some for revenge, while others just wanted to witness the breaking of the bank.

'Okay, but don't blame me if you lose your shirts. Try number one, number nine, nineteen and ten.'

'How much shall I bet?' Sonia called after him as he turned away.

'Suit yourself,' he shouted back as the solid wall of players surrounded the table again. Moving quickly, he intercepted Dieger and Sahara just inside the balcony doors where they had stopped to watch the excitement from a distance.

'You had me worried for a minute,' admitted Dieger. 'What was that all about?'

'Just because I won a couple of times, some crank got it into his mind that I was the man to break the bank,' Scott scowled as the crowd erupted jubilantly again.

'Looks like someone is having a good try,' smiled Sahara, adding, when Scott asked Dieger for a word in private: 'You carry on. I think I'll go and watch the excitement.'

The fever had spread to such an extent that everyone was now taking an interest; even those tending the deserted bar had found something to stand on and were craning their heads to see.

'What's the problem?' asked Dieger.

'When we arrived I noticed two people paying particular attention to us,' explained Scott. 'A young woman dressed as an Amazon and a cave man. When I voiced my suspicions you said you had people covering us.'

'That's right but I didn't pay much attention to those you mentioned. What's bothering you about them?'

'The woman struck up a friendship with me. She's a detective.'

'Did she tell you that?' asked Dieger.

'Yes.'

'Has she asked any questions that might give a clue to what she's after?'

'Only what was I doing here and what did I do for a living,' he admitted. 'Not that I've given her much opportunity. Roulette's a fast game when you're winning.'

Seeing Dieger's gaze focus on the crowd surrounding the roulette table, Scott said accusingly: 'You think I'm cracking up, don't you?'

'I think I know you better than that,' said Dieger. 'I'm simply trying to justify the reasoning behind your fears in order to get to grips with what's going on.'

'My guess is that Sneider is the common denominator,' said Scott. 'He was a pain in the butt at Gatwick airport before we left England, on the flight here and when we arrived. If they think I had something to do with his death and have been checking on me, they'll have found out that I'm working for you – and now, assuming that they are aware of who Sahara is, they'll have linked us to her.'

'Has she mentioned anything about Sneider or ski-cycle

racing?' asked Dieger, as the roulette players erupted again.

'No, but she hasn't yet had the chance. And just for the record, was news of Sneider's death made public? I'd hate to be drawn into a conversation about him, only to find out that it wasn't.'

'No. I found out by accident. The newspapers only reported that the body of a man with a ski-cycle tattooed on his chest had been fished out of the Grand Harbour. The problem is how to warn Sahara without letting her know we suspect that she was behind Sneider's death.'

'Since I seem to be the link between them, perhaps it would be wise for me to disappear,' suggested Scott.

'Maybe we all should,' mused Dieger. 'If they start digging they might start wondering what the connection is between a drugs queen and an international arms dealer. I'll have to make her aware that we're under surveillance before we go, though. Get yourself a drink and be ready to make a move as soon as I say.'

'I'll have to get myself disentangled from Sonia first. She took my place at the roulette table and if I'm not mistaken, she has increased my winnings considerably – which reminds me: I'd better go and pay that visit, if only for appearance's sake.'

The men's room was large and spacious. Huge mirrors were set in marble tiled walls above matching washbasins. Even the urinals and toilet cubicles had been constructed to give maximum privacy with added luxury, and a self-contained bathroom was provided for those who cared to freshen up during their marathons at the tables.

Standing before one of the large mirrors, Scott noticed a smudge of white powder on the shoulder of his dark suit. A casual flick only made the smudge spread, so he tugged the ornate folded handkerchief from his breast pocket to dust the powder away. As it came free, a small, square fold of paper fluttered to the floor, and his blood froze as he bent down for it. He had no need to taste the fine white powder: he knew what it was. And there were only two people who had been close enough to insert it into his pocket without his knowledge.

Filled with a deep, cold anger he left the men's room to

find Dieger, who stood with Sahara at the bar, watching the hysteria at the roulette table.

'Why do you look so solemn?' mocked Sahara.

'With good reason,' he replied coldly, thrusting out his open palm. 'I've just found this in my pocket. It wasn't there when I dressed, and only two people have been close enough to have put it there since then: you and Sonia.'

'You're not suggesting that I put it there, are you?' she flared back in a harsh whisper.

'That would be too simple,' put in Dieger. 'Scott has been riddled with a phobia of being watched ever since we arrived. This proves that something is about to go down. What, or for what reason, I don't know. And I'm not about to wait around to find out. You'd better cash in your chips.'

'It might be a good idea if you both went to powder your noses before we leave,' suggested Scott. 'You might find that you're carrying, too.'

With some misgivings he shouldered his way through the crowd to where Sonia sat at the table. Neat stacks of multi-coloured playing chips stood in front of her.

'You've won a fortune,' she beamed.

'Thank God you've come back,' interrupted the elderly player. 'Haven't won a thing since your numbers ran out.'

'Sorry about that,' replied Scott coldly. 'Maybe you should cut and run while you're ahead. That's what I intend doing. Shall we cash in?' he asked, turning to Sonia. The eager, expectant faces of those who had increased their fortunes soured a little.

'Have you got something to put these in?' asked Sonia, searching his face for a clue to his iciness. Without thinking, he reached for the handkerchief in his breast pocket. A flicker of fear reflected briefly in her eyes. When his hand froze, she instinctively looked up at him, and in that moment she knew he had found her out.

'I think it's time that we had ourselves a little chat,' he said quietly, shaking the folds of his handkerchief.

'About what?' she said uncertainly.

'About small white packets which mysteriously find their way into people's pockets,' he replied. 'And don't bother denying it. The truth is written all over your face.

250

Apart from that, there's a witness,' he lied.

'Could we talk about this over a drink?' she asked, and his cold, curt nod drew a strange smile of relief from her.

At the cashier's cage he showed his appreciation: 'Deduct a blue chip for each of the croupiers and bar staff. Divide the rest into two equal cheques: one payable to Mr James Scott, the other to Miss Sonia Blessed.'

'No,' she protested, 'my bosses would . . .'

'Do it,' he ordered, cutting her off. 'We'll be at the bar. I'd appreciate it if you would be kind enough to bring our cheques over when you're ready.'

Giving her no chance to argue, he guided her towards the bar where they sat alone. Dieger and Sahara were nowhere to be seen, but he guessed that Dieger would not be far away.

'I'll have a G and T with plenty of ice and a slice. The lady,' he added, 'will have a large tonic with plenty of ice.' As the barman turned away, Scott continued with heavy sarcasm: 'I take it that you're still on duty?' She met his accusing eyes, but failed to find the words to answer. 'So, what have you to say for yourself?' he hissed angrily, tossing the tiny packet of white powder on to the bar-top. 'Is it normal practice for the Maltese police to get convictions by fitting up innocent people? Is that how you boost your tally of arrests to justify your existence?'

'No,' she snapped, 'it's how we are sometimes forced to react when high-powered criminals come here to ply their trade and corrupt our people.'

'And the Maltese government condones such actions!'

'No,' she admitted. 'I was acting on my own. I'll be dismissed if I'm found out.'

'So, why don't you tell me your problem?' he invited, mellowing a little. 'Maybe I can dispel some of your fears.'

She gave him a look of disgust as the barman placed their drinks on the bar. 'Get rid of that,' she told Scott, pushing the tiny packet towards him. 'Flush it down the sink.' But before he could reply, a cashier approached.

'Your cheques,' he said, 'and the staff send their thanks for your generosity.'

'You're welcome,' said Scott, offering Sonia the cheque made out to her.

'I can't accept it. It wouldn't look good in the eyes of my superiors.'

Scott glanced down at the cheque and saw it was for £64,500. 'There must be a hundred witnesses to prove how you came by it,' he argued, 'and since you came by it honestly, it can't be misconstrued as a bribe. As for getting the sack because of it – well, with that kind of money tucked away for a rainy day, I don't suppose it would cause much hardship.'

'Why should you care, after what I tried to do to you?'

'It's not a question of caring one way or the other. It's a question of splitting my winnings with the person who helped me win. Now, for the other thing. I'm rather curious to find out what's been going on in that pretty little head of yours. How about an explanation?'

She took the cheque and studied it for a long time before speaking. 'You arrived here with a man called Sneider,' she said at last. 'And are you aware of the fact that he . . .' she paused for a moment to give her next statement more credence, '. . . was tortured to death: murdered, by degrees, for the information he refused to divulge?'

There was no way he could feign surprise. 'I read about a man with a tattoo, like Sneider had, being fished out of the Grand Harbour, but I had no idea that he'd been tortured.'

'You didn't get on too well with him,' she said. 'Your arguments on the flight here are a matter of record.'

'All that was a sham,' he informed her. 'A publicity stunt. We often raced on our ski-cycles for high stakes. His needling me was no more than you see between two professional boxers on the screen, to boost the public's interest and increase the purse.'

'There has never been mention of any such race to my knowlege,' she countered.

'The challenge was to be made after a great deal more aggravation had taken place, but unfortunately he disappeared from the scene before the gauntlet could be thrown down.'

'Why couldn't you just declare that you were going to have a race? And why come to Malta for it anyway?'

252

'You don't just come to a place like this to have a race: it's nowheresville. I doubt if a proper racing ski-cycle has ever been seen here before. An atmosphere has to be created, and sponsors like Dieger and Sahara don't finance the likes of me and Sneider just for the fun of it. They do it for profit as well as pleasure.'

'But why here?' she persisted.

'You should ask that! Look around,' he invited. 'What do you see? Rich people who love to gamble, and calm seas which are perfect for our type of racing. If Dieger, Sahara or I had any motive at all concerning Sneider, it would have been to keep him alive.'

'I'm not sure that I believe you, but I apologize for planting the heroin on you. I had wild thoughts of having you arrested for possession and making you talk under interrogation. It might be a good idea if you found your friends and left the casino now. We know that many people are using drugs at the party and there's a raid planned immediately after the firework display.'

'Fireworks and more fireworks. It seems a shame to let all that excitement go to waste. Why don't we meet later and make a night of it?' he suggested.

'If things go as I expect, I'll be spending the rest of the night carrying out investigations and taking statements, but there's a carnival over at Rabat tomorrow night. You could take me to see that.'

'You've got yourself a date,' he agreed. 'But please put some clothes on – a man can only handle so much!'

10

Sahara soon found out that Sneider's death was a mistake, and to have expected the Maltese police to treat her with the misplaced respect that she received from those back home in Colombia was an even bigger one. The morning after the party she was questioned about being seen riding on Sneider's ski-cycle and managed to lie her way out of what could have been a disastrous situation. Another miscalculation was thinking that she could discover Dieger's secret method of making guaranteed deliveries of drugs to anywhere in the world: the spy she had sent on board the Atlantic Mirage had returned empty-handed, and Scott used Sonia to keep her at a distance until her premature departure.

Dieger spent most of his time on board the Atlantic Mirage pushing the workforce, but when they set sail three days' later, much of the modification work was still in progress. Although this meant that all hands had to work extra duties under the guidance of the engineers, it also removed the boredom from the ship's routine and helped form a genuine bond between the crew. Dieger himself seemed to revel in getting his hands dirty, which earned him the crew's deepest respect.

After cruising for three days and two nights at half speed, the ship was hardly recognisable. The tonnes of old iron and the winches, with their wire hawsers, had been jettisoned into the sea; the decks and super-structure had been de-scaled and the whole ship freshly painted.

Late on the third evening there was an air of excitement on the bridge where Pike kept a constant watch. The night was warm and the brightness of the moon reflected off the calm waters of the Mediterranean to the clear sky. Way over the horizon a golden dome of light mushroomed above the city of Algiers.

'Latitude thirty-six degrees, nine minutes north; longitude seven degrees east. ETA fifteen minutes,' Pike informed Dieger. 'Our supply ship is just over the horizon, sir.'

'Thank you, Mr Pike. All engines stop. I'll stand by up here – you take care of the loading.'

'Yes, sir,' and Pike's large fist hauled the brass telegraph handle back and forth twice. The harsh ringing echoed on the bridge, along with the bell sounding the warning in the noisy engine room below. Seconds later the chief engineer confirmed the order by repeating it on the engine room telegraph.

As the ship cruised slowly to a stop, with a familiar throbbing rumble, it seemed to acquire a strange eeriness. When Pike left the bridge to carry out his duties, Scott joined Dieger. 'It looks as though we'll be under starter's orders pretty soon. Sometimes I can hardly believe that all this is happening to me. It's almost as if I'm living two lives.'

'There are times when I wish that could be possible,' replied Dieger. 'Sometimes I really crave for a life of obscurity; to be a Mr nobody with a dumpy little wife and a couple of kids – just popping into one of your British pubs. It sounds like heaven.'

'It feels about that far away, too. Don't you ever take a few months off, to get away from all this?'

'Every year, just like the average Joe. The only difference is that I'm not like the average Joe. I haven't taken a wife because not only would she be at risk, considering my work, but I'd hardly ever get to see her, anyway. When it comes to friends – well, you don't make many in this business. At least, not the kind you would want to spend a long holiday with.'

'What do you do for relaxation then?'

'Oh, I've got a place tucked away in the hills, back home,' said Dieger thoughtfully. 'It's isolated and there's plenty of hunting. There's one of those woodsy outback towns not far away where a man can really let his hair down without getting coast-to-coast news coverage of his misdemeanours.'

'Looks like we have company,' Scott observed, as a distant craft came over the horizon. 'Moving at high speed.'

A faint smile of satisfaction creased Dieger's brow. 'That will be your brainchild, the fast attack craft. She'll be standing by while the other equipment is loaded. I'm going to be tied up with communications and the like up here but you can go down and watch if you want.'

Sensing that Dieger had things to take care of that he preferred no one else knew about, Scott took his invitation as a polite request and made his way down to the massive docking well. The great stern doors were already open and it had been flooded in readiness to receive its cargo. A hundred yards away was the fast attack craft and beyond that, at a distance of two miles, an Aldis lamp flickered briefly. Minutes later he picked out the dark, squat shapes of four large amphibious landing craft. They forged a passage towards him and two Sea Knight helicopters came in low, large containers suspended beneath them. For several minutes the gentle hum of the ship's generators was shattered by the loud roar of their engines as they hovered, discharging their loads.

Within minutes of their departure, the first of the landing craft entered the docking well. Its four-man crew were dressed in camouflage fatigues and were evidently well-acquainted with their work.

Looking like large, steel, motorised barges, some sixty feet in length, the craft cruised to the forward end of the docking well. Here the first and third ones were loaded into massive lifts which hauled them to stack several feet above the second and fourth ones. The moment they were secure, the crews disembarked and made their way down to the gallery that served as a quay when the loading dock was flooded. An inflatable craft with a powerful outboard motor zoomed in to pick them up, and left again without making any apparent contact with the ship's crew. As it sped off into the night, the fast attack craft nosed in and the stern doors closed behind it with a resounding 'boom'.

Voices began to call back and forth, shouting orders or

instructions, both from on board and from the various galleries. Like veterans, the two crews secured her moorings as she was gently lowered into the purpose-made cradles fitted to the docking well's deck, clamping the hull tight in preparation for the long sea voyage.

During all this activity, Scott cast his eyes over her sleek lines, noting with a certain amount of awe that all of the armaments – which included two 40mm Bofors guns on the forward deck – were still intact.

'She's a powerful-looking craft.' Scott turned to find Pike standing at his side. 'How does it feel to have something like this coming together?'

'I'm not sure,' Scott replied. 'Looking at her gives me a feeling that I can't quite come to grips with.'

'How do you mean?'

For a few moments Scott remained silent, searching for the words to transform his fears into a reasonable explanation of how he felt. Pike sensed his inhibitions and his own mind flashed back, recalling battle scenes which had imprinted their torment forever in his memory. From the battle-weary GIs who had turned to drugs in order to blot out the unending horrors of war, he moved to the slaughter of his entire family, which had happened because of their rivalry and trafficking in drugs. In an attempt to convey his understanding, he gently placed his great paw-like hand on Scott's shoulder.

'At a guess I would say that you've never been to war,' he said quietly, 'and I pray to God that you never have to. By the same token you must try to understand the feelings of those of us who have. What you are looking at is a tool of war which is about to be used to fight a war for which it was never intended. Generally speaking, anyone trading in drugs can just walk away any time he or she chooses. Unfortunately, their victims can't. They are stuck with a craving they can't cope with. Mothers will sell their bodies – and those of their children – in order to get money for drugs; fathers will do likewise. When there's nothing left to sell they turn against society to rob and pillage and very often murder, while the people we are after live in absolute luxury at their expense. Do yourself a favour. When you look at those guns and wonder about the carnage and pain they might inflict, try to imagine the effect if we were really working for the Mafia. At the rate of one trip a month, delivering a minimum of a hundred tonnes of the stuff, I dread to think what the results would be.'

Scott felt deeply touched. In all the time he had known Pike, he had never shown this compassionate side of himself, or such gentleness.

'What bothers me most at this particular moment,' he replied defensively, 'is what damage our first hundred tonnes will cause,' but Pike came straight back with an answer that seemed to echo Dieger's teachings.

'Look at it like a day's fishing,' he advised. 'You bait your hook and cast out your line. When the fish bites you haul him in: hook, line, bait and all. Sure, a few get away, but they're caught eventually because they can't resist the bait. Let's face it, the fish we're after don't come any bigger. Once our hooks are into the Mafia and we've wiped out the bulk of the main producers, trafficking in drugs is going to fall flat on its can.'

Before Scott could answer, a loud, shrieking scream rent the air, and all activity ceased as heads turned in search of the cause. The distance was too great to recognize faces, but high up, on the topmost galleries, several men surrounded a denim-clad figure who was backed up against the guard-rail overlooking the docking well above the landing craft. A torrent of long, golden hair hung over into space as she leaned back in fear of the hungry faces taunting her.

'Jesus Christ!' he muttered. 'It's Sonia.' Fearing that her panic might result in a fall, he and Pike raced up the iron stairways and the long galleries. Pike burst through the tight circle of men to confront them and Sonia flung her arms around Scott's neck.

'Thank God you came,' she sobbed as Pike's gruff voice rang out.

'Okay, the fun's over,' he growled. 'Back to work. You've all seen the female species before.'

'Yeah,' sneered one of the burly sailors, who seemed to be the ringleader, 'but not on board a ship where they have no right to be. Give her to us and we'll see that she

258

keeps what she has seen to herself.'

Sonia shuddered and tightened her grip around Scott's neck. Despite the situation he enjoyed the feel of her against him, but cringed at the ugliness of the sailor's reaction to authority.

'Move it,' demanded Pike, and took a stride forward. His great fist came up like a sledgehammer to catch the sailor squarely on the jaw. The man's head jerked back violently but his body remained unmoved. Raising his hand to touch his jaw he fixed Pike with a deadly glare.

'I figure you owe me for that,' he rasped.

'You know the procedure,' snarled Pike in return.

'Put your name on the list and join the queue along with anyone else who feels he has a grudge.'

'You've got it,' leered the sailor before turning away.

'Now, young lady,' growled Pike, turning to Sonia. 'Suppose you explain your presence here.'

Scott answered for her. 'We were dating back in Malta.'

'Ah, the long arm of the law,' he mocked. 'I'm afraid you're a shade outside your jurisdiction here. I think the Captain will be interested to hear about this.'

Scott nodded and followed Pike, with Sonia at his side.

'What will they do to me?' she whispered.

'I really don't know. What on God's green earth were you thinking about when you stowed away? Surely you must have realized there was no way you could stay hidden for long? It's not as though you could blend in with the crew to get food or exercise?'

'You haven't asked the next important question yet,' put in Pike, without turning round. 'Why did she stow away on this particular ship? If she wanted to travel, finance was not a problem from what I hear.'

'No, but the man I love happens to be on this one, and since it carries no passengers, stowing away seemed the only way of being with him.'

'Love may be blind,' agreed Pike, 'but I'm afraid you may have seen too much for your own good. This is one of those times when I don't envy the man who makes the decisions.'

'If you're referring to your clandestine meetings at sea and your secret arms deals, they mean nothing to me,' she assured him. 'In fact, from what we hear, you Americans are always supplying secret shipments to the Arab countries.'

Stopping at the door to Dieger's quarters, Pike said: 'You'd better make yourselves at home in here. I'll inform Dieger of the situation and no doubt he'll be with you soon.' Looking at Scott, he added: 'Don't expect too much.'

They went inside and when the door closed behind Pike Sonia swung into Scott's arms, kissing him passionately. He returned her fire, recalling better times in Malta.

'I love you,' she whispered, breaking free.

'I love you too. Let's hope that Dieger will believe that's enough.'

'What do you mean, enough?'

'This isn't a pleasure cruise. Our mission is not quite as it appears. Beyond that, I can't tell you a thing.'

'What's going on?' she persisted. 'I can guess what's in those barges, and even the presence of that boat in the hold doesn't surprise me. What does is your reaction to my being here. I can almost smell the fear oozing out of you. What are you afraid of?'

'For the moment,' he said firmly, 'the less I say to you the better. Why don't we have ourselves a drink and be patient? Dieger won't be long now that we're under way.'

'Is it normal for crew members to help themselves to the Captain's cocktails?'

'No, but I'm not a member of the crew. What'll you have?'

'A large brandy would do wonders for my nerves,' she admitted. 'If you're not a member of the crew, perhaps the Captain could put us ashore. Would you like that?'

'It's not a case of what I would like, even if he did agree. I have a purpose in life which I intend seeing brought to a proper conclusion at any cost.'

'Even at the cost of losing me?' she pouted.

'I told you I'd be coming back,' he hedged. 'You should have been patient.'

'You make my presence here sound – well, almost like a death sentence that's hanging in the balance.'

'Quite,' said Dieger from the open door. 'You're a very

persistent lady.'

'What is it the English say?' she said. 'Fools rush in where wise men fear to tread.'

'A very interesting saying as it happens,' he replied smugly. 'How did you manage to get on board without being seen?'

'I sneaked on after Scott and I said goodbye,' she replied readily. 'I tucked my hair into a cap and mingled with some crew members coming back on board.'

'Did you bring any clothes or food? You must be starving after all this time.'

'Just a single change in a duffle bag,' she admitted, 'and yes, I am starving.'

'Why don't you pop down to the galley and get something to eat?' he suggested.

'You're not mad at me for stowing away?' she asked in surprise.

'It does pose a problem,' he admitted. 'It's out of the question to send you ashore but it would be just as bad to let you remain on board. Your movements will be very restricted, I'm afraid. The crew's recreation rooms, their quarters, places of work – specifically the docking well and the bridge – must be no-go areas for you.'

Her face clouded for a moment and then brightened again. 'All I ask is to be with Scott,' she smiled.

'Glad to hear it,' grinned Dieger. 'Welcome aboard.'

Dieger sent her off to get something to eat, after which, he promised, he'd have sorted out a cabin for her. Dieger looked at Scott, who felt a coldness between them which had never been there before. They both knew that Sonia was just using him, but for what purpose remained to be seen.

The moment Dieger was alone he called Pike on the telephone. 'I want her watched night and day,' he said, 'particularly at night. If she is here on somebody else's behalf, she'll probably need some means of communicating with them. Scour the ship for a hidden transmitter. Start with the lifeboats and work down.'

'Your personal launch has a radio,' Pike pointed out.

'Get the chief radio officer to rig a tape to it and check it personally every day. I can't imagine her being so foolish as to leave anything incriminating in her cabin. Check it out anyway, at regular intervals. If she is seen using the radio I don't want her stopped until I give the order. Is that clear? She's to be protected against accidental discovery by unwitting crew members until we find out exactly why she's here.'

'At any cost?' queried Pike.

Dieger thought for a moment about that. 'Within reason – use your discretion.'

'Do you want me to get on to headquarters to see if they can dig anything up on her?' offered Pike.

'Get the duty radio officer on to it right away, and bring me the report as soon as you have it.'

After finishing with Pike, Dieger rang Soames, the chief steward, saying politely that he hoped he hadn't disrupted his sleep.

'You're joking,' replied Soames caustically. 'I've just got in after a hassle with the gunboat crew.'

'What's the problem with them?'

'Your instructions to provide accommodation neglected to inform me that they were all Vietnamese,' he complained. 'I allocated them a mess room of their own and laid on staff to cater for them. They had a steak meal after settling in but the trouble is they're not used to the same diet as us, and I had to detail an assistant cook to liaise with one of them to draw their own rations from the stores each day so that they can cook for themselves.'

'My apologies,' said Dieger. 'I never gave it a thought.'

With that settled, Soames asked what was the present problem.

'If you haven't already heard,' explained Dieger, 'we have a lady stowaway. She'll need a cabin and some clothes.'

'I heard, but all my dresses are at the cleaners,' he chuckled. 'Maybe some of my staff can help out – the sex of one or two is questionable. Is there any truth in the rumour that it's that gorgeous blonde that Scott was sparking?'

'It is. Can you fix her up with some denims or something?'

'Sure. I'll take her down to the stores and she can help

herself. As for the cabin, I thought she'd move in with Scott. After all, their love life in Malta was no secret.'

'I don't want to assume that,' Dieger replied. 'In fact, I very much doubt if she'd appreciate our assuming it.'

'Do I detect a hint of something in your tone?' Soames asked. 'Mistrust, for instance?'

'Let's just say that I'm not entirely happy with what her motives might be for being here. If she's as passionately in love with Scott as she claims to be, the farthest she is going to sneak out at night will be to his cabin.'

'Why not encourage her to move in so that he can keep an eye on her?' suggested Soames.

'Because the more difficult it is for her to move about, the longer it's going to take us to find out the truth. As a precaution, you'd better warn your staff to be wary of her questions. I'd like to know of anything they might feel would be of interest.'

'If you're that concerned, I'll assign her a personal steward.'

'That would be much appreciated. Have him report to me each morning, starting tomorrow.'

When Soames corrected him, with a touch of sarcasm, saying, 'You mean today,' Dieger took the hint with a sly grin and replaced the telephone – only to have it ring again at once.

'Dieger,' he said wearily.

'Jackson, sir. You said to keep you informed of the small radar contact which appears to have been shadowing us since leaving Malta. It closed in during our rendezvous to a distance of twenty-five miles, then remained stationary. No one on board could have seen anything from that distance but it's now closed in to about ten miles abreast of our starboard side and is keeping pace.'

'Are you sure it's the same contact?'

'Yes, sir. It's a yacht. You can see it quite clearly through binoculars from the bridge.'

'I want it kept under constant surveillance,' ordered Dieger. 'We're looking for a possible communication by Aldis lamp, probably a pre-arranged signal and maybe no more than a single flash in response to one from this vessel. I don't suppose you've been able to establish any identification as yet?'

'No, sir. It's too far away,' replied Jackson. 'Nor have we managed to intercept any transmissions from her.'

'Well, stick with it. If our stowaway does communicate from here, they might just pass it on to a third party.'

'You wouldn't have any idea who that might be?' asked Jackson. 'It could make monitoring easier.'

Dieger thought about it for a moment. He had no doubt in his mind that Sonia was using Scott to find out what they were up to, and since she was now well beyond her limits of jurisdiction as a member of the Maltese police force, she had to be involved with some international organization. If it was one similar to the G Force, he'd have been informed, which left two likely alternatives.

'She could be working for Sahara Sediki,' he said at last, 'which means transmitting messages to Colombia. Or it could be the Mafia, in which case, we may well be suffering from the consequences of some sort of feedback from Stoddart's dealings with the Leone family in Palermo. It might be a good idea to check with head-quarters to see if they can dig up any connection between a Miss Sonia Blessed and the Leones, or any Mafia link.'

With a sigh, Dieger dimmed the lights and settled himself into an armchair with a large brandy. He sipped the amber liquid and twirled the remainder of its contents in the glass so that the ice clinked against the sides. Slowly the cube diminished as he pondered on the day's events. Wherever his mind wandered, it always came back to the sudden appearance of this stowaway and the yacht which was never far away on the radar.

His heavy-lidded eyes closed and the goblet fell silently on to the carpeted floor. In the realms of sleep, beautiful long-haired sirens beckoned with taunts of their beautiful bodies as the prize for leaving his chosen path. Squabbles among the crew progressed to violent fights which eventually divided them into two groups: those who stood behind Dieger and his beliefs, and those behind a faceless man who lusted after the sirens dallying close by. At a signal the two sides slowly advanced, hunched in readiness for battle. Then suddenly Dieger's faceless opponent broke ranks to challenge him with a machete, which

264

glinted in the cold light of the moon as he wielded it high above his head. Dieger charged forward, only to find that a long-haired siren who looked like Sonia had swept forward to smite down his attacker, and he stared at her in awe. Perspiration flowed in tiny rivulets down his face and his clothes stuck to his skin. The face of his attacker materialized as his voice boomed in protest.

'Jesus!' cried Pike, as Dieger came out of his chair like a rocket, fists at the ready. 'Hold on, it's me, Pike.' And Dieger stopped, eyes wide and staring, ready to launch himself at Pike who stood just inside the doorway. 'Take it easy,' he continued. 'You must have been having a bad dream.'

'Dieger began to relax and compose himself, wiping away the glistening perspiration from his face with his hands.

'I'm sorry if I gave you a fright,' he apologized.

'That's okay,' said Pike sombrely. 'I guess we all have our bad memories.'

'Do you believe in dreams?' asked Dieger, reaching for a cigarette.

'Only the ones that I can touch – preferably ones with plenty of front.'

Dieger drew hard on his cigarette, taking the smoke deep down into his lungs, as though it were his last.

'She certainly had plenty of that,' he gasped. 'Now, what can I do for you?'

Pike held out a sheet of paper. 'Just a report on our stowaway. This came over the radio about her.'

Dieger took the paper and began to read aloud: 'Sonia Blessed. One of twin girls born July 1st, 1958, Oxford, England. Tutored by father, Professor Reginald Large Blessed. Sister Sabrina overdosed on heroin, 1978. Sonia was with the Metropolitan Police at the time; left the force after being accused of planting half a kilo of heroin on Horace James Callan, a known pusher accused of supplying her sister with the fatal dose. Neither case proven but Callan went down for three years for possession. 1979 Sonia Blessed emigrated to Malta to escape retribution from Callan's friends, and joined the police force. 1980 married Alberto Pucci. 1982 Alberto jailed for ten years for possession of two kilos of cocaine. Divorced 1983. Husband claimed wife set him up. September 1986 she resigned from the Maltese police. Now being sought for questioning in connection with the misappropriation of two kilos of heroin, missing from the strong-room in the Valletta police station.'

'Her presence here doesn't take much working out,' remarked Pike.

Dieger agreed. 'But it does give us food for thought,' he went on. 'Our manifest states that we're running in ballast to Santa Marta in Colombia where we shall pick up a cargo of high grade coffee beans. Let's suppose that she knows we're going to pick up cocaine there, and hopes to betray us when we make the delivery. She can't guarantee that we'll allow her to stay on board that long. If she did, there wouldn't be any point in her planting the heroin on this ship as we left Malta. So she must be banking on us making an unscheduled stop where the charge of trafficking against us would bear some weight without harming her too much.'

'Gibraltar,' suggested Pike.

'That's my guess. Which brings us to how she can guarantee that we'll dock there.'

'Sickness – a fake appendix, or something like that.'

'Something a little more Draconian, I think. Something that would guarantee a docking or beaching at least.'

'An explosion that would hole the hull or a fire that would cripple us?'

'Since she had no idea that we were about to pick up a dangerous cargo, you could be right – in which case she has probably planted a device of some sort in the docking well where she was found. Now she knows that the docking well is loaded with a dangerous cargo, she's going to have to move it or run the risk of blowing herself up along with us. That is, of course, if she hasn't already moved it.'

'No chance,' Pike assured him. 'She hasn't been able to go to the john in privacy since we discovered her. You want I should have the docking well searched?'

'Yes, but if you find anything don't remove it. Just make it safe and install a video camera out of sight to watch over it. We'll work on the theory of letting her re-site it before tossing it over the side. By the time she realizes the truth, we'll be out in the north Atlantic.'

'Surely you're not going to keep her on board throughout the mission, are you?' asked Pike.

'I'm open to suggestions.'

'You could have some of our own people meet us as we go through the Straits of Gibraltar and take her into custody – or even leave her on some remote island.'

Dieger's face looked thoughtful for a few moments, before breaking into a sly grin. 'She's a gutsy little broad, isn't she?' he smiled. 'I suppose we could do worse than recruit her into our ranks. At least it would keep her quiet.'

Pike grimaced. 'No comment. And she isn't so little, as I recall.'

'It would solve a lot of problems,' Dieger pointed out. 'Invite her and Scott to have breakfast in my quarters in half an hour. You can join us, if you've a mind to.'

'Problems I've already got,' Pike groaned, turning away.

'By the way, is that yacht still shadowing us?' asked Dieger.

'No, it headed off towards Spain a couple of hours' ago. There was no sign of any attempt to communicate with anyone on board here – or anywhere else, if it comes to that.'

After a leisurely shower, Dieger found that his elusive steward had laid out a complete change of underwear and a fresh set of tropical whites. The chink of cutlery and china filtered through from his day room, and the appetizing aroma of percolating coffee, bacon and eggs filled the air.

'That smell never ceases to make my mouth water,' he said to his personal steward.

'Mine too,' the steward replied, 'and I've already eaten more than my fair share. I hope your guests won't leave it too long, or the eggs will be spoiled. Will you have coffee while you wait, sir?'

'No, the grapefruit looks about my mark. You carry on: I'll help myself and my guests can do the same.' With a glass of cold, refreshing juice in one hand, Dieger lifted the silver-domed lids and the steamy aromas filled the cabin. On the first platter were a dozen freshly fried eggs surrounded by three large, succulent ham omelettes. The second was filled with crisp rashers of thinly-sliced bacon surrounded by larger rashers of lean back bacon and small griddled lambs' kidneys. Another was heaped with sweet-breads and tomatoes. A selection of individual packets of cereals, cold milk, coffee, toast, marmalade and preserved fruits completed the array.

'Come in,' he called in answer to a knock on the door.

Pike poked his head in. 'We've found the heroin and what appears to be a time bomb of some description,' he said. 'Kolme reckons it's safe. Do you still want them left?'

'Yes, just keep a man watching them. It will be interesting to see what she does with them if she accepts my offer.'

'I've had your launch radio set up and I've instructed the radio officers to listen in on any calls made from it and to jam any transmissions that might prove embarrassing for us.'

'Good. Are you sure you don't want to stay for breakfast? There's enough here to feed half the damn ship's crew.'

Pike considered for a moment. The thought of a woman like Sonia on a ship dominated by men of the calibre of their crew was not pleasing, for her beautiful body was bound to cause problems if she were allowed to display it without restrictions. From this point of view he should remain distant and aloof so that he could speak his mind to the lady without prejudice. On the other hand, he understood and feared that the same beauty might blind Dieger's judgement, or serve to hide her true thoughts during their expected confrontation.

'Well, I haven't eaten yet,' he said grudgingly, 'and if I don't make myself unavailable, I can't see me stopping this side of supper time.'

'What you really mean is that you're caught between a tight spot and a hard place,' smiled Dieger, reading his thoughts. 'She's just too beautiful to be trusted; isn't that the truth?'

'Near enough,' Pike grinned back.

'Come,' Dieger called as there came another knock on the door. Scott leaned in to push it open, and then withdrew to allow Sonia to enter first. She was wearing tight denim shorts and a white, short-sleeved shirt which left little to the imagination. Pike's expression was bland, giving her the feeling of impending doom, but Dieger's face lit up with a bright smile which reflected his appreciation of her beauty, and she consequently felt more at ease with him.

'This is Mr Pike,' he beamed, 'my first officer.'

'Pleased to meet you,' she smiled, meeting Pike's direct stare, 'and thank you for looking after me last night. I dread to think what those men might have done if you hadn't come along to save me.'

'What might have happened then is nothing to what might happen after they've been at sea for a while,' he said darkly. 'They're a rough handful at the best of times.'

'Come now, Pike,' soothed Dieger, 'they're not so bad. Shall we serve ourselves?' he continued, turning back to Sonia with a smile.

'I'm easily pleased,' she told him pleasantly. 'Fruit juice, one slice of buttered toast and white coffee – otherwise I'll get fat.'

'So be it. You'll excuse us if we indulge, I hope?' While both Dieger and Scott helped themselves to a breakfast of omelette, four rashers of bacon and kidneys, Pike heaped his plate high.

'I hope you'll forgive my bluntness,' said Sonia, 'but I have a feeling that your invitation to breakfast here in the privacy of your own cabin was more of a royal command.'

'Well, there are things to talk about which are better said in the privacy of my cabin,' he admitted and took out the report on her. 'As you're aware, we are carrying a shipment of what many people might construe as contraband arms. It is also possible that some rebel Arab organization may have persuaded you to join our ship so that you could previl upon us to hand over the cargo to them. An act of piracy, in fact.'

'You're joking,' she laughed. 'How could I, a woman alone, persuade you and your crew to do anything against your will?'

'The threat of a time bomb hidden where it could cripple the ship might help?' he remarked, handing her the report.

'You're well informed,' she said when she read it, 'but after my efforts to frame Scott at the casino, I'd have thought this would be self-explanatory.'

'Oh, it is,' he agreed. 'The death of your sister has obviously inspired in you the need to wipe out these drug dealers whenever or wherever you're able – and as far as you're concerned, the end justifies the means.'

'I'd sell my soul to the devil to put just one away in prison if that's what it takes,' she admitted with some passion. 'But why should that give you cause for concern?'

'You didn't just happen to be in the casino. You were primed and waiting for us,' Dieger said accusingly.

'That's not quite true,' she argued. 'The raid had been planned weeks ahead, but then, quite by chance, I recognized Sahara Sediki and knew her for what she was. After I saw her virtually seducing the man called Sneider I began to wonder if she was planning to use him to smuggle drugs into Malta from Sicily. It's only ninety-three kilometres away, and the ski-cycle would be much more difficult to detect than a powerboat or yacht. In an effort to prove my theory I approached him with an offer that was similar to the one I thought she might have made. He laughed in my face but despite that we became friends. I continued to badger him in the hope of finding out the connection between them, and eventually he told me that he'd come to Malta hoping to seal the deal of the century.

'I began to check on every visitor and Scott was an obvious suspect since they travelled there together and shared an interest in ski-cycle racing. As he was staying on board this vessel, it was easy to link him to you. Anyway, Sneider let slip that Sahara was interested in where you were and when you were expected to arrive. Although I wasn't aware that you were going to the casino, I did know that she'd be there and hoping to meet you. We also knew that Mohammed, who's a big wheel in the drugs world, was going, so apart from being drawn to Scott I had already singled him out as my best chance of gaining more information.'

270

'That's all very interesting,' admitted Dieger, 'but it doesn't explain why you stowed away on my ship – and please spare me any more of this "love at first sight" talk,' he added bluntly.

Her eyes flicked to Pike's face for a moment and the look in those beady eyes made her squirm and feel unclean. As she shifted her weight in the chair her leg came into contact with his and she quickly withdrew it as though she'd been stung. Her eyes immediately returned to his face as she offered a polite apology. If anything, she thought him to be ugly – yet his touch excited her in a way that she had not experienced before.

Feeling slightly off balance but believing that she still had the advantage, she answered Dieger.

'I knew that you had a meeting with Sahara and I believe that you agreed on a deal to purchase a large amount of cocaine, although I'm not so sure about the arms. They could be her price for the cocaine, I suppose. As for my objective, I had hoped to gain your confidence. Then, when my fears were proved, I planned to report you to the authorities at the first opportunity.'

'And how would you expect to do that?'

'You have a radio room. I was going to lure the duty officer to where I could render him unconscious and then use your radio to pass on the information,' she lied.

'You do realize that you've said enough to get you killed, don't you?' Dieger pointed out.

'Only if my assumptions are correct.'

It was checkmate. A smile teased his eyes when he realized that she had manoeuvred him to a point where he had three options: to let her remain on board, either as a passenger or a captive, and hope to hide their smuggling activities from her; to put her ashore with her suspicions, which could have serious repercussions; or, if they were the criminals she judged them to be, go to the extreme of eliminating her permanently.

Pike, chewing a grilled kidney, watched them blandly, knowing that Dieger was nobody's fool. He was about to reveal their true mission to her. He knew that if she wished them harm, then sooner or later she would use the radio or the bomb, or both.

'Have you heard of the G Force?' he asked.

'Only vague rumours which remained just that, despite my efforts to track them down,' she admitted. 'Personally I think they are a myth, invented by certain governments in the hope of frightening the barons out of business – or at least reducing their dealings by making them more cautious.'

'From your form sheet, I'd imagine that a woman of your calibre would be a great asset to such an organization,' said Dieger smoothly. 'So far you have planted evidence, married a suspect in order to get evidence against him, used your obvious charms and now placed your life in jeopardy – just for the privilege of finding out information which you may never live to pass on.'

'There are people who know where I am and why I stowed away,' she argued. 'If I were to go missing you'd have an enquiry on your hands.'

'Many strange things happen at sea,' he retorted. 'Now, how do you feel about joining our happy little band? We are currently engaged in a contract to supply the Canadian and United States Mafia with a billion dollars' worth of cocaine.'

Her face blanched as she raised her hand to her throat. Somewhere in its depths she tried to clear it with a rasping sound as if she was choking.

'The only difference,' Dieger went on, 'is that we are the G Force and it is our mission to break them – and the likes of Sahara – in the process.' She gasped, looking from Scott to Pike and back to Dieger, her expression a mixture of fear, shock and disbelief. In those seconds she recalled the loading of their cargo of arms at sea, where alien eyes could discern neither their source nor the supplier. If they were the G Force it was reasonable to assume that those supplied had been authorised by the American Government and delivered by a vessel from the Seventh Fleet, which continually cruised the Mediterranean. On the other hand, it seemed out of character for such a force to enlist crewmen of the type who had caught her spying in the docking well after the loading was complete.

'I'm speechless,' she said at last. 'Of course I'd love to join you.'

272

'Welcome aboard,' grinned Dieger, raising his glass of fruit juice. 'Scott can explain our mission – and, of course, you may now have the freedom of the ship. Be wary of the crew on the lower decks, though; they're a rough bunch with a rough job ahead, so don't make any snap judgements about them.'

'Is that it?' she answered in surprise. 'Don't I have to be sworn in or something?'

'To what?' he smiled. 'Your own enquiries have already proved that the G Force doesn't exist. Now, if you will excuse us, Pike and I have to make our rounds to see that everything is shipshape.'

When they had gone, she said sheepishly: 'I don't know what to say. I'm thrilled to have been asked to join you but embarrassed that you've found out how I have used you.'

'Consider it to be water under the bridge,' said Scott simply. 'But if you have any ideas about letting the side down, I should give them a great deal of careful thought before doing so. Dieger can be a hard taskmaster when the need arises. He'll be watching you like an old cat watches a mouse: one wrong move and it's what he calls "room 101" for you.'

'What's that?'

'Death by the thing you fear most,' he warned, and she shivered.

'Don't you trust me?' she asked.

'It's not a case of what I think. I know Dieger and he's got something up his sleeve. You only have to prove to him that he's made a bad choice and he'll prove to you that he's smart enough to have allowed for it.'

'Don't worry. Whatever fears you may have about me, I'll show you they're without foundation – so long as you prove to be what you say you are. Now, are you going to tell me what this mission of yours is all about?'

'It's quite simple. We're heading for Colombia to pick up one hundred tons of cocaine from Sahara. From there we head for the United States and possibly Canada to deliver it to the Mafia. Once they have it, the G Force – or the relevant authorities – will gather enough evidence to prosecute them. But before news of that breaks, we'll return to Colombia, ostensibly to collect a second cargo but really to destroy Sahara's base of operations.'

'Surely someone is going to wonder how you're able to deliver such an amount with immunity when no one else could?' she argued.

'As you well know, somebody already did: Sahara had Sneider tortured to death to try to find out just that.'

'How do you plan to get it ashore?' she asked.

'The arms shipment isn't for sale,' he confessed. 'While this ship is hundreds of miles out to sea, the fast attack craft will leave it, head towards the coast, fire its torpedoes – whose warheads will be loaded with cocaine – and then return. G Force agents will then collect the torpedoes from the beaches and later hand over the cocaine to the Mafia.'

'God,' she whispered, 'that's an ingenious method. If an organization like the Mafia got wind of it and decided to cut you out, I dread to think of the consequences.'

'So now you know what's at stake,' said Scott, adding deliberately: 'Any treason from within the G Force will be dealt with without mercy.'

She reached across the table: 'I can understand that now. My mistrust of all of you caused me to take certain precautions. The only way I can think of at the moment to prove my loyalty is to tell you what I planned to do if you really were big-time smugglers. While I was with the Maltese police I went on a bomb disposal course – quite a lot of them from the Second World War are still being unearthed there. During that time I also learned how to make them – smaller ones, of course,' she smiled. 'I brought one with me to cripple the Atlantic Mirage so that it would have to be towed into port. Then I was going to inform the authorities of the whereabouts of two kilos of heroin which I also brought on board.'

Dieger turned from the close-circuit television monitor with which they were able to view almost all of the ship. 'Well, it looks as though we've won ourselves another agent,' he remarked.

'It does look that way,' replied Pike, with a trace of scepticism. 'Have you anything particular in mind for her?'

Dieger turned back to the screen. 'She's a beautiful

274

young woman, with a way of moving that stirs a man's blood – and she isn't opposed to using her assets to ensnare a victim. I was wondering if we could use Stoddart to get her introduced into the Mafia circle.'

'For what purpose?'

'A little pillow talk could give us a good insight to what's going on,' he mused. 'And another thing: as far as our Mafia friends are concerned, we have to somehow collect payment for the cocaine.'

'I thought Stoddart was going to accompany them while they put the diamonds into a safety deposit in each of the cities where we deliver. Then, when they receive the goods, all they need to do is hand over the key and we can collect at our convenience.'

'Precisely,' said Dieger, 'but I wonder what we could do to help our cause if we used those collections as a lure.'

'Sometimes I wonder about you,' reflected Pike. 'The line between the workings of the criminal mind and yours doesn't exist.'

'The tragedy is that if all those so-called criminals were to put their minds to doing something which would benefit mankind, instead of grabbing everything for themselves, the world's problems would be solved overnight.'

'There's no harm in dreaming, I suppose,' replied Pike caustically. 'Right now, though, I'd better get on with my rounds, or tonight's show won't get off the ground.'

'Show? What show?'

'Boxing, wrestling and the sod's opera,' he retorted impatiently. 'Don't you ever read my reports?'

'It slipped my mind. I suppose there will be the usual line of defaulters waiting to iron out their grievances with you?'

'You can bet on it. Don't expect me for lunch.'

Pike went back to the main bridge. He stopped to check their position and chat with the officer of the watch before walking the decks to see that the crew were carrying out their duties. On reaching the massive afterdeck, which covered the docking well, he stopped. The two Boeing Sea Knight helicopters had been secured to the port and starboard sides. With their rotors swept back and the sun glinting on their dark, tinted windows, they had an awesome, waspish look. Benches and a variety of chairs spread back on all sides from the boxing ring which was to double as a stage during the evening's entertainments.

The beefy sailor whom Pike had hit the previous night was being coached while sparring with another sailor. Seeing Pike watching, he threw a wild punch as though to intimidate him. The hit laid his partner low, provoking a grim smile from Pike as the coach vented his anger over the pointless act. Meeting the sailor's insolent glare with contempt, Pike took the time to light a cigarette, shielding the match's flame from the breeze with cupped hands before flicking it aside.

He waited as he watched Scott, clutching a package in one hand, escorting Sonia along the deck. 'Taking your constitutional?' he asked when they reached him.

'Not exactly. Sonia asked me to dispose of the heroin she brought on board. We were just about to throw it over the side.'

'Best place for it,' he remarked, noting that the package was too bulky to contain just heroin. Giving Scott a broad wink, he tactfully changed the subject. 'Are you coming to the sod's opera tonight?' he asked.

'What's that?' enquired Sonia.

'Big ship's entertainment,' he explained. 'Members of the crew sing, tell jokes, stories and so forth to entertain the rest. Anyone can have a go. Can you sing by any chance?'

'I can, but not everyone would call it entertainment,' she said modestly, glancing beyond him at the boxing ring. 'Judging by the stage, I imagine a few of the audience could make a violent protest.'

Pike turned for a moment to follow her gaze. 'It's not quite that bad,' he smiled. 'We have a few rounds of boxing first. I expect Kolme's engine room staff will put on a martial arts exhibition, too.'

'I wouldn't miss that for anything,' she beamed, with interest. 'It makes the self-defence we learn in the police force look like child's play. I'd love to take some lessons.'

'They normally work out every day,' said Pike, 'so maybe they'll be willing to teach you during your stay with

276

us. If nothing else, it should ease the boredom of a tiresome sea voyage for you.'

'Would you ask for me?' she said, turning to Scott.

'Just as soon as we've got rid of this excess baggage,' he promised.

'I'll have a word too, if I see him while I'm making my rounds,' said Pike, and went on down into the docking well to check on the security of the landing craft and the removal of their lethal cargo.

His nose sensed a familiar tang in the air, high up on top of the gallery, and for several minutes he stood gripping the guard rail, looking down. Members of the crew busied themselves with general maintenance chores while beneath him the deck officers were supervising a gang of sailors as they unloaded the long wooden crates containing the torpedoes from the landing craft. Each one had to be raised in its sling by the overhead crane which then ran towards the desired gallery and settled it upon the deck. Here the case was prised open and the torpedo removed by a miniature version of the large crane. With the torpedo hanging clear, a purpose-made silver alloy cradle was placed over the packing case. Then the torpedo was lowered into it. This done, the sailors stood aside while two other men removed the explosives from the warheads. When they were safely set aside, the warhead was replaced with the torpedo to await replenishment.

The offending tang still hung in the air and Pike's eyes scanned the vast interior of the docking well until his eyes came to rest on the fast attack craft at the far end. Looking down at his knuckles, he released his grip on the guard rail and then each step he took down through the galleries to the gangway was like a key winding up the tension behind him.

'Captain Tsi,' he demanded, crossing the gangway. A small, flat face with an even flatter nose and dark yellow skin peered out from the wheelhouse doorway as Pike strode towards it.

Aware from the look on his face that he was in trouble, Captain Tsi stepped out on to the open deck. 'Sir!'

'My nose tells me that someone down here is smoking grass!' growled Pike angrily. 'And so far I haven't seen any of my own crew disobeying the no-smoking order. My guess is that it's one of your men. Root him out, get rid of the stuff and see that it doesn't happen again. Is that clear?'

Tsi's dark, cod-like eyes shifted uneasily as they searched Pike's angry face. He had known him for many years; but for Pike and Dieger, he and his crew would have been left to face the Vietcong when the Americans withdrew their forces from Vietnam.

'It grieves me to think that a member of my crew has given offence,' he said, sounding as though his nose was obstructed, 'but I would ask that you try to understand that our way of life differs in many ways from your own. What you judge to be wrong may be quite normal in our culture. I am aware that the smoking of grass gives great offence to you, and for this reason I have ordered my crew to limit their use of it on this vessel to below decks. Should you demand that I order a total abolition, I will do so – but I fear it will cause much unrest, possibly to the point of desertion.'

Tsi's quiet rebuke took Pike by surprise and it worried him. His mind flashed back to his days in Vietnam where, due to the pressures of the horrific war they had fought, many GIs had resorted to using grass, or worse, to ease the traumatic memories of combat. Yet these gallant, displaced persons had not only lost their country and their way of life, they had also seen family and friends butchered after the American forces had withdrawn.

'You know well enough what our task is,' he replied more gently. 'You must also know what the Mirage's crew are going to think if they realize that I am aware of the marijuana and have done nothing to stop it.' Tsi nodded. 'Then you must make sure that the grass smoked on this vessel cannot be detected by sight or by smell. Is that understood?'

Tsi's smile revealed a mouthful of yellow teeth. 'It is a wise man who makes a judgement to satisfy the guilty as well as the innocent,' he observed, with a slight bow of the head.

'And you're full of bullshit,' Pike growled back in a friendly tone. 'Just keep the lid on it and we'll say no more

278

about it.'

'I see that the torpedoes are being re-packed after the explosives have been removed,' Tsi queried. 'Why is this?'

'Because we don't want prying eyes to see them when we pick up the cocaine shipment. If anyone manages to sneak on board during our stay in Colombia, it's hoped they will assume your boat to be our method of transporting it to the rendezvous.'

'So far, we have only been given a very vague outline of our mission,' said Tsi, 'and this has led us to much speculation. When might we expect a full briefing?'

'Only Dieger knows the answer to that.'

'Rumour has it that we are to be sent into the jungle to fight, as we did in Vietnam,' he persisted. 'Is that true?'

'To a small extent,' he admitted. 'I've been told that our path will be cleared, way ahead of us, so our casualties should be light to zero – but keep that under your hat. We don't want the whole damn ship's crew to know what we're about in case someone runs off at the mouth.

'Now, you get this smoking business out of the way because I have better things to do than chin-wag with you all day long.'

As he turned away, Tsi said: 'I understand that we are to replace our Bofors guns.'

'All in good time,' he replied. 'For the time being, just concentrate on making sure that this boat of yours doesn't let us down when we need it the most. When your new gun is installed you'll be the first to know. Don't worry.'

Pike continued his tour of the ship, skipping lunch, and towards three o'clock he reported to Dieger by telephone from the privacy of his cabin. Stretched out flat on his back in the deep comfort of a leather sofa, Pike closed his eyes to listen to the noises of the ship. Visions of the beautiful Sonia and Sahara returned to brighten his dreams and when he awoke, hours later, they remained imprinted on his mind. While taking a shower he continued to enjoy the memory of those visions. Yet no matter how hard he tried he could not recall the contents. They just seemed to be standing in mid-air, the dark-haired, tantalizing Sahara symbolizing evil, while the golden-haired Sonia outshone her.

In a clean set of whites, with golden epaulettes of rank gleaming on his shoulders, Pike set out from his cabin to check that all was well with the duty watch on the bridge.

'So you've surfaced at last,' chaffed Dieger playfully. 'No lunch and no dinner. You haven't taken to getting seasick, I hope?'

'No, I have not,' Pike replied in a precise, clipped tone. 'And any deep rumbling you may hear won't be distant thunder. I could eat a horse just now – shoes and all.'

'You should have joined us for dinner then,' jibed Dieger. 'I'm sure the chef used one to make the curry.'

'I hope this Manhattan Mauler hasn't been eating it or I'll be out for the count just by the smell of his breath.'

'As a special favour to you I'll instruct the seconds to put some mouthwash in his water.'

Pike shot back with: 'Your consideration for my welfare overwhelms me.'

'Oh, I wasn't thinking of your welfare,' Dieger assured him playfully. 'I was thinking of the crew. It would be a shame to deprive them of their few moments of glory.'

'A man should be blessed with such friends,' retorted Pike, tossing his head. 'Now we must be about due to start. Shall we get moving or does the thought of so much activity tire you?'

As they left the bridge just after eight o'clock, the duty watch was changing. The outgoing watch handed over with great speed, a measure of the enthusiasm they felt for the coming entertainment. Even at this hour the sun still shone brightly over the calm seas but it had lost its sting and there was a gentle, refreshing breeze.

Practically all the off-duty crew were present on the afterdeck when they arrived. Seated in ever-decreasing circles around the boxing ring they listened quietly to the compere telling a children's story.

'And then Janie, Dieger's little daughter, stood up to address the class,' he continued.

'"When my daddy came back from a shopping trip one day he had so much shopping he could hardly carry it. There was one large plastic bag hanging from each arm and a big tray of fresh eggs in his hands. As he walked up the garden path he tripped over and broke all the eggs."'

'And what is the proverb?' asked the compere, playing the part of the teacher.

'Don't carry all your eggs in one basket!' called several of the crew.

'Right. Next,' he went on, 'little Magnus Pike stood up to address the class.

'"When my dad was trapped in a cave during the war all he had left to fight with were a thousand bullets and a bottle of bourbon. So he drank all the bourbon in one go and went out and shot a thousand Vietcong dead."'

Scratching his head the compere asked: 'So where's the proverb in that story?' Without waiting for the crew to answer, he quickly took the pupil's part by dropping down on one knee.

'"That's easy, sir. Don't upset Pike when he's had a drink."'

Shouting and jeering, the crew hurled a mixture of verbal abuse and empty beer cans into the ring.

'Take it easy, lads,' called the compere, holding the microphone to his mouth while raising his free hand above his head. 'We don't want to make the canvas soggy, now do we?'

As the jeering abated, two seamen jumped into the ring to start clearing the debris.

'Did you know that it was a Polack who invented the toilet seat?' continued the compere. 'But it was an American who put the hole in it.'

'Get off and get Pike up there,' yelled someone, and moments later the audience began to chant his name.

'Okay, okay,' cried the compere. 'If you don't want to hear our guest sing we'll get Pike up here. Would you care to explain to the lady in question why a bunch of jerks like you would prefer to watch a fight than hear her sing? She's right there, behind you,' and he waved his arm.

A bright spotlight beamed down on Sonia, and even though the daylight robbed the event of its true glamour, she still looked beautiful. Dressed to kill in a revealing midnight blue dress, hastily tailored for her by the catering staff, she walked seductively forward. Hungry eyes followed her progress towards the improvised stage and their appreciation was shown in continued applause and a chorus of wolf-whistles and howls of delight from all sides. In the centre of the ring she turned full-circle, while the compere took his leave.

The crew, of around a hundred and fifty, came in all shapes and sizes. Most of them were dressed in grubby white T-shirts and shorts, while a few wore cut-down jeans. Many were bare-chested. Only the officers in their tropical whites appeared to have taken any particular trouble over their appearance.

'Well,' she began when it grew quiet, 'I can see that singing lullabies is out; a more rugged bunch of men a woman couldn't wish to meet.' Her comment drew more wolf-whistles, and one beefy crew member stood up on his chair to show off his powerful bare-chested torso.

'I'll go fifteen rounds with you any time,' his deep voice boomed – before the chair collapsed under his weight to raucous laughter and a shower of beer cans.

Pike, in the front row, stood up, his face like thunder as he hauled himself into the ring. 'Let's get one thing straight!' he roared. 'This lady has come here to entertain, so I suggest that those of you who have no wish to be entertained go below. If anyone present cares to disagree, let him come up here right now!' The scowls on some of the faces mirrored the respect he commanded, and when order was restored he clambered back down to his seat.

'Under the circumstances I think I have just the song for you,' Sonia continued. 'I first heard it in one of the bars back in Malta, and out of curiosity I tried to trace its origin. You may well be familiar with it, if you ever visited Malta and went to a place called The Gut. It was a popular song back in England shortly after the war. If you know it, join in the chorus – Cigarettes And Whisky And Wild, Wild Women.' She turned to peer over the ropes to confer with the ship's band, who were sitting in one of the front rows, and soon a few bars of music brought a satisfied smile to her face.

As she began to sing, members of the crew joined in, many rising to their feet and holding their beer cans aloft as they sang the chorus. Having succeeded in diverting their humour along a more amicable avenue, she moved on to a lively calypso called Caribbean; another old song

282

but still well-known among the crew. Two sailors began to dance in the aisle, their antics crude but hilariously funny. When the lyrics told of a Cuban queen they faced each other, and one bowed while the other curtsied, before striding arm-in-arm down the aisle once again. When the music ended there was a thunderous applause, and calls for 'More!' were met with smiles of dismay from Sonia. Holding up her arms in mock surrender, she waited.

'You're gluttons for punishment,' she panted. 'Not being a singer by profession, my repertoire is a bit limited. How about a nice gentle ballad?'

'Sing us the Ballad of Palladin!' someone shouted.

'I was thinking of something soft and mellow, like Bright Eyes from the film Watership Down,' she suggested. 'I'm not quite sure what the author had in mind when writing the lyrics, though. The book was about rabbits and their desperate plight to escape an unseen scourge, but when I first heard the song it put me in mind of a family trying to escape a cloud of nuclear fallout. Then, after a while, I began to wonder if the lyrics were better suited to parents suffering the agonies of protecting their children from the scourge of drugs, and the trauma of watching their loved ones fade and die when they failed.' Her words had brought the whole crew to a thoughtful silence, which continued throughout the song.

At the end there was a standing ovation, unmarred by jeers or shouting, which lasted until she had exchanged places with the compere at Dieger's side.

'You have a great deal of potential as an entertainer,' he told her.

'As the only woman on board, I'd say the audience were captivated by circumstances rather than my singing,' she replied.

While the compere began to tell another of his jokes, the crew grew impatient for the thrills of the main attraction and the chanting began as a low rumble, which soon escalated to a full-blown demand.'

'Pike, Pike, Pike!' they thundered. Dusk was falling, and when one of the spotlights, brighter now, swung to the outer circle beyond the audience, the sailor who had threatened to assault Sonia the previous night stood in its golden glow.

'Ladies,' the compere began, pausing long enough to give a sarcastic cough before adding, 'and gentlemen, and others. Our next act for your entertainment is the long-awaited grudge match. The challenger chosen to represent the defaulters among you, weighing in at two hundred and thirty pounds: the Manhattan Mauler!' Beer cans sailed high into the sky as their calls for judication rent the air. 'And in the other corner,' bellowed the compere, 'the pillar of authority: Hard Man Pike!'

'Lynch him!' yelled someone above the chorus of abuse smothering the compere's voice, and belatedly a second bright finger of light stabbed down from above to illuminate Pike. He strode forward wearing a dressing robe over his shorts, his stern face looking neither to right nor left in response to the scorn. As he approached the ring, two seconds bounded ahead to spread the ropes for him. When Pike climbed up, the Manhattan Mauler crossed to his corner to intimidate him, and fearing that he might strike, one of the seconds let go of the ropes and turned to ward him off. The Mauler reacted by throwing a sharp left-hand jab to his solar plexus and the second doubled over, winded, only to duck into a right upper cut that laid him low. To cheers, jeers and boos, the referee pounced on the Mauler's back in an effort to draw him off. Pike waited passively, looking up at the bear-like figure, until the remaining second joined in the struggle to restrain him. The floored second was now struggling to his knees, and Pike helped him to the stool provided for himself between rounds.

'I don't envy you,' the man mumbled. 'If I didn't know his seconds, I'd say he had a couple of horseshoes stashed inside his gloves.'

'I'll keep that in mind,' said Pike, 'and maybe I'll lay one on for you while I'm about it.'

'I'd appreciate that. He needs to be taken down a peg or two. He's bad news, even on a good day. Watch that left of his, though; what you saw him do with me was put on for your benefit. He's a natural south paw, despite what he leads you to believe.'

'I'll remember that. Thanks.'

'And now, gentlemen,' began the compere again, 'for the benefit of those who came to see some professional boxing and missed my announcement, in the blue corner, wearing white shorts, is Mr Pike, who also weighs in at two hundred and thirty pounds. I hasten to add that in his known forty-five bouts he is as yet unbeaten. You will notice that Pike is considerably smaller than the Manhattan Mauler, despite their being the same weight.' Turning to the Mauler with a look of disgust, he added: 'This is because the Mauler is nothing more than a tub of lard.' The Mauler immediately strode across the ring to menace the compere and, as the referee sprang between them, Pike turned away, making his contempt obvious.

As one of the seconds helped Pike to disrobe, Dieger watched Sonia's face. The sight of Pike's powerful torso, with its masses of rat-bite scars, was not unknown to his eyes, but Pike always kept it covered when in company. Sonia gasped in horror, her hand at her mouth, for there was hardly room to place a small coin on any part of his torso without touching scar tissue. For a moment Pike held her gaze, all of the hardness drained from his eyes as though begging her to accept his unspoken apology. Then he raised his gloved hands high above his head and turned in anticipated triumph to challenge the crowd and his opponent.

'God!' she gasped, turning to Dieger. 'Whatever happened to him?'

Dieger, taken by surprise, had found it hard to understand just why Pike had chosen to display his battle scars so flagrantly when he'd always fought shy of it before. Was it an unspoken threat, he wondered, to intimidate Sonia in case she chose to betray their cause? Or had Pike at last found a woman he'd like to know better, and had simply prepared her for what she must bear witness to, sooner or later?

Pike strode out to the centre of the ring, even the hardbitten crew shocked to silence, while the referee's voice droned on.

'During the Vietnam war,' explained Dieger to Sonia, 'it was common practice for the Vietcong to put American prisoners in cages submerged in rivers. For some reason, which I could never fathom, they took great delight in watching swarms of rats eat their victims alive. Rumour has it that Pike bit off the heads of over five hundred live rats before managing to escape. Originally he was worse than you see him now: he spent a great deal of time in hospital having skin grafts.'

The bell rang loud and clear, and Pike immediately assumed a semi-crouched position with gloved hands guarding his face. The Manhattan Mauler did likewise but with none of Pike's poise. For a few moments they circled each other, looking for an opening. The Mauler was an awkward, lumbering man, yet Pike moved constantly and easily on his feet while balancing from the waist up, rather like a cobra.

Confident that he could smash through Pike's guard, the Mauler threw a right to his jaw, at which Pike danced back a step, swinging his torso clear. They continued circling. Pike kept his eyes locked on to the Mauler's, dancing clear at the first sign of movement and knowing that a gloved fist would follow. Facing in again they prowled, each waiting for the other to drop his guard and ready to take advantage of a brief lapse in concentration. Somewhere a voice urged them on and Pike deliberately moved his eyes as though to look. The Mauler, taking the bait, let fly with a pile-driving left to his jaw. Pike moved lightly away but came back quickly to land a punch that stung the Mauler's ear as he staggered off balance.

Now there was a mocking glint in the Mauler's eyes – a weakness of which Pike intended to take advantage. As they sparred, Pike saw that the Mauler had realized that his own inferior footwork put him at a disadvantage. To combat this he began to crowd Pike into a corner, and Pike deliberately obliged. As soon as he touched the ropes the Mauler let fly with a powerful right, but Pike's hours of martial arts training with Kolme enabled him to dodge clear. Mauler's fist rocked the post, dancing back with a short sharp right-hand jab to the jaw which stunned him.

Angry at being out-manoeuvred, the Mauler turned and found himself in the very position in which he'd tried to catch Pike. Pike's fists jabbed out from their guard position, jerking the Mauler's head back and forth before he could cover up. Senses reeling, the Mauler bulldozed his way out into the open, swinging wild punches, catching Pike on the jaw with a left-handed haymaker just as the bell rang out to end round one. Pike's head jerked, and as his body hit the canvas the Mauler crouched in waiting like a great, triumphant bear. When he ignored the referee's demand to stand aside, Pike hooked his toes behind the Mauler's ankle to hold him fast then rammed his legs hard with his other foot, sending him sprawling backwards into the ropes.

'If he lands another left like that in the middle of a round,' warned Pike's second, 'you've had it.'

'I know it,' he panted. 'Give me some of that water, I'm as dry as an old bone.' He swilled the cold water around his mouth and then spat it into a bucket in a long stream. Aware of Sonia's gaze, he turned and gave her a broad wink to ease her concern.

By the time the bell rang for the second round, Pike had formulated a plan which he hoped would secure a knockout win. As the round progressed he kept the Mauler at bay with his superior footwork and occasionally managed to land a good, pile-driving punch – apparently with little effect. Anything he delivered to the Mauler's body seemed to be soaked up in his bulk. Whenever he could, the Mauler used his right hand in order to give the impression that he was right-handed. However, as Pike deliberately dropped his guard, he would memorize the look in the Mauler's eyes the split second he let go with another of those powerhouse left-handed haymakers that had already laid him low.

They entered the third round, Pike relying on his footwork to keep him out of trouble, and within a minute the Mauler was trying to crowd Pike into a corner again. When Pike danced clear, waiting in the middle with a mocking smile on his face, the Mauler took the bait. Angry and brooding he approached Pike, who stood his ground, using only his agility from the waist up to dodge or deliver blows. With cold precision Pike provoked another wild punch and when it landed squarely on his jaw Pike closed his eyes to the pain and nausea, then spun like a programmed robot on the ball of his foot, his gloved fist at the ready. The blurred image of the Mauler came into view, still leaning forward after delivering the blow, with the side of his face completely exposed. Pike's fist continued on its wide arc, its momentum increased tenfold by the Mauler's punch, to land squarely on his exposed jaw.

The sheer power behind it sent the Mauler reeling across the ring, the ropes stretching under his impact, before catapulting him back to crumple on the canvas, unconscious. Pike, his momentum stopped dead by the impact from his fist, stood still for a moment, fighting the nausea that threatened to drain his senses. Faces became blurred and the jubilant shouts and jeers of the crowd became warped in his mind. Slowly his legs gave way and he sank down on all fours, just one voice penetrating his head as he slowly shook it in an effort to regain control. All he could think of was that he was down and the referee was counting. At 'four' he barely managed to lift his head towards the direction of the voice; at 'six' he could just see the blurred visage of the referee, who was crouching as though sitting on an invisible chair. Seeing both hands rising and falling with each second of the count, he realized that the Mauler was still down.

He lay flat on his back, his head lolling from side to side, his limbs flailing the air limply as he tried to right himself. Knowing that the man's legs would not support him long enough to beat the count, Pike made an all-out effort to scramble to his feet, hauling himself up on the ropes. The crowd erupted with cheers and the referee dashed to his side to declare him the victor. At once several of the crew invaded the ring, but their cheers were not for Pike. Stooping down they hauled the semi-conscious Manhattan Mauler high into the air and bore him on their shoulders as though he were the victor.

'I don't understand,' said Sonia.

Dieger turned to her with a knowing smile. 'A ship is like a small, isolated village,' he explained. 'When there's animosity on a ship it affects everyone on board. There's nowhere to run so any trouble is contained, like a powder keg ready to blow. In order to defuse such situations we have a ruling that the winner pays the crew's bar bill for the whole of the evening. Since the crew look upon Pike as an ogre of authority, the Mauler has become their champion. By losing, he's making Pike pay for the privilege of winning.'

'I can see I'm not going to be very popular with Pike, since the fight started over protecting me,' she said. 'I dread to think how much they can drink between them.'

'Pike is dedicated to our cause,' Dieger assured her. 'You can repay him by taking part in a mission I have in mind, if you care to.'

'I'm all ears.'

'We can't talk here, with all this activity. Would you care to walk for a bit?' She nodded and stood up, and seeing Scott's look of enquiry, Dieger asked: 'Would you care to join us, too?' Leaving the excited melée behind them they strolled out of the limelight into the comparative semi-darkness of the falling night.

'I've been toying with the idea of sending you to the United States,' began Dieger. 'Sooner or later we're going to have to organize the collection of payments for the cocaine. At the moment all that our contacts have to hand over in payment for the cocaine shipments are the keys to safety deposit boxes in secure banks, which will contain diamonds to the appropriate value. It's just possible that the Mafia dons we are dealing with are harbouring thoughts of stealing the diamonds back when we try to collect them.

'What I'd like you to do is go to the States and – through Stoddart, one of our agents – work your way right into the heart of the Mafia families. Your target will be the family of the Godfather who oversees the whole US Mafia operation, one Mario Leone Cantilano. The operation we're involved with at the moment won't gain his conviction but when the lower echelons of his empire begin to crumble because of it, it's more than likely that he and his close family could be tempted into making a play for the diamonds.'

'Payment for one hundred tons of cocaine must run into billions of dollars, so what makes you so sure that I won't double-cross you?' she asked.

'I'm not so naive as to discount the idea,' he told her,

'but after studying your record I can't help but wonder how long you could live with yourself, knowing that in betraying us you also betrayed the memory of your sister.'

Sonia's face hardened, as distant memories came flooding back. 'When do I start?' she asked quietly.

'I'll have you put ashore in Gibraltar as we pass through the Straits,' he replied. 'You can fly out from there.'

11

The Atlantic Mirage seemed strange without the beauty of
Sonia to brighten the boring routine of long days and
nights at sea. Leaving the Mediterranean, they tramped
steadily south-south-west across the vast North Atlantic
Ocean to Trinidad, for refuelling and replenishment of
food supplies. Being a man's man, Dieger remained in
port for a second night, in order to allow the crew to rid
themselves of their pent-up feelings courtesy of the local
bars and female population.

By the time they put to sea again, the ship was abuzz
with the crew's exploits ashore. Although there was many
a battered and bruised man around, spirits were high.
Without exception, all defaulters brought before Dieger
to answer for their misdemeanours concealed a smirk as
he docked them a day's pay. With the pleasures of their
conquests still fresh in their minds, they cruised just out of
sight of land along the Venezuelan coast and on to
Colombia. At Santa Marta they entered port just long
enough to take on their legal cargo of coffee beans before
leaving in the early evening to follow the coast. In the
early hours of the following morning, Dieger transmitted
a message to the coastguard saying that owing to minor
engine problems the Atlantic Mirage was anchoring
offshore for repairs.

Immediately after dropping anchor, Captain Tsi took a
party of six men ashore under cover of darkness to search
out Sahara's headquarters and reconnoitre the thick forest
between it and their anchorage.

Within minutes of their leaving, a powerful cabin
cruiser came alongside. 'Welcome to Colombia,' smiled

Sahara.

'My pleasure,' said Dieger, smiling in return as he eyed her companion, a small, dark-skinned man of about sixty in a grubby white tropical suit. He wore silver-rimmed spectacles with thick lenses, and revealed a mouthful of yellow teeth when he smiled.

'This is Sanchez,' she explained. 'He will value the diamonds for me. If it meets with your approval, we can begin loading while he carries on.'

'By all means,' Dieger agreed, 'and I'll have one of my men take random samples to check the quality as the goods come on board. Do you have boats to transport it, or would you rather I use my landing craft?'

'Is that how you intend landing it when you reach the States?'

'It's food for thought,' he hedged. 'Do you need them?'

'No,' she smiled. 'It's already loaded on a fleet of small boats waiting in the creek. You can have it on board and be on your way in a matter of hours.'

'We have to make some engine repairs before we leave,' he said, 'so there's no hurry as far as that goes.'

'Nothing serious, I hope? It wouldn't do to have the coastguard embarrassed by your continued presence here.' Her statement suggested that any embarrassment on the part of the coastguard would be in their explaining why no investigation was carried out; and that, he assumed, would be because she had paved the way with a handful of dollars.

'No, just preventative action,' he said smoothly. 'I'd hate to have a serious breakdown at sea for the sake of a few hours here.'

The beach, which ranged from nothing where the trees came down to the water's edge, to a fifty-yard width of sand, was barely three hundred yards away. At night the creek was hardly visible in the darkness, but after peering shorewards for a while it became evident that the brushwood growth choking its entrance was not quite as it appeared. In the next few minutes, large clumps of green snaked out and spread apart giving a clearer view of the creek. The low growl of outboard motors began to filter ahead of the camouflaged boats and Dieger, guessing that each craft would only carry about a tonne, began to count them. At twenty he stopped, estimating there'd be at least twice that number in all. His first thought was to take on ballast and allow them to enter the docking well for unloading; but the longer the operation took, the better for him. Apart from keeping Sahara's mind occupied, it would serve to deflect her attention from his real purpose for delaying their departure.

'Mr Pike,' he called through the darkness, 'have those deck cranes manned, and get that cargo stowed below as quickly as you can. If you want me, I'll be in my cabin.'

'Aye, aye, sir,' came the brisk reply.

In the privacy of his cabin, Dieger carefully placed a smart wooden chest on the coffee table, handed Sahara the twin keys to its locks and stood aside while she opened it. Never, in all his experience of women, could he recall one who looked as radiant as Sahara when her eyes fell on the diamonds. With cheeks flushed and eyes sparkling, she dipped her hands into the chest to lift up a handful of gems.

'This is better than your greenback dollars,' she beamed, letting them trickle through her open fingers.

'There's one hundred million dollars' worth there, as agreed, and plenty more where they came from. I could be back here in a month with another chest, just like that; and I could keep on coming for as long as you can supply me with cocaine or until the diamonds run out.'

'That could be when I have them all,' she beamed, and turned to Sanchez, saying: 'Check half a dozen stones and we'll take the rest on trust for the moment – I don't think it would be in either of our interests to cheat each other, or to haggle.'

'I'll agree to that, providing the quality of your goods is equal to mine,' said Dieger. 'Can I offer you a drink, or would you rather go on deck to watch the loading?'

'Why not delegate such tiresome tasks and join me for breakfast at my hacienda?' she suggested. 'We can be there in half an hour – and you'll be back by mid-morning, if you care to rush things.'

Once again Dieger's thoughts returned to his true mission. There was no doubt in his mind as to Sahara's sincerity and the opportunity to spy out the land for himself in broad daylight was something he could not afford to let pass.

'I hear that some of your haciendas are very beautiful,' he replied, 'and having breakfast with a beautiful lady in an exotic jungle oasis sounds fine to me. As soon as you're satisfied with your end of the bargain, I'll inform my first officer that I'm going ashore.'

'You carry on,' she suggested. 'We'll meet you on deck when Sanchez is finished – unless, of course, you're worried that we might steal the family jewels while you're gone,' she joked.

'When you leave,' he said flatteringly, 'there won't be anything worth stealing.' As he stepped back out on deck, dawn was breaking, and even at that distance the sound of the jungle creatures came to them on the cool breeze. Mostly it was the multitude of birds, singing and screeching their dawn chorus, but mingled with it were the calls of the animals, echoing beneath the dense umbrella of foliage until they escaped across the sea.

'That racket brings back some sour memories,' remarked Pike, jerking his head towards the shoreline. 'I hope those screams are not from any of our lads.'

'I doubt it,' said Dieger. 'They're veterans in that sort of terrain, as you well know.'

'They're strangers here, though.'

'Agreed, but I'll bet my shirt on them any time. No matter how well-trained Sahara's men might be, they're not likely to have had actual battle experience, as ours have.'

'Let's hope they don't need it just yet,' said Pike. 'It would be a shame to foul things up.'

'Everything's going to be just fine,' said Dieger reassuringly. 'How's the loading coming along?'

'Fine. The first wave of boats are well under way, and ten have already returned ashore for another cargo. If anything's going to hold us up its that.'

'Well, don't rush it. We might as well give Tsi's men as much time as we can to finish the recce. Anyway, I've been invited ashore to have breakfast with Sahara at her hacienda. That will at least let us see the lie of the land.

Can you handle things here while I'm away?'

'There's nothing much to handle, if we're left alone. You go and have yourself a nice breakfast,' grinned Pike, 'and don't mind us slogging it out here, while you're getting yourself laid.'

'Now that is food for thought,' Dieger grinned back. 'I've got just the thing to hang round her neck.'

'What's that?'

'Her ankles,' he laughed.

'You just make sure she doesn't hang your balls around yours,' warned Pike as she approached.

Promising to see him for lunch, Dieger turned away to meet her. He hadn't really paid much heed before to the way she was dressed – it had always been her face which had captivated his attention – but now that the seeds of lust had been sown in his mind, he began to pay more attention to her body. Above soft, white high-heeled boots which reached just below her knees, well-tailored white trousers were loose-fitting to enable easy movement in the heat of the day. The matching blouse was also loose, with men's long shirt sleeves folded back to the forearm. One of its six pearl buttons, he guessed, was tucked out of sight below the waistline of her trousers, and the next two were buttoned, leaving the remaining three for display only. Her walk was very seductive, and if she wore any undergarments there was no evidence of it. Her full breasts moved beneath the material and he found himself staring.

His obvious attention made her feel good, and her pulses began to race, her nipples standing proud – riveting his gaze even more.

'You like?' she whispered huskily, turning full circle for his inspection.

'My apologies,' he said to hide his embarrassment. 'I guess I've been at sea too long.'

'Don't apologize,' she smiled. 'When a woman fails to draw a man's attention she's over the hill – and being at sea isn't so very different from being hemmed in the middle of this jungle with a bunch of half-wit natives,' she added with a broad wink.

'There are plenty of towns and cities within easy reach,'

Dieger pointed out.

'Alas, the Colombians are not my cup of tea. What I really crave is a good old Westerner – they have the bodies, the beauty and the brains. How a woman can love and respect some of these creatures is beyond me. Why, most of them are greasy-haired, short by our standards, and smell as though they've just feasted themselves on garlic.'

Dieger gave her a sideways glance, and could easily understand her reservations about having a mate smaller than herself, for she matched his own six feet plus. Even he might soon begin to suffer an inferiority complex in her constant company if he was just a few inches shorter, and that in itself could make her feel unfulfilled.

Reaching the gangway to her cabin cruiser, she slipped her arm through his for support in case she missed her footing. Sanchez trailed behind, clutching the chest of diamonds, and her touch sent a tingle of excitement through Dieger. As they descended, she turned slightly towards him in order to negotiate the steps more easily in her high-heeled boots and instead of holding the handrail she gripped his arm, bringing them even closer, their hips rubbing, her breast pressing against his arm.

Unable to resist the temptation, he looked down and the glimpse of her unsupported breasts was too much. He stopped and she took a step further before turning enquiringly. This only made matters worse, for now the view down the front of her blouse was unobstructed. When he looked up and met the impish smile on her face, her dark, seductive eyes seemed to trace even the slightest movement of his own.

'Lady,' he sighed, 'I'm not sure that I can handle this.' Her eyes sparkled in quiet appreciation of the passion she had inspired in him, and for what seemed to him like an eternity she just stood there.

'I'm no lady,' she smiled, 'and I doubt if you've been at sea so long that you've forgotten how to please one – even if I was.' Without waiting for him to answer, she pressed her hip into his crotch, and at the same time tugged on his arm, making her expectations of him quite plain.

Like an obedient lamb, but with the heart and mounting

passion of a rampant lion, Dieger fell into step again.

Her cruiser was a twenty-footer, with a cabin situated below the foredeck. The wheel-housing, amidships, was open-backed, reaching to the stern with comfortable leather seating around its edges. Moving forward behind the windshields, Sahara took her place at the helm, only releasing her hold on him when his arms were about her waist, hands clasped on the flat of her belly.

The powerful engine began to throb and she swung the helm to ease the craft clear of the gangway. While enjoying the comfortable sensation of her body leaning into his, Dieger watched the small boats queueing to unload their contraband cargo. As each empty one moved away, another took its place beneath the jib of the overhanging crane.

The sea around was littered with the discarded green foliage which had been used to camouflage the small craft as they waited for the Atlantic Mirage's arrival. The mouth of the creek, barely forty yards wide, had narrowed to half that width in the first fifty yards. Tall trees and thick undergrowth came right down to the water's edge, hanging over with thick vines that trailed in the gentle current. The small log quay to which the boats returned for more cargo lay right inside the overhanging vegetation, and would have passed unnoticed without the presence of the boats. Dieger could not detect any tracks or pathways to indicate just how the cargo had arrived at this point. Beyond the quay, where the creek narrowed to a mere twenty feet, the branches of the trees entwined overhead to form a canopy. Monkeys screeched in protest at having their privacy invaded. Multi-coloured parrots and parakeets took to the wing in fright and, where the canopy was incomplete, large, colourful orchid-like blossoms hung from the vines.

'This sure beats the hell out of looking at painted iron,' remarked Dieger.

'It's beautiful,' she agreed, 'but lonely. I long for the lights of the city but after a while I crave to be back here. I used to wonder why until I realized what I missed most was the quiet security of it. Access to my place is limited and the jungle is too dense for anyone to get through without one of my outposts hearing about it first.'

'I'm surprised you need to worry about such things,' lied Dieger. 'Who would want to invade your privacy out here?'

'There are a number of syndicates who would love to take over my operation,' she assured him. 'Even some of the friendly officials, the ones I have to pay for protection against the law, have been approached with large bribes to close me down. Fortunately I've taken the precaution of covering myself; if anything happens to me a good many heads in high places will roll.'

'You could get out altogether,' Dieger suggested. 'You must have enough put by to keep you in luxury for the rest of your life.'

'I've thought about it often enough but I just can't see myself settling anywhere. In its own way, my operation has its good points. Once every couple of weeks I saddle a horse and visit the growers – I would say plantations, but that sounds a bit exotic.'

'Sounds like something out of the old South back home, when the cotton plantation owners used to make their rounds.'

'More like the hillbillies with their illicit stills,' she chuckled. 'It wasn't so long ago that we had feuds between the growers just like the hillbillies did in the films. Poaching crops was commonplace until I took over.'

'How did you manage to combat it?'

'I invited the growers to meet and got them to guarantee to supply me with all the cocaine they could produce at a stable price. In return I supplied them with radios so that they could call for help if they got raided by poachers, or thieves after the finished product. I have a mercenary squad to respond to such calls, both to retrieve their goods and to see to it that the culprits never try again.'

'Do you still get poachers?' asked Dieger.

'Very rarely!'

'It must be expensive paying your mercenaries to sit around on their butts.'

'It's a necessary evil,' she replied, 'but they don't spend much time at my base. I have a system of outposts to keep me informed of what's going on. Every week several of them come into base which gives them the chance to relax and enjoy a little social life.

'You see the big fig tree up ahead?' she asked. 'Well, that's as far as we go. My hacienda is just a few minutes' walk through the jungle.'

They had come about three miles, thought Dieger, and among all that beauty he had seen no sign of any other means of travel. The fig tree, about a hundred feet tall, was like a giant umbrella. It overhung the creek and obscured a log jetty from view. Nothing grew under it and the rotting leaves gave off a musky odour. Sahara's glance up into its dark recesses did not go unnoticed by Dieger, who found it unnecessary to search for the reason why: the odd silver gum wrapper and cigarette end on the ground told of hidden eyes watching from above.

The narrow path they trod showed little wear or damage to the foliage, which suggested that it had not been used to transport the cocaine to the coast. For five minutes they walked in silence. Then the gloom of the forest gave way to the early morning sunlight and Dieger found himself in an area a thousand yards wide where the forest had been cleared. The levelled area was surrounded by a wide band of rough grass, which showed signs of having been used for horse-riding. Inside that was a neatly-mown band with flags marking the holes for golf, giving the impression of home luxuries – but also serving as a clear zone for security purposes. Within this was an area devoted to the growing of vegetables, bush and tree fruits, all well-spaced and in lines running diagonally towards the hacienda, so as not to obstruct the view.

There were several buildings, including the hacienda, set inside a white perimeter wall, some four feet high. All were of a similar design, with smooth, white-plastered walls. The roofs looked as though they had been constructed from short lengths of red-glazed clay pipe, cut in half lengthwise. The first layer had been laid down the pitch of the roof with the curve lying on its back, the second placed half astride the first but the opposite way up, so as to weather the joins between the rows.

Dominating the far corner of the compound was a

large, two-storey barn, whose solid outer walls had only small windows and formed part of the compound wall. The inner, front wall was completely open at ground level, but had large wooden doors above, giving access to a hayloft. Inside, a stable-lad groomed one of the horses, while outside, in complete contrast, a mechanic carefully serviced Sahara's private helicopter. Several small chalet-type buildings were obviously for the use of guards on leave from their normal patrol duties. The hacienda itself, dominating the centre of the compound, was large, square and sprawling and had been constructed around a former courtyard, converted into a patio area with a large swimming pool. Verandahs with tinted-glass patio doors gave access to the upper rooms, overlooking the pool. Rich vines, heavy with grapes, climbed the stout beams supporting the verandah and entwined themselves in the safety rails before continuing up to the roof. Tables, chairs and sun loungers were situated on the patio along the east and west sides, close to the building, so that the sun or shade could be enjoyed at leisure.

Dieger's eyes were everywhere, collating information which would provide invaluable on his return visit. Normal access to the hacienda was via a tall, wide, ornate arch through the ground floor of its eastern flank.

With the early morning sun warming their backs, they meandered in, the singing of the birds diminished by the hollow echo of metal-tipped, high-heeled boots making contact with the herringbone-patterned red briquette paving.

'It's like another world here,' said Dieger.

'It's beautiful,' she agreed, 'but, alas, boring after you've been here for a while. Would you like to freshen up in the pool while breakfast is being prepared?'

'Sounds great to me.'

'What would you like?'

'Chilled grapefruit juice, half a dozen lean rashers, a couple of fried eggs easy over, toast and a gallon of coffee,' he smiled. She turned to Sanchez, following like a devoted lap dog with the small chest of diamonds clasped to his chest.

'Will you ask Maria to prepare that for us?' she asked.

'I'll have chilled melon followed by an omelette, toast and coffee. We'll eat out here in the sun when we've finished our swim. You can leave the chest on the table.'

Sanchez smiled and obediently shuffled off as Sahara turned towards the pool. Dieger soon realized why. At the water's edge she began to undress and it was obvious that she intended them to enjoy their swim while also enjoying the beauty of each other's bodies. After removing her blouse she turned, shaking her long hair back into place like a wild horse tossing its mane. His eyes were on the movement of her breasts while her own were on his as she balanced one foot to remove the first of her boots.

'You're shy,' she teased provocatively.

'No,' he replied, reaching for the buttons of his shirt. 'You're a woman of rare beauty, but the trouble is that the beauty of the body is difficult to appreciate at close range.'

'And the pleasures of the flesh?' she gave him that special look which she knew fired his emotions.

'That kind of close combat is best enjoyed in the privacy of the bedroom – or barn,' he said, dropping his shirt to the ground.

'Close combat,' she echoed. 'That sounds interesting.'

'It can be. The rules are that each partner must strive to please the other by whatever means necessary.'

As the second boot dropped from her left hand, the long, tapered fingers of her right hand tugged at the zip fastener of her trousers. Lifting her right leg a little, she waggled it until the hem of her trouser leg dropped over her foot. Wedging it against the ground with the toes of her left foot, she gradually drew her leg clear. While she repeated this performance with the other leg, Dieger stepped clear of his own shorts, then removed his underpants, socks and shoes.

'My, you are a big boy,' she smiled admiringly, as he ogled her full-frontal view.

'I never had any toys when I was a kid,' he grinned back, 'so being poor did have its compensations.'

To hide his embarrassment he raced past her to dive headlong into the pool, where the water struck cold after the humid early-morning heat. Surfacing on the far side he turned to watch Sahara as she approached the edge.

301

She looked like a goddess with her arms swept back behind her back and her shapely legs bent slightly at the knee. Revelling in his admiration, she brought her arms slowly forward, wriggling her toes forward to grip the edge of the pool, and gave the impression that she had been unsure of her footing. Crouching slightly again, she swung her arms back in preparation for her forward thrust but, at the point of springing, her head whipped upright with such force that she toppled over backwards.

Dieger's warm glow of passion died of shock as he pushed powerfully against the side, cleaving through the water towards her. He hauled himself out of the pool to find Sahara lying just as she had fallen. Her expression was serene and calm and it was obvious that she had died without ever knowing why or by what means.

Looking away from the dark bullet wound in her forehead, he peered into the gloom of the rooms beneath the verandah opposite – the only sound apart from the birdsong was the beat of his heart. At first he could see nothing, then a slight movement in the depths of one of the rooms caught his attention. Slowly it took on the form of a man wearing a beige uniform and Dieger, knowing that he had indeed been caught with his trousers down, stood up with hands raised.

The man, who wore the uniform of a Colombian police captain, emerged into the bright sunlight, making a great show of unscrewing a silencer from his pistol. Several of his colleagues came out onto the verandah above to support his authority. Only one other entered the area at ground level. He was ushering two captives before him, one of them Sanchez. The other, a man in an expensive-looking safari suit, was carrying a black leather bag.

'You must be Captain Dieger,' said the officer, replacing the pistol in its holster. 'I am Captain Ruez. My apologies for spoiling your little romp. Such beauty; she will be sadly missed by many, although I hasten to add that you owe me a debt of gratitude.' Turning to the other captive, whom he fixed with a cold stare, he said: 'Why don't you tell the brave captain why you were summoned to the hacienda?'

'Your food was to be drugged,' said the doctor sheep-

302

ishly. 'While you slept I was to administer a truth drug so that Sahara could question you.'

'What about?'

'I have no idea,' said Mendosa. 'All I can tell you is that she was prepared to pay any price for the information she believed you to have.'

'Sahara might not appreciate it but I guess you did her a big favour,' said Dieger, thinking that at least he had been spared the awful task of disposing of the beautiful Sahara at some time in the future. 'Having died when her radiance was at its peak, her beauty will never fade in our minds as we grow old. Now, if you have no objections, I'd like to put my shorts on.'

'Are you so sure that you are not to share her fate?' asked Ruez, as Dieger strode confidently away to retrieve his clothes.

'To be honest,' Dieger remarked, 'I think that you were on a percentage of Sahara's business but that on this occasion she may have neglected to inform you of our dealings. Shooting me a few minutes ago would have achieved nothing – whereas the threat of it might. If you're wondering what brings me to that conclusion – well, I don't really see you shooting anyone out of hand in the line of duty – not even me.'

'You are very astute,' Ruez remarked, as he walked towards the table bearing the chest of diamonds. 'The keys?' he asked, looking at Sanchez, and the old man shuffled forward fumbling in the grubby pockets of his shapeless coat.

Ruez took the keys without a word and opened the chest, staring at the contents in disbelief for several moments. Telling Sanchez to bring a tray of drinks he directed a look of enquiry at Dieger, who replied: 'Whisky on the rocks.'

Ruez turned to his colleagues guarding the doctor. 'In life Sahara was an inspiration,' he said. 'In death she is just another body. Get rid of her and the doctor. Now,' he continued, turning back to Dieger, 'shall we discuss your future visits in the shade? As I understand it, you have devised a method of delivering large shipments of cocaine which the authorities would be hard-put to detect. I also understand that Sahara wanted that knowledge so that she could use it to sell her produce direct to the market, cutting out the likes of you. Would you agree to that?'

'It sounds about right.'

'Well, I don't pretend to be in this for the benefit of my health,' he declared, 'but on the other hand, I'm not opposed to making a fortune. Unlike Sahara, I would be more than satisfied with sticking to supplying you, while you do your part in supplying the market.'

'Being greedy does have its drawbacks,' Dieger observed, nodding towards Sahara as her body was being carried away. 'For all her sins, I'd like to think that she'll have a good Christian burial.'

Ruez followed his gaze. 'Alas,' he said. 'Unfortunately, her death must remain one of life's mysteries. A simple, unmarked grave in the jungle with a friendly prayer of farewell is all I can promise. Anything elaborate would only draw attention – and we wouldn't want that, would we?'

Dieger had to agree. Sanchez brought a tray containing a bottle of twelve-year-old Glenfiddich malt whisky, another of cheap brandy, an ice bucket and a jug of water. Evidently he knew Ruez' requirements without being told. Dieger gave a curt nod to indicate the level of whisky he required.

'Is it common practice for you to pay for shipments in diamonds?' Ruez asked.

'Always,' Dieger assured him. 'Admittedly, it does cause some inconvenience in getting a valuation, but once that obstacle is overcome, diamonds do have the advantage of being easy to transport – they are also indestructible. Dollar bills are not and they don't have the added attraction of accumulating value when not invested. Diamonds appreciate in value, no matter where they are kept.'

Ruez' eyes strayed to the chest, aware of the truth of Dieger's words. The diamonds' carat value was currently reported to be one hundred American dollars. If he buried them in the jungle for safekeeping their value would increase daily and no amount of research into his financial status by interested parties could uncover his hidden fortune. Paper money, on the other hand, could depreciate to the extent of becoming virtually worthless if it was not invested properly.

'When do you return for your next cargo,' he asked. 'And how much do you expect to require?'

'At least double the hundred tonnes I'm taking on this trip. As to the timing, I should think in about a month's time.'

Dieger could almost hear Ruez' mind working. Many governments believed that the Colombian authorities only paid lip service to their demands to crush the illicit narcotics trade. It could not be proved, of course, but it did inject millions of much-needed dollars into the country's sagging economy, and gave many under-privileged people the means of earning a living. There was no doubt in Dieger's mind that Ruez was answerable to a person – or persons – more powerful than himself and that he was now contemplating skimming off some of the profits for himself. Dealing in diamonds made that so much easier. It was also safe to assume that rather than allow him to come in contact with his superiors, Ruez would arrange for Dieger to mysteriously disappear. Even the likes of Sanchez would be at risk if Ruez decided to deny any knowledge of the diamonds he had valued for Sahara.

'Two hundred million dollars' worth of diamonds,' mused Ruez. 'That would be something worth waiting to see. Does acquiring such vast amounts cause many problems?'

'Not for me,' replied Dieger. 'Since I demand payment for the shipments in diamonds my only inconvenience is getting them valued before trading. Sanchez' expertise in that field will prove invaluable to you. He must be worth his weight in gold.'

At the thought of having to keep the man around with the knowledge he possessed, Ruez' eyes lost a little of their glitter. 'Yes, a diamond of a man,' he agreed, 'although I think Sahara must have treated him shabbily.'

'If his dress reflects the esteem in which she held him, she must have paid him peanuts,' remarked Dieger.

Ruez agreed, adding: 'I think perhaps a little more

appreciation is in order. Sanchez?' he called.

When the man shuffled over to the table, he asked: 'Were you in love with Sahara?'

Sanchez fidgeted, shifting his weight from one foot to the other, before replying evasively: 'Wasn't every man with eyes to see?'

Ruez smiled, and leaning forward he pulled open the chest. 'Captain Dieger has gone to some pains to point out that payment for your expertise is not reflected in the way you dress. I am inclined to agree. A man of your skills should dress to suit his position. He should also live in a modest home and have a beautiful young wife to tend his needs.'

Feeling that he was being ridiculed by Ruez, as he had often been by Sahara, Sanchez was angry but he stifled it. At the whim of his tormentor he could be marched off into the jungle and shot out of hand and Sanchez decided that it was better to grovel.

'I am but a poor man,' he pleaded, stepping back a pace with his hands spread to show his shabbiness. 'At forty years old, I look at least sixty. The modest fees I earn, combined with my appearance, hardly make me a good catch for a beauty such as you describe. As for living in a fine house – even if I could afford one, I could not rely on my earnings to maintain it.'

'Loyalty is a rare commodity these days,' observed Ruez. 'When a man in my position finds it, I think he should repay it with something more tangible than words of thanks. So, as of now, you will live here in the hacienda as my representative. You will liaise between the Captain and myself and speak of our dealings to no one. As for payment, take ten diamonds of your choice from the chest. They are for you to do with as you see fit.'

Sanchez staggered and had to hold on to the back of a chair for support. For all Ruez' generosity, Dieger knew that he was just buying the man's loyalty in readiness for making a killing out of their dealings.

'I don't know what to say,' gasped Sanchez.

'Just what I tell you to,' advised Ruez, giving credence to Dieger's thoughts. 'In the meantime, I suggest that you sit down and help yourself to a brandy before you suffer a heart attack.'

Hand shaking, Sanchez poured himself a large brandy into the glass offered by Dieger. The glass rattled against his teeth as he gulped it down. To add to the dismay of Sanchez' good fortune, Ruez, sensing his reluctance, dipped his own hand into the chest and brought out the first ten diamonds that came into it. He placed them on the table and demanded: 'Where is Sahara?'

Sanchez' baffled gaze lifted from the diamonds to stare into Ruez' eyes. He squirmed in his chair as he contemplated his reply. Under the circumstances he guessed that diplomacy was the best course of action. 'I heard her riding out during the early hours,' he began in a quiet, lilting tone. 'She loved the cool of the dawning day. I heard one of the natives speak of a large American ship which had stopped just off the coast to make repairs. She loved to be in the company of men in uniform – especially Americans because they wooed her. Perhaps she paid them a call, to ease the boredom of her daily routine life here. You could ask the Captain, of course.'

Ruez laughed aloud. Obviously Sanchez knew what was required of him. 'And the Captain?' he persisted. 'What do you suppose the Captain might have to say if he were questioned about the events of the day?'

'Perhaps that his concern for his ship was such that he had no time to entertain his goddess even if she had happened to drop by,' Sanchez replied. 'As I recall, I often warned Sahara about the dangers of riding alone through the jungle. The pathways are often narrow and the animals love to prowl during the cool of the dawn in the hope of catching their daily meal. She might have been swept from her horse by an overhanging branch and devoured while she lay unconscious on the ground.'

'You missed your calling,' said Dieger, patronizing him. 'And if I don't get moving I'll miss mine.'

'Leave us,' said Ruez sharply to Sanchez. When they were alone, he told Dieger: 'There are others above me who will want to know what has been happening. I have it in mind to deny all knowledge of these diamonds.'

'I had that figured out for myself.'

'And it doesn't bother you?'

'Not in the slightest. I have what I came for and that's all I'm interested in.'

'I'd feel better if you would accept some small payment as a token of good faith,' said Ruez. 'The diamonds, I suspect, are not of great interest to you. No doubt you can replenish your hoards without effort whereas I cannot. On the other hand, I can replenish our stocks of cocaine without effort; it's cheap to produce out here in the jungle wastes. Might I make you a gift of, shall we say, one tonne?'

'Ah, now that does have some appeal. I accept your offer with thanks.'

'I can see that you and I shall become great friends,' beamed Ruez, taking his hand. 'It will be delivered before you leave. Now, how would you like to return to your ship? By the way you came or would you like me to take you in the helicopter? I could show you our plantation if it is of any iterest to you.'

'I'd like that,' said Dieger, seizing the chance.

'Then it's settled. Sanchez!' he called as they rose from their seats. Shuffling back to them, Sanchez' eyes immediately strayed to where his diamonds still lay on the table.

'Pick up your diamonds,' said Ruez, 'and put mine away in a safe place until I return. Then I want you to organize the transportation of a further tonne of cocaine to the Captain's ship.'

'Yes, sir,' he smiled. 'Immediately.'

'I can see that he is going to be a great asset to you,' remarked Dieger as they walked across towards the barn where the helicopter stood.

'He is quick to learn,' Ruez agreed. 'Let us hope that his diplomatic prowess continues to smooth the troubled waters I see ahead.'

'As they drew closer to the barn, Dieger peered inside to where horses stood in a row of stalls facing them. One whinnied at their approach, provoking a chorus from the others. 'Are they bloodstock?'

'Sahara has always said that they are. I like horses but breeding has never been one of my aspirations. She loved them. Would you care to browse for a few moments before we leave?'

'If you don't mind,' said Dieger appreciatively. They entered the barn and crossed to a midnight black which continually tossed its head in the hope of gaining attention, and tried to bite Dieger's outstretched hand when he came close enough. As he recoiled, cursing, he noticed a large room to the left of the main entrance. The door was open to allow a flow of air, and he could see several white-coated people weighing clear plastic packets of white powder.

'I don't suppose you've seen anything like that before?' Ruez boasted. 'The cocaine is brought here from outlying plantations. We check its quality then package and store it here. The building was filled to capacity before your arrival. Until your order came in we were in a slump thanks to the crackdown by the major powers. That's why Sahara was so desperate to find out how you operated.'

'Aren't you curious?'

'Of course,' admitted Ruez, 'but not stupid. By dealing with you I know that we can move all our produce. If your method were known to all and sundry the authorities around the world would soon get wind of it. You'd soon be caught and we'd be unable to proceed. The profits in that are only short-term.'

'Wise words. I can see that it's going to be a pleasure dealing with you.'

Returning to the sunlight they climbed on board the helicopter and took off with Ruez at the controls. From above the compound, with its red-roofed buildings, looked like a jewel. A single track, angled towards a distant road, appeared to be the only life-line to the outside world, and Dieger knew that the nearest town was at least fifty miles away. There were several other buildings, barely more than rusty, tin-roofed shacks, hidden beneath the heavy foliage. Moving in a circle inland, skimming the tree tops, it soon became evident that parts of the jungle had been cleared of trees and covered with camouflage netting to conceal the illicit crops beneath.

'Don't you have any roads out here?' shouted Dieger above the roar.

Ruez turned, shaking his head. 'Just narrow tracks for

the pack horses beneath the trees,' he yelled. 'Their isolation is their protection as they see it. They feel that if roads are made for easy access, progress will follow and they will be put out of business.'

Dieger nodded and looked back at the jungle below. As they swept out towards the sea, he managed to pick out the creek, although only a few pools of water could be seen through the heavy foliage.

'Your ship,' called Ruez, as they drew close. 'It looks odd.'

'She was purpose-built. Basically, it's a floating dry-dock used for picking up stricken ships at sea and carrying out repairs. It serves my purpose well. I'd like to return your hospitality by showing you around, but that wouldn't be in my interest.'

'I understand,' he smiled. 'I get seasick, anyway. I'll drop you off and head back to the hacienda before Sanchez decides to abscond with the diamonds.'

Under Pike's sceptical eye, the helicopter came in and Dieger disembarked. Standing clear, he managed a friendly farewell wave while shielding his eyes against the draught of the sweeping rotor blades.

'Was that the local law,' asked Pike, 'or was I seeing things?'

'It was, if you could call it that.'

'That sounds ominous. Did he give you any trouble?'

'Apart from scaring the crap out of me, I'd be more inclined to believe that he has saved us quite a lot of trouble,' admitted Dieger. 'Is Captain Tsi back yet with his men?'

'About ten minutes ago. They're waiting to report their findings to you.'

'Good. By the way, there's another tonne of cocaine due. Detail someone to see it on board. Better make sure it's thoroughly checked – it was a present from our friend in the helicopter. He's taken over from Sahara and the extra cargo is a token of his good faith.'

'What happened to Sahara?'

'He shot her. Now he's the boss.'

'It's the same old story,' remarked Pike laconically, dismissing her death as if it were a mere statistic. 'Get rid of one and another pops up to take her place before you can bat an eyelid. Your trip must have been worth the effort though: nobody gives a tonne of coke away for no reason.'

'He had reason enough. He shot Sahara for skimming off too much cream. Somewhere along the line the diamonds I handed her seem to have got mislaid, along with her body. The extra cocaine is to keep me quiet.'

'Sometimes I have the feeling that we're in the wrong game. Surely there'll be some repercussions? One hundred million dollars' worth of diamonds don't go missing without someone getting their head lopped off.'

'As far as anyone else is concerned, Sahara has disappeared with the loot,' explained Dieger. 'What the Colombians make of that is their business. Where's Scott, by the way?'

'He's around but bored out of his mind. Can't you find something to keep him occupied?'

'If I hadn't needed him here, I'd have sent him to the States with Sonia. The trouble is that he needs something to keep his brain moving otherwise he feels he's being left out.'

Captain Tsi had debriefed his men and taken the trouble to draw a rough map of their findings. Dieger immediately recognized what he had seen from the air. There were fifteen plantations, all of them small and situated in an arc inland, around the hacienda, linked to one another by a track. A second track led directly to a larger one which Dieger had seen from the air, making the diagram look like the exploded view of the segments of three-quarters of an orange. The only link missing was one leading from the hacienda to the jetty at the mouth of the creek. The creek itself was marked on Tsi's map, but Dieger was confident that this was not the route used to transport the cocaine to the coast.

'Your map confirms what I've seen from the air,' he said, 'but there's no way you can convince me that they moved that amount of cargo down the creek.'

'That was my guess,' agreed Tsi. 'They'd need several packhorses, making many trips, and there's no damage or horse droppings. There is a possible alternative, though.

311

After reaching the shore, we pushed through the jungle to the hidden jetty at the mouth of the creek. Just here,' he said, pointing to a small circle close to the creek's bank, 'is a cave. We couldn't see exactly what it was because there was too much activity around it so I left a man there to check it out. So far he hasn't returned.'

'That could be nasty if he gets caught,' remarked Dieger.

'He's a veteran and can't talk, if that's what's worrying you. The Cong cut out his tongue for collaborating with your forces back home.'

'That's something I suppose. What was so special about this cave that you should risk a man's life?'

'The lie of the land had a familiar look about it. Between the jetty and the cave the ground is flat but there also appears to be a shallow, dry river-bed. It's seen a great deal of wear over a short period of time, and it's probably where the cocaine was stored before loading. However, after exploring the track from the hacienda to the creek I realized that how it arrived there was still a mystery. It's my guess that many centuries ago that creek was part of a large river. Then, somewhere deep inland, there was a great volcanic eruption. The molten lava followed its course down to the sea leaving only the creek, and the exposed lava cooled to form a protective shell which now forms the forest floor. Beneath it, where the molten lava continued to flow down to the sea, I think you'll find tunnels. One of these probably passes close to, or under, the hacienda and ends at the cave's mouth.'

With an aerial view of the hacienda in mind, Dieger began to recall what he had seen down to the minutest detail. 'What did you drink while you were out?' he asked Tsi.

'Water from my canteen.'

'Did you drink any from the creek, by any chance?'

'Yes, it was cooler than my own. Why do you ask?'

'I was just thinking. It seems strange that someone should build a luxurious hacienda in the middle of the jungle with an absolute disregard for the nearest natural water supply.'

'Perhaps they pump their water through an underground line from the creek,' suggested Tsi.

'Or from a well. That would be more plausible. They have a pool, where I had a dip, and that was no creek water. It was more like a good mineral water. What's puzzling is there's no sign of a well up there. Now I'm wondering if, in the digging of their well, they inadvertently hit one of those tunnels. When the cocaine trade began to boom, they could have built the barn and stables right over the top of it, to hide it from view.'

'Any particular reason for it being under the barn?' asked Pike.

'That's where the cocaine is stored and checked,' explained Dieger. 'If my assumptions are correct we can formulate the perfect plan of attack.'

'Shall I take a search party ashore?' asked Tsi.

Dieger thought about it for a moment. Losing one man, even though he was incapable of speech, was bad enough; losing the knowledge he may have gained could mean the difference between suffering heavy casualties when they returned or just a few.

'We can't stay here any longer,' he said at last. 'Send two of your best men ashore – the rest of us will leave as planned. When we're out of sight of land we'll discharge the fast attack craft. You can lie-to until dusk and then come in to pick up your men. You shouldn't have any trouble catching us up with your superior speed. Let's get one thing quite clear, though. Under no circumstances are you to risk your boat. Without it, our mission is sunk. Get fully armed and don't hesitate to use your muscle if that's what it takes to get clear.'

'Yes, sir,' responded Tsi, coming smartly to attention.

'We'll weigh anchor just as soon as the rest of our cargo is stowed,' Dieger continued, turning to Pike. 'If I'm wanted I'll be in the radio room or on the bridge and don't forget to send Scott to see me.'

An hour later, Ling and Chek splashed into the water on the seaward side of the Atlantic Mirage. The sun was high and many of the crew were already in the warm water enjoying themselves in noisy horseplay to help cover the exit of the two men.

Making their way towards the bow, they submerged and

swam towards a clump of the discarded foliage. They used it to conceal themselves as they proceeded towards the shore, where the trees ran down to the waterline. For several minutes they remained motionless, with only their heads protruding from the water so as not to disturb the birds and animals. With the greatest of care Ling edged his way ashore, to wait quietly in the clinging heat for Chek to follow. While they waited for the creatures of the jungle to accept their alien presence, voices from the ship carried to them on the still air.

They removed the waterproof wrappings from their weapons and equipment and looked around them. The trees were tall, with straight trunks and few branches near the ground. This part of the jungle was covered with thick brush, tall clumps of reed-like grass, and long-stemmed bright orange amaryllis lilies, which filled the air with their musky scent. There were no paths or tracks to indicate penetration by either human or large animal life.

Rising to a crouch, they began to creep towards the cave above the creek's mouth, dropping to their bellies when they could hear voices and crawling the rest of the way to the clearing. Only the heads of four men could be seen from where they lay, sitting in the dry gully around the fire whose smoke drifted lazily upward. Cautiously, the two men turned inland to slither up the long, shallow rise where the ancient lava flow had stopped. They circled until they were directly above the cave looking down on the foursome, who chatted and smoked around a skinned rabbit roasting on a crude spit. Although dressed in shabby battle fatigues, each man sported a modern sub-machine-gun with several clips of spare ammunition, a pistol and a machete. There was no sign of Harry Tet, the two men's missing comrade. But since his orders had been to explore the jungle terrain between the cave and the hacienda, it was easy to pick up his trail. Following the tell-tale signs of his passage, they tracked him for two hours until they reached a large thicket. A discarded cigarette end and a small patch of trampled grass showed where he had stopped to rest in the shade of the trees before moving on.

Puzzled by his insistence on sticking to a strict compass

314

bearing, right through the heavy thicket, the two men also paused for a smoke, both agreeing that skirting the tangled mass would have been easier. As Chek drew the smoke from the cigarette deep into his lungs, his face soured, and he began to peer into the gloomy depths.

'I smell kerosene,' he whispered harshly, 'and it's coming from in there.'

Without waiting for an answer, he turned to climb a tree and found signs that Tet had done the same. From his perch all he could see was a haze of smoke hanging lazily in the upper foliage, right in the centre of the thicket. There was not even a suggestion of human occupation to make him wary of trouble; yet his senses screamed out warnings.

'Something tells me that all is not what it appears to be,' he whispered on his return. 'There's smoke, or fumes, coming from the centre, but no sign of life. Nor is there any pathway to suggest that anyone has passed through.'

'Maybe it's just a natural ventilation shaft for the tunnel,' speculated Ling.

Chek nodded, but he was unhappy as they crawled on all fours through the thick undergrowth as Tet had done only hours before. Several minutes later they found themselves peering down a large, natural vent into a tunnel which spewed kerosene fumes out into the heavy growth around them. It hung there like a blue mist, trapped by the dense leaves.

A patch of freshly-disturbed earth told the story. Tet had secured a rope to some brush in order to climb down but the earth had been too shallow. The brush had torn out by the root and he had fallen some fifteen feet.

The tunnel was not as Ling expected – round, long and running directly from A to B – but more like a honey-comb. Large boulders of rock wedged in the ancient lava flow divided the main stream and caused walls to build up behind them. It was into one of these small annexes that the two men finally dropped. The main tunnel, just seven feet high, was easy to locate by the flickering light of the crude Aladdin-type paraffin lamps placed in niches along the walls. As they stood in the shadows, peering along the annexe, a tiny marble of lava bounced on the floor in the main tunnel and they strained to listen. They heard what sounded like a man trying to stifle cries of pain while dragging his tortured body along the floor. Guessing it must be Tet, they peered out again as he crawled into view from a similar annexe a little further down.

'Both of his legs are broken,' whispered Chek.

Ling looked down at Tet's tortured face. 'What happened?' he asked, but Tet's head lolled from side to side and he waved his open hands in front of his face to indicate he was in too much pain to answer. 'Were you tortured?' Ling persisted, but to this Tet shook his head. 'We don't have any field medical kit,' Ling went on, 'or morphine to kill the pain. I'm going to put you to sleep so that we can move you.'

He placed his hands at the base of Tet's neck and gently pressed his thumbs against the skin. Tet's eyes closed as he slipped into the painless mercy of unconsciousness. They carefully hoisted him through the hole and once outside Ling slung him across his shoulders in a fireman's hold, while Chek led the way back through the jungle.

They arrived at their pre-arranged rendezvous and Chek hauled out the bag of equipment they had left hidden in the brush. He immediately inflated a small rubber dinghy into which they gently placed the injured man. Squatting in the dinghy, they looked out from beneath the overhanging trees and vines. Not a single cloud drifted in the clear night sky to blemish its translucence, nor was there moonlight to pick out any dark shape on the silvery surface of the sea.

'This is Charlie One calling Big Brother,' said Chek quietly into a walkie-talkie handset. 'Do you read me? Over.'

'We read you, Charlie.' It was Tsi's voice. 'Do you have our stray? Over.'

'We do. He's got two broken legs but otherwise he's okay. We are going to push off. Can you pick us up? Over.'

'Can do. Head straight out to sea. We'll give you ten minutes to get clear of the coastline before we come in. Over and out.'

Soon they were heading for the open sea and paddling

against the incoming ripples of water. There was nothing in sight, yet both felt the tension nagging at their nerves the further they ventured onto the mirror surface.

'I've got a bad feeling,' moaned Chek, voicing his fears.

'Me too,' admitted Ling. 'Stuck out here in the open I feel like a big, juicy fish in a small barrel. Keep that walkie-talkie handy. I've got a feeling that we're going to need it.'

Even as he spoke, Tsi's voice called: 'Big Brother to Charlie One. Do you read me? Over.'

'Reading you loud and clear. Come on in,' responded Chek.

'We have a radar contact about ten miles south-east of your position. We are lying about the same distance away to you, north-west. I'm pretty sure it's a coastguard cutter looking for pirate dealers – and they are monitoring our progress. If we each maintain our present course we're going to meet. So that they can't pick you up on their radar I suggest you continue on your present bearing. I'll run out to sea to lead them away then dodge back to pick you up.'

'What if they chase you?' asked Chek.

'If we can't outrun them there are going to be some fireworks,' declared Tsi flatly. 'That is unless you have any suggestions?'

'Anything's better than nothing,' moaned Chek. 'I only hope they don't call for air support. Over and out.'

Within minutes, the silhouette of the coastguard cutter was cruising along the horizon like a ghost ship in pursuit of a ghost. More than an hour passed before Tsi called to give warning of their return. With the land now no more than a dark sliver between sea and sky, they stopped paddling and sat watching the north-western horizon. A single flash gave warning of the fast attack craft's speedy approach. Chek replied with a single short flash every five seconds while Ling strained his eyes and searched for the coastguard cutter.

Knowing that they had been spotted by Tsi, Chek stopped signalling until the tiny speck could be recognised. Then he began again so the pilot could plot his manoeuvres and speed in order to make a fast rescue. After heading for a point some five hundred yards to their port side, the growl of the powerful engines diminished to a steady throb as the craft made the final approach under its own momentum. Dark silhouettes became the distinct, friendly faces of concerned comrades waiting eagerly to help them on board. Seconds later the engines roared again and the craft surged forward. Then, as they began to pick up speed, there came the screaming whine of a shell from the coastguard cutter. It hit the water more than two hundred yards away, sending a great white plume towards the sky. Tsi's crew immediately answered with a token warning barrage from the Bofors guns. A second flash, followed by the instant detonation, drew Chek's attention to the position of the cutter as the shell screamed towards them; once again it fell short.

But that proved to be the least of their troubles: Thant turned from the radarscope with its greenish glow reflecting in his flat, impassive, cod-like eyes. 'We have bandits approaching from the north,' he warned. 'Two helicopters, by the look of it.'

Tsi nodded. 'Dieger was right about one thing: pirates are not welcome. You'd better call in reinforcements.'

'This is Big Brother calling Angel's Wing,' called Thant. 'Do you read me?'

'Loud and clear, Big Brother. We see your problem and are moving in to intercept,' came the reply.

Out-running the cutter was child's play but the helicopters coming in at sea level posed a threat. When the steady stream of white-hot tracers began to search them out, Tsi's Bofors guns retaliated. Cocksure, the helicopters came in two abreast – until the Bofors guns forced them to change tactics and they parted, banking to left and right while climbing sharply.

The Angel's Wing swept down upon them from high above and took them unawares with a salvo of rockets. The exhaust streamers sped to their targets, which blossomed into great mushrooming glows of orange flame and black smoke. As the wreckage fell in to the sea, the Angel's Wing discreetly retreated to continue their guardian role from a distance. Baffled by the ferocity of the attack the cutter radioed back to base for help.

Tsi anticipated this turn of events and radioed ahead so

that Dieger would have the Atlantic Mirage ready and waiting to receive the fast attack craft the moment it arrived.

Within minutes of its embarkation, a searching aircraft passed overhead but made no contact. Confident that the crisis was past, Dieger sent for Tsi for a report on the findings of Tet's exploration of the cave and tunnels.

'Any comment?' he asked Scott when Tsi had left.

'The fact that the tunnel exists is not necessarily to our advantage,' he replied. 'Obviously we could find our way through to the compound, but the problem is, could we wipe out the guards at the entrance before they alerted those at the hacienda and the plantations? My previous suggestion is clearly out of the question, unless we can think of some method of leadership. It's a bit much to expect our carnivorous army to find their way through on their own. They're known to bivouac at night and it's a three-mile trek through honeycombs of tunnels. By the time they arrive they'll be down to half their original strength and we shall have lost the initiative. Since they're at their peak in the jungle I suggest we look for ways of getting through it rather than under it.'

'It's your baby,' said Dieger. 'When you've figured it out, let me know. If there's anything I can do, or anything you need, don't hesitate to ask.'

12

The crew members of the Atlantic Mirage had one thing in common – somewhere in the past, each one had suffered from or been tainted by illegal trading in drugs. Following their departure from Colombia, Dieger devoted much time to making an itinerary of his deliveries. Due to the unprecedented amount of cargo and his insistence that payment be made in diamonds or shares in Mafia holdings, orders for only fifty tonnes had been confirmed. In normal circumstances this would have been considered a disaster but in this particular case it was treated as a great triumph.

Every man not on duty – or who could be spared from it – was gathered on the docking well deck to witness one of the factors that had drawn them into Dieger's force. Fifty one tonnes of cocaine were brought out and stacked on the open deck. Then, each man pierced as many packets as he could, before throwing them into the sea. When the last was gone, the sailor known as the Manhattan Mauler stood proud among his comrades and called for three cheers for the Captain. The crew responded heartily before demanding a speech.

'For the life of me, I can't see what you have to be pleased about,' Dieger began. 'You've just thrown a billion dollars' worth of cargo into the sea.' This only brought forth a demand for more, and when they had quietened down he went on: 'Well, I must admit that it feels good to have you all gathered here, where you can see and take part in what we've been preaching to you for so long. However, many of you will be unaware of the fact that the real glory for this mission belongs to a man you refer to as 'Limey', or the 'Pom'. He doesn't say much, but he's the one who started this particular ball rolling. Now, I'm not going to put him on the spot by asking him to give a speech because he's not much of a one for talking. Just keep it in mind that but for his ingenious ideas, that particular billion-dollar cargo wouldn't be where it can do no harm. As for the rest, let's hope we can achieve our objectives by netting some of those big wheeler-dealers and get them put away for a good long term in the prisons where they belong.

'The next part of our mission, as far as you're concerned, is quite simple. There's no danger at all in making our deliveries but when we return to Colombia things could well be dangerous. From Captain Tsi's recce we know that there's no way we can destroy the plantations in a commando-type raid so all arrangements will be above board. This means that everyone must be on his guard when he's ashore. If word gets back to Colombia that we intend wiping them out, all hell is going to break loose when we make our bid. So, be your brother's keeper. That's about all, gentlemen. Dismissed.'

The feeling of having achieved something boosted the crew's morale. In the days that followed the torpedo warheads were re-packed with cocaine and the torpedoes themselves were loaded into their storage racks, ready for use. By-passing the exotic island of Haiti, the Atlantic Mirage entered the vast Atlantic ocean, maintaining a north-westerly course for two days and nights as though heading for Miami. After a hundred miles she swung round to run north-easterly, parallel with the United States coastline.

It was the moment they had all been waiting for. The ship's engines had stopped pulsing and the feeling of being driven was replaced by a quiet gliding which became a slow rolling as the ship wallowed in the gentle swell. Those who were able to went up on deck.

The docking well had been flooded and the stern doors were open. At precisely two o'clock, Captain Tsi eased the fast attack craft out into the night. For a while it, too, wallowed in the swell after clearing its mother ship, almost reluctant to embark on a mission alien to its nature. Large, dark, rain clouds hung heavily in the night sky, and lent an eerie sense of foreboding.

Suddenly the tranquillity was broken by the echoing boom of the docking well doors closing and, as though they'd been waiting for that, the attack craft's engines began to roar. Her low bow raised a little in the water and a bow wave began to build up as the propellors thrust it forward through the sea.

'Steer two-seven-oh west for Miami Beach,' ordered Tsi, before turning to the radio officer. 'Have you made contact with Stoddart yet?'

'He's on the line now, sir.'

'This is Captain Tsi speaking. How are things in Miami?'

'Bustling,' replied Stoddart. 'Word has got round that there's a big shipment due. The law has put the lid on things good and tight. Nothing has been getting through and prices on the streets have hit an all-time high. We're hungry and waiting for your shipment. What is your ETA?'

'Around four am, I should think. We have a little swell running out here. How is the weather in Miami?'

'Like a duck pond and the forecast is good.'

'Do you have any problems I should know about?'

'No, bonny lad. You just keep coming and deliver the goods. I'll head on out and be waiting.'

After signing off, Stoddart remained seated for a moment and reflected on the situation. Dieger's first shipment consisted of ten warheads, each one packed with two hundred and fifty kilos of cocaine with a street value of around seven hundred and fifty million dollars. Dieger had pressed him to bargain hard with Francesco Di Carlo, the Mafia's Florida Godfather, and as a result five hundred million dollars' worth of diamonds had been deposited in a safety deposit vault across the street from Stoddart's hotel.

Swinging around in his chair, he leant his arm on its uncomfortable, straight back while he studied one of the two keys which would open that vault. Di Carlo had insisted on retaining the second key himself, promising to hand it over personally on receipt of his consignment. Looking up, Stoddart gazed round the room. It wasn't

322

much: just a walk-in wardroom on the first floor, utilized to house the transmitter, yet somehow it put him in mind of a prison cell. Shuddering at the thought, he turned towards the door.

Sonia was leaning up against the frame, wearing a pale blue robe, tied at the waist, which didn't quite reach down to cover her white lace panties. From her long, shapely legs his eyes travelled up to meet hers.

'Eat your heart out,' she cooed.

'All the time, bonny lass,' he replied, letting the key fall from his grasp to hang on the chain around his neck. As he walked towards her, she stood aside, then followed to stand behind him as he peered through the narrow slits of the vertical blinds. The street was wide and well-lit, with not so much as a tiny scrap of paper to mar its tidiness. Even the trunks of the tall royal palms, which lined the pavements and central reservations, were so smooth and round that they might have been carved out of stone. The bank where the diamonds were deposited stood prominently among the shops and drugstores opposite. In the parking lot, a dark blue van which had been there since the deposit was made had gathered a thin layer of dust.

'Don't let it bug you,' she advised.

'I've seen too many double-crosses,' admitted Stoddart. 'It's the not knowing that bugs me. Is it as innocent as it looks? Has Di Carlo, or the vice squad got us staked out in the hope of making a killing?'

'The vice squad?' she echoed. 'I keep forgetting that although we consider ourselves to be on their side, they're still not aware of our mission.'

'Consider that a blessing. I'm not so sure about trusting myself in this business let alone some crooked or power-hungry cop.'

Turning away, he walked through to the verandah at the rear, which skirted a large patioed area. On three sides there were holiday apartments on both levels and also a cocktail bar at the rear of the ground floor. A restaurant ran through to the front of the building. Across the patio, close to the hotel's private swimming pool, was a round, gazebo-style bar with a thatched roof; beyond the pool another gazebo housed a barbecue, from which

323

plumes of blue smoke drifted all day to entice holiday-makers with its rich aromas. Beyond that lay the world-renowned golden sands of Miami Beach and the open sea.

'Quiet as a grave,' he remarked, scanning the multitude of boats lying just offshore. 'The tourists must be hard-put to believe what really goes on here when they're out enjoying themselves.'

'Maybe it's just as well,' she replied. 'You'd better get going or you'll be late.'

Reaching around his neck, he unclipped the gold chain with the key attached. 'You'd better take this. That, at least, will keep me from getting tempted when Di Carlo hands over the other key.'

Taking it, she stretched up to give him an encouraging kiss on the cheek, saying teasingly: 'There's only one place to run and that's back here to Momma.' When she withdrew, he looked into her deep, bewitching eyes and smiled, but did not speak. The promise in them was not for him, he knew that; but he also knew that she was destined to bewitch shrewder men than himself before her beauty faded. Di Carlo was her target, if Stoddart failed to ensnare him, and he had already made his feelings about her quite plain, despite being many years her senior.

He left the apartment and made his way towards the little wooden jetty where a small boat bobbed on the gentle waves. Releasing the mooring, he stepped on board, and as the boat drifted clear he hauled on the starter cable. The engine fired into life with a roar, shattering the tranquil silence of the night. Manoeuvring his way through the maze of smaller craft moored in the shallows, he tied up alongside a larger, powerful deep-sea pleasure fishing boat, where several tall, whip-like rods, mainly used for catching marlin or shark, protruded from their mountings.

He moved forward on the after-deck and tapped on a door, which opened immediately. Captain Stewart, the owner, stood in the darkened cabin, running his fingers through his uncombed hair. A short, squat man with a deep chest and broad, weatherbeaten face, he was thought to have been a drug smuggler himself until his own addiction had earned him the reputation of being un-reliable.

'It's time to go,' said Stoddart, stating the obvious. 'You get started, while I check my gear.'

'I'm being well-paid for my services,' replied Stewart, 'and maybe I should mind my own business, but I figure I ought to tell you that I think my boat is being watched.'

'To be honest, bonny lad, I'd be surprised if it weren't. You can take my word for it, you don't have a thing to worry about. Whatever it is I'm up to won't be causing you any grief. Just get those engines started and head out to sea. I'll be up to use the radio as soon as I'm through down here.' Clawing his hands through his unruly hair again, Stewart departed.

When he had gone, Stoddart unstrapped the wicker-work fishing basket he'd brought with him. Inside was a micro-computer homing device which would first attract the torpedoes and then shut down their gas turbine engines as they passed twenty feet beneath the surface.

Deeply curious, Stewart watched covertly while hauling up the anchor and making his way to the bridge. But what he saw meant nothing to him. The engines roared into life and he began to head out to sea as instructed, passing a large sea-going yacht called the Sea Queen, which lay at anchor several hundred yards offshore. He scanned its quiet, deserted decks for the hidden eyes which he felt sure were watching his every move, but there was no sign of life on board. Stoddart joined him when the vessel was barely three hundred yards away and told him to cut the engines and drop anchor.

The moment Stewart was out of earshot Stoddart switched on the radio and began to call Captain Tsi on board the fast attack craft. 'Saratoga calling Big Brother. Do you read me? Over.'

'Big Brother receiving you loud and clear. We should reach our rendezvous in thirty minutes. Are you ready to receive your fish? Over.'

'Just sitting out here waiting. Just let them go when you're ready. Over.'

'Will do,' promised Tsi. 'They'll come in pairs, approxi-mately five minutes apart. Good hunting. Over and out.'

Leaving the bridge, Stoddart began to inspect the tall fishing rods before selecting two and taking them to the stern.

'Surely you're not going to cast out there?' said Stewart reproachfully. 'Any fool knows that my gear is totally unsuitable for fishing from a stationary vessel, even if there was anything worth catching this close inshore.'

'Well, you know what they say about us crazy English,' replied Stoddart mockingly. 'I'm just a little old country boy, bonny lad. You just brew us a nice cup of tea while I see if I can't catch us a couple of tadpoles for breakfast.'

'Tea!' he scoffed. 'All I have is beer, coffee and bourbon. Take your pick.'

'Black coffee with a dash of bourbon – just to keep out the early morning chill, you understand.'

'Early morning chill?' echoed Stewart in exasperation. 'I'm beginning to wonder if you're not some kind of nut.'

'For a thousand dollars a day to rent your boat, you should care,' Stoddart retorted. 'Just get the coffee and then go read a book or something.'

Stoddart selected one of the two seats mounted at the Saratoga's stern, strapped himself into one and prepared to cast out his lines. Several minutes later, Stewart returned with a large, steaming mug of coffee, which smelled strongly of bourbon. On hearing his footsteps, Stoddart swung around in the swivel chair, leaving the rods in their stands. 'Pass me my basket, bonny lad,' he asked, after taking the coffee.

'Tell me something,' Stewart remarked. 'Are you one of a kind or are they all like you back home?'

'I guess they broke the mould after making me, bonny lad,' Stoddart smiled. 'You can go about your business now – I'll call you if I need any help,' and he turned back to face the sea, waiting until Stewart's footsteps died away before opening the basket. With his bulk shielding it from view, he switched on the homing and tracking devices. The latter emitted a steady bleep, indicating that the homing mechanism on the torpedo warheads was still a great many miles away.

Cupping his mug in his hands, he began to sip, every now and then glancing furtively towards the Sea Queen.

Memories came flooding back of the night Scott had been shot by Haynes. McNalty was another of that stamp, and as Stoddart's gaze traversed the distant multitude of craft closer to the shore, he felt sure the man would be out there, watching him, with similar motives in mind. Just like his Mafia contacts, he knew that the shipment was due. All he needed to know was how.

Alerted by the shortening time lapse between the bleeps on the tracking device, Stoddart nonchalantly hauled in one of the fishing lines, hooked on a piece of bait, cast out into the sea, and then repeated the procedure with the second line. Adopting a relaxed pose, he waited, eyes alert on the open sea. There was nothing to see out there but miles and miles of water until it met the sky. Studying the sea closer at hand, he saw in his mind's eye those long, sleek shapes speeding twenty feet below the surface towards his baited hooks. When the bleeping grew rapid, he searched for the only visible indication of life beneath the gentle waves: a steady stream of bubbles, scarcely noticeable in the early dawn.

Suddenly the fast bleeping changed to a very slow pulsing, which meant that the first two missiles had arrived and the computerized homing system had shut down the gas turbines, leaving the torpedoes to glide gently onward under their own momentum. In the tranquil world forty feet below the surface they came to rest on the soft, golden sands, where four frog-suited divers wearing aqualungs immediately set about preparing them for the next stage of their journey. To ease the burden of moving such weighty objects, they attached large rubber balloons which they then inflated by use of a small compressed gas cylinder. With the missiles gently suspended, they guided them carefully over the sea bed to where a hook hung suspended from above. Securing the first one, the divers followed as it was hauled up into a pressurized diving well, situated in the Sea Queen's hull. As the torpedo warheads broke the surface, the divers gave the thumbs-up sign before returning to the depths.

When the tailfins cleared the water, eager hands attached a second line so that it could be placed horizontally in a cradle for its warhead to be removed while the hawser returned to the depths. Three minutes later, when the second torpedo surfaced, the warhead of the first lay to one side with its priceless filling stacked close by. A highly efficient team, the eight men unpacked each warhead and reassembled it before securing the torpedoes in racks fitted to the bulkheads along both sides of the vessel.

When the last had been hauled safely on board, one of the divers returned to where Stoddart's fishing lines hung in the water and gave one a hard tug. Stoddart nonchalantly hauled in both lines and re-stowed them, while Stewart looked on.

'Had enough?' he mocked, shaking his head.

'I have, that, bonny lad,' Stoddart replied, ignoring the man's obvious contempt. 'I can smell a whole mess of bacon and eggs cooking someplace close by, and it's making my belly rumble.'

'That'll be the Sea Queen,' Stewart remarked, stating the obvious.

'That's what I figured,' he agreed, 'and, as it happens, the Captain and I are acquainted. You can drop me off there.'

'Will you be needing me any more today?'

Stoddart handed him his fee, saying: 'I guess not; my business here is all but finished.'

With a brief nod, Stewart went forward to haul in the anchor, Stoddart watching him from the stern while mulling over the events of the morning. The feeling of being watched persisted, and brought a broad grin to his face. Di Carlo's face was something he could only visualize, but he guessed that there would be some repercussions if the man had indeed kept him under constant surveillance, as he suspected.

When the Saratoga eased alongside the Sea Queen's gangway, he stepped aboard without so much as a backward glance, and made his way up to the Captain's cabin, where he knocked before entering. Only her new Captain's personal effects had changed since Dieger's day. His successor was also American, but unlike Dieger, he was not tall: barely five feet six inches in his stockinged feet, he weighed in at a meagre one hundred and fifty pounds. And where Dieger had an air of 'savoir faire', Captain Maurice Cheto's Indian blood showed in his wiry build and searching dark eyes.

'Congratulations,' he smiled now, looking up from his breakfast. 'I hope you're hungry. I took the liberty of ordering for you.'

'Hungry as a bear,' he replied cheerfully. 'It must be all that early morning fresh air. Did everything go as planned, your end?'

'Like clockwork. The man who figured it out must have been some kind of villain in his day.'

Sitting down opposite, Stoddart poured himself a mug of coffee, saying: 'As it happens, I doubt if he ever harboured a bad thought until he met me.'

'It happens,' Cheto remarked, as Stoddart removed the silver-domed cover from his plate of eggs and bacon.

'Did you happen to notice anyone else taking an interest in me while I was out there?' he asked.

Cheto smiled. 'No, but that's hardly surprising, is it?'

'It was just a thought. Maybe it's my guilty conscience that's making me feel as though everyone's watching me.'

'I doubt it. There's a lot at stake.'

'That's a fact,' Stoddart agreed. 'I'd give a lot to see Di Carlo's face, when I call to let him know that the shipment has arrived, safe and sound.'

'I'd give a whole lot more to see it when he realizes the truth!'

'Do you think he'll come on board personally to complete the deal?' asked Stoddart.

Cheto shook his head. 'I doubt it. When are you going to call him?'

'As soon as I've eaten. I'm sure he's had me under surveillance, so I'll let him sweat it out for a while.'

'People like him don't sweat so easy,' said Cheto, 'and if I'm any judge of his kind, the chances are that he's too busy trying to figure out how to get his hands on the shipment without parting with the diamonds.'

'That wouldn't go down too well with his Mafia friends in other parts of the country – it would lead to our putting a stop on their shipments, unless they made good our losses.'

'Well, let's hope that the day progresses as we expect,' said Cheto. 'Worrying about what might happen will only give you ulcers.'

Eating his breakfast, Stoddart's thoughts returned to the vehicle in the bank's parking lot. Obviously it wasn't there just to wait for him to pick up the diamonds, because Di Carlo would not have bothered until his shipment had been safely delivered. On the other hand, it could be one of Di Carlo's colleagues using it to keep him under surveillance while he stayed at the hotel.

'Why don't you make the call?' suggested Cheto, noticing his worried frown.

Stoddart met his dark-eyed gaze across the table. 'I must be getting too old for this game,' he said. 'There are gremlins everywhere I look, these days.' Refilling his mug, he sat on the corner of Cheto's desk and tapped out the digits of Di Carlo's private number.

'It's Mr Stoddart,' he informed the female voice that answered. 'Mr Di Carlo is expecting my call.'

'Di Carlo speaking,' said a deep nasal voice with a Sicilian accent, moments later. 'Have you any news?' he asked, guessing that he had not.

'Your shipment has arrived,' said Stoddart. 'When can you pick it up?'

Di Carlo was furious; keeping Stoddart, and everyone who had come into contact with him, under surveillance had been both expensive and time-consuming. However, he held his anger in check and asked levelly: 'Where is it?'

'On board the Sea Queen. Two thousand five hundred kilos in all, as agreed.'

'Can you hold the line for a minute, while I get my act together?'

'Take your time,' Stoddart invited. 'There's no rush.' Covering the mouthpiece with his palm, Di Carlo looked through the open French doors of the library. Outside, the happy voices of his two young grandchildren rang with laughter as they played in the early morning sun on the vast lawns reaching down to the river where his luxury cabin cruiser was moored. Somewhere out of sight a battery-powered lawn-mower whined, and he could visualize the ageing gardener sitting hunched on it as he

330

trundled along.

'Don!' he called, and his son-in-law, Don Cantilano, stepped into view, his lithe body clad only in a pair of swimming trunks. For a man of thirty years, he had a great deal on his shoulders, but his swarthy Castilian handsomeness often drew him away from the responsibilities of business to indulge in the pleasures of his many female admirers. 'Somebody goofed,' declared Di Carlo angrily. 'The shipment is on board the Sea Queen.'

'That isn't possible,' argued Cantilano, as he entered the room. 'She was clean when she arrived, and there's no way it could have got on board without our knowledge.'

'Has she taken on any stores or fuel or laundry?'

'You know that our companies are taking care of those contracts,' retorted Cantilano. 'There's no way anyone could have moved that amount of stuff without our knowing. Apart from the crew's liberty boats going to and from the shore, the only other vessels passing near to the Sea Queen was Stewart's Saratoga.'

'What's he got to do with this?' demanded Di Carlo.

'Stoddart hired him for a fishing trip. That guy's crazy, though. He was using deep-sea gear for angling, a thousand yards off shore.'

'Did Stewart go near the Sea Queen?'

'Only when he dropped Stoddart off. He didn't stop for longer than it took Stoddart to cross over. Barely a second or so.'

'Damn! I was banking on finding out how they got the stuff in. You'd better get things organized to move it. I'll go on board to check it out.'

'What about the crew at the bank?'

'Leave them there until we're in possession, then pull them out. If it gets robbed after that, it's Stoddart's worry.' Turning back to Stoddart, he said: 'Hello, sorry to keep you waiting. I'll be along shortly to check out the goods. If they come up to expectations, we'll move as planned.'

'Suits me fine,' said Stoddart affably. 'Need I remind you to bring the key?'

'How could I forget?' responded Di Carlo curtly.

'Sounds like he's coming himself,' remarked Cheto, as Stoddart put down the telephone. 'It's a pity our laws of entrapment won't allow us to have him charged while he's here.'

'Knowing my luck, I'd probably land up in jail myself, doing life,' said Stoddart. 'Apart from that, his immediate arrest would implicate us – and that would queer our deal with the rest of the mob.'

'Give Di Carlo to me for twenty-four hours and you wouldn't need to bother about him,' Cheto boasted. 'I'd have him singing like a canary in no time.'

'Winning a few battles isn't what this is all about,' Stoddart reproved. 'When Dieger pulls the plug, he intends winning a war against the Mafia and anyone who deals with them.'

'So they say,' agreed Cheto, without much enthusiasm. 'Let's hope his dream materializes before someone pulls the plug on him; keeping this project under wraps is going to take some doing.'

Stoddart slid off the desk. 'Fear is the key,' he replied. 'Have you checked to see if the videos are loaded and working? I'd hate to have Di Carlo slip through our fingers after going to all this trouble.'

'It's fine – stop worrying.'

'In that case,' said Stoddart, moving towards the door, 'I'm going to check in the dining saloon before I get changed.'

Waiting was not one of Stoddart's favourite pastimes, and after double-checking all their arrangements, he prowled the decks like a brooding mountain cat. At noon, when the sun was at its zenith, Di Carlo's cabin cruiser approached from the direction of Fort Lauderdale and moored on the landward side of the Sea Queen. Cheto immediately headed for the bridge to supervise the recording of Stoddart's meeting in the supposed privacy of the officers' dining room.

Di Carlo entered first, and was visibly surprised to see that no attempt had been made to cover the neatly-stacked plastic packets of cocaine. Alfonso Siracusa, his chemist and colleague, a short, dapper man with an olive skin and a taste for expensive suits and heavy gold jewellery, gulped so much that his Adam's apple kept bobbing up and down.

'Christ!' he gasped, pushing past Di Carlo. 'You must have friends in high places to have got this past the customs.'

But Di Carlo, who had friends in that department himself, knew that the Sea Queen had been clean when she arrived. 'Just how did you manage it?' he asked. 'I'd pay good money to know.'

Stoddart smiled. 'Competition is something I can do without and operating the way I am suits me fine.'

Di Carlo nodded while Siracusa selected several packets at random. After each test, his answer was the same: 'Quality, ninety-six per cent proof.'

'If I might beg the use of a telephone,' said Di Carlo politely, 'I'll get the transportation organized.'

'You can use the one in the Captain's cabin – or I can plug you one in here, if you wish,' Stoddart offered.

'Here will be fine,' Di Carlo agreed.

Taking a spare telephone from the steward's cupboard, Stoddart pushed the jack-plug home. 'For the Captain's convenience during meals,' he explained; then, as Di Carlo began tapping out the digits, he asked: 'How will you get this ashore?'

'You are due to take on fresh laundry, fuel and victuals,' he replied. 'The companies involved belong to my organization.' When Cantilano answered the telephone, he grunted: 'Di Carlo. The stuff is here, so get things moving.'

'Would you care for a drink while we wait?' asked Stoddart.

'I have business ashore to take care of,' he replied. 'Alfonso will stay to keep an eye on things and will hand over the key when it's all loaded.'

'Suits me fine,' agreed Stoddart, and held out his hand. 'I'll be looking forward to doing business with you again sometime.'

'Me, too,' agreed Di Carlo, thinking of the two hundred and fifty million dollars profit he expected to make on the deal.

The minute Stoddart and Di Carlo left, Cheto replayed the video tapes: a perfect recording of everything that had taken place. Setting them aside, he inserted fresh ones to record the removal of the shipment, and double-checked the videos that had recorded Di Carlo's arrival and departure from the outset. Using the camera's all-seeing eye, via the monitors in the radio room behind the bridge, he watched the progress of the small refuelling tanker and the ship's chandlers' vessel. The latter moored on the leeside of the Sea Queen and there seemed nothing out of the ordinary as stores were transferred from one vessel to another. With all the victuals loaded, several large oblong cane laundry baskets were deposited on the deck via the vessel's derrick cranes. Quickly the clean linen was removed, replaced with two thousand kilos of cocaine, and the baskets returned.

On the seaward side of the Sea Queen, where all the activity was out of sight from the land, the remaining five hundred kilos of cocaine were loaded on board the tanker while refuelling took place, and although all was quiet as the crew feverishly stowed away the contraband, all was not as it appeared. A simple order over the telephone from Cheto sent out a diver from beneath the Sea Queen to attach a small explosive charge to the tanker's hull below the waterline, with a radio detonator. When Cheto received confirmation that this order had been carried out, he picked up the ship to shore telephone.

'Senator Angus McCluskey's residence,' his private secretary replied. 'Can I help you?'

'The name's Maurice Cheto and I would like to speak to the Senator, please. It's urgent.'

'I'm afraid he's in conference at the moment. Can I help you?'

'Sure you can,' he said angrily. 'You can get off your frigging butt and tell McCluskey that Captain Maurice Cheto is on the line, before half of Fort Lauderdale goes up in smoke!'

The secretary swallowed hard. 'Yes, sir,' he gagged, 'I'll get him right away,' and, as if stung, he hurried out into the garden where Senator McCluskey was practising his putting on the lawn.

'There's a man called Cheto on the line,' he panted, 'ranting about blowing up half of Fort Lauderdale.'

'Jesus Christ!' exclaimed the senator, dropping his club.

'What in hell's name is going on?'

When he repeated this question into the mouthpiece of the telephone, Cheto asked: 'Are you alone?'

McCluskey looked at his secretary and said: 'It's private.' The man left, and he said: 'You can speak freely now.'

'You know who I am?' asked Cheto, as though unsure of who he was talking to.

'Of course I do; you're Captain Maurice Cheto, one of Dieger's colleagues. We had a secret meeting a couple of weeks ago, and another two days ago. What's all this about blowing up half of Fort Lauderdale?'

'We have ourselves a whole new ball game out here,' began Cheto. 'The shipment has been loaded on to two vessels, one of them a refuelling tanker which I have mined. I figure that if I put a hole in its hull after it leaves, and the second boat goes to pick up any survivors, it will create a prime situation for the proper authorities to accidentally find the cocaine. It will give them just the excuses necessary to investigate a great part of the Mafia holdings.'

'Sounds perfect,' praised McCluskey. 'You have my approval.'

'There's just one snag,' Cheto warned. 'Since they'll have just left the Sea Queen, any questioning of the two crews could implicate us.'

McCluskey searched for an answer. The G Force were doing a good job – one that needed to be done – and having them arrested would foul things up and possibly hinder the rest of their mission. On the other hand, he could see Cheto's point; an accidental explosion would keep the narcotics from ever reaching the street, and also bring the Florida Mafia to financial ruin. 'Have you got the tapes you promised?' he asked.

'Sure. At the moment we have Don Cantilano and Alfonso Siracusa supervising; Di Carlo was here earlier, and we have him on film checking the goods.'

'It's too good an opportunity to miss,' McCluskey decided. 'Can you follow the tanker's progress on radar and detonate your bomb at the last minute without endangering innocent lives?'

'No problem.'

'Then I suggest that you do so. Weigh anchor the minute your transaction is concluded. I'll cover you as much as I can by placing a security blanket over a G Force participation.'

'You've got it!' said Cheto. 'I'll send a messenger with the tapes before we leave. Have a nice day.'

Within minutes of their conversation, the small tanker began its journey back to base, the ships' chandler boat following, a quarter of a mile behind. Cheto immediately sent a crew man to McCluskey with the video tapes, and gave the order to set sail.

Surprised by their sudden departure, Stoddart joined Cheto on the bridge and was given an explanation. The two men hovered over the radar. Their course took them directly out to sea, and by the time the two smaller craft were nearing their destination, they had long since disappeared from view. With an evil glint of satisfaction in his dark eyes, Cheto detonated the charge. They were too far off to hear the explosion, but their success was soon verified by the frantic calls from the authorities ashore. Within thirty minutes, intercepted calls told the story of hundreds of packets of narcotics floating on the sea amid a thin, widespread layer of powdery oil slick. Soon the air was alive with messages about the biggest illegal narcotics find ever known in the United States.

Satisfied with the outcome of the day's events, Cheto relayed their success to Dieger on the Atlantic Mirage. In the days that followed, secret messages from Senator McCluskey kept them informed of the situation in Florida. The arrest of Siracusa, Cantilano and the crew members of the two boats, led to many more arrests ashore and this, combined with the loss of the shipment of cocaine and the diamonds he had handed over as payment, caused Di Carlo's empire to crumble overnight. Faced with ruin, and the inevitable life sentence behind bars, he took his own life as the easy way out.

Days later, a massive ten tonne shipment of cocaine found its way ashore at Jacksonville. Eight tonnes were loaded on to a truck, to be taken to destinations as far away as New Orleans, but this was hijacked by a G Force team of agents posing as thieves. Eventually they dumped it in the Gulf of Mexico where it could do no further harm. The remaining two tonnes was destroyed, thanks to other G Force agents, when a gas main exploded in the warehouse where it had been stored to await distribution.

Apart from the actual loss, the Mafia suffered a far reaching investigation after its official discovery by the fire department. In Savannah, a rival gang was informed of the location of a further fifteen tonnes, and a gang war broke out for possession; but this only resulted in its confiscation, and many arrests were made. These led the authorities deep into the Mafia network, and many high-ranking members were convicted as a result.

The G Force's greatest coup by far was the New York operation. The fast attack craft spent most of the night launching torpedoes right into the heart of the harbour, where the Sea Queen divers worked feverishly to recover the warheads. By morning, twenty tonnes of cocaine had been stored on board, destined for Baltimore, Washington, Pittsburg, Philadelphia, Cleveland, Detroit and Chicago. In order to protect their investment, the Mafia employed a whole army of enforcers. Under their watching eyes the Sea Queen discharged her cargo and after receiving the keys required as payment, she sailed.

That evening, when she was many miles out at sea, a G Force agent, high up in the cab of a dockside crane, began to act like a crazy man, shooting at anything that moved. The steady report of his high-powered rifle soon attracted squad cars to the scene, and as more and more police arrived the Mafia guards were forced to seek refuge in the shadows. Using megaphones the police tried in vain to talk their man down, and no amount of shooting from the ground could penetrate the crane's control cab floor to force him out. In desperation, marksmen climbed to the cabs of adjacent cranes and on to the rooftops of warehouses, but as the night wore on he still evaded all efforts to bring him down.

As the new day dawned he still kept the authorities at bay, and in an effort to gain maximum cover at close range during the daylight hours, the police forced open the doors of several warehouses in order to seek refuge. Their action provoked great criticism from the warehouse owners, which fell on deaf ears. By mid day the whole area was under siege, both by the police and by legal representatives of the owners who were trying to evict them.

Then, suddenly, at about three o'clock, the G Force agent's presence became a minor matter as all attention turned towards a dog. Its yapping echoed continually inside one of the warehouses, as it frantically clawed and chewed at a wooden crate. At once an officer sealed off the area, and requested sniffer dogs and more positive legal advice before investigating the suspect crate.

Having achieved his objective, the gunman let his weapon clatter to the ground. 'Hold your fire!' he called. 'I am unarmed and coming down.' Half-expecting to feel the thud of a bullet at any time, he made his way down to where Captain Joseph Lloyd awaited him.

'Grab yourself a piece of iron,' growled the Captain, pushing him back towards the crane. 'And what's your name?'

'Baines. Robert Oliver Baines,' he replied with a cheeky grin as he leaned forward, spreading his legs. 'Rob for short, to my friends.'

In seconds he had been frisked, his hands dragged behind his back and put in handcuffs.

'You have the right to remain silent . . .' began Lloyd, but Baines interrupted him.

'Cut that crap and get me out of here, before some damn fool takes a pot-shot at me,' he growled, adding in an undertone: 'What took you so damn long, anyhow?'

'These things take time,' Lloyd replied quietly. 'You know how the law is: one tiny slip and the fish slips off the hook, no matter how guilty they are. You did a good job. Nice going.'

Turning away, he beckoned a patrol car over and shoved Baines roughly inside, muttering: 'You'd better play dead on the floor until you're clear – I'd hate to see some crank blow your fool head off after this. Take him to wherever it is he wants to go and set him free, Barney,' he instructed the driver.

'You're some kiddy to have as a friend,' groaned Baines. 'I sit up there cold and hungry, getting shot at all night,

338

while you get all the goodies and promotion.'

'Take a flask and some sandwiches next time,' Lloyd chuckled.

It was inevitable that, with such losses of Mafia men and finances, there would be repercussions. Word spread through North America to such an extent that the Canadian Mafia cancelled any part in what they considered to be a jinxed contract, and this pleased Dieger. Although none of the Mafia's recent tragedies could actually be attributed to him, it was better to ease off before an ambush was sprung on his force on the mere assumption that he was behind it.

Although total victory had eluded him, the achievements of the G Force had reached deeper into the dark recesses of crime than any other body ever had. Arrests ran into many hundreds, and the tally was still rising. So far, the diamonds handed over for no return stood at seven thousand five hundred million dollars' worth, while the total of seized Mafia assets was many times greater than that and still rising. Dumping of narcotics, including the remaining unsold two and half tonnes – but not any which had been dumped after being sold to the Mafia – totalled fifty three and a half tonnes, worth more than fourteen thousand, three hundred and twenty million dollars on the street.

Such an impressive record deserved recognition, and standing on the bridge, Dieger related the figures to the entire crew, over the tannoy system. When their jubilant cheers had died away, he informed them of a change in course to allow them a short, well-earned holiday in Bermuda.

13

Dieger had only intended to stay in Bermuda long enough to replenish the stores and refuel, but after Scott had voiced a thought which had been nagging at him since they left Colombia, he kept the Atlantic Mirage at anchor for a full week. Careful research proved Scott's fears, that Ruez would be unable to meet their contract for a further two hundred tonnes, were not without foundation. Only a limited amount of cocaine could be produced in a season and since Dieger had borne witness to the fact that they had depleted Ruez' stocks, they obviously couldn't produce double the original quantity during their absence without buying in massive stocks from elsewhere. The only other explanation seemed to be that Ruez might have ideas of joining the queue of those trying to make a final killing before departing to foreign parts, in order to enjoy the proceeds of their ill-gotten gains.

Every avenue that Ruez might conceivably tread was explored, and counter-measures allowed for. By the time the Atlantic Mirage sailed, Stoddart had already begun his diamond run, picking up the Mafia payments. Sonia, who had inveigled her way into the upper echelons of the Mafia, had sold her knowledge of Stoddart's diamond run to Antonio Monte Leone for the promise of a nominal million dollars. Leone was chairman of International Finance, a company that managed billions of dollars of Mafia money after it had been laundered.

He proved to be as shrewd in his dealings in crime as he was in the world of high finance. When his henchmen were ambushed as they tried to rob the man they thought to be Stoddart making his last collection in Miami, none were prepared to give evidence likely to incriminate anyone other than themselves.

With the bulk of the Mafia millions left in safe hands, Stoddart finally approached the Atlantic Mirage in the fast attack craft, many miles out to sea, with Ruez' two hundred million dollars' worth of diamonds. In the greyness of the early dawn, low cloud shed a fine drizzle over the lazily rolling swell. With virtually no wind, the only brightness on the drab waters, apart from the occasional white top of a wave breaking, was the wake left by the attack craft.

While the mother ship waited, with engines quiet and stern doors gaping, Stoddart witnessed for the first time the idea he had once scoffed at. Captain Tsi piloted his way expertly into the vast cavern of the ship's docking well. Voices echoed back and forth as both crews prepared to secure the smaller craft, while the great doors were already swinging in to hide its existence. Beneath the echoing boom of their closing, the Atlantic Mirage's engines began to throb, sending the familiar, comforting vibrations of life throughout the ship again.

Hoisting the ornate chest of diamonds to his shoulder, Stoddart crossed the gangway to the lower gallery and made his way up through the decks to Dieger's cabin, where he was waiting with Scott.

'You're a sight for sore eyes, bonny lad,' beamed Stoddart, and Scott's pleasure at seeing him showed in his broad smile.

'I never thought I'd be so glad to see your ugly face again, but I am,' he said, offering his hand.

Placing the chest on the coffee table, Stoddart took it in his own firm grasp. 'I've missed you,' he said sincerely, 'and I've got to admit,' he added, turning to Dieger, 'I owe you a debt that I shall never be able to repay. In the past few weeks I've seen more than enough villains pay the price for their crimes, and I can't help thinking that, but for you, I would be among them.'

'You did a fine job,' said Dieger approvingly. 'The intrigue seems to be doing you good – you look ten years younger.'

'That's through not having to worry about having my

collar felt by the Old Bill,' he grinned. 'And what other occupation offers free world travel, the best hotels, luxury yachts and unlimited travel expenses?'

'Which brings us to the next part of our mission,' said Dieger sombrely. 'I don't really see any need for you to come to Colombia with us. It's been a long time since you saw your wife and daughter, and the Caribbean is nice at this time of year; I could have them flown out for a holiday, if you like, so that you can spend some time with them – all expenses paid, of course.'

Just thinking about a holiday with his wife set a warm glow burning deep inside Stoddart's chest, but he asked suspiciously: 'You wouldn't have an ulterior motive in mind? Work is work, but using my family is another matter entirely.'

'My motives are to keep you safe until your services are required elsewhere,' Dieger assured him. 'The Sea Queen is due to dock soon at Port au Prince in Haiti. When our business in Colombia is concluded, Scott and I intend joining her ourselves, for a break.'

'It sounds appealing,' Stoddart admitted, 'but I'd like to see this mission through to the end, having come this far.'

'As you wish,' Dieger conceded. 'Now, let's have a look at those diamonds.'

Stoddart handed over the keys and Dieger inserted them into the twin locks, turning them in opposite directions. All eyes looked down in ancitiation, and there, beneath the rounded ornate top, were many shallow trays. Access to all but the top one was gained by releasing two tiny catches inside, allowing the front of the chest to swing down. The trays, an inch and a half deep, two feet long and one and a half feet wide, were upholstered in rich midnight blue velvet, and displayed large, quality diamonds set out in neat lines. Beneath each one was a description of quality, colour and weight. None was priced, but a wad of documents in the rounded lid provided this information, together with the date of valuation. Dieger slid the trays out, one by one, to inspect their contents. Stoddart swallowed hard, for only a few weeks earlier, under different circumstances, he'd have moved heaven and earth to gain possession of them.

'Are you really going to hand them over,' he asked.

'Of course,' smiled Dieger, turning towards his desk. 'Our deal was to exchange them for two hundred tonnes of cocaine, and I see no reason to deviate from that.' He took out from a top drawer a minute tracking device, no larger than a shirt button. Removing one of the diamonds, he made a small incision with a knife in the dimpled velvet where it had rested, eased in the device and replaced the gem. 'On the other hand,' he continued with a grim smile – and left the threat unspoken.

'Say no more,' said Stoddart. 'What's the form, apart from that?'

'Hard to say. There's some doubt as to whether Ruez can actually supply the tonnage required. There's a lot of jungle out there and we could be wrong about his production capacity. If they can meet our demands, then their operation is at least three times bigger than we first thought – which will mean a much bigger job breaking it up. If Ruez can't honour our contract and doesn't admit it in the early stages, it's a fair bet that he's going to make a grab for those diamonds, and what he's planning for us is anybody's guess. He could have us marched into the jungle and shot, to cover his crimes, or he could confiscate the diamonds and have us arrested for what we appear to be.'

'I'm beginning to wonder about the wisdom of coming along with you,' said Stoddart. 'Dare I ask what precautions you've taken, since we're undermanned for a full-scale assault?'

'Don't underestimate our strength,' said Dieger solemnly. 'We have a secret army of jungle troops at our disposal. They're in cold storage at the moment, but you can take my word for it; they're hardened troops and will eat anything Ruez or his like can throw against us.'

Stoddart groaned. 'Sounds like we're about to start a regular war.'

'You look tired,' observed Dieger. 'Why don't you get some breakfast and a couple of hours' rest? Then perhaps Scott will show you around. You could find yourself in for a few surprises.'

'His delivering those diamonds like a good little boy was

surprise enough for one day,' grinned Scott. 'I'm not sure he could handle much more.'

'Stoddart swung a playful punch to his jaw. 'Have you had any more bright ideas, bonny lad?' he beamed.

'Just the odd one!'

'Get out of here,' growled Dieger. 'I have things to do, even if you haven't.'

Outside, the gloomy drizzle persisted. Eyeing the wet decks and the depressing atmosphere, Stoddart remarked: 'Bed seems a good place to be on a day like this, bonny lad. It's been a long night but I doubt that I'll sleep.'

'A good hot breakfast will work wonders,' Scott suggested. 'You can tell me about your escapades in the United States while you eat.'

'Don't you even think about the States and food without taking a deep breath between,' Stoddart advised. 'Have you ever been there?'

'No. What's it like?'

'Like nothing else you've ever seen,' he declared admiringly. 'Just about everything is bigger and better than back home. Take breakfast, for instance: you want a dozen eggs and a whole pound of bacon? You just help yourself. It doesn't cost any more and no one gives a toss. And coffee: they'll keep topping you up for as long as you like. The first time I went out for a steak was an experience in itself. These Yanks start off with enough salad to keep the likes of us going for a week, and that comes free while waiting for what they call a steak. Basically, they tear off the cow's horns and wipe its butt before you get it served up on a plate the size of a dustbin lid.'

'You must have been out there too long,' laughed Scott.

'To be honest, bonny lad, I'd like to go out there for keeps, when this is all over. It's a grand place and that's a fact.'

While they were chatting they'd walked on aimlessly, and had arrived at the vast docking well. Stoddart barely glanced at one of the more recent additions: looking like a small crane with twin jibs protruding from beyond the operator's cab at shoulder height, it in fact concealed within those telescopic jibs the barrels of an Emerlec

344

thirty-millimetre cannon, capable of firing twelve hundred rounds per minute. Between this and the two helicopters – transformed now into seaborne gunships – stood two medium-sized refrigerated freight container units.

As the two men passed, an engineer officer approached from behind them to check that the heavy doors of the units were secure, and the temperature correct. His dark, impassive eyes seemed to rivet on Stoddart, giving him an eerie feeling.

'Don't worry, bonny lad,' he mocked. 'We're not about to plunder your cargo.'

The engineer's head turned slightly, the beginning of a smile creasing his flat, tanned, pock-marked face.

'Special cargo,' he explained in broken English. 'The temperature must be kept just so, or the contents would spoil.'

'That's just how this weather affects me,' said Stoddart, smothering a gaping yawn. 'I think I'll skip breakfast and turn in with a good book.'

The next few days followed the tedious routine of life on board ship, but for Stoddart there were a few surprises. Deep in the docking well where the fast attack craft lay secure in its berth, he saw the Bofors guns being replaced by a thirty-millimetre cannon, similar to the one on the Atlantic Mirage's deck. This, too, was made to look like a crane, and located with its twin jibs protruding over the stern. Only then did he realize exactly what the innocent-looking piece of machinery was. Two of the four amphibious landing craft had been deliberately scuttled after serving their purpose of supply depots for the fast attack craft during its deliveries of torpedoes, thus allowing the Atlantic Mirage to continue its voyage. The remaining two were now prepared for the assault on the Colombian jungle plantation.

Scott made a few practice flights in a flimsy microlite aeroplane, whose engine could be jettisoned to convert it into a glider. Numerous meetings, too, added to Stoddart's enlightenment. These were to discuss tactics to perfection, and every single meeting made Stoddart's skin crawl, so much so that his continual scratching became a joke.

Leaving the North Atlantic behind, they entered the Caribbean as though heading for the Panama Canal, and then, fifty miles off the coast of Santa Marta, the engines fell silent. Under cover of darkness the fast attack craft and the two amphibious vessels eased out into the night, and while they drifted the helicopters took to the air, one of them transferring a refrigerated container on to a landing craft.

Last to leave was Scott, in the flimsy microlite. Heading towards the hacienda he quickly climbed to two thousand feet and located his specified target area, using a hi-tech night sight, before checking his equipment. Looking up, he scanned the flimsy, billowing, triangular cloth sail as it strained against the lightweight alloy tubular framework. Next he pulled a small lever, while looking at the two pressurized tanks fitted on either side of his seat. Satisfied with the misty brown spray emitting from them into his slip-stream, he shut them off and double-checked that he had an aerosol can of insect repellant.

'Nighthawk to Mirage,' he called into the walkie-talkie set. 'Do you read me? Over.'

'Loud and clear,' answered Dieger.

'I'm all checked out and making my home run. Over and out.'

An hour later he was approaching the coastline at a height of one hundred and fifty feet, and when he was the same distance from the trees, he jettisoned the engine into the sea so that he could continue his journey in silence.

Now he was over the jungle, on a course aligning the gully to the cave and the hacienda, and he began to spray his flight path across the jungle. Using skill acquired during his business days, he stayed aloft without much effort. After sweeping directly over the hacienda compound he turned to pick out the first of the plantations on his extreme left, from which point he circled right to spray a narrow path over all of the outlying plantations.

With that part of his mission complete, he skimmed silently over the dark, foreboding jungle to the far side of the clear zone round the hacienda, where he landed close to the forest edge. With quick, deft movements he stripped the sail from its frame and then reduced the frame itself to so many pieces of alloy tubing, hiding it all in the dense undergrowth before reporting to Dieger.

'Nighthawk to Mirage,' he called quietly. 'Do you read me? Over.'

'Loud and clear. Over.'

'Everything went as planned. I am on the ground and waiting. Over.'

'Good. Did you see any signs of life on your travels? Over.'

'Just a few lights. The hacienda itself is well-lit but I saw no activity. There were several vehicles and two small helicopters in the compound, otherwise all was quiet. Over.'

'Good. Carry on as planned. We'll be dropping anchor in a few minutes. Ruez has made contact and should be on board soon. If we don't make contact every hour on the hour, you know what to expect. Good hunting. Over and out.'

Dieger, standing on the bridge's wing, turned towards the vast emptiness of the open sea. Toward the shore, a single dim light burned beneath the overhanging jungle as a guide to their anchorage. The main engines no longer throbbed beneath his feet, for the Atlantic Mirage was cruising in under its own momentum, and as it made its final approach a cabin cruiser quietly led a fleet of small camouflaged boats out from the creek, as before. Pike gave a brief order, which was answered by the harsh rattle of the anchor chain and the splash of the heavy, barbed hook when it hit the water.

Guessing that Ruez would be on board the cabin cruiser, Dieger made his way down to meet him and Sanchez at the head of the gangway. 'Welcome aboard,' he smiled. 'I see that you're ready for us.'

'But of course,' smiled Ruez, shaking his hand. 'Did you have a good voyage?'

'A quiet one, at least.'

'I see that your Mafia contacts were not so lucky, if the news bulletins are to be believed,' said Ruez seriously. 'Many arrests have been made over the past month, and a great deal of narcotics seized.'

'Most unfortunate,' Dieger agreed, recalling the vast tonnage he had dumped, which could not be accounted for by any amount of news coverage. 'I should think that only half of our original cargo got through. Perhaps our Mafia contacts will be more cautious this time around.'

'Let's hope so. Would you like to check your cargo before we proceed?'

'I think we can leave that to my first officer, while you and Sanchez check the diamonds. Shall we adjourn to my cabin for a drink?'

'Ah,' beamed Ruez, 'I was hoping you might say that. It's been a long day organizing and there's been no time to relax.'

'Mr Pike,' called Dieger, and Pike turned from where he stood by the crane at the ship's side. 'I'll be in my cabin if you need me.'

'Yes, sir.' For a few moments Pike's dark eyes followed them as they walked along the deck. The uniformed Ruez reached briefly to touch his holstered pistol, drawing back immediately after reassuring himself that it was still there. Turning away, Pike looked down as the first tonne of cocaine was lifted from the small boat. The moment it was clear the boat moved away, and the next edged into place. Two minutes later the first tonne was landed on deck, where his own crewmen unslung it and began random tests before moving it away for stowage below decks.

In less than an hour, five small boats had discharged their cargoes and then, without any warning, everything went quiet behind Pike as he continued to peer over the side. When he turned to find the reason, the crewmen in charge of stowing stood with their hands held high, and beyond them, in a semi-circle, were several ragged natives holding machine pistols at the ready.

'What the hell's going on?' demanded Pike.

'You are under arrest,' said the spokesman in broken English.

'You're joking!' he scoffed. 'If you're the law around here then I'm Father Christmas!'

'You will put up your hands or I will shoot. Tell your crane man to come out or I will shoot him also.'

Obediently raising his hands, Pike called: 'Hey, Schultz! You'd better come down here and join the party. Don't try anything, unless you want to get yourself shot.'

When Schultz had meekly come to join them, the spokesman said: 'All of you stand along the side and lean over as though you are looking in the water.'

When the natives in the boats below saw them doing this they pulled aside the camouflage to reveal reinforcements who at once headed for the gangway and streamed aboard to take over the ship, marching the entire crew out on to the open decks where they could be kept under guard.

Not a single shot had been fired to give any warning to Dieger, but the lack of normal ship's activity aroused his suspicions. The chest of diamonds stood on his desk, many of the trays exposed, while Sanchez scrutinized each gem in turn through an eyepiece as Ruez looked on expectantly.

'Did you encounter any problems explaining the disappearance of Sahara and the diamonds after our last trip?' asked Dieger.

'My colleagues were most upset,' said Ruez, 'but what could they say? She was nowhere to be found and I had you and Sanchez to back up my story – you, incidentally, have been invited to dine at the hacienda to give your account of what happened. I presume that I can count on your support?'

'Of course,' he agreed, emptying his glass. 'Can I get you another drink before I check up on what's happening on deck?'

'Beautiful,' muttered Sanchez as he held a large gem up to the light.

Ruez glanced at it while handing Dieger his glass. Guessing that his plans to steal the diamonds were under way, the last thing he wanted was for Dieger to leave his cabin without him. When Dieger was at the cocktail cabinet, with his back towards him, Ruez drew his pistol and shot Sanchez through the back of the head.

'What the hell!' cried Dieger, spinning round to face the pointing weapon.

'Just let them drop to the floor,' said Ruez, indicating the glass and decanter.

349

Letting them go, Dieger's eyes strayed to Sanchez' lifeless body sprawled over the chest on his desk. 'Is he to be another missing person?' he rasped.

'One of many, I fear. Lift his body clear of the chest and then re-pack it.'

'You'll never get off this ship alive,' Dieger threatened. 'My crew will have heard that shot and they'll be out there waiting for you.'

'I think not,' said Ruez. 'Your crew will have been arrested by a group of natives who are under the impression that they are my deputies. By the time they realize the truth it will be too late.'

'You seem to be taking a great many unnecessary risks. Why don't you just make the trade as before, and then disappear with the diamonds?'

'I'm afraid I brought you here under false pretences,' he admitted. 'You see, I can't meet your order. All we have is ten tonnes of cocaine. As you will appreciate, I couldn't have told you that or you would not have returned with so many diamonds – and now that you have, the last thing I need is for you to meet my disgruntled colleagues.'

'So where do we go from here?'

'First we are going out on deck to reassure your crew that you are still among the living. Then you will all be safely locked up while I make my getaway. I'm sure my disillusioned colleagues will set you free when they hear your tale of woe. And, just for the record, don't bother trying to convey my intentions to my men. Only one or two speak English; I specified that before enlisting them. Now, if you would be so kind as to carry out the chest for me, we shall get started. Don't be so foolish as to think that I won't shoot you if you give me just cause. Two hundred million dollars' worth of diamonds is worth any risk.'

'Three hundred million,' Dieger corrected him. 'Let's not forget the first payment.'

'All the more reason for you to take care,' Ruez pointed out. 'Just keep in mind what might happen to your crew if mine take fright and start shooting. They're not civilized to your standards; life out here is cheap, and the jungles are vast and deep. The only law they understand is survival.'

'I get the message,' said Dieger, and picked up the chest. Clasping it against his torso he waited for Ruez to open the door, stepped through and walked towards the docking well deck, where the crew were under guard.

'You seem a little short-handed,' remarked Ruez. 'Where are the rest of your crew?'

'They got sick after being bitten by some of your insects last time we were here,' Dieger lied. 'I paid them off. I had to issue those who remained with cans of insect repellent, to protect them this time around.'

Ruez nodded absently, preoccupied with the problem of getting rid of the witnesses to his crime without risk to himself. A whole month of careful planning had gone into his escape with the diamonds. Few of his men could understand English, and only two could swim. Both had served at sea, one as a junior deck officer and the other as an engineer. His plan was so simple: to tie up the whole of Dieger's crew, take the Atlantic Mirage out to sea and then sink it, with them and his own men still on board. There were to be only two survivors apart from himself, the deck officer and the engineer, and he would dispense with them at the first opportunity, once he was safe on board his cabin cruiser and heading for a new life.

While Dieger struggled to see the time, confirming that his G Force colleagues would soon be coming to the rescue, Ruez was considering the possibilities of the container standing on the deck. Large enough to hold Dieger's crew as well as his own, if they were squeezed in, it was also as stout as any prison cell and would be easier than trussing up all of his captives.

'Open the container,' he said to one of his own men in his own tongue, and then to Dieger: 'Put the chest on the deck and lead your men inside.'

'I wouldn't do that,' Dieger advised. 'The freezer unit broke down a few days' ago and the smell might make you heave, even at this distance.'

'It can't be worse than whatever it is you and your men are using for insect repellent,' Ruez observed. 'You ought to try taking a bath now and then.'

Dieger, smiling, allowed himself to be marshalled ahead of his own men by the band of ragged guards. Pulling aside the man Ruez had ordered to open the door, he slid out the long bolts holding the double doors closed, stepped back and hauled them open, while his men fanned out in a wide semi-circle at the yawning mouth. Unseen by Ruez' men, a writhing brown mass of carnivorous army ants, just out of hibernation in their previously chilled home, surged forward on to the deck. Uninterested in Dieger's crew, who were all smothered with insect repellent, they advanced in their millions on the unpro- tected men behind them. In seconds the guards were screaming in terror as the tiny creatures swarmed up their legs, ripping at them with their sharp mandible jaws.

Many men just dropped their weapons and leapt into the sea to douse their tortured bodies. Others started shooting, but soon realized that guns were useless against such a foe. Ruez, standing well back, stood dumbfounded for a few seconds. His first thought was to gun down Dieger for his trickery, but there were too many people in his line of fire; so instead he bent down for the chest of diamonds, hoping to make a speedy exit; but the swarm had already covered the chest and were advancing up his legs. Sick with fear he took several backward steps, stamping his feet. Many ants fell off but most did not, and fearing the fate which had befallen some of his men already – now writhing in agony on the deck while being eaten alive – he raced for the gangway.

'Get the engines started!' he shouted at the pilot, who stared up at him in bewilderment from the cabin cruiser. Men were in the water, some trying to scramble aboard the small boats as they bobbed about, while others cried for help as they floundered helplessly. To his pilot's distress, Ruez ordered the man to leave the stricken men and make a speedy retreat.

Dieger, meanwhile, headed for the bridge to contact his incoming force. 'Get that container and drop it smack in the middle of the hacienda,' he growled; then he turned his attention to Scott. 'Do you read me, Night Hawk?'

'Loud and clear,' Scott replied.

'Ruez made his play and we've routed him,' panted Dieger. 'You can expect company soon. How are you doing?'

352

'I've disabled all the transport and I'm standing by.'

'Ruez will head for the jetty, by the looks of it. Get there as soon as you can and use his boat to travel back here the minute he's out of sight. Over and out.'

Grabbing an aerosol can, Dieger raced down to the docking well, but found that Pike had the situation well in hand. Several of his men had dived over the side to retrieve some of the small boats, and were now waiting with them at the bottom of the gangway. When Pike sprayed a trail of foul-smelling scent from the deck to the boats, the army of ants hungrily followed. When each boat was filled to capacity with the heaving brown mass it was pushed towards the shore to pick up the trail laid by Scott during his flight.

During this operation the helicopter carrying the second container of army ants flew over with its escort, and minutes later Captain Tsi arrived with the fast attack craft, to stand by in case his services were required. Even as it cruised to a stop, the twin thirty-millimetre cannon at the stern swivelled menacingly towards the coastline.

'Keep an eye open for Scott!' shouted Dieger. 'He should soon come out of the creek in a small cabin cruiser. Hello, Delta Force – do you read me?' he called into the walkie-talkie.

'Loud and clear, Captain,' replied a voice in a lazy Texan drawl. 'Our bomb has gone and our guests are having a ball – at least there's plenty of dancing going on down there. Over.'

'High-tail it out of there and head out to sea to our rendezvous – no point in wasting valuable fuel hanging around,' said Dieger. Signing off, he said: 'Get us under way, Mr Pike. Captain Tsi can wait for Scott and catch us up.'

By the time he reached the bridge, the heavy anchor chain was being winched up, and he had barely warned the engine room to stand by when he followed up with: 'Full speed ahead.' The engines began to throb and as the propellers churned the still waters, he gave the helmsman the order to 'steer three-zero-zero degrees', adding: 'And keep your eyes open.'

'Three-zero-zero degrees coming up,' echoed the

helmsman, spinning the spoked wheel. As the helicopters bypassed them on their way out to the open sea, Dieger, worried about Scott, walked on to the bridge's wing to look back. The white cabin cruiser had just appeared at the mouth of the creek where Captain Tsi was waiting to pick him up, and just for a moment Dieger allowed himself the luxury of contemplating the consequences of their night's work.

Somewhere back there the millions of carnivorous ants would now be settled after their disturbance and waiting for the dawn. When the sun came up they would begin their march of destruction, eating anything alive and unable to get out of their path. Stopping such army ants was virtually impossible; once they had decided on a direction – which altered each day by one hundred and twenty degrees – nothing would deter them. Death – or the fear of it – was beyond their comprehension, and since they carried the eggs of their unborn young at the rear end of their column, and they had a prolific reproduction cycle, their numbers were unlikely to be depleted. It would be many a long day, thought Dieger, before the jungle for many miles around would be able to be used again; and with any luck the ants would multiply further in their new, warm environment and spread to clear a much larger area.

He watched as Scott abandoned the cabin cruiser and boarded the fast attack craft, which then, in turn, sped out to sea to form a protective screen for its mother ship, with the beleaguered helicopters. When the landing craft, carrying the reserve assault group, came into view, scrambling nets were thrown over the side and the craft itself, having served its purpose, was left to drift with an explosive charge on board.

Tense minutes became hours in which no force arrived to retaliate, so it looked as though dropping the carnivorous ants on the hacienda had indeed prevented anyone from using a transmitter to call for help, as Dieger had predicted.

When the sun came up there was still no sign of any alien craft on the radar.

'It looks as though we've made it,' observed Dieger.

'Recall Captain Tsi and the Delta Force. Better dump that cocaine, too.'

'Yes, sir,' said Pike. 'The pleasure's all mine.'